Soul
Bonded

A Haven novel

Dria Andersen

Dedication

To my husband who was my sounding board, my cheerleader, my critique partner, and all the things I needed to finish this project. I appreciate every hour, every word of input and most of all, your unwavering support.

To my family who had to deal with mommy being on in another world for hours at a time. Thank you for your patience.

To my sister Tina, who reads everything I write and gives me honest feedback and encouragement, thank you mucho mucho.

Thank you to every fan who continues to stick with me while I tell the stories playing in my head. I appreciate each and every one of you.

Table of Contents

Chapter 1

Pain was the first thing Brianna Watson noticed, the hot sting of scrapes along her legs and arms. Her ribs ached. Even breathing became a chore as she pushed through the fog of sleep. Brianna opened her eyes and winced as light pierced her pupils. She shut them quickly praying the headache that accompanied the move would disappear. She battled confusion and struggled to lift her body and get her bearings. The pain was excruciating, a whimper escaped.

"Settle, Brianna." Heat moved through her body as a deep voice murmured to her.

Calloused hands pushed back her thick, curly hair from her forehead, their touch gentle on her face. Her reaction was extreme, as need poured through her body, nearly taking over the pain. Curiosity propelled her lids open and the eyes that met her gaze mesmerized her. Hazel, the color was pale and smooth with a ring of green circling the irises. Exotic, but what entranced her was the concern, and genuine affection she saw in them. It matched the need pulsing through her body. They pulled her in, held her captive. Perhaps she was hallucinating, but she could've sworn they glowed.

Cool hands touched her abdomen, the sensation jarring. She tilted her head to look around him, but his large hands held her chin still, forced her eyes back up to meet his. Warmth flooded her insides, floating out towards her feet, taking her pains with it. It did the same with her back, the hands now warm, gently touching her skin. She took a deep, relieved breath.

"Better?" Her stranger asked.

Her stranger? She'd need to examine the possessiveness she felt about a man she'd never met. His voice was deep, the rumble tightening her body with feelings she didn't understand. She nodded, chin still in his hand. He leaned over and kissed her lips lightly. The air stilled in her lungs at the light contact, heat bloomed in her chest and she wondered if there was a tell-tale blush on her cheeks. The scent of his cologne wrapped around her, its fragrance making her a little dazed. She leaned closer, chasing the scent.

"Commander," a woman's voice called softly.

Jealousy rose, sharp and insistent and Brianna's hands curled into fists. A snarl escaped before confusion took over. He chuckled softly, amusement for her reaction in the hazel depths of his eyes. He kissed her cheek and rose. Brianna's eyes widened. He was shirtless, his back carved mahogany. The muscles were defined, and his skin looked smooth and touchable. A pair of jeans hung negligently on his hips, lovingly cupping a butt that made her mouth water.

Her breasts swelled, she dampened at the vee of her legs and her nipples hardened until they poked through the thin tank top she wore. What was it about this man that caused these reactions? She couldn't remember ever being this turned on by any man, let alone a stranger. He spoke with the woman across the room, their voices only a murmur.

Brianna used the time they were occupied to check her surroundings. The bed she lay in was plush, the feather soft cotton sheets heaven against the scrapes on her body. She glanced around the room. Despite the opulence of the bed, the rest of the place was Spartan in comparison. The walls were painted a warm yellow, but nothing graced them. A single lamp sat on the bedside table. The only other furniture in the room was a wooden high-backed chair next to the bed. The room was large. Half of her tiny studio apartment could probably fit into it.

Brianna frowned. Why was she here instead of at her apartment? She adjusted and pain pierced her back. Her eyes darted around the room, seeing no tell-tale equipment. Better question, why wasn't she at the hospital? The last thing she remembered was crossing the street to go to work. She closed her eyes and attempted to focus. Her thoughts were scrambled, muddied. She tried harder and winced as a sharp pain pierced her head. She pushed up, intending to move from the bed.

"Don't, Brianna," his voiced ordered from across the room.

"Where am I?" Her voice was hoarse, throat scratchy.

Immediately he rushed to her side and lifted a glass of tepid water to her lips. It felt good. She downed the glass in dragging gulps. "Slow down, babe." He murmured and pulled the glass away.

She clutched his wrist to bring it back. The contact seared her. He took the glass from her and cupped her cheek. His eyes devoured her face, his gaze hungry as it lingered on her lips. Her body buzzed, her skin tingled as he took her lips in a kiss that further clouded her mind. The kiss was possessive, but his lips were soft, coaxing, as his tongue danced with hers. Brianna was dazed when he pulled back. His full lips turned up in a cocky smile as he watched her.

Who was he that he felt he had rights to her?

Her gaze roamed his face, taking in his high cheekbones, broad nose and squared chin. He was a god.

He groaned and laid his forehead against hers. "You're at Haven."

"Haven?"

He kissed the corner of her mouth and inhaled a shuddering breath. "Gods, I thought I'd lost you." His whisper brushed her lips.

Her stomach pitched, her sex clenched and tears burned her eyes at his desperate tone. Who was this man? "Where is Haven, exactly?"

"What's the last thing you remember, Brianna?" His gaze sharpened, the lust clearing from his eyes.

"I got up this morning to go to work." She tried again to sit up. "Can I borrow your phone please?"

He frowned, his face darkening. "That's the last thing?"

Brianna backed up from the rage. "If you can just let me borrow your phone, I'll call my friend and have her pick me up." A spurt of fear went through her as a growl rumbled through the room. It was an animalistic sound, one unfamiliar to her.

"You don't know who I am?"

She shook her head and regretted the motion. Her head throbbed. "I'm sorry, I've never met you."

Her body protested the statement. Somehow it knew him well and mourned the distance between them. He stood, shock etched on his face and backed away from the bed. He turned and left the room, blanketing her in silence. The door reopened before she could panic and he re-entered wearing a collared shirt and a small cell phone in hand. He toyed with a large coin in his other hand, nervously rolling it across his knuckles.

"I've called Cassie, she'll be here in thirty minutes or so." His face was closed, the affection she saw in his eyes earlier, hidden behind an icy demeanor.

Relief at hearing her best friend's name overwhelmed her. If he knew Cassie, her situation wasn't nearly as dire as it seemed. "You know Cassie?"

"I know *you*, Brianna."

His mask fell for a moment, his stricken expression stalling her breath. He set the cell phone on the table and left the room.

She felt guilty, though she didn't know why. She picked up the phone and dialed her best friend.

"My God, Bri, are you okay?" Cassie was out of breath, her voice tight with worry.

"I think so, are you on your way?"

"Yeah, I stopped by your place to pick up some clothes and make sure the shop was okay. Fallon called and said you were awake. You scared ten years off my life, Brianna. You've been in a coma for nearly two weeks."

She pushed the panic aside momentarily, resolute in finding out where the hell she was. "Fallon is?"

"What?"

"Who is Fallon? The guy taking care of me? Why am I not in a hospital?" Brianna worried at the sudden silence on the other line.

"I'll be there in another ten minutes." Cassie ended the call.

She dropped the phone on the bed. Confused and exhausted, she closed her eyes. She would sleep for a little longer, and then wake up and plan her way out of here.

***

"What do you mean, she doesn't remember anything?"

She remembered nothing. Dazed, Fallon stared at down at his hands and fought the grief shredding his insides. She'd responded to him. Damn it, she'd been as into their kiss as he was. He licked his lips, tasting her. His body shuddered. The confusion on her face prodded him.

It hurt.

"Did you hear me? Her memory is gone?"

Fallon shrugged his shoulders, tuning back into the conversation. "Just what I said, X." He kept his face neutral to keep the rage and pain circling his gut from broadcasting to his brothers.

"What does she remember?" His youngest brother Leo was stretched out on Fallon's leather sofa, his shoeless feet propped up on his coffee table.

"I didn't get that far, Leo. She was afraid of me." Fallon didn't know what hurt worse, the fact Brianna didn't remember him, or that she would feel even a moment's fear around him.

"I'm sorry, Fallon," Leo said softly.

Again, he shrugged. "We didn't find the book on her. I'm not sure, in this state, she'll know what happened to it."

Xavier slammed his hand against the coffee table in anger, cracking the wood. Leo jerked his feet from the collapsing table. "How could this happen? Have we found the guards that were supposed to be watching her?"

Fallon stared at his brother in irritation. Xavier

grimaced. "Sorry about the table."

He raised an eyebrow.

"I'll get you another one."

"I made that one." It was one of the many hobbies he'd tried in his quest to keep himself from going after his mate. He'd made the table with her in mind. He'd even chopped the tree and had the wood blessed and everything.

"It's not that great of a table, though," Leo commented.

His brother was right, but still, he'd made that ugly table with his bare hands. "Fuck you, that's not the point. I bet you couldn't do it."

"I mean, if I did, it certainly wouldn't look like that." Leo frowned at the ruined table.

"Enough about the damn table." Xavier sighed and waved his hand over the splintered wood, fixing it.

"Thank you." Fallon rolled his shoulders to release the built tension, stored after weeks of worrying about Brianna. "The guards watching her were found dead just this morning. They were dumped outside of town."

A fresh wave of rage washed over Fallon. He'd assigned the guards watching her, personally. The failure was his. He flexed his hands and rolled his neck as the beast within him fought to be released.

Leo sat up. "How did you find them?"

"We didn't. A human found them in the woods behind her house." He held up his hands before Xavier released his growl. "It's taken care of, the human shouldn't remember anything."

His older brother scowled all the same. "You managed to do all that without leaving her bedside?"

Fallon shrugged. He'd done nothing save sit next to her bed for the last few days as she moved in and out of consciousness. Today was the first time he'd been in his apartment since Brianna had been dumped at their doorstep. He'd tried to sleep but every time his eyes closed, he saw her body tossed from the moving car. The sick crunch of her hitting the pavement in front of Haven was a sound he would never forget. So, while he sat next to her, he'd worked. And when her parents visited, he did the work that couldn't be done from her bedside.

The soldiers felt the rough end of his ire as he barked orders through the phone, pushing them through shifts that went past twenty hours every day, looking for answers. Exhaustion pulled at him until he could barely keep his human form.

"Killed two Demi? You had Demi guarding her, right?" Leo frowned,

Fallon sent him a scowl. "Yes, they were Demi. Do you think I'd trust my-"

Leo raised his brows at his brother's slip. He leaned over and lifted Fallon's wrist, and examined the glowing Sanskrit in the middle. It was Brianna's family's name, showing all who saw with who he had been mated.

"Strange business, this mating thing."

"I had no choice, Leo."

"You had a choice," Xavier argued, as he'd argued the day before when Fallon proposed initiating the mating bond to save Brianna. It was risky, but he couldn't see her languish away any longer.

"And now you've tied yourself to a female you're not sure will accept you. What will you do in the next twenty-nine days if she doesn't accept you?" Xavier crossed his arms over his chest.

He wouldn't think about that outcome. "It worked, she's awake, and that's all that matters to me."

"Yeah, okay, tell your dick that in thirty days," Leo muttered.

Xavier shook his head. "It's done now. What were you saying about the guards?"

Fallon sighed, no use taking his frustration out on his brother. "I haven't been able to figure out how they died, I have the Kira, Ade, looking over their bodies."

Leo whistled. "That's a big favor to ask."

"Yes." He would ask anything to have his mate safe.

The Kira were healers, a gracious race who used their gifts to heal the Demi. Ade was one of the elders, a noble only a few steps from their royalty. It was a big favor to ask him to leave his peaceful realm to help Brianna.

"Fallon, you have to rest." It was an order, Xavier's tone implacable.

Yeah, right, like he would sleep when his mate was in the infirmary scared and in pain. He'd snatched a few hours each night, Brianna wrapped in his arms, the skin contact helping according to the healers.

Damn it.

His mate.

He'd known it since the first moment he'd seen her a year ago, but instead of claiming her, he'd run. Instead of initiating the mating frenzy, he backed away from her to give himself time. Even after what he did yesterday, he wasn't altogether sure he wanted to be tied down with a mate. He'd roamed the Earth for a good portion of his adult life finding and researching magic. It was only in the last century that he'd settled and taken the position Xavier had given him at Haven. And still, he traveled between all the Havens in the world to make sure the wards that hid them from humans held. A mate involved settling down, continuing the family line, all ties that made him claustrophobic thinking about them.

But now, with desperation riding him, he'd initiated the bond anyway to save her life. Yesterday when he'd done it, it made the most sense. She would wake, and they would build on the tentative relationship they'd had prior to her accident. Surely it would've been easy to build their bond. But with her memory gone…He shook the bad thoughts from his head.

"I'll be fine, Xavier."

"Like hell, bro. You're about to fall down, and don't think we don't notice your magic wavering." Leo snorted and crossed over to his brother. He lifted his arm. "Unless you think humans have marbled skin?"

Fallon looked down and sighed. His skin was onyx, marbled with copper lines, proof that he couldn't hold his human skin. He couldn't let Brianna see him that way, especially with her memories gone. He gave up the magic and allowed his body to take its natural form. His skin tightened and stretched as he grew to his full six-feetseven inch height. His hands burned as the black-tipped claws were unsheathed. The soft silk of his hair brushed his shoulders and Fallon nearly slumped from the relief. Holding on to the power with no rest had been harder than he'd realized.

"When did you last feed, Fallon?" Xavier grabbed his brother's arm and slung it over his shoulder.

He searched his mind but his thoughts were jumbled, the days running together. Goddess, how long?

"Fallon?"

"I don't remember."

Leo cursed and grabbed his other arm, and his brothers guided him to the master bedroom of his apartment, lifting him into the bed. "What the fuck, Fallon? You know better."

He did, but it seemed irrelevant with everything going on. He opened his mouth to explain, but no words came out. Damn, he was exhausted. His brothers damn near carried him across the thick carpet in his bedroom and deposited him on the California king-sized bed in the middle of the room.

"Sleep," Xavier ordered. "Tomorrow is Saturday, if you're not on the floor at midnight, I'll chain you to a stripper pole."

Gods, Fallon winced. The thought of strange hands running across his body brought the sharp edge of hunger stabbing into his belly. Guilt pushed it back as he thought of his mate in the infirmary. But just thinking about Brianna's hands exploring his body brought it back, doubled. Lust tore through him and he growled, his vision sharpening as his teeth lengthened.

How long had it been since he'd slacked the lust clawing his chest, hardening his dick to a steel pike? A year, at least.

Since the night he'd met Brianna.

Somehow, he didn't think his brothers would want to hear that. He'd fed from a distance, skimming magic from the air during club nights, allowing it to dull his hunger, but not sate it. The magic from sensual energy worked the best for Cagyns, but it had him hard and achy most days. He'd tried feeding on the aggressive energy of fight night, but it'd only made battling his beast and his hunger a constant war. There were many nights he wound up on her doorstep with no memory of how he got there. His beast pushed, battering at his defenses until he'd finally decided to give in.

The night Brianna was kidnapped.

"Leave, I'll rest." He'd try.

Though sleep pulled at him, dragging him under, it didn't necessarily mean it would be restful sleep. The visions and dreams that haunted him since his traveling days didn't usually allow for it. He could pray he'd sleep long enough to be alert and able to help his mate when he woke.

Xavier and Leo both eyed him suspiciously.

"I'm posting up outside your door," Leo growled.

"Go to your mate, Leo. Liliana is due any day now. Don't use Fallon to avoid your grumpy mate." Xavier pushed a protesting Leo out the door.

Fallon listened to them argue until their voices faded. He closed his eyes, and sleep claimed him quickly.

Chapter 2

The quiet snick of the doorknob woke Brianna up. It took moments of disorientation for her to remember where she was.

Haven.

Where ever that was.

Brianna squinted as her best friend of more than twenty years rushed into the room, rolling a suitcase behind her. She let out a breathy sigh of relief.

"Thank God." Cassie left the suitcase against the wall at the door and rushed to her bedside. "I brought clothes for you."

Cassie wore a pair of leather leggings and a bright red, bulky knit sweater. Her hair was braided back in cornrows, and gold rings adorned them from front to back. It made her friend's high cheekbones stand out, her brown skin flawless and makeup-free, which was unusual for Cassie.

Brianna nodded and moved to sit up. She closed her eyes and pinched her lips together as pain radiated from her ribs and back with her every adjustment. While daunting, it wouldn't stop her from leaving. She didn't know what the heck Haven was, and as far as she could tell, no one had been in the room since the man named Fallon left. There were no nurses, no machines beeping or i.v. hookups, which was suspicious enough to make her nervous. She couldn't afford a private facility, so unless she spoke to someone with actual medical credentials she was hightailing it out of this place.

"I don't think it's a good idea for you to be up, Brianna." Still, Cassie gripped her under her arms and helped her to a sitting position.

She snorted. "I'm leaving here, so, you can help or you can nag." She took another deep breath and swung her legs, placing her feet on the floor. Cassie groaned and went over to the suitcase, grabbing a few items.

Brianna may have winced the whole time she struggled into the t-shirt and yoga pants Cassie brought for her, but she put them on all the same. She groaned as they wrestled a sweater over her head. She breathed from her mouth and leaned over her knees to catch a second wind once they were done.

She held a hand out for her friend to help her up. "Now, Cas, let's go."

Cassie sighed and pulled out her phone instead of reaching for her hand. "Hey, she says she wants to leave, but I'm worried she's not healed enough to go home." She paused and listened to the other end. "I know, I know. You don't have to tell me. Can you send someone to just look her over?"

Another pause and Brianna growled. Her best friend was snitching, but to who was the question.

Cassie hung up and eyed her. "There's a healer coming to look at you before we leave."

Her mouth hung open. "A healer?" She didn't bother disguising the scathing skepticism in her tone.

Cassie shrugged. "It's complicated."

"Complicated? Why am I not in a hospital?"

"I mean, you are, of sorts." Cassie grimaced. "It's hard to explain. What's the last thing you remember?

She frowned and thought about it, her head throbbing as she tumbled through memories. "Crossing the street to head to work."

Cassie's eyebrows bunched. "Work?"

Crap, yes, work. She needed to call her supervisor and explain why she hadn't made it in. Odds were though, she was fired. Cassie told her she'd been out for two weeks and her boss Frank was an asshole. So, she was as good as fired, and now she would need to find a way to pay rent. She sighed.

"I need to call Frank and find out if he sent out my final check yet." She was mentally doing the math on how long that check would stretch.

Cass stepped closer and touched her arm. "Sweetie. You don't work for the magazine anymore. You haven't for a year."

Her mouth dried, she took a rough breath. "What do you mean a year, I thought you said two weeks on the phone. I've been in a coma for a year?" she whispered.

"No! God, no. I'm sorry. It's only been two weeks, but from what Fallon tells me, and what you're saying now, you've lost a year of your memory." She sat down next to her on the edge of the bed.

"How is that possible?" She wracked her brain going through the endless amounts of information she stored there. Losing just a year of time? Did amnesia work that way? She'd have to research when she got home.

The door opened again, and the man who walked in brought an insane amount of energy with him. His presence soaked up all the air in the room, and not in a good way. He was nearly as handsome as Fallon, but his demeanor and 'don't fuck with me' attitude had all her fight or flight instincts engaged.

"We've had a few healers examine you, and none of them can tell us why you've lost only a portion of your memory." His deep voice matched him to perfection.

She shivered. He was huge, his arms hung at his sides, an irritated look painted on his face. A tall woman, braids trailing her back, shook her head at him and walked slowly to Brianna.

"If you don't mind?" The woman's voice was soft, soothing, but Brianna growled all the same.

A healer, what did that even mean? The woman smiled and examined the lacerations on her body. She moved Brianna's hair around to check her head. A tide of warmth suffused her body, and the soreness she'd felt since getting dressed, dissipated a little. She didn't want to believe in this woman, but she did feel better, so she thanked her.

"You really should allow your body a few more days of rest."

"I think a coma counts as rest."

A soft snort was the woman's only answer. She stood, nodded to Xavier and left the room. He studied her, the color of his eyes a warm hazel, but none of that warmth transferred to his expression.

"You should stay."

"I don't even know where I am or who you are."

"I'm Xavier and you're at Haven. I know you don't remember anything, and asking you to trust us is a stretch, especially for you, but I'll advise you that we can keep you safer here."

She frowned. "Why would you need to keep me safe?"

And why would they bother? He spoke to her and about her in a way that spoke of familiarity. It was disconcerting for someone to know her, and her not have any memory of them.

He exchanged a glance with Cassie whose eyes widened.

"Someone dumped you here. You were kidnapped and held for an undetermined amount of time, at least three days, though we can't ascertain when you were actually taken." Said in a detached manner, he folded his muscular arms across his chest and glanced at Cassie again. "We don't know who took you or necessarily what they wanted. I feel like it would be best if you stayed here."

"Well, that's not an option."

Though goosebumps chased up her arms and down her back, she kept her face neutral. Kidnapped. Yeah, he'd scared her, but she'd feel safer at her own home. Plus, she had an idea who would want to kidnap her. Not that she was telling this guy she didn't know.

He grunted. "Fallon will set up guards for you. Don't be alarmed if you see them around." It sounded non-negotiable.

She didn't do orders.

"I don't know you, so you can chill on ordering me around." She stood, thanking the unnamed woman for the fact that her body didn't buckle in pain.

He put his hands in his pockets and jingled what sounded like keys. "So, you're refusing help? On the basis of what?"

"What exactly is Haven?" She asked instead.

"It's a private club." Was his stiff answer.

"Private, as in members only?" She gave Cassie a hard look.

She would be asking her friend about it as soon as they left this place. She grabbed her suitcase, popped up the handle and walked towards the door, not missing the look passing between Xavier and Cassie.

He turned to track her movement. "Brianna, it would be easier for everyone if you stayed."

The scent of his cologne seemed to get stronger, the smell distracting, and enticing her for a long moment. She leaned towards him but jerked backward in surprise when she realized what she was doing.

"Who is everyone, you got mice in your pocket?"

"Goddess above, you get on my nerves, female."

"Female? You're an ass."

Xavier sighed and raised an eyebrow at her best friend.

Cassie grabbed her arm. "Brianna please, consider it."

"I want out of this…private club, now." She was not budging on it.

Cassie groaned, and Xavier raised his arm towards the door for them to precede him out of the room. She could see what Cassie meant when she said of sorts. It was a small facility, there were a few rooms in a circular pattern around a large wooden nurses' station in the middle. The woman who'd helped her looked up and gave a small, rueful shake of her head before going back to her paperwork. The place was quiet, with not even chatter from a television. It was eerie.

Further creeping her out, she was led into a corridor, a steel corridor that seemingly went on forever. Xavier led them through a myriad of tunnels, which really made her happy to be leaving. She slowly edged towards a panic attack, not sure of the source. Something about the hallways creeped her out, though she'd never been claustrophobic as far as she knew. She took a deep breath once they pushed out of a set of double doors and walked outside. The cool, fall air brushed her skin and she took a deep, grateful breath.

They'd spilled out of the doors into a small parking lot with only two cars in the lot, which was alarming. What kind of facility was it? There were at least three women at that nurse's station, and unless there was a parking garage in the back, those ladies had all rode in the same car. She shot her friend another disgusted look.

Shady shit.

She'd made the right decision. She shuffled her sore body into Cassie's expensive coup, sighing in relief when she sat, the white leather of the seat hugging her body. Though the healer's touch helped abate a lot of the pain, the walk out had aggravated her injuries, and now she sat sullen, waiting on her friend to get them out of this place. She watched Cassie and Xavier talk outside of the car for a few minutes, before she leaned over and tapped the horn in irritation. She knew they were talking about her, and she hated being left out of the loop. Cassie knew that better than anyone.

They both gave her incredulous looks.

Cassie entered the car and slammed the door. "Real mature, Brianna."

"A private club, Cassie, one that doesn't let people leave?"

"We're leaving, aren't we? No matter how stupid it is," she muttered.

"I don't know how we got caught in something like this, but I don't like it." Brianna shot back.

"It's not like you're going to listen to reason." Cassie sniped. "You were kidnapped, Brianna. I was scared out of my freaking mind while we looked for you. Fallon and his brothers moved heaven and earth to find you and they couldn't. We had to wait until you were dropped off in the street like garbage."

A shudder wracked Cassie's body and she held her head on the steering wheel a moment to compose herself. Sending Brianna a scathing look, she stabbed the button to start the car and peeled out.

Brianna took a deep breath, wincing as her ribs started to ache again. "I'm sorry, Cas, but I didn't feel comfortable there. Did you see the maze we went through to get out? We could disappear in there, and no one would ever know where to come to look."

"Well, you got your way." Cassie shook her head and turned the music up and tuned out her best friend.

Chapter 3

Brianna shuffled her sore body through the familiar door of her aunt's apartment. Grief had her hands shaking as she gripped the doorknob. She opened the door and wrinkled her nose at the smell of stale air, another indicator that the place had sat empty for some time. The faint smell of Cassie's favorite perfume lingered, probably from her coming to get clothes. She took another breath, almost willing her memories to come back.

When nothing happened, she sighed and stepped inside. Cassie was on her heels, her rolling suitcase behind her. Cassie had explained a little of her life in the year she was missing as they rode over. They'd lapsed into a tense silence as Cassie explained her aunt's death. How could she forget something that big in her life? She searched for something to say to break the awkward silence.

She sighed. "Look, I'm sorry, Cassie, I'm grouchy and lashed out at you."

"It's fine. It just sucks that your memory is gone. All of the issues from the past are clouding your judgment."

Brianna rolled her eyes. "We both know the Esin are the ones who kidnapped me. I don't know why you can't see it. Nothing could have happened in the past year to make me not suspect them."

Cassie frowned. "We left them years ago, I was Chosen, why would they kidnap you and not me, and why now?"

"Well, who the hell else would have a reason to kidnap me and bring me back?"

Cassie clammed up, but on her face was a secret. Brianna had known her nearly their entire life, she knew when Cassie was hiding something. She was too tired to deal with it, so she let it go. If Cassie wanted to believe she didn't know who kidnapped her, then who was she to shatter her illusions.

She looked around. The apartment was familiar, but it should've been. She and Cassie had spent the end part of their teenage years in it, though, everything inside was different. From the furniture to the paint color. The place looked modern, sleek. Everything her bohemian Aunt Sarah wasn't. Gray paint, the color cool and soothing covered the walls, replacing the turquoise color her aunt had splashed on every wall. There was one bright tangerine wall in the dining area, one of the few remnants of Sarah's quirky taste. As she looked around, Brianna spotted more of her aunt's artwork hung around the apartment. Her crystals were on a bookshelf against the wall. She swallowed the lump in her throat.

She'd made all these changes?

She spun in a circle. All of her stuff was there. Pictures of her and Cassie, a picture of her parents. She felt a small pang at that. They were still with the Esin and she doubted they even got her letters to them. She traced her finger over their picture. Her elephant statues were there, her books, even her laptop lay on a side table.

It was strange. The last time she'd lived in this apartment, she and Cassie had been sixteen and running for their lives. They'd lived with her aunt until they were old enough to move out and get jobs. It was eerie seeing her stuff up instead of her aunt's.

Cassie touched her shoulder. "Nothing?"

Brianna shook her head and regretted the motion. "Nothing new anyway. Remembering when Aunt Sarah let us live here for the first time." A sharp pang of grief brought tears to her eyes.

Cassie sighed and looked around. "It felt like a castle. Two young girls from a trailer park, this place was like a dream."

Her ribs ached as she turned to her friend. "Tell me again why I couldn't go to a hospital?"

Cassie sighed. "We were afraid if we took you to a hospital, whoever took you would try again."

She was skeptical. "Why kidnap me, drop me off and kidnap me again?" It didn't make sense.

Cassie didn't answer.

"Well, I need to go see someone with a medical degree to make sure there's no lasting damage from whatever happened to me. I can only assume there's no police report?"

"The police won't help you with magic," was Cassie's answer.

Um, the fuck? Her mouth dropped open. "Magic, Cassie?"

Surely she couldn't be serious. Next, her best friend would tell her that she not only believed in Santa Claus, but she also helped him deliver toys. She shook her head.

Cassie's shuddering sigh brought her attention to her friend's face. Tears streamed down her cheeks.

"You almost died, Brianna," she turned her head and wiped her face. "Were it not for Fallon, you would've wilted away. I would never do anything to endanger you and you know that."

"I'm sorry I don't believe in magic."

"I don't care if you don't believe in it, Brianna. It saved your life!" A sob racked Cassie's shoulders and she rushed to her, enfolding her into her arms.

Cassie's grip was light. Even as she cried, she was considerate of Brianna's pain. Cassie cried for a few minutes, hiccupping sobs that made Brianna feel guilty for doubting her friend.

"I'm sorry, I'm a bitch." She said as Cassie stepped back.

"You're not…without your memory, everything will seem suspicious to you, I know that. It's just…" Cassie sighed. "I watched you lie in that bed, writhing in pain some days for hours. I'm happy you're alive and I won't apologize for the measures we took to make it so."

Brianna nodded, had it been Cassie in that bed, she would've done anything she could to help her. "I'm sorry."

Cassie wiped her face and sniffled. "Sit, let me make you some coffee."

Brianna rubbed her hands down her thighs, the raised seams of the pants scrapping her palm and grounding her. She hadn't believed in magic when they were growing up in the Esin, she for damn sure wouldn't spend her adult life looking for magical remedies. It wasn't worth hurting her friend again to argue about it, so she dropped it.

She had no idea what had happened to her, or what kind of condition she was in. She was a person that needed information, and she would get it from a source she trusted and knew, at least. She'd just make an appointment with her doctor when Cassie left and file a police report when she was done. Once she had concrete medical information on her condition, she'd work to find out how to fix it.

A year, a whole year she'd lost. How was that possible? She sat on the leather sofa in the large sitting area. It was a spacious apartment. The high ceilings and polished wood floors lent an elegant feel to the place. She'd knocked down a wall that used to separate the kitchen from the living room, giving the place an open floor plan. She liked it a lot. It was eerie that she didn't remember doing it. She pushed her hair off her forehead. She was the lucky owner of the entire building both her apartment and a beautiful bookstore downstairs.

Cassie hadn't given her much of an explanation as they came through the building, only that her aunt had left everything to her when she'd died. Sorrow clenched her chest as she thought of her aunt. Sarah had helped her and Cass when they'd left the cult they'd grown up in, giving them a place to stay, and helping them as they navigated Atlanta. She'd helped them both get their GEDs and offered to pay for their colleges. Cassie had taken her up on it and had made monster bucks as a stock analyst until she'd tired of that. She was now a wedding photographer, a highly sought after one.

Brianna had gone a more circuitous route for her education, but she'd finished her bachelors and landed at a magazine on their research team. Not the most glamorous job, but it was one she enjoyed. Even if it didn't pay much.

She frowned. Cassie said she didn't work for the magazine anymore. It made sense since she now owned a bookstore and café. That was something to figure out on another day. For now, her head was reeling with the changes in her life.

She stretched out on the large red couch that was definitely to her taste, laying her head on the armrest and staring at the ceiling. So, let's see if she had the details right, she was a detail person. Reciting them would help calm her and keep her from the freak out she felt brewing in her chest.

She was kidnapped possibly up to three weeks ago.

Two weeks ago she'd been dumped at Haven, the place where she'd just awakened. According to a stern-faced Xavier, she'd been in a coma for two weeks, only now waking.

She thought about Xavier and shuddered. Dude was seriously scary. Completely drop dead gorgeous with an intense demeanor that said he didn't take shit. If she closed her eyes she could probably still see his cold eyes staring her down. It was so different from Fallon's warm gaze. Everything about Fallon was warmer than Xavier. They looked similar enough to be brothers, and for all she knew, they were. She pushed aside her body's reaction to Fallon to dissect later.

Xavier hadn't wanted her to leave, telling her she could heal there, but she'd not escaped one cult to get sucked into another. He'd called it a private club, but yeah…she'd pass. Anything the rest of the world couldn't know about, she didn't want any parts of.

Cassie came out of the kitchen with a steaming cup of coffee, and she sat up, grateful.

"So, I'm going to stay with you here until you're completely healed."

"You don't have to do that, Cas." She clutched the hot cup inhaling the wonderful scent. "This coffee smells expensive, I can't afford expensive coffee."

Cassie snorted. "Child please, with the amount of money Aunt Sarah left you, you could buy coffee pooped out of a rare goat's ass, and bathed in unicorn tears."

"Jesus, Cassie." She muttered taking her first sip. It was quite good.

"So, as I was saying. I'm staying here with you until you gain back your memory."

"We'll kill each other before then."

It had been years since she'd last lived with her best friend, and if she remembered, Cassie didn't understand the meaning of the word tidy. She operated under the rule of, what's yours is ours. Brianna was obsessive about what she deemed her space.

Cassie waved off her concern. "After all these years, I've learned to stay out of your space, and you've learned to tolerate my messy streak."

Brianna snorted.

"Anyway, Xavier said he would send a healer over here every day to check on your progress and I'm sure Fallon will have someone watching the place in case something else happens."

Her body warmed at the mention of Fallon. Her lips tingled in remembrance of their kiss. That man should not be loosed on the female population. Cassie was looking at her strange which meant she'd missed some parts of the conversation.

"Sorry." She took another sip.

Cassie sighed. "I need to leave and get some stuff to stay here, I'll be back in about an hour. Will you be okay alone?"

She tilted her head and raised an eyebrow.

Cassie smiled. "Right, sorry, who did I think I was talking to? We can chat when I get back and I'll fill in more of your missing year."

Brianna nodded her assent and Cassie left.

She sipped her coffee, looking around the space. It was a beautiful apartment, arched windows with a couple of walls with bare brick. She stood, clutching her cup and wandered around. There were two bedrooms with ensuite bathrooms. One she'd once shared with Cassie, and the master bedroom once belonging to her aunt. From the looks of it, she'd redecorated in the last year. None of her and

Cassie's teenage paraphernalia littered the walls as it had when they'd lived here. She passed the office that they never used and paused.

The small room had been redecorated as well, but more to her taste. The white walls lent an airy feel to the room. Built-in bookshelves covered one wall to the left of her desk and oversized, framed black and white pictures adorned the wall on the right. They were all Cassie's images, taken at her friend's favorite wedding venues. She loved the images, but then, she loved all of Cassie's work, so it was no surprise. Her desk was a simple white table with shiny gold legs. It faced a large picture window that looked out into the street. The sheer curtains let in the morning sun, bathing the room in muted light. She drifted into the office and observed the neat-as-a-pin desk, her distinct loopy writing covering the notebook left open next to a large monitor.

She smiled.

Cassie had once said her writing was the only romantic thing about her. The way she'd decorated the whole apartment called her friend a liar. The place was modern and functional, but there were whimsical touches everywhere that pleased Brianna on a very feminine level. She and Cassie just had different ideas of romance.

She flipped through the notebook. Her eyebrows lowered as she read the contents. It was about the Esin, but the notes hinted at differences between their story and the Demi's story. Who were the Demi? She sat at the comfortable leather chair and was soon lost in her notes. She laid her head on her desk to think about the things she'd read and fell asleep.

Chapter 4

Shaking the sleep from his head, Fallon swung his feet off his bed and sat on the edge. He was not much more rested than when he'd went to sleep. It was the price for the power he'd gradually collected over the years. The nightmares…that and being tied to a god who ruled the hell realm.

He sighed.

He wanted to check on Brianna, but from their last interaction, he didn't know if he should. Either way, he needed to take a shower first. He made it quick, going over the list of things he wanted to get done today. First on the list was food. His stomach agreed with a loud growl. Next would be checking on his mate. Since she was awake, he could probably go down to his office for a bit to see what else he could find out about her kidnapping.

He walked into the kitchen, his towel hanging on his hips. There was fruit in a bowl on his kitchen counter and he devoured it, searching his cabinets for something easy to make. He could call down to the kitchens, but it would take time he didn't really feel like wasting. Finding nothing, he sighed.

He'd been at Brianna's bedside for the past two weeks, of course, his cupboards were bare. He would stop by the kitchens on his way down to his office. He wondered if Brianna was able to eat now that she'd awakened. He walked over to the comms panel in his living room and punched in the number for the infirmary. It was answered immediately, the image of the healer at her station popping up. Just as quickly, her serene expression unchanging, she told him Brianna had left.

"What do you mean, left?" He tamped down on the panic building in his chest.

The Kira made a sympathetic sound and shrugged. "The Marshal gave permission for her to leave."

He growled and ended the call, dialing his brother's office.

"Yes." Xavier's assistant was not any nicer than her boss.

"Where is he?"

"Unavailable, Commander." She flickered an impatient glance at the screen and continued with her work.

He cursed and slapped the comms panel to end the call, knowing he'd get no further information from her. He rushed to his bedroom for his personal communicator. He dialed his brother's direct number. It took a few rings, but his brother's image flipped on the screen, a scowl covering his face.

"What?"

"Where is she?" He used magic to manifest his uniform, black cargo pants and black short-sleeved button-down shirt on his body, along with his black boots.

Xavier sighed. "She went home."

"What? Are you serious?"

"Tone, little bro," Xavier growled.

Fallon glared at his brother's image. "How could you let her leave?"

"She didn't want our help, and you know I can only deal with her attitude for like, a hot second. I let her go." Xavier waved away his concern and went back to whatever work he'd been doing when Fallon called.

Gods, but Xavier could be a dick when he wanted to be. His brother and Brianna butt heads every time they talked, so he knew the attitude to which Xavier referred. With no one there to intercede the two could and would argue until one of them got mad and left.

"You shouldn't have let her leave." Fallon corralled his temper as best he could.

"As it is illegal to kidnap on this realm, I had no choice." Xavier groused.

"Who's watching her?"

Xavier sighed and shuffled through the papers on his desk. He pulled up a small note. "Leo sent Roy after her and Cassie. I assumed you would assign someone when you woke. I didn't expect you to sleep for two days."

"Two days!" His stomach dropped and he nearly swayed with worry.

"Yes, two days. So, now that you're awake you can do your job and I can focus on more important shit, namely finding the book your human can't seem to remember losing. Hopefully, she doesn't die out there while you're in here napping."

Fallon growled. "Your compassion knows no bounds."

"Fucking right." Xavier flipped his brother the bird and ended their transmission.

Despite his brother's callous words, he knew Xavier wouldn't let harm come to Brianna while he'd been asleep. Besides the fact that she was his mate, his brother took his job very seriously. They'd been tasked by their god, Rugaba to keep her safe, and X would do that with or without input from Brianna.

Fallon rushed into his office on the third lower deck while trying to reach Cassie. It was the same place they kept their cells, so there was minimal personnel on this floor. Just the way he liked it. He was in charge of the soldiers and their assignments as well as security for the Haven. He maintained all the wards keeping the Havens from being seen by the public. Keeping his office down on basement level three kept him from visitors and general complainers. The silence on this floor was deafening and rarely did anyone venture down to the B3 level.

Cassie finally answered. "Fallon, hey."

"How is she?"

"She's Brianna, so, I don't really know. She doesn't seem to be in pain. She slept the past couple of days and barely ate. Your brother sent healers here and they've been in and out. She's up and out today, she went to see a 'real human doctor', her words, not mine."

A weight lifted and he slowed his steps to his desk. "How many guards are on her?"

"I have no idea. Xavier arranged everything, but I haven't seen anyone hanging out looking buff and bodyguard like."

He grunted. "If they're doing their job, you won't ever see them until you need them."

"That's only slightly creepy." She muttered.

"Well, I'm up, so if you need anything from now on, call me, okay."

"Sure, no problem."

"Thanks, Cassie."

Ending that call, his first order of business was finding a replacement for her current guards. He shuffled through the personnel files on his computer looking for a suitable replacement for Roy. Not because Roy couldn't handle the job, but because Roy was Lily's personal guard and he was sure she was complaining about being stuck in Haven until he came back.

He called Leo. His youngest brother was in the kitchen of his apartment, sitting at the table.

"Who else have you trained besides Roy and Paul?"

"What do you mean?" Leo put a hand to his chest, his eyes wide with fake innocence.

He sighed. "I know you've been harassing my trainers and taking over their classes."

Leo shrugged. "Well, not being able to hunt sucks."

He knew his brother had been antsy since he'd been ordered to stop hunting. He had wandered around Haven looking for something to do until he'd finally settled on 'helping' the trainers Fallon had assigned.

"You don't trust your trainers?"

"It's not that. You're better." He reluctantly relented.

"Of course." Leo laughed.

And Fallon rolled his eyes. The modesty in their family was astounding.

"Liliana marked it in their records, as she said you would want to know."

He quickly went through his records and found her mark, thanking the gods for his sister-in-law.

"Thanks." He hung up on his little brother.

He recognized two of the guards as having been assigned to Brianna before her kidnapping. He called them and sent them over to Brianna's bookstore with implicit instructions to be careful of magic.

He would assign two more when he had a little more time, so they could rotate and rest.

The next order of business was checking the Oras. He hadn't been able to do it when he'd sat at her bedside, but now he could take his time and look through the footage. He queued it up for the day he went to visit her and found her missing.

He moved through the images, working backward to see if he could find the exact time she went missing. The Oras used the magnetic fields around the earth. Their magic allowed them to use those fields to record and monitor any place of the Earth. It worked exactly like humans used satellites, but it was more accurate, the images clearer.

He filtered the images down until he found her bookstore the day before he visited. He watched as a vehicle pulled up in the alley behind her place and sat idle. He frowned as the van sat idle for five minutes with no movement. A moment later the guards he'd assigned to Brianna slipped out of the shadows around the building. There was what looked like a scuffle. He flipped the image, coming in from the other side, to see the fight better.

He cursed. It looked like his guards were fighting…nothing. Air, they were punching and kicking at the air.

"What the hell?" He whispered.

He moved past the images, and moments later, Brianna came out of the building, struggling, fighting. Again, there was no one there. They were invisible? What kind of magic hid from the Oras?

Everything on the Earth had an energy signature, and the Oras picked it up. Why was it coming up blank? He fast-forwarded through and watched as the guards were ostensibly picked up by ghosts and tossed into the panel van. He checked the Oras around the time she was dumped and the same thing. A van pulled up, stopped and Brianna was tossed from the same panel van. What the hell was going on?

He had tried to view the video from the cameras he'd set up around her building the day she went missing and they had come back blank. The whole day had been completely erased. Two separate security measures skirted. Her kidnapping was getting complicated as evidence came in.

A knock on his door had him looking up. The healer, Ade, entered. The tall male was shirtless, the rings on his shoulder reaching his chest, in tight concentric circles. It denoted both his age and status. The older a Kira was, the more the rings on their chest filled out. Tree branches, resembling dreadlocks were pulled back into a low ponytail and trailed his back. Ade emanated peace, his magic filling Fallon's office with its calming presence.

"Ade, please, come in. What did you find?" Fallon was anxious to know what happened to his guards.

Ade sat in the chair in front of his desk. "Well, the eeriest thing."

Fallon leaned forward and took the comms tablet he held out. He skimmed through the images of his dead soldiers, anger, and grief making his head pound.

"It wasn't Demi magic."

Fallon frowned and went to the actual report. "No?

"No, it was from the Divine." Ade leaned over the desk and pointed out the section of the report on how they died.

Fallon reeled. The only divine Esin in their area was closely aligned with them. They had a shaky truce with them dating back at least three decades. What reason would they have to go against the Amanda?

"It was death magic, magic I haven't seen in some centuries. Not since the Divine started reproducing with Neanderthals."

"So an old Esin?" He used his fingers to scroll through the other details of where they'd found them.

"That's the thing. An Esin old enough to know this magic would know not to use it. The karma that comes with it outweighs its use."

"So whoever used it?"

"Is probably dead or dying." Ade raised his eyebrows. "I'm sorry for your loss, but I'd be damned interested in seeing the effects of the spell on whoever wielded it."

Fallon grunted. It wasn't unexpected. The Kira were scholars, he could understand Ade wanting to study the results of the spell.

"Is it something we'll need to worry about in general, this death spell?"

"I really don't think so. This is a specific threat." Ade supplied, standing to leave. "Still, I'll get with an archivist and see what I can find. I also assigned someone specifically to your mate. Hopefully, we can figure out this memory thing."

Fallon called down to Xavier and told him he needed to see him with an update. He gathered the comms pad and stood. This case was getting stranger by the minute.

Chapter 5

Keyboard keys clacking followed by the occasional curse word were the only sounds in the office. Brianna growled as she came up against another dead end in her internet search. Her notes were all about 'Demi', but the only thing she'd found on the Demi was vague notations in old African folk tales. She thought back to her time in the Esin. There had never been a lot of mention of the Demi when they were younger, outside of stories the children passed around to scare each other. Her notes made reference to recent interactions with them which was why she'd tried scouring the internet. She was frustrated and it was not a nice look on her. Luckily she was alone and had no one to take it out on.

She'd slept for two days. Two more days of her life gone! All she could remember about the time were bits and pieces of Cassie bringing her in food and strange women checking over her, waving rocks over her body. It was all a blur, a big, frustrating blur.

She stood and stretched out her back, having been in the same position for at least an hour. She thought about her doctor's appointment earlier that morning. He'd saw the bruising and said that from the looks of it, her injuries were a few weeks old, which didn't gel with what Cassie had told her and she wouldn't let her self believe that the 'healer' Cassie convinced to let her see had done anything in any meaningful way that would've healed her wounds. The doctor had told her that it was possible for her brain block memories a traumatic event, and to give her body and mind time to process what happened. He told her that it was best to rest and take it easy. She didn't know if she could necessarily do that. But, as far as she was concerned, research didn't require physical effort so technically she was following his orders.

She picked up her notebook and walked to the bookshelf that housed books her aunt had treasured. Some of them were listed in her notes as sources. She'd assumed they would also be on the internet and she'd been wrong. She would have to do her research the old fashioned way.

Cassie came around the corner with a towel wrapped around her body and one drying her hair.

"Hey, Cass, why do I have notes about the Demi?"

Cassie sighed and stopped at the door. "I knew it wouldn't take you long."

Her eyes widened in surprise. Had she been searching all morning for answers when she could've just asked her best friend? She walked over and sat back in her office chair and awaited the response.

Cassie plopped into the armchair in the middle of the office. "What do you know?"

Brianna growled. "Not much, the notes I have are vague and, I've managed to lock myself out of a ton of files on this fancy computer."

"You, are…the you of a year ago, I don't know that you'd believe anything I tell you."

"Try me."

Cassie stood. "This conversation definitely calls for liquor and clothes."

She walked over to Brianna's desktop and pulled up the files she'd been trying to get into all morning. With a few clicks of the keyboard, she opened a massive file with multiple smaller files hidden in it. Giving Brianna a pitying glance she left the room.

"I'll meet you in the living room when you're ready." She said over her shoulder.

Brianna opened a random file and her mouth dropped. Information on the Douglasville Esin, the cult she'd grown up in, was broken down by their beliefs and compared to….no that couldn't be right. Compared to a thriving Esin here, right outside of the city. An Esin this close to metropolitan Atlanta? She scoffed. She found it hard to believe another cult doing what Elder Cedric had done in his Esin could operate so close to law enforcement.

She knew Aunt Sarah had once been a part of an Esin, but since she and Cassie had come to live with her, Sarah had either stop going or kept it from them. She'd never seen a clue that her aunt was still involved. Grief struck her anew. She shook it off and went back to her notes.

"What grown adults believed in magic?" she muttered to herself.

Not only believed in it but if her notes were right, actively practiced it. She pulled her thick hair back into a ponytail searching her desk for a tie. Finding it, she bound her hair and dove into the research it seemed she'd collected these last few months. A lot of it was from a Demi library? Twenty minutes later Cassie once again entered her office. This time with a bottle of brandy and a plastic cup. She had a soda in the other hand.

Handing the soft drink to Brianna, she dropped into the armchair. "I figured you'd be stuck on your notes and forget I was waiting for you in the living room."

"There is an Esin in Roswell and you're wondering who kidnapped me? Why wouldn't they have done it, if you don't think it was our old Esin?"

Cassie sighed. "They for sure didn't kidnap you, Bri. Your aunt was an elder in the Roswell Esin, they would never. And, we left our Esin when we were sixteen, why would they wait this long to come after you?"

"Maybe." She tapped her chin with her pen and conceded Cassie's point. "So Aunt Sarah was still practicing? Do you believe this stuff, like about magic?" She asked indicating her computer.

"We've lived that stuff for the past year, *you* believe in it, hell, you're a lot better at it than I am."

She snorted. Her doing magic? "I seriously doubt that."

Cassie shrugged instead of answering.

"So who are the Demi?"

Cassie tucked her legs in the chair and took a big gulp of her brandy. "Certainly not the boogieman of our childhood. According to their records, they're the children of the gods and the first humans."

Brianna sat back in her desk chair. "What kind of records?"

She could get with records. Documentation was something she wholeheartedly believed in. It was something a lot more tangible than magic.

"They have archivists who have kept track of their recorded history. The gods made the first humans from clay and fell in lust with their creations. The progeny from those unions are the Demi."

"Hmm," she grunted. "I haven't gone through all the files, but the majority of them come from the Demi's library. Why would we have been given access to something like that? They didn't trust humans. That's what we were taught, right?"

"It's true they don't trust humans, but it didn't pertain to us." Cassie lowered her eyes.

She growled, sensing her friend's evasion. "I want to go there, then. To the Demi library."

Cassie sighed. "I'll call Fallon and arrange it. Since we're talking about the Esin. You probably want to see your parents."

Brianna gasped, her heart ached. "My parents escaped?" She whispered.

"Escaped, dragged out forcibly, ransomed, either of those would apply." Cassie gave her a sympathetic look.

"Ransomed?"

"You wanted your parents out. Remember, we weren't allowed to visit them since we're persona non grata with Elder Cedric, but you being you, found a way to get a message to them. The Oliri found out about it and offered to let them go for a price. Your parents didn't know you had the money from Aunt Sarah, so they tried to stop you, even going so far as refusing to leave. You took a hundred thousand dollars and a couple of guards from Haven and forcibly removed them from there."

Tears gathered in her eyes. "Where are they?"

Cassie looked away.

"Cassandra."

"They're staying with the Roswell Esin."

"What?!" Her voice bounced off the walls. "Why in the hell would I rescue them from one cult and put them in another?"

Cassie sighed. "Brianna, with your memory gone, there's so much context you're missing."

"I want to see them." She demanded.

"Of course. We can go now. They're worried about you. They came to see you, when..." she cleared her throat. "Aunt Deidre will be happy to see you up and out of the bed."

"They were allowed to see me?"

She slightly adjusted her view of both the Haven and the Esin where her parents lived. Not enough to quell her distrust, but still. There were strict rules about allowing Esin members to fraternize with those they considered outsiders. At least at the Douglasville Esin, could this one be that different?

"Allowed. Brianna." Cassie ran a hand through her hair. "Yes, your mom stayed with you the first week, the only reason she wasn't there when you woke, was because Uncle Henry made her get some rest. She's anxious to see you."

"Can I, can I talk to them?"

Cassie got up and came back a few moments later with a slick cell phone. "The number's in there. Take all the time you need."

***

Fallon knocked on Leo's door before punching in the code and entering. It was quiet, but the fragrance of flowers filled the foyer. He walked into their living room and saw the source of the scent along with gifts on nearly every surface. He didn't want to announce his presence, knowing the baby could be somewhere sleeping. Liliana had delivered his first nephew while he'd been asleep and he would be kicking his brother's ass for leaving that out when he'd talked to him earlier.

He moved silently through the living room and opened the bedroom door. Liliana was sleeping on top of the blankets, her arm resting on the small crib next to the bed. He tiptoed in and peeked. His heart stopped a moment and expanded when he looked saw his nephew's little face. Loose black curly hair covered his head, and his skin was a beautiful chocolate color. He was completely swathed, so Fallon couldn't see the amber whorls that would cover his body, showing his Cagyn heritage. He was half Eshu, but his winged tattoo on his back wouldn't show until he was a little older. He couldn't resist running a finger across his nephew's soft hair. Kell moved a little, his mouth making a moue of irritation.

Fallon smiled, and let himself out of the room. He found his mother in the kitchen making tea. Her face lit as she saw him.

She turned and gave him a hug. "You want a cup of tea?" She kept her voice soft.

"Yes, please." He sat in the chair, the lack of sleep and feeding catching up to him. His body was exhausted despite him having slept two days. He gratefully grabbed the cup from his mother.

"Did you see the baby?" She asked, blowing into her cup.

"He's very cute."

"Kell is the most handsome kid in the world."

He squirmed in the chair, finding a more comfortable position, laughing at Sharine's enraptured face. "You're going to spoil him rotten."

"Of course." There was no shame on her face.

"I should probably warn Liliana that you'll be unbearable for the foreseeable future."

"Don't you dare." Her quiet chuckle made him smile. "I'm barely back into her good graces after the wedding."

He snorted. "She should've made you work a little harder for it."

"Psh," she waved away his words. "It's been a year, over a year."

"Mother, you taunted the queen until she couldn't even maintain her social face. You two were arguing like fishwives."

"I hate Kaylin." She muttered, sipping her tea.

"What? I couldn't tell." He rolled his eyes.

"She tried to kill my son, you know. She's lucky I didn't use that fancy silverware to carve away her face. I'm glad she's dead."

He groaned and sipped on his own tea. Gods, but his mother was dramatic…and violent, no doubt she would've put hands on the queen, had she not promised him to be decent. He knew he couldn't ask her to behave. No, that would've been asking too much of Sharine, but he'd begged her, before the ceremony started, right as she'd started tearing into their father, to at least curb her more violent tendencies, if only to keep from embarrassing her sons.

"And Liliana's so-called mother, ugh." She made a disgusted sound.

"Enough mom, as you said it was a year ago."

"Well, not that I'm happy they're estranged, but, I do relish having Kell to myself." She lifted her cup to her mouth, a selfsatisfied smile curving her lips.

"You're impossible." He shook his head, but couldn't help but smile.

His mother was an acquired taste, not all got her biting and sarcastic humor, but he did, and he was regularly amused by it.

She touched his hand. "What's going on with you?"

He shrugged. "Work stuff."

"You're labeling Brianna under 'work stuff'." She raised a brow.

"Mother."

She held up her hand. "I'm not butting in, I told you I wouldn't." She grabbed his hand. "You look exhausted, my love. Are you feeding, eating, sleeping?"

None of those things, but telling his mother that was a surefire way to have her hovering over him for the next few weeks. "I'm fine, *Iya*."

She fiddled with the linen at the table. "Fallon, you're not…I know your father and I aren't a stellar example of a mating, you're not letting that stand in the way are you?"

"*Iya*," he whispered and sighed. "That's…you and dad treated each other like shit. But I don't harbor much resentment from that, and this thing between Brianna and I has nothing to do with the two of you." He gripped her hand.

"I can't help but feel a little responsible."

"You and dad are you and dad. It's not the same."

She nodded. "I just get so angry with your father."

"Then why did you do it?" Neither of them had heard Leo enter the apartment.

Sharine sucked in a sharp breath. "Leo."

He stood. Sharine waved him back into his chair and approached her youngest son. "He asked." She whispered. "I don't know if you can understand how crazy in love I was with your father, but he asked and I just couldn't…" She shrugged her shoulders.

Leo stood stiff at the entrance to the kitchen.

Sharine stood in front of him, her hands fisted at her sides. "It wasn't the first time he'd asked. He'd asked me at least a dozen times before I finally said yes." She rubbed her arms. "We were so close, the four of us. Ray and the king were best friends and Kaylin and I sort of tagged along whenever they met. He was desperate and your father desperate to help his best friend retain his kingdom. The way he'd explained it was that you were the last resort. If they tried to remove the king from his throne, then he would produce you as his heir. If Kaylin had a child before that happened, then we agreed not to put you through any of it." The words spilled from her mouth in a flurry.

Her eyes welled and Fallon couldn't help but get angry at the manipulation he knew it would take for his father to convince Sharine to do it. She'd been a totally different person before the birth of his brother. There were many years after Leo was born where he'd hated the intrusion of his little brother's birth. It had taken a while for him to warm up to the kid.

"I made him promise that you would stay with us, that I could raise you until you were needed. I knew Kaylin wouldn't accept you and I knew after carrying you for a year, I wouldn't be able to give you up. You see, I had asked your father for more children, and he told me, with his new responsibilities it wasn't possible, so, in the end, it was a chance to have another child." She lowered her head. "Your father reneged though. He promised to let me have you, and he turned around and turned you against me. I will never forgive him for that." she whispered.

Leo stepped fully into the room.

She lifted her head. "I apologize to you, for dragging you in the middle of it when I left. I…you looked at him with such love in your eyes, and you didn't give me a chance."

Fallon closed his eyes at the pain in his mother's voice. He and Leo had fought over their differing feelings about their father and this was why. He knew the Sharine prior to Leo, and she was a hard woman, yes, but one who loved her children hard.

"I'm sorry, *Iya*," Leo whispered.

Sharine gasped, tears, cresting her eyes and falling down her cheeks. Leo hadn't called their mother, mom, in a very long time.

"No, I didn't know the truth, but there was no excuse to treat you the way that I did." He wiped a hand over his face. "I held Kell in my arms," he held open his hands. "I looked into his face and fell in love. Just imagining him not being in my life, or treating me in the way I treated you. I'm sorry and I forgive you."

Sharine sobbed. He and Leo both rushed to her side. She hugged tight to first Leo and then him, not leaving him out.

She wiped her face and laughed. "This is probably the best day of my life outside you guys' birth."

Fallon smiled at his brother, happy he'd been able to get closure with their mother. He was still fighting with their father, but that was a whole separate situation. One, he reminded himself, he wouldn't interfere with. He would not come behind Leo and mediate between the two.

The communicator at his hip vibrated. He looked down and saw the guard who was watching Brianna. He kissed his mother's forehead and excused himself. He stepped into the hallway and took the call.

"Commander, we're following Brianna and Cassie to the local Esin to visit her parents, do you want us to follow them in?"

"Absolutely." He thought about Ade's report. It was Divine magic that had killed his guards, he didn't want her alone anywhere for now. "Did you relieve Roy before or after Brianna's doctor's appointment?"

"Before. From what I could glean, she took a lot of tests but nothing came back."

"Do I want to know how you found that out?"

"You do not. But I'll let you know the results once they come in." Isaiah answered.

"I'll call over to the Esin and let them know you're her guard. Stay on your toes though, the Divine are entangled in her kidnapping in some way."

"No problem. I'll let you know if anything happens." Isaiah assured him.

Isaiah's report matched what Cassie had told him earlier this morning. He yawned, rolling his shoulders to remove some of the tension. He needed to eat and to feed, and not necessarily in that order.

He headed down to his office, doing neither, wanting to keep working on Brianna's case.

Chapter 6

"Holy crap," Brianna whispered as they went through a gated entrance.

For all intents and purposes, it looked like a gated community. Very much different than the dusty trailer park in which they'd grown up. There were houses in neat little rows, gardens in the front yard of a good portion of them. They drove through slowly. There was what looked like a temple, with farmland spread behind it.

"What is this place?" She couldn't keep the awe from her voice.

"This is what a real Esin is supposed to look like." Cassie made another turn.

There were statues of a stern-looking god flanking the temple and she turned around in her seat, fascinated by the familiar expression on his face as they drove past it. Cassie took a couple of turns, slowing past kids playing in the street. There was shouting and squealing as they passed a park.

Her eyes widened. "There are so many kids here."

Cassie nodded. "Happy kids."

She turned down another street and parked in front of a house with a porch and flowers.

"Is this their house?" A lump swelled in her throat. Her mother had always wanted a porch.

"Yes, and as you can tell by the crazy amount of flowers, Uncle Henry has settled well." Cassie laughed.

Cassie switched off the car and the front door opened. Her parents came out onto the porch looking happier than she'd ever seen them. Her mother's kinky hair was in its normal braid, trailing her back, her father's locks were pulled back into a bun. They looked younger than their fifty-six years and she'd always been fascinated by that. Her mother wore a pair of loose pants, flowers in blinding colors adorning it. Her simple tank top hugged her trim body. Her father wore a pair of worn overalls, the dirt on the knees telling her what he'd been doing all morning. Tears escaped and she rushed from the car. They both enveloped her in their arms and she sobbed.

"I can't believe this is real." She whispered.

Her mother sniffled and pulled Cassie into a hug. "Come inside you two. Despite Henry's fondness for the outdoors, it's too cool out here today."

She shuffled them through the well-kept house, way bigger than the small trailer where they'd lived. Deidre settled them at the kitchen table and moved around to make them tea. Her eyes widened at the fancy equipment everywhere.

"What is all this stuff?" It looked like nothing she'd ever seen.

"Well, the Demi share some of their technology with us. It's like living in the future," her mother laughed.

"Yes, and annoying to boot, but every time your mother goes to solstice worship, she comes back tinkering with another gadget."

Brianna laughed. Her father was a simple man, his garden, and his family his only needs. Her mother, on the other hand, had an obsessive need to know how things worked.

"How many has she taken apart?"

Everyone in the room laughed.

Deidre swatted the air. "I joined a club. I get to take things apart there."

Brianna stared at her parents in awe. "You're really happy here?"

Deidre sighed. "It was an adjustment I can tell you. It took a lot of convincing on your part and in the end, it took you having us kidnapped. You can't imagine how scared we were waking up in a strange hotel with actual Demi looking down on us." Her mother put a hand over her heart.

Henry laughed. "I gave them a fight before you came in and calmed us down."

Deidre laughed, but it went away when she saw the look of confusion on her daughter's face. "Oh, my baby. When Cassie told me your memory was gone, I didn't want to believe it. But you really don't remember?"

Brianna shook her head.

"This Esin is so different than our last, sweetheart. They practice the old ways, not the bastardized rules Elder Cedric enforced upon us. We go to temple, we worship at the solstices and we take care of our little slice of earth. There is no in-fighting, no backstabbing and certainly no stealing of innocence."

Brianna shifted uncomfortably and avoided her friend's gaze.

Her father had no such compulsion, he grabbed Cassie's hand and gripped it. "The children here are cherished, well taken care of," he whispered.

Cassie nodded and swiped away a tear.

"I don't know how you got a letter to us, but you did. It outlined all the differences between the Esins and showed the ways the Oliri was perverting the Divine text. Well, we didn't believe you and had you not kidnapped us we would still be there, wilting away under his rule. You saved us, my love."

"So, you're happy here?"

"Happy doesn't describe it, baby girl." Her father knocked on the table.

"We're using magic, actual magic." Her mother put a hand to her warm cheeks. "You know your father can make anything grow, we didn't imagine it was a part of his natural power."

"I'm in charge of the Esin's farm," her father said proudly. "There I was used like a slave, here, I make all the decisions on what to plant, where we plant and I can actually read the soil, Brianna. You can't imagine the sense of purpose I've known since being here."

Her parents grabbed hands and kissed, her eyes widened in shock.

Cassie snickered next to her. "Yeah, they do that a lot."

Deidre pulled from her husband and smiled.

"I can't believe this," Brianna murmured. "I don't want to see my parents making out."

"Would you rather us argue the way we used to?" Her mother scolded.

"No, I'm unbelievably happy that you two are closer."

"I wish we could talk you into attending, darling. There are a lot of good single men in the Esin if Fallon doesn't do the right thing."

Her cheeks burned. She would not be discussing Fallon, nor the fevered dreams she'd had of him.

"Deidre," her father muttered and took a sip of his coffee. "Don't start with that."

Deidre sighed. "Well, I can want my baby married, that's not a crime."

Brianna smiled, her eyes misting. Her parents looked happy. Certainly closer than they had been when she was growing up. There was none of the tension that used to coat her childhood home.

"Nothing is stopping me from lighting a candle in Rugaba's temple tonight for my daughter's happiness."

"Woman, give it a rest." Henry fussed.

Brianna laughed outright.

"If you thought getting her to temple was hard before, it will be twice as hard now." Cassie shot her a withering glance. "Brianna believes the Douglasville Esin kidnapped her."

Deidre will shake her head. "Besides the fact that they wouldn't have the money to do it, I honestly don't believe they have the resources."

"Why not? If it's money they need I seem to have it in spades." Brianna pointed out.

Her father frowned and thought about it. "She has a point."

Cassie groaned. "Uncle Henry."

"What? Elder Cedric has to be desperate. She had to pay a ransom to get us out of there. Who's to say he wouldn't come back for more? She was living outside the protection of both this Esin and the Haven, it wouldn't be hard."

Brianna slapped her hand on the table. "See, I'm not crazy." She ignored her father's point about her not living under protection.

"No one said you were crazy, Brianna, calm down." Cassie rolled her eyes. "If it was money they wanted, then why would they let you go without a ransom?"

Brianna put her head on the table. "I can't argue with you about this, Cassie."

Cassie raised her eyebrow at Brianna's parents.

Henry held up a hand. "What does Fallon say about it?"

Her head came up. "How do you know Fallon?" It was the second time they'd mentioned him.

Her mother smiled and sipped from her cup. Brianna

narrowed her eyes. "He's been here?"

"Several times," her father answered.

"Who *is* this guy?"

"What does he say about it?" Henry asked again.

"I haven't talked to him." She muttered.

"What do you mean you haven't talked to him?" Deidre's voice went up an octave.

"We're staying at Aunt Sarah's until Brianna figures out who kidnapped her. All by herself, no help from anyone." Cassie didn't mask the sarcasm.

Deidre's cup hit the table, hard. "You cannot be serious, Brianna. Why would you turn down help from the Haven?"

"It's a cult," Brianna said stubbornly.

"It's not a cult!" Everyone around the table said.

She growled.

"You were just kidnapped because you wouldn't accept protection from neither this Esin nor the Haven. And even now you're refusing help?" Deidre took a deep breath.

"Honey, surely you can see how much happier we are here? You can't still think this is a cult." Henry stared, his gaze making her feel guilty.

Brianna averted her eyes.

"Well!" Deidre scoffed. "She's your child, Henry."

Henry laughed. "She's certainly stubborn as hell, and there's plenty of women in this family she could've gotten it from."

"Honey, we can show you around, this isn't a cult." Deidra grabbed her hand.

"Let's not, for now, mom." She shook her head.

"Why won't you accept help from Fallon at least?" Henry gripped his coffee cup.

She crossed her arms over her chest and barely kept herself from pouting like a child. "They put guards on me." She muttered.

Everyone around the table sighed.

"Fallon is your best chance to get the answers you want." Her mother explained gently.

"Mom."

"Fuss all you want. Xavier runs a good Haven, I would much rather you be under their protection. You don't believe in anything the Esin taught us, so surely you don't believe all that crap about the Demi being out to steal our magic and being untrustworthy." Henry's look dared her to disagree.

Brianna refused to speak. Her father did have a point though. The best way to find out what she thought about the Demi would be to read through her notes. Get a full understanding of what they were and did.

"I'll think about it." She acquiesced.

"That's all we're going to get from her, let it go, Deidre," her father said when her mother opened her mouth.

"Fine." Deidre picked up her teacup.

"What are they doing about your memory, sweetheart?" Henry changed the subject.

She shrugged. "I've seen a few of their 'healers', Papa. It seems to me all they do is wave their hands over my body and hum. I haven't gotten any answers."

"Is there anything we can do to help?" Her mother covered her hand with her hands, warmed from the teacup.

"I wouldn't object to one or two prayers to your god."

Her father sighed and touched her mother's shoulder to stop the argument he knew was coming. "We will pray, sweet pea."

The rest of her visit passed with her catching up on her parents' life in the new Esin. By the time she'd left, she had some insight into the difference between the two Esins but remained skeptical.

"You gotta call Fallon," Cassie said as she maneuvered her car out of the gated community.

Brianna sighed. "I'll see how I feel about it tomorrow."

Chapter 7

It had been over a week since he'd seen Brianna, well, eight days exactly, but it felt longer. Frustration and need was a living, breathing monster on his back as each day away from her passed. Although he'd been getting reports from the men he had watching her, he ached to see her. He'd thought giving her time and space would help, he was starting to reevaluate that.

He stomped through the portal room in Haven, ignoring the looks his soldiers sent him. He was going to see his friend Tahir in the hopes he could help him decide what to do. He slapped his palm against the corridor wall of the officer's portal in irritation, activating the portal spell. He moved through the spell, bringing up the symbol for Edin. With a few more hand movements, he moved through the top-level restrictions placed on the realm to finally open the gateway.

The cool, calming air of the mountainous realm blew across his face. He inhaled deeply, taking in the soothing breeze. He stepped through, the bright light blinding him momentarily until he stepped fully into the sedate portal station of the Kira realm. Unlike the portal station at Haven, this station was restricted, so there were no crowds milling about. The Kira didn't allow travel to Edin unless invited. It was very rare for the Demi to have any illness, and although they lived in relative peace, curses, serious injuries, and trauma, much like PTSD was not rare. Only those with the most severe cases were allowed on the Kira realm for healing. The elders on Edin wanted to keep the essence of the realm pure, untarnished by the energy most Demi had.

He waved at the guard on duty and pushed through the doors. Cold air blasted him as the doors slid open. Tahir stood waiting for him, leaning against the giant leg of the iron vehicle they'd nicknamed the Spider. A gift from the Gu, it looked like a dune buggy. Instead of wheels, it had long iron legs with metal claws that connected to the natural magnetic lines of the mountains as it climbed or descended. Several of the vehicles could be seen traversing the land as they traveled around the mountainous part of the realm, never disturbing its natural beauty.

Tahir gave him a head nod as he left the warmth of the portal station and entered the dawning frigid evening. He and Tahir had been friends for near a century, the two met while they were both in Europe in search of magic. They'd hit it off immediately and traveled together for years before he was called back to Haven.

Despite the cold, Tahir had his arms crossed over his bare chest, the branches of his hair draped across one muscular shoulder. In his natural form, his friend's skin resembled that of tree bark, no doubt the reason the temperature didn't bother him. He wore loose, wide-legged cotton pants that hung on his trim hips and scraped the ground, covering his feet completely. He and Tahir clasped hands and touched foreheads.

"You look like shit, brother." Tahir's eyes roamed his face.

Fallon laughed. "What would a man do without you stroking his ego?"

Tahir laughed and launched up into the cab of the spider. Fallon walked over to the passenger side and jumped up behind him. Tahir activated the vehicle, and the windshield dimmed, a topographic map glowing on the screen. Pulling up to release the brake, Tahir moved the behemoth machine down the mountain towards his home in the village.

The view outside the cab was always breathtaking to see. Mountains and hills folded into one another creating lush curves and valleys where all manner of greenery thrived. Giant Phoenix-like birds swept casually through the sapphire skyline as the sun was beginning to set on the day. The occasional call from various birds of paradise and other creatures stirring as their night began, filtered in through the windows. The Spider locked from ley line to ley line as it worked its way smoothly over the canopy making its way to the valley below.

They rode in silence as the Spider moved quickly through the terrain. The first sign of civilization came into view as they passed the common plaza in the larger patch of trees woven through the branches well above the ground. The shop and stand clusters were linked together by vine bridges and swings allowing Kira to move about as they pleased.

They arrived at the end of the magnetic path, the valley spread before them. Tahir's arbor home was beautiful. It was a lush landscape full of the trees, shrubs, and alcoves the inhabitants themselves resembled. A grand pair of perennials marked the entrance to Tahir's land, and he stopped his Spider on the edge of the forest a few yards from it. The cab rested on the ground as the metal legs retracted into itself cleanly.

"We walk from here, my friend," Tahir said, same as he did every time Fallon visited. Tahir walked to the first of the giant trees looming over his property. "Thank you for your protection and shade," he whispered lovingly as he always did when returning home. He repeated this as he passed the other remaining sets of paired trees lining the path to his alcove.

Fallon knew the drill, he hopped out of the vehicle and stretched, taking in the soothing energy emanating from the trees, Tahir's ancestors. He rolled his neck and shoulders, happy he'd decided to come. His friend lived towards the edge of the village, his house resembling a log cabin, if say, a millionaire decided to rough it

59 |

in the wild. The large porch wrapped around the ground level of his two-story home.

They went through the large front door and warmth wrapped around Fallon as he stepped in.

Tahir pulled his hair back and bound it with string. "I'll have to do a lot of sweeping when you leave. Your energy is all out of whack."

"That's seriously an understatement," Fallon said over his shoulder as he walked through the foyer, straight back, past the living room and kitchen, and into a small room, his friend kept towards the back of the house.

Candles sconces covered one wall of the room, and bamboo mats covered the floor. Tahir entered the room and lit the candles along the wall with a sweep of his hand. The room filled with a scent that put Fallon's body immediately at ease.

Tufts of natural earth and grass were arranged around the room like furniture with stone tablets acting as tables in opposing corners with books laid out where they'd been left undisturbed. The western wall was translucent allowing the fading sunlight through and a view of the natural beauty of the land outside. The eastern wall was filled with small planters holding all sorts of growing exotic seedlings of various colors and scents. An intricate water feature flowed through the wall like a meandering river feeding the seedlings and stirring the energy of the room washing out through several holes in the bottom of the wall out of the room.

Fallon sat on the floor with his legs crossed, closing his eyes focusing on the gentle babble of the water. He started his deep breathing, the way his friend had coached to him in the years that they'd been doing this. In all the trips they'd taken together, the magic they'd seen and dabbled in, he'd mastered the drill and knew how to get ready for Tahir to clear his aura.

Tahir kneeled behind him, and wind from his hands brushed across Fallon's back as he started the sweeping process. Tahir hummed quietly behind him, and Fallon soon fell into a semi-sleep state.

"So tell me why you initiated the mate bond with Brianna."

His voice shook Fallon from his daze and he opened one eye. Tahir sat across from him, legs crossed, expression serene. He didn't even feel his friend stop, never mind move. He must have really been in a trance. Fallon closed his open eye and took catalog of his body before he answered. He felt lighter, less stressed, but no closer to purging the need for his mate from his body.

Fallon sighed. "It was the only way to save her life, but with her memory gone, I have to wait to finish the bond."

Tahir hummed.

Fallon frowned, not sure what the sound meant. "Don't go all Kira on me, tell me what you think."

Tahir shrugged. "You know what needs to be done. If it will make you feel better I'll say the words aloud."

Fallon sighed. "I want her, now."

"But not a year ago?"

Fallon growled at his best friend. "You know…"

"I know you have a mate and you ran away because you weren't ready to give up what you called freedom."

He wanted to argue and deny Tahir's words but even when he didn't want to hear it, the Kira would give him the truth. "I fucked up."

"For lack of eloquent words." Tahir tipped his head. "The question again, is what do you plan to do about it?"

"With her memory gone, I don't want to push."

"Oh, we're being noble now."

"Fuck…Tahir, what can I do? I feel like it'll be taking advantage of her."

"You've already started the bonding process, Fallon. I can see the ties from here. Can you imagine how your mate feels? She has no memory of her relationship with you, and yet, her body and probably her mind are having feelings she can't explain." Tahir's face held no judgment.

And yet…guilt punched him in the gut. Fallon wiped his hand over his face. "So what should I do?"

Tahir sighed. "If you want your mate, go after your mate, if your lifestyle is more important to you than that which the ancestors have chosen for you, then leave her the fuck alone. Once the new moon has passed she can move on with her life."

Fallon hung his head. "I want her."

"Her body, or her?"

Fallon clenched his teeth unable to answer the question. He didn't know enough about Brianna to say whether or not he wanted her. He'd spent the last year avoiding being in the same room with her. The only things he knew about her were second hand. Stories from her parents and Cassie were his only glimpse into his mate's life. So, he couldn't say for certain that he wanted her, but he absolutely wanted her body.

"Leonalph had to give up hunting to be with his mate, has he complained?"

"He's always complaining about being bored," he muttered.

Tahir snorted.

"Okay, not often."

"You'll do as you feel, Fallon. In the century I've known you, you've searched the world for something. What if your mate is it? Think about that, brother. And for the love of all, feed. Your aura is weaker than it should be."

Fallon brushed a hand over the top of his head. "I've already got the lecture from Xavier."

Tahir raised a brow and shook his head. "As I said, you'll do as you feel. Are you staying the night?"

"No, I have to get back on duty and as you said feed."

Tahir stood, his graceful movements belying his tall stature. "Let's move then."

***

Brianna sat in the café, her café, she reminded herself, trying to get through the passwords on her laptop. Cassie had given her a list of passwords that she'd remembered, but none of them opened the hidden file she'd found. She rubbed across the top of the laptop, still in awe of the sleek machine. She'd not been able to afford a computer this fancy on her last salary. Her previous one used to sound like a marathon runner on their twenty-sixth mile. This baby made no noise despite the several windows she'd opened. She frowned as she got another wrong password error.

"So, you've lost the book."

She jerked to attention, swallowing her yelp. She peeked over the edge of her laptop and saw a dark-skinned male, who could be described as nothing less than perfect. His massive bulk completely took over the chair in which he sat. His dark sooty lashes framed hazel eyes that burned through her. His full lips were pressed in a tight line, his chiseled jaw jutting forward, indicating she should close her laptop. She slid it closed with a small click, curiosity burning through any fear she should have had.

"Who are you?"

He grunted. "So you *have* lost your memory. I didn't quite believe that part."

"Who are you?" She repeated and squinted her eyes. He looked vaguely familiar.

Instead of answering, he drummed his fingers on the tabletop, staring at her until she lowered her eyes and squirmed. He was powerful, whoever he was. She found it hard to keep his gaze.

"What do you remember about the book?"

"What book?"

"Hmm," he murmured, his gaze turning speculative.

"Brianna?"

She turned her head and frowned, as a man from her past rushed over to her table from the counter of the coffee shop. "Darren?"

She didn't stand. He'd never been what she'd call a friend, despite his family's effort to force the two of them to marry.

"How are you?" He smiled wide.

"I'm a little busy now." She arched her head in the direction of the male sitting across from her.

"I don't..." Darren's smile dimmed as looked over and frowned. "Are you waiting for someone?"

Brianna blinked, her brows knitting. She looked again at the man sitting across from her. The corner of his mouth went up into an impertinent smile that didn't reach his eyes.

"You don't see-" She broke off, tilting her head. Surely, he saw the massive man.

Darren looked taken aback. "Can I sit there?" He gestured to the spot the man occupied.

Confused, a touch scared, Brianna shook her head. She hurried to cover her blunder. "No, you're right, I'm waiting for someone." "Oh." Nonplussed, he clasped his hands in front of him and he looked around. "It's nice to see a familiar face," he rushed to fill the awkward silence.

She glanced back at her mysterious guest who waved an impatient hand towards Darren. She sighed.

"Are you visiting?" Darren tried again.

"No, I live here." Not quite curt, her tone still conveyed her disinterest.

"Umm," he scrambled into his pockets. "Well, I don't want to disturb you while you're working or whatever. Here's my card, when you're not…waiting for someone, or busy give me a call, perhaps we can go out sometime?"

She nodded and extended her hand, intending to chuck the card the moment he left. "Yeah, sure, that sounds great." She waved as he walked away. She turned back to her guest.

"What was that, why couldn't he see you?"

He leaned forward. "What if I told you, only those purest of heart could see me."

She snorted. "Then I definitely wouldn't be able to see you."

He gave her a small smile. "You'd be surprised what is in your heart, Brianna. Now," he tapped the table, "Back to the matter at hand. The book."

"You gotta be specific, I know a lot of books." She held her arms out. "This is a book store. Who are you?"

"Depends on who you ask. You may call me Rugaba."

Her eyes widened, and she sat back in her chair. "The god of fate?" That would explain the familiarity. His statue stood tall in front of the temple in the Esin she'd just visited. She scanned his face, amazed at the amount of detail they'd correctly captured in the statue.

In her old Esin, there had been some tales of the god, but not many. There had been no offerings to Rugaba in Douglasville. Still, she was in awe that she'd warrant a visit from a god. Especially one of which she knew.

"As I said, I'm known to different people as different things." Said without a hint of arrogance, he studied her.

Her hands shook as she picked up her coffee cup and took a sip. "How…why would you come see me. My parents have prayed to you, you could've chosen them for a random visit."

He shrugged, dismissing her snark. "Your parents don't work for me."

She choked on her coffee. "Excuse me?" She, Brianna the skeptical, worked for a god? "What kind of work would I do for a god?"

"You were set as guardian of a very important spellbook, and within a year of your post you lose the book." He sighed. "Tsk tsk, Brianna."

She pushed her lips out and gave him an incredulous look. She didn't believe in magic, why would he put her in charge of a spellbook.

He ignored her disbelief and leaned over and placed his hand on her forehead. Heat emanated from his palm, warming first her head, all the way down to her chest. He pulled back with a hiss. His eyes narrowed on her a moment, his mouth pursed in concentration. "Interesting," he murmured and disappeared.

She gaped at the now empty seat, rubbing her forehead where it was still warm. That was… she shook her head. Strange did it no justice, and weird was an understatement. She'd been visited, by a god, why was that not the strangest thing that had happened to her this week? She whipped out her phone and called her mother. Joy suffused her that she was able to call her parents anytime she wanted. Her mother answered, breathless.

"What are you doing?"

Deidre giggled, giggled! "Nothing." There was some shuffling, her mother squealed, "Ok, not nothing, stop," she laughed, "It's our daughter."

"Call back later, Bri Bri." Her father shouted from the back.

Brianna groaned, "You guys are…never mind, I don't want to know. I, mom, I think I met a god."

Her mother gasped. "Oh my goodness, who, what happened?" "Rugaba just popped up in the middle of the café."

"Brianna," her mother said breathlessly. "You should come to temple."

Brianna snorted. "Mom, let's get real here."

"You just met the god of fate, a creation god, you cannot possibly scoff our beliefs."

Deidre had a valid point, and it made her feel petty. "I'm sorry."

Her mother sniffed. "If you didn't call to get advice, what do you want me to say, love."

"I don't know. I was hoping maybe you would know something about him."

Her mother hummed as she thought about it. "Well, I know you, nothing I can tell you will help. You spent a good amount of time in the library here before the accident. You'd find better answers there."

Excitement bubbled through her. "Yes, oh my god, yes. You know I love libraries."

Her mother laughed. "I love you. You know, most people would be awed to be in the presence of a god. You don't sound nearly reverent enough, I shudder to think of how you spoke with him."

She cringed but didn't answer. "I love you too, mom."

She hung up and pumped her arm. A library, yes, she could get behind that.

Chapter 8

Fallon adjusted the sleeves on his dress shirt, rolling them up to his forearms. He usually dressed in his all-black uniform, but it was sensual Saturday and per orders from his best friend, as well as his brothers, he needed to feed. He sighed and finished getting dressed. Power saturated his apartment a moment before their god, Rugaba, popped into the room. He went to his knee.

"My lord."

Rugaba waved him up, but Fallon kept his gaze lowered. "Tell me about the girl."

Fallon cleared his throat. "We don't have any further information as of yet. The two I had guarding her are dead. According to the Kira, Ade, it was Divine magic, some kind of death spell. Xavier and I have met with the local Esin and they don't know anything about it."

"I tried healing her and could not get past the block over her mind." Rugaba frowned. "Not necessarily because it was powerful, but rather shoddily done. It's twisted in a way, I can't make sense of. What are you doing to recover her memories and the book?"

"We're nearly certain whoever kidnapped her didn't take it. From what her friend says, Brianna never carried it around."

"And Brianna says?" His sharp tone brought Fallon up to his full height at attention.

"She hasn't been back to the Haven, we haven't as yet convinced her to come in for an interview."

"And why is she given the option?" Power sent Fallon to both knees.

Speaking took effort as the god's magic settled atop him. "My lord, you've had dealings with Brianna yourself, she can be stubborn. I felt that if we pushed her, she would clam up worse. We're not entitled to the Book of Divine, and she could run if we push too hard."

Rugaba released him from his thrall with a growl. "You may be right. I want her interviewed as soon as possible. I will see to the guards who died and find out what they know."

Fallon nodded and swayed as Rugaba left the room. He took a deep breath, still on his knees. That could've gone a lot worse than it did and he sent up a prayer of thanks.

He checked the time and cursed, it was way too late to go through his pre-checks. Though only after nine pm, the floor would be full of humans, anticipating their night. He ran into Xavier coming out of the living quarter's wing.

Xavier eyed him. "You're late."

"I know." Fallon held up his hands. "I trust my staff."

"I didn't say otherwise, I'm just curious, you're never late." Concern lingered as his brother raked another look over him.

"I got a visit from Rue."

Xavier whistled. "And you're intact."

"Just barely," Fallon said. "He wants Brianna in so we can question her and I agree."

"Well if your mate wasn't such a-"

"Watch your mouth X." Fallon cut him off.

Xavier sighed. "She makes everything such a damn chore."

"I'm going to go after her."

"Not tonight you aren't. You need to feed, Fallon. You've been skimming."

"I know, X. I'm going tonight."

"Don't leave this Haven without feeding. That's an order."

Fallon clenched his jaw, not wanting to get into a fight with his eldest brother. "I will feed," he said through gritted teeth.

"Fine. I'll follow you up."

Fallon frowned. "You never go to the club floor."

"I too need to feed, brother."

"But you always do so on the observation deck."

"And that's where I will be."

"You never-"

"Gods above, Fallon, can I not walk with my brother?"

"Sorry," he muttered. He kept an eye on Xavier, stealing glances at him. "What's going on, X."

"Nothing I can't handle." Xavier held open the door to the club floor.

Loud music and magic blasted them as they entered. They separated, Xavier going up the stairs to the observation deck and

Fallon headed towards the entrance of the club. Like he'd told his brother he trusted his staff, but it didn't stop him from checking after them. He was waved down as he neared the front.

"Yeah?"

One of his bouncers slid a nervous glance to the coat check room. "We have a little problem."

"This early?"

The bouncer nodded and led him deeper into the coat check room to a lounge they kept in the back. It was where they let women wait on cabs, or rides, keeping them from having to wait alone in the front of the club. His eyes narrowed as he found the room full with two bouncers, a Demi patron and a human, nearly unconscious, laid out of the couch.

Fallon growled. He didn't allow drugs into the Haven, especially on sensual nights. The magic in the club took down most of the barriers humans had over their minds. Drugs would make them much more susceptible and was not at all safe.

"What's going on?" He asked the room.

"I demanded to speak with someone in charge," the Demi demanded haughtily.

He ignored the pretentious ass and instead turned to his bouncer. "You stopped him from leaving?"

"She's clearly out of it," the bouncer explained.

Fallon went to the female and stooped down to her level. He lifted her chin with his finger. "Hey, you okay?"

She rubbed against him, mewling, the sound more distress than lust and anger filled him. Not at her, but at the Demi trying to lead her out. He whispered a spell over her and put her asleep. He straightened and turned back to his bouncer.

"Check her pockets to find her address and see her home personally." He ordered.

"Yes, Commander."

He addressed the Demi. "You know the rules."

"How was I supposed to know she was on drugs?" The male shrugged his shoulders.

"You know the fucking rules! You don't take advantage of the humans inside the walls of Haven."

It was a rule he'd put into place when he'd taken over security for the Havens. Yes, they all used the humans to feed, whether it be lust or sadism. But, they needed to be mindful of the fragility of humans. Taking advantage of Haven's patrons would get them booted or banished, depending on the infraction.

"What are you talking about, the magic in the air is enough for me to get laid. I don't need to drug some pathetic human." He looked defensive though.

Fallon stared at him as he pulled out his communicator. He snapped a picture of the Demi and sent it down to the surveillance room. He then called down there and instructed them to track the Demi's movements. He hung up and waited on them to call back.

The Demi opened his mouth to speak. Fallon held up his hand. "Don't even."

His communicator beeped with a single message.

He slipped something in her drink.

He smiled and by the way the Demi backed up, it wasn't a nice smile.

"Avail this gentleman to our fine hospitality on B3 please."

The Demi shook his head, panic blanching the color on his face. "You can't do that, you can't keep me here."

Fallon stepped closer to him. "As I am in charge of security here, I can do whatever the fuck I want. You'll spend a few days downstairs until I decide what your punishment will be."

He nodded his head for his bouncers to take the Demi into custody. The Demi cursed, fighting against the bouncers attempting to detain him. Fallon watched his guards struggle for a moment before he hauled and punched the guy in the head, knocking him out.

"Put him in a cell." He ordered and rubbed his knuckles. He turned to the only bouncer left in the room. "Replace the bouncer at the door and send him to me."

It only took moments for the bouncer assigned to the door to come in.

"You're checking for drugs, yes?"

The male held up his hands. "I swear, Commander, I put up the spell and had someone check behind me."

"There are drugs coming in this door, if I find out you're being lazy, you're fucked, understand?"

"Yes sir," he stammered.

Fallon dismissed him and left the lounge, nodding at the attendant. As he exited the coat check room, he saw a human male, half dragging a woman to the exit. It wasn't even ten yet, what the hell?

"That's a negative, Hoss." He took the girl out of his arm and passed her to the attendant at coat check. She would make sure the woman got home safely.

"Hey, what's the big idea," the human protested.

Fallon whispered a spell to wipe his memory and sent him out the door. He sighed and shook his head. It was early and already the night had gone to shit. He went about his rounds edgy and irritated. He double and triple checked the spells surrounding the dance floor, and swept the upstairs rooms to make sure nothing out of the ordinary was going on. The last thing he wanted to be doing, was chasing after over-inebriated humans.

His mind drifted to his mate, as it always did and he tensed in need. He wanted to go to her, but he knew Xavier would probably have someone watching him, at least until he fed. He headed to the dance floor to get it over with. He was going for his mate tomorrow morning, work be damned.

He found a woman as he came downstairs. He crooked his finger and her eyes lit up. He guided her out on to the floor, letting the driving bass empty his thoughts. He let down his shields releasing the pheromones natural to Cagyns. The woman's lids lowered, a drowsy look suffusing her face. Her motions were more sensual as he pulled her hips closer to his own. He normally would kiss the human, feeding from her, but he had to think of his mate. His beast wouldn't allow it anyway. As it was, his close proximity to the woman was making his magic flare wildly.

Guilt for what he had to do, nearly made him stop.

He skipped the kiss but trailed his arms across her skin, feeding her sexual haze and taking in the magic to feed himself. She leaned her head back, and her mouth open as she moaned. He backed up a small touch as she tried to grind on him, searching for release. He let his nails grow just a little, trailing his claws down her neck and she shuddered. He pumped out more pheromones as her lust-filled his pores.

He could've skimmed the magic from the room from the top floor, as he'd been doing for the past year. He should've done as his brother and fed from there, but here, in the thick of the dance floor, he would get the most energy. He didn't want to hear shit from Xavier when he left to go after his mate.

His dance partner's breath hitched, and he hovered closer, as he sensed her getting closer to release. Her nipples poked out of the barely-there shirt, and he was not in the least bit tempted. She closed her eyes and threw her head back. Magic flared, her orgasm bowing her back with its intensity.

He opened his mouth and hovered over her hers, taking in the energy with her every exhalation, feeding it into his body, feeling his skin heat, dispersing the lustful energy. While the magic energized his body, he knew one woman wouldn't suffice. He danced with her until she came down off her high, giving her a smile when her eyes focused on him again. He thanked her for the dance and set her aside. She waved and happily grabbed another dance partner.

It took him six dance partners to replenish his energy, the sensual haze feeding him and energizing his body. By the time he was done, his body buzzed, the beast in him, sated...at least for the moment. A part of him still felt guilty, but at the end of the day, it was in his nature. He'd not touched the women any more than he'd had to.

Finished with feeding he left the dance floor and headed for the back. Once the door to the club level closed he loosened the magic holding him in his human form. Whorls raised on his skin, lighting the dim corridor, pulsing along with his heartbeat. He released his hair, sighing as it brushed his shoulders. He reigned in his magic, not wanting to completely release his true form. He ignored the females brushing against him in the hallway, called to him by his Cagyn magic. Only one woman would do, and she was not available. He could nothing while he was on duty, but wait out the magic coursing through his body. He'd go back and resume his duties as soon as he could corral the power.

Chapter 9

"I can't believe you're sold out of 'Donor'. I've been waiting months for the release."

"We're out of stock." *Except for the thirty in a box in the storeroom.* But did she really want to tell her customer she was too scared to go back and retrieve it? That there was a two hundred plus pound stalker locked in the room? She pursed her lips.

Answer: She didn't.

She pasted on a sunny smile. "I ordered more. If you give me your number, I can give you a call the minute they come in."

"Thanks, I'll just see if I can find it online." The customer moved on.

That was close.

She rolled her eyes up to the clock on the wall. She'd told Lucy, one of the employees of the bookstore, she'd cover for her as she ran an errand. She was supposed to be back in another thirty minutes or so. Surely Brianna could keep it together until then. Her hands shook as she skimmed her ponytail debating what to do. Keeping an eye out for customers she pulled out her cellphone.

Who to call?

She could call Fallon, her parents vouched for him, but, she'd been having increasingly hot dreams about him. Like, repeated sessions with her vibrator, hot. They were becoming hard to ignore, to the point where her body was craving to see him. She didn't know if calling him, seeing him in person, was such a good idea. Didn't seem smart to tempt fate. As it was, just thinking about him raised her body temperature until sweat beaded and gathered on her forehead.

She swiped a hand across her skin and breathed deep, willing her body under control. She wanted her memory back before she even attempted to go there.

She could call Xavier, after all, he did say to call him if she had problems. Though he made it clear Fallon should be her first call. She chewed her lip, maybe she should call Fallon.

Nope, not going there.

Her phone beeped with an incoming text message. She frowned, not recognizing the name. Who was Isaiah? She opened the message.

Hey, can I have snacks while I'm back here?

Oh God. She swiveled her chair and glared at the storage closet where she'd locked him in. He had her number? She growled. Of course, he had her number, he was one of Xavier's cronies. She dialed king jackass.

Xavier answered on the first ring. His tone brusque, irritated.

She cleared her throat. "So…umm…you told me to call you if something happened."

"What's happened?" His voice sharpened.

"There is a guy, locked in my stockroom. He was following me, so I lured him in there. He's been in there for thirty minutes. I'm pretty sure he could be yours."

"You're just now telling me?"

"Well, I had to open the store, and then people started coming in and other employees, I-"

He cut her off. "Let me call you back."

She blew out an irritated breath and glanced back at the stock room. She'd told her other employees to avoid the room, and so far there wasn't any bumping to indicate her prisoner wanted out.

Her phone rang again and it was Xavier. "Hello."

"Let your guard out of the closet please." His voice was terse.

Which of course, irritated her. She sucked her teeth. "So he is yours."

"I assigned guards to protect you, remember? You've locked one in your stock room, please let him out."

"That isn't the same man who was following me before. It's bad enough you insisted I have guards. The least you could've done was told me when you changed them."

"Since they require sleep, genius, there have to be shift changes. You're not going to recognize every guard watching you. Hell, Fallon trains his men well enough that you may not even know they're there."

She let out a disgusted sound and ended the call. She stared at the door to her stockroom and bit her lip. She debated whether or not to leave him in there to rot for a while. It wasn't the guard's fault that his boss was an ass, though.

Sighing, she walked to the back and opened the door.

Her stalker-turned-guard, sat on the stool she kept to reach the higher boxes, reading a new thriller. "Isaiah?"

He nodded and closed the book. Dark skin, full lips, and narrow sooty eyes, he was very handsome. He stood, his large bulky figure filling up the stock room.

"I thought you were a stalker."

He raised an eyebrow. "You yelled, 'oh my god, please help'. Do you imagine a stalker would've rushed to your aid?"

She bit her lip to stem her giggles at his dry tone. "I didn't think about that, to be honest, I was hoping it would make you run away, I didn't expect you to go charging into the stock room." He grunted. "Did you not get my text?"

She wiggled her phone and nodded.

He rolled his eyes. "And you didn't bring me any snacks? Cold, Brianna."

She smiled, ok, so he was funny. "I'm sorry?"

He snorted and pulled out some kind of high tech phone and spoke softly into it. "There is a team of four of us rotating, would it make you feel better to know who we are, so this doesn't happen again?"

She nodded.

He waved his hand to indicate she walk in front of him. She led the way out of the stock room and another large guy came into the store. Clearly, along with well trained, Fallon only employed behemoths.

"This is Michel."

The guard nodded his head in greeting. His hair was pulled up into a bun on top of his head, the hair tapered, the lines sharp and framing his chiseled face.

"Kegan and Brian take the shift after us. Fallon handpicked us so please don't worry. We'll be around, if at any time you feel threatened or unsafe, let us know.

She frowned. "How?"

He held out his open palm. "Give me your phone."

She did.

"I programmed all of our numbers in your phone." He showed her their info.

What? "When?"

He gave her a droll stare but didn't answer the question.

She growled. "Fine. I don't know if I like having guards, though."

Michel grunted. "You've never liked having us around. The Commander scares me more than you, so we'll take our chances."

Isaiah smiled and shrugged. "Being locked in a comfortable room is a lot better than what Fallon or the Marshall will do."

She scrunched her face. "How long have you been following me?"

"We were told to be discreet. You shouldn't have even known we were following you this morning." Isaiah admitted, his face chagrined. "I don't want to imagine what Commander Tegan will say when he finds out."

They left and she followed them with her gaze, realizing they hadn't answered her question. She frowned when they disappeared.

Like, into thin air, disappeared.

She looked around trying hard to find them. How did they do it? She realized it had been a stroke of luck that she'd seen Isaiah this morning. A cyclist was up on the sidewalk and had nearly run into her. Had she not turned to avoid him, she wouldn't have seen Isaiah duck out of the way at the last minute. She thought her instincts had been honed a little better, but clearly, she'd grown soft since they'd left the Douglasville Esin.

Taking her post behind the counter, she sat on the stool and waited on Lucy to come back. She could've probably put someone else on the counter, but quite frankly, she was bored of inaction and frustrated that she couldn't remember the passwords to her laptop.

Ten minutes later, Brianna looked up from the customer she was helping and sucked in a sharp breath of need. Her body started to thrum, and her sex throbbed in time with her heartbeat. What was it about this man that set her senses on fire? Just his mere presence was enough to melt her. He entered the bookstore portion of the café, his confident gait drawing stares. He radiated intensity and purpose, but there was no impatience in his manner. He wore navy pinstriped slacks with his white button-down open to mid-chest and a matching suit jacket on top. He should've looked pretentious, but the way he filled out his pants.

God.

She would not drool. She licked her lips, only ten percent sure she could keep that promise to herself.

She hadn't seen him since she'd left the Haven and her eyes drank in the sight of him. It didn't make any sense. She didn't know this man, but her body and heart told her she did, and both raced as he neared her. This was the reason her horny ass had called Xavier instead of him.

Her customer cleared her throat and it startled her out of the erotic images playing on a loop in her head. She quickly apologized and finished the transaction. She stole another glance at him, their eyes meeting. Surely the lust in his eyes couldn't be for her. She was nothing in the way of sexy. Despite the fact that she could not starve herself out of her size fourteen jeans, she still remained stubbornly flat-chested. Her barely B cups, barely got notice from the other sex. She'd straightened her kinky hair and wore it pulled up into a ponytail today and she wished she'd put in the effort of a little bit of make-up.

She sent her customer a smile and a good day, fussing at the counter to cover up her nervousness. Xavier must've told him she'd called. She pasted on a polite smile as he stepped closer. His eyes were gentle as they scanned her face but decidedly covetous. His gaze was a caress, her skin heating every place he looked. Lust surged in her body, and she gripped the counter to fight the urge to sail across it.

"Brianna."

That was all he said, just her name, so why did her stomach tighten? Why did moisture gather between her legs in preparation to take him? God, why did she want to sit on the edge of the counter and allow him to do wonderful things to her body?

She cleared her throat. "Hi, Fallon, right?" She hoped she sounded casual.

He smiled, seeing straight through her false nonchalance. "Why did you call Xavier and not me?"

"I didn't want to bother you." She lied.

He smiled again and her clit throbbed as though he'd actually touched it.

"I'm responsible for you, Bri, so next time, save me the asschewing from my brother and call me."

The docile bob of her head was her answer since she was struck mute.

He leaned over the counter, "So, how are you feeling?"

Hot and bothered. "I'm fine, thanks. Did you come by because your brother told on me?"

"I was headed here anyway. I wanted to see you." He murmured.

He trailed a finger lightly across her hand on the counter and she felt it all the way to her toes. She went slack-jawed, her body damn near entering meltdown phase. Her late-night dreams of him played out in her mind in stark detail, and she barely stopped her moan. She stepped back from the counter recalling where she was.

"Why did you want to see me?"

If it was for sex, she was saying yes, and worrying about consequences later.

He remained leaning against the counter watching her a moment before he spoke. "We would like to speak with you, get details about your kidnapping directly from you. It will help us, hopefully, fill in some of the parts we don't understand."

She cleared her throat and quashed her disappointment. "You want me to come back to the Haven? Why? I don't remember anything."

He shrugged, continuing to stare at her. His cologne scented the air around them. He smelled amazing.

She leaned forward a bit. "What could you possibly do that the police couldn't do?"

Not that she'd gone to the police. The doctor's office she'd visited had barely believed she was attacked, no way did she want to experience that same disdain on the police's face.

"The police won't be able to help, not with this."

She thought about her visit from a god. It was definitely outside of the local police's scope.

"If you come to Haven, we can explain a lot of this to you." He smiled, a dimple in his right cheek charming her.

"I'll have to think about it, I'm a little busy right now." She hedged, not quite sure if she wanted to go back to the dark caves of Haven.

As if on cue, a small line of customers gathered behind him. She narrowed her eyes at the woman leering at Fallon's butt.

"Come tonight. It's a club night, so they'll be lots of people, bring Cassie if it will make you more comfortable." He pulled a card out of his jacket pocket.

There was only an address on the card front, and on the back, it said plus one. She looked at it and then him, still not agreeing to anything.

"You have my number if anything comes up. I'll expect to see you tonight if I don't get a call from you."

He turned to leave and gave the woman behind him a smile. The lady came up to the counter fanning. Brianna eyed the card he'd given her. He promised answers. She just might take him up on it.

Chapter 10

Fallon walked along the observation deck, his mind half on whether or not Brianna would show, and half on the task he was supposed to be doing. He shook his thoughts clear and focused on the wards protecting the flow of magic at Haven. He'd learned the hard way to do it closer to opening time, versus when he used to do it at the beginning of the day. Last year someone had spiked the spell during a fight night, and the ensuing chaos had left enough Demi injured that liaisons from across all seven realms had raised an alarm. He and Xavier audited the security policies across every Haven, and they'd spent the last year cleaning up the mess.

There had been soldiers taking bribes to look the other way while illegal shit was going on, soldiers giving out confidential information and lazy spell casting. Were it not for the trouble Liliana had been in, they may have gone longer without knowing. It was an oversight he took personal responsibility for, one he put every bit of his energy into over the past few months into fixing.

His punishment for every infraction had been increasingly harsh as they got further down the wormhole. He'd had to rework his security policies from top to bottom. He'd rooted out spies in his surveillance room, and instituted a check and balance system for any spell work they used to secure the Havens.

He could easily say it was one of the reasons he'd waited to claim Brianna. It wouldn't be true, though. Yes, he'd been busy, yes there had been chaos, but it didn't negate that he'd run from his mating. Despite his instincts, against the demands of his soul, he'd ran.

He rolled his shoulders and fought to concentrate on the task at hand. He walked to the far corner of the top deck and prodded against the ward set up there. The spell held, the normal power levels emitting the sensual magic that would eventually fill the club. It was probably a bad idea to ask his mate to visit tonight, knowing he was already having a hard time controlling his need for her. Vivid dreams about Brianna had him spending the time he was able to sleep hard and achy. Just thinking about them had him adjusting his slacks.

He opened a couple of the doors to the private rooms on the floor to be sure there wouldn't be any surprises for any patrons that ended up in them. He went down two floors to the ground level and popped by the front entrance. The bouncer assigned to the door waved.

"Spells up?"

Even as he asked, he probed the spell that kept drugs, guns and any harmful magical items from being brought into Haven. Per protocol, any bouncer on door duty had to add their essence within the spell to ensure that he'd be alerted if someone attempted to bring in contraband.

"Yes, sir, up and double-checked." Jin answered.

"Brianna and Cassie will be stopping by tonight, keep an eye out for them please."

Jin saluted and wrote it down on his clipboard.

Satisfied that everything was set, Fallon headed to his brother's office to give his nightly report. He walked in and found his nephew in a swing next to Xavier's desk.

"Why do you have babysitting duties?"

Xavier looked up from his display screen and squinted. "Liliana and Leo are going to the floor tonight. They needed some time."

"Aren't you sweet?" He walked over to his swaying nephew and smiled.

Kell was a cute baby. He could be biased a bit, though. Kell's hair was a riot of black curls taking after Leo, his piercing green eyes all Liliana. Those eyes watched him as he got closer. He squirmed in his swing, making a gurgling sound. His skin and hair color changed from dark brown to a lighter toffee color as he moved and cooed. A blast of wind emitted from his hands and papers on Xavier's desk went flying.

He smiled as his brother cursed. He lifted the tiny two weeks old out of the swing and nuzzled him. The kid had a strong soul, it reached out to him as they cuddled. He'd connected to Kell during his parent's bonding exercises, so he wasn't surprised his nephew knew him. Liliana had hated her bonding exercises, her impatience making the unborn Kell anxious. He'd had no such issues and as a result, his nephew recognized him easily.

He sucked in a breath as his vision went dim and the small peek of the future flashed across his mind. He saw Kell tearing through Haven with two other kids behind him, one, a little girl with silver eyes, and the mischievous smile Leo had worn as a kid. He sucked in a breath as it faded.

'What did you see?" Xavier asked, not looking up from his work.

Fallon smiled and his heart warmed. "This little male is going to be a terror. He and his siblings will use this Haven as their playground."

Xavier smiled, and it was the first smile he'd seen from his brother's in a while. Stress was a normal part of his job, but the last year had brought down a lot of trouble. They'd discovered the Kokoro souls were loose in the world, there had been a cult trying to free an evil being, and someone had been trying to kill Liliana. Xavier had ended up punishing nearly an entire royal line, leaving only King Leander to rule until Kell was old enough to take the crown. It had been a lot to juggle, and now that they'd lost the *Book of Divinity*, it was another layer. Understandably, his brother had to be more stressed than usual.

He put Kell back in his swing. "You ok, X? Is the stress getting to be too much?"

"I'm in the middle of a pile of help reqs and the person who had taken it off my plate is taking time out for that monster, so no, I'm not ok." Xavier waved off his concern. "It's nothing I can't handle."

Fallon stared at his brother not sure if he was telling the truth. There was nothing he could do if Xavier wouldn't accept help. Still, it was in him to make his brother's life easier if he could.

"X, I can take some of it for you."

Xavier sighed and looked up. "Fallon. You have a mate now, it's not your job to take care of us anymore. She should come first."

"That's not-"

His brother rolled his eyes and went back to his paperwork. "Stop it, Fallon."

He sighed and let it go. "The floor is ready and I have the front door on the lookout for Brianna if she shows up."

Xavier grunted and continued his work. Fallon looked over to his nephew swinging happily, his eyes enraptured with the mobile hanging from his swing. He frowned.

"You gonna be okay with a newborn baby?"

"My nephew and I have an understanding. He's going to be a good baby until mommy and daddy finish feeding and come to pick him up or until the Kira Liliana hired comes first."

Fallon snorted but said nothing. If X said he could handle it, who was he to say otherwise. He left him to his babysitting. His gut was churning as he left the office. He shrugged the tension off his shoulder and went to the security office to make sure everything was running smoothly there.

Ade caught him as he was leaving the surveillance room. "Hey, I checked with some of the archivists about that spell."

"What did you find?"

"The local Esin is doubling down on denying they had anything to do with it. The archivist there gave me a list of Esins she thought may dabble in spells of that nature." Ade held up his comms pad. "I sent it over to you since investigations are not my strong suit."

"Of course, thank you. I'll go through them. Anything else?" Fallon asked.

"Nope, but I'll keep you posted." Ade walked off, his head bent over his comms pad.

Fallon stood with his hands on his hips. He really wanted to go to his office and get started on the list, but he wanted to be there when Brianna arrived. Hell, if she arrived. Hopefully, she showed. He desperately wanted to see her.

***

Brianna sat in the parking lot with a death grip on the steering wheel of a car Cassie said was hers. Cassie fluffed her hair next to her and reapplied her lipstick in the small mirror on the sunshade. What was she thinking about coming to Haven? Did she really want information bad enough to go into the dark cave she'd waken up in? She shivered as she remembered. She wanted answers though, so she'd suck it up. Every day that went by, she was steadily loosening her stubborn views on magic. She'd talked to a god, an actual god of myth. After her talk with her mother, she'd visited the Esin library.

The documents she'd seen in their library made a mockery of all she thought she knew of the world.

It was time for her to fling away the blinders over her eyes.

Cassie flipped up the mirror, smacked her lips and smiled. "This is going to be fun. You've never wanted to go to an actual club night. You spent all your time in their library."

That sounded exactly like her, so she didn't bother with denial. She glanced down at her lap, nervous. The bandage dress Cassie made her wear clung to her every curve. How she let her best friend talk into it was anyone's guess. She didn't wear 'sexy' clothes. Not that she was ashamed of her curves, it was more practical than that. She spent a good portion of her days in front of a computer or chasing down obscure facts. Comfort was the name of her game. But, she'd wanted to impress Fallon. She could admit that. And now she was wrapped in an emerald green skintight dress. She would never admit to Cassie how much she loved the black beaded jacket she wore over it. She'd argued her friend down about the whole get up, she couldn't cave and let her know how hot she felt in it.

"We're not coming to party, I don't know why I let you talk me into getting so dressed up." She muttered, even as she ran her hands lovingly over the beads.

"You may not know this, due to your lack of social life, but when most people go out, they dress up." Cassie dropped her lipstick in her purse and snapped it shut.

"I look trashy."

Cassie snorted. "Not in Givenchy you don't. You look hot as hell, now shut up and get out of the car."

Brianna growled but did as she was told. They parked in a different place than before. The lot was huge, full of cars, the gravel crunching under their feet as they walked towards the building. She pulled out the card Fallon had given her and followed Cassie over to the line of people waiting to get in. Her friend flounced towards the crowd in a long tutu skirt with a sequined halter that she managed to pull off without looking anything but chic. They weren't in the line but a second before the bouncer's head snapped up. He leaned to the side to see around the line. He waved them over.

"Yay, it's Jin, come on." Cassie grabbed her arm and they skipped through the line.

Jin smiled as they reached the door. "Hey Brianna, hey Cassie, Fallon's expecting you two. I'll let him know you're here." He moved the rope and let them through.

"Thanks, you're the best." Cassie smacked a kiss against his cheek and flounced through the door.

They walked in through a tunnel, and the muted baseline of the EDM playing shook the walls around them.

"That guy knows us?"

Cassie looked back over her shoulder and gave her a sympathetic smile. "Sweetie, you know a lot of the guys here."

Brianna sighed in frustration. She wanted her memory back.

She gaped as they emptied out of the tunnel they'd entered, into the cavernous club. The place was certainly bigger than the outside appeared. Their heels click-clacked along the hardwood floor and they walked to a glass guard rail circling their whole floor. She noted there were bars on each level, the closest just to their left, and a few booths on the right side.

The dance floor was in front of them, but a full floor below. A DJ booth was above them a level. The DJ wore a LED computerized lion, dancing and hyping the crowd as he prepared for the next song to pound out of the sound system. The guard rail circled not only the floor they were on but also two more floors above them. Thick privacy glass separated a few private rooms, or maybe VIP areas on the floors above them. The spotlights that highlighted the dance floor bounced off the coating on the glass, glinting metallic. Curiosity had her stepping closer to the railing to see if she could get a peek inside.

Servers and bartenders worked in and out of the crowd like smoke through tall grass swaying to and fro. The movement of the crowd captured her attention for a moment. Bodies in every direction pushed and pulled and wove around one another, dancing. Provocative, passionate, the dancers were lost in lust. She stepped back, her skin flushed from the sight.

She had to admit, even if just to herself, the place looked cool. Mauve lighting danced along with the patrons below, painting the whole place with a pink hue. From the moment they'd stepped out of the tunnel, a languid heat grew and overtook her body. It was an odd thrumming, as though a live wire sang through her bloodstream.

"Oh God, my body is buzzing," Cassie shouted over the music, her body shuddering as her eyes drifted closed, and her lips parted.

So it wasn't just her.

Not that the information relieved her at all. They turned from the rail to look around, in time for her to notice Fallon moving through a crowd that easily parted around him. Brianna's breasts swelled, her stomach clenched, and her palms dampened the moment she saw him. He was wearing a pair of slacks and a crisp white dress shirt unbuttoned to the top of his chest beneath a vest the same wine color as his pants. The color against his brown skin was just…

She took a deep breath and squirmed. He was entirely too sexy for her peace of mind. He stopped in front of them, a smile covering his face. She wanted to peek and open the shirt wider, instead, she stepped closer to him and straightened his collar. She also brushed a hand across his head, concern for him drowning out her reticence and dampening her lust a touch. He looked exhausted and she wanted to do something about it. It was a caring gesture, one that had her staring at her hand in confusion.

By his stunned look, he too didn't expect it. "What was that for?"

"I don't, I don't know." She couldn't think of a single reason for what she'd done, other than she'd wanted to take care of him.

His narrowed eyes studied her a moment, before nodding. He leaned over and kissed her cheek where he lingered. Air moved across her skin as he inhaled deeply.

"I'm glad you came." His whisper carried over the music.

Her heart fluttered and she forgot to breathe. She stepped back from him, hoping the distance would bring perspective. He looked over at Cassie and smiled an easy, familiar smile. He kissed her best friend's cheek and Brianna wanted to rip them apart. Where in the hell did the jealousy come from?

He reached his hand out to her and she grabbed it. The heat of his palm comforted her, which, she'd examine later. He led them downstairs, through the crowd waiting at the bar. Whether it was his size, or demeanor, the crowd parted quickly moving from their path. As they walked through the club, there were people who stopped what they were doing to look. She looked at Cassie and her friend shrugged.

"We're going to meet in Xavier's office. The sexual pressure is less there." Fallon guided them through a door behind the dance floor.

Sexual energy? She frowned. Had she been that obvious? Fallon was using his thumb to stroke her wrist as he held her hand. It was clouding her thoughts, making her forget to ask him for clarification. His appreciative gaze traced her face, working down her body and back up. He gave her a smile and he led them down a corridor that was only slightly less crowded than the dance floor. They passed a busy kitchen, where the sound of shouting orders and clanging dishes reached out into the hallway. She was growing uncomfortable under the stares.

"Why are people staring?" Her curt voice carried throughout the hallway.

Fallon growled as one guy came close to them. The guy quickly scrambled back down the corridor. "The Divine don't visit our Havens. You and Cassie both stick out. You have a different magic to us, it's...heady."

"It's never this bad, though," Cassie said, stepping closer to him.

"Well, it's a club night and your magic stands out." He answered.

Their magic? She added that to the many things she'd ask later for clarification. She didn't bother tracing their steps or taking in the sights they passed. He distracted her. Plain and simple. The way he prowled the hallway, the way his ass moved in his slacks. She was quite honestly distracted enough that her usual panic at being in tight spaces didn't trigger.

They reached a door and a tall dark skin woman in a simple strapless dress was coming out. She had a baby bundled in her arms, but that wasn't what had her gaping. The woman had her hair in a high ponytail, but it looked like there were leaves and branches coming out of her hair. She turned to watch the woman leave as Fallon pulled her through the door. She lost sight of her as she rounded a corner.

Cassie closed the door behind her and took a seat on a supple maroon leather lounge chair next to the door. Brianna looked around to see where they were. The lighting seemed almost harsh compared to the rosy tones on the dance floor. It was a large office. The floor wood, the walls a sedate gray with large fantasy landscapes on each of the walls. They were beautiful images, the scenes pulling her in, making her wish such a place existed. The one behind the massive, hand-carved mahogany desk was a beach scene, unlike anything she'd ever seen. The sand was jet black, and yet glittering like diamonds, the sky a hazy purple as the sun came up or went down, she honestly couldn't tell.

A tall bookshelf and file cabinet sat in the corner filled with various binders and books with text she couldn't read. Floating just above the desk, with nothing seemingly connected to it, was a seethru glass monitor. Symbols and writing she didn't understand floated across the screen. She wanted a closer look but didn't dare take another step.

The office smelled faintly of burned paper, and gas. She frowned and Fallon looked around in confusion.

Xavier growled. "Ignore the smell."

Fallon glanced down at the trashcan.

"And the fire," Xavier said. His hands were working through a holographic screen emanating from his glass monitor, moving objects around. It looked even fancier than the computer her parents had in their house.

Brianna was impressed by the office and intimidated by the man behind the desk. He looked no nicer than he had when she'd first met him. His hazel eyes pinned her, once he turned his attention to her.

"Are you feeling alright?"

She nodded, unsure of how to act. At first, Xavier said nothing, just continued to stare at her as though waiting for something. She stared back, intrigued by the ring of green around his pupils. She looked up at Fallon and noticed he had the same eyes. A Demi trait? She'd have to write it down in her notebook to research later.

She turned back to Xavier and his jaw was working, his irritation plain to see. Was there some type of protocol she was missing? Why wasn't anyone saying anything? She looked back to Cassie who had made herself comfortable on the small sofa in the office. She suppressed a growl and the silence stretched.

Xavier sighed. "Did your visit to the Roswell Esin yield anything?"

She blinked in surprise. "How did you know about that?"

He raised an eyebrow instead of answering.

"You're having me followed?"

"What part about the guards are you not understanding?"

"I didn't know they'd also be snitches."

"Father of gods, did you imagine the guards following you wouldn't report your whereabouts?"

"You obviously are looking for something from me. I don't know what it is, and having someone follow me and report back won't help you."

"We're trying to protect your stubborn ass."

"I don't need protection from the people that kidnapped me. They were after my money, they didn't get anything, I don't think they'll be back. Besides, who are you to even offer me protection?"

Xavier shot Fallon a look and waved his hand in her direction as if to say, 'See what I deal with'.

"X." Was all Fallon said.

"We work for the same god you work for and until you remember why you were kidnapped, the guards stay. Hell, even after. Clearly, you need protection."

"This is ridiculous."

"How much does she know?" He directed the question to Cassie.

"Her laptop was encrypted. I thought I knew the password but it was different than the last one she gave me." Cassie spun the ring on her finger around in a nervous gesture. "I told her some about the Demi, she certainly knew much more than I before her memory loss, so there wasn't much I could tell her."

Brianna sat and pulled out the small notebook she always kept on her. She came to get answers, instead of arguing about guards, she would focus on that.

"So you work for Rugaba, doing what?"

Fallon shifted. "There are two groups who govern the Demi, us, the Amanda, and our ancestors, the Eminzu. The Amanda are in charge of the Demi's policing and protection."

She frowned, her pen poised. "A-mahn-da?"

"You're pronunciation is off. Short A's." Fallon told her.

She heard the difference, but still…

She wrote out Amanda like the girl's name anyway and looked up. "What do you mean by your ancestors?"

Xavier sighed. "It has no bearing on the present problem."

He had a point so she dropped it. "So you're in charge of the Amanda?"

"I am." Xavier crossed his arms over his chest.

Explained his demeanor. "I want to know what I was doing here, what I could've been researching."

Xavier sat back in his seat and put his arms behind his head. He was silent a moment, seemingly studying her. "I don't know the particulars of what you were researching. You'll have to talk to Liliana about that, you spoke with her about it more. I know you were working on translations for the *Book of Divinity*."

"Which is what, exactly?" She had her pen poised to write.

Xavier frowned his gaze flickering back to Cassie. "I thought you asked her about it."

"I did, you don't remember our conversation, Brianna?" Cassie's brow furrowed in confusion.

She licked her lips and stalled. As she perused her memories, a low throbbing started in her head. "I don't know anything about a *Book of Divinity*."

A spike of pain went through her head at saying it. She hissed in a breath and grabbed her head in pain.

Fallon sat in the chair next to her and leaned over, his hand resting on her shoulder. "You okay?"

She nodded.

"Interesting." Xavier murmured and exchanged a look with Fallon.

"What is the *Book of Divinity*?" Another sharp pain pierced her brain. She hunched over and took shallow breaths.

"Are you okay?" Cassie rushed to her side.

"Fine." She whispered and waved her away.

Xavier leaned back in his chair and eyed her with concern. Somehow, she knew it was not usual for him. His face was wiped clean, passive by the time she looked at him again.

"*Book of Divinity*." She whispered. Pain shot through her again. What the hell?

"Don't, Brianna." Fallon rubbed her back and some of the pain ebbed.

She straightened once she could get her breath. "What is…it, the book, what is it?"

"A spellbook," Fallon answered.

She looked up.

Xavier's face was back to the stoic expression he'd had when they walked in when. "As it is with us, it is with the Esin, there are archivists. The Divine, for all their secrecy only had one, Leah, Lalah, Liane, her name depends on who tells the story. She collected spells, from as far back as their creation. One of those ancient spells was used to bind Ofeere. That's the only reason we care about it and you, no offense. Only one from her line, one it's been 'willed' to can read the book. You're that person. You were given it when your aunt died. You're its new guardian."

Rugaba had told her she was the guardian of a spellbook. Were they one and the same? She wrote down spell book in her notes.

"I don't know you well enough to guess at your passwords, but what I know about you assured me you'd keep the book safe."

Cassie snorted. "She couldn't have predicted being kidnapped, Xavier."

"All the same, the extra protection must have been your way of keeping the book safe."

"And you don't know where it is?" She looked up from her notes.

"No one but you," Fallon answered.

A weight settled on her shoulders, one she didn't bring in, the responsibility weighing on her. "So not only do I have responsibility for the book, I have to now find it."

Xavier crossed his arm and gave her a short bob of his head. She looked to Fallon who stared back at her grimly.

"Would I have hidden it here?" It would make sense if, as they said, she'd visited a lot.

"No way, you wouldn't bring it in past our doors," Xavier told her.

"What?" She darted her glance back to Cassie.

That sounded very much like her. She didn't trust but a handful of people, and obviously, neither of the men in the room counted. Though, she looked at Fallon. She had a draw to him, some instinct that made her feel safe with him. She looked to Xavier, not so much with him.

Fallon as though sensing where her thoughts went spoke up hurriedly, "No, not wouldn't, you literally couldn't."

Xavier nodded. "There's a spell on the book that prevents it from entering any Haven."

She let out a breath. "My aunt?"

"It's part of the magic of the book. The Divine in the Esin were understandably suspicious of the Demi. Their Elder Divines may have worked to lock away Ofeeree with us, but it didn't mean they trusted them with their book of spells."

Her mind whirled. "I don't… none of that rings a bell. What is the contention between the Esins and the Demi? At least from your perspective. We barely learned anything about the Demi when we were with the Douglasville Esin."

"We were warned never to interact with them. Half the Esin didn't even believe they existed." Cassie added.

Fallon crossed his legs at his ankles and crossed his arms over his chest. He seemed to come to some type of conclusion as he stared at her. "It goes back to the beginning."

"Of what?"

"Of time," Xavier said on a sigh.

She frowned.

"Our gods created the first humans, the Divine humans. The Divine paid homage to their creators every Solstice, each worshiping the god that fit their needs, offering gifts to said gods."

She nodded, the Esin she'd grown up in had a bastardized version of the ceremony, but according to her parents, their current Esin in Atlanta practiced the solstice offerings.

"Some gods and goddesses lusted after the divine and demanded sex as their offering. Soon babies, half god, and half human were born, Demi-gods, which is why we're called the Demi." Fallon supplied.

It was fascinating and along the same lines of what Cassie told her. She leaned forward in her chair.

Xavier picked up the tale. "The Divine, for all the gifts they received from the gods, were mortal, and once they figured that out, they started to look for ways to extend their existence. They grew jealous of their progeny and the first war between the two started."

"How many wars were there?" She scribbled his accounting into her notebook.

"Maybe skirmish is a better word for the initial fighting between the two groups. The Divine in their quest for immortality offered up a gift, one they thought one of the creation gods could not refuse."

Her stomach churned, already sensing where the story was headed. "I take it they killed someone important."

"Someone important to the very god they were hoping to appease. What started as petty skirmishes, turned into full war once that god shortened their life span in retaliation."

"The great war, we call it," Fallon said.

"The divine unleashed an evil this dimension and others couldn't contain nor defeat. Ofeeree was born of magic and held no soul, nothing that tethered him to humanity. He was wholly evil." Xavier spread his hands.

Other dimensions? "Wait, what? This was all starting to get to be a little much." She was breathless.

"The part of the story that pertains to you," Fallon started.

103

"Me, personally?"

Fallon nodded. "To end the war, the Divine and the Demi came together to bind Ofeeree. The strongest elders from each of our species got together with the Divine. It was the only time during the war they all worked together. After he was bound, the archivist for the Divine documented everything needed in case he was to ever escape his prison. It's been passed down, and since they didn't trust the tentative truce between the two, only the guardian of the book has the key to unlock the book. You have an added complication."

"Oh God, what?"

"Once bound, the knowledge of how and where were seared onto the souls of three people. You're one of those people." Fallon laid his hand on top of her now cold hand, as shock went through her system. "You're what's known to us a Kokoro soul."

"What? Why me?"

Fallon shrugged. Her head was throbbing and suddenly she wanted to get out. Her breathing accelerated as panic reared up to choke her. She'd come for information and for the first time, she thought perhaps, she had too much information.

Scary information.

She got up from the seat and bolted for the door.

Chapter 11

Fallon waved Cassie back into her seat. "I'll take care of it."

He had monitored Brianna's face as they recited their history, watching the panic grow as she absorbed what they told her. He sensed that she would run. With every bomb his brother dropped, he saw her tense to run.

He raced from Xavier's office after her. By the time he'd caught up with her, she was deeper into the tunnels than she should've been. Her face was fixed into a scowl.

"You're going the wrong way, shorty. The exits back that way." He jerked his thumb over his shoulder.

"You guys deliberately made the corridors confusing so y'all can kidnap people." Her accent had thickened, fear, bringing out the country girl she mostly kept suppressed.

Fallon laughed, her words catching him off guard. "You don't believe that, Bri, you know better."

Her face was so confused and so beautiful when she looked up at him that his chest hurt.

"That's just it, I don't know. I don't know anything about what's happening to me. About the Demi and the Divines. I've lost a whole year of my life, and I'm not handling it as well as I thought I would be." She ran a shaking hand through the curls sprouting around her face. He loved the way her curly afro framed her face. "I mean, you look at me as though you expect something from me and I'm getting all these feelings for you I don't understand."

Lust tore through him and he stepped closer to her. He remembered Tahir's words about how confused she would be. He debated telling her what he'd done. An audience was gathering around them, drawn to Brianna's magic. Wild and untamed, it flickered around her in bright colors that only the Demi could see and recognize. He had no idea how the Divine saw their own magic.

"Let me take you somewhere we can talk?"

She nodded and he led her up a back stairwell, to the upper level. He found an empty room and with his hand on the small of her back, guided her into it. He watched her walk in, an appreciative glance going over her ass. He loved the way she wore the dress. He'd never seen her in something so revealing. The heels she wore made her legs look longer, and longed to have them wrapped around his waist.

He went to the window to compose himself. He looked out onto the dance floor. Humans and Demi both danced, the energy pulsing in the air. Instinctively he pulled some of it in, skimming as he usually did when he couldn't get his mate out of his mind. The energy was high enough, that had he been standing there for an hour or so he would be energized enough to go without feeding for another week. He fought to keep the sensual magic from overtaking his body as he pulled in energy from it.

It was a stupid idea to bring her out to the club area. He could see that now. But Cassie had told him she nearly had a panic attack the last time they were in the catacombs. He knew being above ground would make her feel better. Plus, he didn't think he could trust himself with her in his apartment. He checked the time. A little after eleven.

He caught Brianna's reflection in the glass and she was looking at him with those beautiful dark eyes and he was having a hard time focusing.

"Fallon, what are we to each other?" She whispered it, but that whisper traveled into his heart. "Why does it feel like you're mine?"

He sighed. "Little Love."

Unable to take another minute separated from her, he marched over and pressed a scorching kiss to her lips. He was swamped with the sensations. His tongue explored her mouth and her body relaxed into their kiss. He told himself he wouldn't lose it. But the magic was thrumming over him. He let down his shields and selfishly drew it in. He fed from his mate, wanting to feel the closeness with her. Allowing the energy to sink into him. It built, the power rushing through him like a high.

Leo had been right, feeding from his mate was a whole different experience. The magic was amplified, potent and strong. He was in no way near starving, and yet, his cells soaked up the magic from Brianna as though he hadn't fed in a month. Her magic mixed with that of the club's and a wave washed over him, dragging him under.

His hands roamed her back and he walked them back until they met a wall. She moaned, wrapping her arms around his neck, tiptoeing to get closer. The energy flowed over him and he pulled it in, feeding his suddenly starving body.

With no outlet for the lust, he'd not allowed himself to feed this way in ages. Guilt had assailed him anytime he tried to do anything other than the barest touch of another female. Two nights ago had been the first time in a year that he'd fully fed, and being with his mate made a mockery of that. The floodgates opened and Brianna's energy inundated him, cascading through his body. Her thoughts, her fantasies, the confusion and fear all rolled over him as his magic poured into her and bound them through the temporary spell used on club nights.

Brianna pulled back to get air and he leaned down, trailing his teeth along her neck. The tips of them elongated, the need to claim his mate slamming into him. Just a little taste, a tiny bit of her blood and she would belong to him, and no one could take her away. The temptation nearly sent him to his knees. Tahir's question looped through his mind, did he want Brianna, or did he only want her body? With her in his arms, her every breath feeding him, giving him life, he found it hard to separate the two.

She arched her body, pressing her breasts into his chest to relieve their ache. She yanked at his shirt in desperation to feel his skin.

107

"Yes," he purred. "Touch me, sweetheart."

She ripped the buttons on his vest, and shirt and lifted the shirttails from his pants, sliding her hands underneath. His skin was burning, his muscles firm everywhere she touched. He moved up her neck and reclaimed her mouth. The kiss sent her spinning. She gripped him tightly. It was like something took over her body. She wanted to crawl into him, anything to be as close as possible.

"What is happening to me?" She whispered.

He stiffened and backed up. His chest moved up and down with his harsh breathing. His hazel eyes were now metallic, glinting in the dim lights. For a moment she'd forgotten that he was a demigod.

He turned his back to her. "It's the magic."

His hoarse voice raised goosebumps on her arms. She was confused, yes, but she still wanted him… no…

Craved him.

She closed her eyes and fought to breathe normally. He moved to the window and put his hand up, resting his head on the glass. It took her a minute to gather her thoughts together, and even still, her body shook with her need for him. It was scary and so confusing. She walked to him and touched his shoulder tentatively.

He stiffened and relaxed with a rough exhalation.

"It's the magic." He repeated. "See the dancers down there? They're feeding the lust in the air. It starts with a spell. One that sends out a pulse of magic to lower inhibitions and amplify lust. A little spark is all it takes, once it starts, the humans and Demi both feed it. It grows into a mass of energy that the Demi take in and use to fuel their bodies and magic."

Somehow she didn't care about that. She couldn't think about anything but what was between the two of them.

"You didn't answer my question. What am I to you?"

He didn't say anything for a moment and she thought he wouldn't answer the question. He turned around and she gasped at the torment in his eyes.

"Everything." Said in the faintest whisper, the impact of it stunned her.

She stiffened, fear and excitement racing through her. It was so unlike her, this wanton woman. It equal parts thrilled and alarmed her. Another thing to ponder later. Right now? Right now, she wanted to see how far the wanton would carry her.

He closed the distance between them and grabbed her, kissing her senseless. His hands lowered to her ass, lifting her to deepen their kiss. She wrapped her legs around his waist, feeling his erection through his pants. Her dress was up around the top of her hips, her cheeks out, the thong offering no coverage or modesty and she couldn't find it in her to care. He growled into her mouth, his hips jerking into hers.

She lifted her hips, riding the thick ridge poking through his slacks. Her breasts warmed, the nipples tightening, adding to the maelstrom of lust. She rode his erection, wanting very much to feel him inside of her. His hands gripped her ass, lifting her, rubbing her clit against him. She needed…his tongue mimicked exactly what she needed. It stabbed into her mouth, his full, soft lips covering her own. His hands tightened their grip and heat, like she'd never felt, assailed her body. Her skin tingled, the nerve endings buzzing. Her mind was cloudy with need, drunk off the lust.

"Oh God." She moaned.

Her body tightened and he ground his hips into her with just the right amount of pressure. The orgasm swept over her. From the top of her scalp to the tip of her toes, shockwaves engulfed her. She threw her head back and moaned as he held her in place, prolonging it. She closed her eyes as amber light bathed the room. Even behind her closed lids, she saw the glow.

109

She opened them, drowsy, still seeing the amber light, but this time it almost seemed to surround Fallon. It was gone before she could think of remarking on it.

She pulled his head down for another kiss. One hand reached down for the button of his pants, she wanted him. Now.

Fallon pulled back with a groan. "Not here, little love. Not now. Not when you're high off magic. Our first time won't be in a night club."

She froze. It was as if a bucket of cold water had doused her. Their

first time?

It meant she'd never slept with him. Oh God, she didn't know him, not really, what was she thinking?

"I have to go," she whispered.

Fallon grabbed her arm. "No, *ife,* don't go."

She snatched her arm away, jerked down her dress and fled the room. She didn't know what to feel. She was mad, but mostly at herself. Everything she'd heard about Fallon led her to believe they had a relationship. Hell, he talked to her parents regularly. They spoke highly of him. Why would she have these feelings for someone she wasn't dating? She didn't do casual sex, ever. She ran into Cassie on the way down the stairs.

"I want to go."

"Of course," Cassie answered quickly, looking behind her.

Almost unbidden, she turned her head to look. Fallon stood at the top of the stairs, at the door to the room she'd just fled. His clothes were immaculate, no trace of what they'd done marred them. The need in his eyes seared her, sent her heartbeat skittering in her chest. Oh God, what had she gotten into?

Chapter 12

The sun had only been up an hour and he was on the rooftop groggily moving through the canopied chairs scattered around the Olympic sized pool. Behind the lounge chairs, there were Haven employees cleaning up, putting up cabanas and setting out café tables and wicker chairs. It looked like a luxurious resort and ran as proficiently as a five star would. Behind the cabanas on one side was grass spread to the edge of the roof, with plenty of room for blankets and beach towels. Already families were set up with their blankets spread out on the grass taking in the sunrise, basking in its energy.

He waved as he passed them, headed to the corner of the roof. There were wards built into the building that kept prying eyes from seeing what was going on in Haven, and it was his job to keep them up and functioning. There were two on the roof that he checked weekly to be sure the Demi had their privacy as they lay, reenergizing from the primal source. It was the only reason he was up at such an ungodly hour.

It was part of his job as the head of security of Haven. It wasn't a job he thought he'd ever have, but his father had been adamant that all three of his sons served. His family had dismissed the years he'd spent away as flighty, not understanding his need to center himself and escape the heavy tension that had blanketed their home. He'd spent those years searching out magic, honing his own. And while there were scars, hard lessons he'd learned while out, he wouldn't change it for a moment. Without it, he wouldn't have had the power or even know how to perform the spell that had kept his mate alive.

Speaking of his mate, he thought about the Oras he'd seen around her disappearance. She'd vanished into thin air and he was still puzzled days later after seeing it. He'd been in their library with the archivist trying to find out what type of magic could hide from the Oras. So far they'd come up with nothing. He reached the corner of the roof and stopped. He took a deep breath, cleared his mind and meticulously worked through the spell making sure there were no breaches. Finding none, he turned to move on to the next one.

He caught sight of his sister in law, wearing Kell across her chest and directing employees, making sure the area was cleaned and ready for guests. She waved him over with a huge smile, obviously having no problem being up so early. He walked over and rubbed the top of Kell's head, peeking out from the baby wrap.

"You look exhausted."

"Good morning to you too, sister dear. I was up late."

"And you have nightmares." She held up her hands, "sorry, good morning."

"How would you know that, Trouble?"

"I know lots, Fallon. If you haven't noticed, I've built a vast network here."

He snorted. That was an understatement. He now understood how Liliana had evaded the soldiers his brother had sent looking for her when she'd been on the run. No one made friends the way she did.

"How much longer are you on maternity leave?"

She sighed. "I'm already bored. I promised Xavier I'd take over the help reqs next week. The nursery he set up next to my office is beautiful.

Kell will be well taken care of, and I'll be on hand to feed him when needed."

"My mother hasn't offered to take him during the day?"

She gave him a droll stare. "Don't get me started on Sharine and the help she offers. Anyone who can ruffle a Kira, is something of a special snowflake."

His bark of laughter stirred the baby sleeping against her chest. "*Iya* is an acquired taste."

"Between his uncles and his grandmother, Kell is fully protected." Liliana bounced the baby back to sleep.

He had to agree with her on that point. "I'm going to finish my rounds." He leaned over and kissed her cheek.

"Leo and I are setting up over there," she pointed to a secluded spot far from the pool. "Come sit when you're done."

He nodded, not making any promises.

He finished the last ward less than an hour later and turned to leave. He seriously debated going back to sleep or taking his sister in law up on her offer. He glanced over at the area Liliana had pointed out and saw his brother sitting alone with Kell.

His little brother looked peaceful. It reminded him again of his conversation with Tahir. He cursed, mad he could hear Tahir's words in his head. Even as he made out with Brianna, he couldn't get the Kira's words out of his mind.

He walked over and took a seat on the blanket. There were fruits and pastries spread out on a large tray. He assumed Liliana was expecting company. He smiled at his nephew who was no longer sleep. Kell's eyes were wide and happy as he gazed at Leo.

"Little brother." He grabbed a cup and poured coffee from the thermos.

"It's Uncle Fallon," Leo said in a voice that could only be for the benefit of his newborn.

"How are you enjoying fatherhood?"

"It's lots of tears, dirty diapers and daydreaming about sleep," Leo said with a satisfied smile. He kissed his son on the top of his head. "How's it going with you? Fully mated yet?"

"You know I'm not." He grumbled. As if he could finish the bond outside of the *di êjê*.

He'd considered taking her blood last night, but while it would've bonded them, without the *di êjê*, it wouldn't have been a soul level bond.

"What's stopping you?"

"Are you happy?"

Leo blinked in confusion at the change of subject. "With life?"

Fallon sighed, unable to explain what he wanted.

"You don't want to mate?"

"I do, I mean eventually."

Leo gaped at him. "Why the fuck did you initiate the mating bond if you weren't ready?"

"She would've died."

"That was up for debate at the time. We could've found another way." Leo argued.

"A more dangerous way." He insisted.

"I'm not butting my head against that brick wall, what's done is done."

"Thank you." Fallon breathed out.

Leo narrowed his eyes. "I don't understand you and I thought out of me and Xavier, I knew you the best. Not to diminish you or your position, I know I didn't want to mate because I would be forced to give up hunting. What about your position can't be done with a mate?"

"I don't…" he stopped and thought about his brother's question. "It's not my position that's a problem. I don't love my job the way you and Xavier love yours."

"Then what is it?"

"I spend a good portion of my life taking care of everyone. Xavier was groomed to lead the Amanda. You knew you would be in the Amanda without a doubt. Meanwhile, I was left to make sure nothing got in the way of either of your dreams. No one, at any time asked me what I wanted out of life."

Leo rubbed his son's head, bending down to kiss him. "I didn't realize you felt that way."

"It is what it is."

"So you don't want to be tied down to someone you'll have to take care of?"

"Is that selfish?

"I mean, kind of." Leo held up his hand to stem his argument. "It's your life, you can be selfish all you want. However, when your selfishness affects others, it becomes a problem."

"How?"

"You started a bond, Fallon. I distinctly remember our older brother yelling at you about the decision. But you were sure, you were adamant and now you're…not?"

Fallon sighed and wiped his face.

"You're a 'runner, Fallon."

"What does that mean?" He debated whether or not to take offense.

"When shit gets too complicated, you bounce. You go off to another far corner of the world in search of some mysterious magic.

Being with a mate, a human one no less is complicated. I'm quite frankly surprised you haven't found a reason to go 'check the wards' at another Haven."

He growled, pissed that his brother knew him as well as he did.

"Look, we had no reference for a decent relationship, so I get it."

"Speaking of childhood, have you talked to baba?" He changed the subject frustrated he still couldn't articulate his issue with the mating.

Leo looked away. "I'm having a hard time reconciling the great father I knew, with the shitty things he's done."

Fallon snorted. "You romanticize a lot of our past, Leo. As the baby, you were sheltered from a lot. Since I did most of the sheltering, I'll take both your thanks and the blame."

"Thank you?" Leo gave him an incredulous look.

"You're welcome." He took a pastry from the tray.

Leo smiled a little and shook his head. "He was the only one there for us."

"He was not, little brother. You saw him so much because you spent all your free time following him around like a little duck. Ranolph spent his every waking moment at Haven and mostly left our raising to whichever nanny mom had not run off at the time. Once I was old enough to feed us, even the nannies stopped."

Leo closed his eyes and lifted his head to the sun. "Shit, you're right. How did I forget that?"

117

Fallon shrugged. "I'm good at what I do. Whether it be making sure the Havens function or making sure our family functioned without anyone being inconvenienced, it's all the same to me."

"You know, all this time, I assumed we were hiding the grittier parts of our job from Xavier when it seems as you were hiding it even from me."

"It's not gritty, Leo. Tiring, sometimes monotonous, but for the most part, it's a simple matter of paying attention. Facilitating others is something I've done my whole life, it's no different now."

Leo hummed. "So, you have no problem catering to people, making sure their lives are easy and run smoothly, but you won't apply that to your life."

Fallon frowned. "What do you mean?"

"I love you, brother, and I love Xavier, but this kid and Liliana come first, in everything, and my life has been the better for it. Take care of yourself and your mate, and you'd be surprised how much your life will line up."

Fallon looked away, Xavier had said something similar to him last night.

Leo sighed. "But you're not ready. You have what, three more weeks before the decision is taken out of your hand?"

Fallon nodded.

"You'll do what you want, you always have."

Fallon growled. "That's the same thing Tahir said."

"Well, there you go."

They lapsed into silence and Fallon stretched out and closed his eyes. He could both rest and fuel his body. He sighed as the heat of the sun touched his skin. His body relaxed as it soaked in energy from the sun's radiation. Thoughts of last night drifted to the forefront of his mind. He couldn't figure out what went wrong, Brianna had been as into it as he was. What made her stop? He needed to find out and soon. He was fast running out of time.

Chapter 13

She stared at the ceiling, debating if she wanted to get out of bed. Brianna's body was still buzzing. Buzzing, languid and sated. God, what had she been thinking? She wanted to run to the other side of the globe to avoid Fallon, but, last night, she'd had nightmares. Nightmares about her kidnapping. How much was real, she didn't know, but instinct had her wanting to tell Fallon about it. Plus, she wasn't a coward, she would face this thing between them head-on.

Eventually.

She sighed and got out of bed. Her cell phone buzzed, it was a text message. Darren was asking her out to lunch. Had she been in her right mind, the answer would've automatically been no. But, she agreed to go out to lunch with him. She didn't think it was a coincidence that she was kidnapped and all of a sudden someone from her past would appear. It was not because she was avoiding Fallon.

She blew out a breath, okay, that was a lie.

She needed perspective. Lunch with Darren could give her something other than Fallon to focus on. She could ask him some questions and prove her theory that the Douglasville Esin was behind her kidnapping. She walked to Cassie's room and knocked.

A groggy Cassie answered the door. "Why do you insist on being up so early?"

"Do you remember Darren?"

"Ew, skinny guy, followed you around, told everyone not to touch you because you were his." Cassie scrunched her face.

"Yep, one and same."

"What about him?"

"He just asked me to lunch." She avoided her friend's eyes.

Cassie straightened, fully awake. "What? How? Are you considering it?"

"Yep, I just wanted to let you know in case I went missing again."

"One, do not joke about that, and two, I don't think it's a good idea."

"I thought you said the Esin didn't kidnap me."

Cassie flipped her the bird. "Doesn't mean his crazy ass didn't. Maybe he thought he could convince you to finally be with him and when it didn't work, he let you go."

Brianna snorted. "Now who's making up wild theories?"

"It could happen, I watch enough t.v. so I know."

"You watch too much t.v. Go back to bed, I'll text you the address, you know the drill."

"Yeah, yeah, text you in an hour with a work emergency." She started to turn but then whipped back around. "Are you going to tell Fallon?"

Her stomach fluttered. "Why would I?"

Cassie raised an eyebrow. "Oh, ok. We're playing that game."
"Whatever, Cass, besides, he has people following me anyway. I'm sure they'll let him know."

"Mmhmm." Cassie rolled her eyes and shut the door in her face.

"Forget you, then." She murmured and went to make coffee.

Her morning went by quickly with her waffling about going to lunch. Was Cassie right? Should she tell Fallon? Maybe after, she decided around ten o'clock. She got dressed and left the apartment to meet him. He'd asked her to meet at The Bag Lunch, a café all the way downtown. Traffic had completely aggravated her by the time arrived, and looking for street parking added another level. Her mood was well and truly spoiled when she'd found parking a couple of blocks away from the restaurant. Luckily, she'd dressed casually, just a pair of skinny jeans with a cute blouse. Her flat Mary Janes made the walk easy enough.

He waved her over to a table away from the window, it looked shadowy in comparison to the other tables near the front. He stood as she reached the table, his features gaunt and pale, not much different than how he'd looked as a teenager. By now, she assumed he would have filled out. She dismissed the thought because of course, he wouldn't be able to compare with Fallon's muscular body. The man was a behemoth, no human would be able to compare. She waved Darren back into his seat and sat across from him.

"I took the liberty of ordering for you if that's okay." He indicated the drink in front of her place setting.

She frowned at the glass on the table. "No, that's fine." She waved the waitress down and handed back, whatever had been sitting in the cup. "I'd really just like some ice water please."

He frowned but covered it quickly when she glanced over. "You don't drink sweet tea anymore?"

"I'm sort of on this diet," she lied.

He nodded, and his face cleared. "Well, you are a lot…bigger than you were, so I understand."

Did he really just say that? She glared. Strike one for him.

"Thanks so much for meeting me," he said again. Ignoring the glare on her face.

"Yeah, how did you get my number?"

"Well, I have to admit, the first thing I did when I arrived in town was to search out your aunt. I thought she'd know where you were." He reached out and covered her hand with his own. "I was really sorry to hear about her passing."

She gave him a tight smile and pulled back her hand. He didn't answer her question, strike two.

"Thank you. You've just arrived in town then?"

"Yeah, I finished my degree and thought Atlanta would be an easier place to find a job. I left the Esin not much longer after you did. Once you and Cassie left, I started, I don't know, looking around, noticing things not quite adding up."

She snorted. "What, you were manifesting this magic they promised before that?"

He grimaced. "What kid doesn't want to believe they're magic?"

"But at what cost?" She asked, taking a sip of her water.

He sighed. "Apparently at the cost of our freedom."

"There were enough restrictions to make prison seem appealing," she remarked.

"You never told me what happened to make you and Cassie leave. I mean, she was Chosen, she left a potentially cushy life."

She swirled the straw around in her glass and stared into its contents.

Potentially cushy.

Clearly, he knew nothing about what went on behind the Oliri's closed doors. It was not her place to inform him, so she went with her standard answer when asked about her childhood or why she'd left home.

"It's not something I discuss."

"Fair enough. For a while, I'd assumed you left to get out of our betrothal." He joked.

She barely withheld her snort of disdain. Instead, she took a sip out of her straw and didn't answer.

"I was looking forward to life with you."

"I somehow doubt that." She couldn't keep the contempt from her tone.

"It's true!" He insisted, once again, grabbing her hand.

She patted his hand with one hand and extricated the other. His touch made her uncomfortable, and not just in the sense that he made her skin crawl. It made her think of Fallon and had some measure of guilt attached to it. She should've called him and told him where she was.

Ever since their heavy make-out session, she'd been antsy and restless. Her body was craving his and she didn't know what to do about it. Though she had to be honest, it had been more than just making out. But, she wasn't a person that 'checked in', and the compulsion to do so was a foreign feeling to her.

She noticed Darren staring. She shook her head to clear her mind. "I'm sorry, I missed what you said."

He smiled. "You're distracted. What's going on?"

"Not much. I was in an accident." She paused, wondering if he would take the bait. When he didn't leap in to say anything, she continued. "I've been having some issues and not quite up to 100 percent. I probably should've declined this lunch, I'm sorry I'm such bad company right now."

He smiled, looking relieved. "That would explain the awkwardness. Would you like me to take you home?"

How she kept from rolling her eyes was nothing short of a miracle.

But, he sounded sincere and she felt bitchy for lying to him. Not guilty enough to stop trying to interrogate him, though.

"No." She sat up straight, "no. Let's have a nice lunch." She said as their food arrived.

He'd ordered her a turkey club and she couldn't much fault him for that, no matter how barbaric she found his ordering her lunch. He smiled bigger as she started eating.

"Do you miss it?" He asked after they'd been eating a moment.

She shrugged and finished chewing. "I miss some of the people." Another lie.

"When have you last spoken to your parents?"

She stared at him for a moment, wondering how he knew her parents had also escaped the cult if he himself didn't have a way to communicate with the Esin. The half of sandwich she'd eaten sat heavy in her stomach. It was forbidden for them to speak with their family members once they left the Esin, so he wouldn't have asked that question unless he knew. Perhaps she'd been hasty in dismissing his motives.

"Years." Thank the Lord no one but she was keeping a tally of the lies she was telling. "And you, do you still talk to anyone from Douglasville?"

"Yeah, I've tried to talk to my parents and cousins since leaving, but no response. They're all under Elder Cedric's pull, I can't get through to anyone."

She felt some empathy for him, her parents were thriving in the Roswell Esin. It gave her both peace and happiness. She didn't want to remember how it felt to know they were in their old Esin wilting under the Oliri's rule.

125

"What have you been up to?" She prodded, she didn't want to feel anything for Darren. She wanted answers.

"Well," he sat back in his chair. "I left the Esin and went to live with my father's sister. She helped a lot with…deprograming. I went to college as I said, and now I have a new job working at a marketing firm here in Atlanta."

"Wow, marketing. Interesting."

"It has its moments. How about you, still asking questions? Did you ever become a reporter?"

She tilted her head, she hadn't talked to him enough as a child for him to even know that.

He gave her a sheepish grin. "I remember overhearing you tell Cassie once that you wanted to be a reporter."

"Oh." She forced her mouth into a smile. "Not quite. Before the accident, I did work for a national magazine."

Her phone beeped, thankfully, her signal from Cassie that she'd been gone longer than her friend was comfortable with. She checked the time, it had been nowhere near an hour, which told her how anxious Cassie was. She smiled and sent her back a message that she was leaving. She wasn't as good at investigating as she thought she was.

"So this has been great." She pulled out her wallet. "But I have to get to work."

"No," he hastily waved away her money. "Lunch was on me. Next time we'll do this after you're done working for the day."

She gave him a tight smile and waved goodbye. She definitely wouldn't be seeing him again if she could help it. She headed out of the restaurant, back down the street to her car. The hair on the back of her neck stood up, and her stomach started a slow roll.

Someone was watching her.

She needed to apologize to Xavier when she saw him. Knowing there were guards somewhere behind her was the only thing keeping her from panicking. Still, she picked up her walking speed. Her phone beeped. It was a text message from Isaiah.

Don't freak out.

Beep.

I'm with you but you have a tail.

Beep.

Don't look.

Her shoulders tensed and she slowed a little. Now that he'd made her aware, the temptation to look overwhelmed her. She inched her head a little to the right as it beeped again.

No, seriously, don't look. You'll blow my cover.

She growled and picked up her speed towards her car, staying just under a run. She had to look silly speed walking down the sidewalk.

Beep.

Black SUV, coming up on your right.

Oh shit, was she supposed to avoid the car, get in the car, what? Jesus, talk about vague? She glanced off her right shoulder, just in time for a truck to pull up next to her and stop. Isaiah came up on her left side and grabbed her elbow. She squelched her scream and instead just cursed. He shuffled her into the back seat of the SUV, going around the back and getting into the front passenger side.

"Wait, what about my car?"

The driver looked into the rearview, it was Michel. "We'll send someone to bring it to Haven."

127

Of course, they were going to Haven, the one place she wanted to avoid.

Chapter 14

Haven was right outside of Atlanta, Michel drove and occasionally checked his mirrors for anything following behind them. After exiting the highway, Brianna lost track of the turns and backtracking they did but felt better knowing these guys were obviously well trained. After a while, they were on a long-isolated road cruising along. They passed a gas station on the corner turning into the plaza, a large grocery store anchored the place with the standard fare of pizza, nails, and coffee shops surrounding it. She recognized some of it. She lived not more than twenty minutes from this part of town.

Oddly, Michel didn't slow at all as he made the needed turns to glide the black oversized SUV to a small alleyway between the plaza and a bank offering free check cashing. Passing between the bank and plaza, two lanes were available. One direction lead to a drive-thru for the bank, the other into a bay of garbage bins and truck unloading for the grocery store. Michael kept pace, headed right for a wall at the end of the lane.

"Uhh, Michel." Brianna took another nervous look around. It wasn't the same route she and Cassie had taken when they'd come to Haven.

Michel looked up at her in the rearview mirror with a smirk. "Wow, you really don't remember."

He didn't slow their speed as they neared the wall. She closed her eyes, bracing for impact. She opened one eye after a moment when nothing happened. They'd passed through the wall without incident. She scrambled in the seat and looked behind them. The wall was behind them, intact. What the hell?

"Yeah, I definitely don't remember driving through a wall." She put her hand over her chest.

Isaiah snickered. "The gateway's open during club nights. Fallon keeps it closed during the day to keep humans from wandering back here looking for trouble."

She marveled at the kind of power Fallon had to have to pull something like that off. She peered around the front seat to see where they were going. She recognized the modern-looking brick building. All of the windows on the upper floor were giant glass fixtures. Four lined the front of the building, with an oversized glass double door entrance in the center of the front-facing wall. Warehouse doors on either side of the doors were also glass but as hard as she looked, she could see nothing inside. Along the side of the building, a tree-lined walkway led to the back and out of sight. Brianna recalled coming out of that walkway when she left last time. To her left was the gravel parking lot that was full when they'd visited on club night. It was empty, and now she understood why.

She was sure none of the shop owners on the other side of the wall even knew the building was here. Haven fascinated her as she saw it in the light of day. Michel pressed a button in the console and one of the warehouse doors opened, allowing them entrance into a garage. As they passed through the entryway, the entire place came to life. Staff members were busy moving palates about on forklifts, a full parking bay went on for what seemed like forever.

Michel drove past a fleet of cars in the warehouse, expensive ones, both foreign luxury cars and mean-looking muscle cars. She wondered who owned them all. Their car stopped at the end of a row of matching SUVs and they all piled out.

Isaiah held out his fist for a bump. "Good job following instructions. The old Brianna would've asked a hundred questions before following one simple direction."

She bumped his fist and rolled her eyes. Michel snickered next to her. It was weird that they knew her so well, and she had no memories of them outside meeting them the other day.

"Who was following me?"

"I don't know, but they followed you to the restaurant and waited until you left. Better safe than sorry, so the protocol is to bring you back to base." Michel answered.

She nodded, thankful they were there. They walked to a door at the end of the garage near where they'd parked. There was a guard at the door.

"Yo, where's the Commander?" Isaiah bumped elbows with the guard.

The guard pointed up, and she frowned. "Just up?"

That was the only answer they were getting? The brick building that housed Haven had maybe three floors, but still, that wasn't an answer. The guard didn't elaborate and Isaiah didn't ask for clarification, just walked past him to the brick walkway that connected Haven to their garage. She assumed they were going inside, and would pass the club floor. Instead, they veered and went up three flights of stairs at the side of the building.

The guard had meant literally up, they were going to the roof. She gaped as she came out of the stairwell. It looked like a luxurious resort. There was a giant pool, lounge chairs and gazebos, and a bar? There were children running around squealing, their parents laid out on beach blankets and towels sunbathing. There was a lot of splashing in the pool, and more than one lifeguard on duty. It was like a whole different place. The temperature up there didn't reflect the rest of the city's temperature. It definitely wasn't swimming weather. How in the world were they hiding something like this in the middle of a shopping plaza?

She was shocked. So far, she'd seen so many sides to the Haven. The healing ward where she'd awakened, the club, the underground corridors, Xavier's office and now this place where kids frolicked and squealed in pleasure. It made a mockery of everything she'd accused the Haven of when she'd awoken. It looked nothing like a cult. Isaiah smiled at her open mouth staring and led her to a grassy area away from the crowds.

Fallon was laid out on the ground, relaxing on a blanket, a baby cooing on his chest. She didn't know which sight surprised her more. Him relaxing, or the cute baby he was making faces at. The baby turned his eyes to her and she was smitten by the serious emerald stare that scrutinized her. A beautiful woman lay across from him on the edge of the blanket, a bikini barely covering her slender body. Her bronze skin gleamed metallic as the sun danced over it. She had a waterfall of red, yellow and orange shiny hair laid along the side of her. She looked every inch the Demi-god, and suddenly the jeans she wore felt frumpy, the blouse she had on, inadequate.

Jealous was an ugly emotion, and it dug its claws into her, making her insanely, irrationally angry at the scene before her. Who were these people to Fallon? Surely he wouldn't touch her the way he did and have a whole ass family? She dug her nails into her hand and bit her lip to keep from saying anything.

"Yo, boss. Brought you some company." Isaiah gave her a salute and waggled his eyebrows, just leaving her there.

Fallon turned his head to her, and she was pissed at the way her body reacted. She wanted him. Even with him laying with his family, her body coveted his. She glared at him, wanting to punch him in his gorgeous face. The woman opened her eyes and turned to glance at her. She had the same startling green eyes as the baby and disappointment weighed Brianna's shoulders. The woman sat up and smiled at her.

"Brianna, hi! How are you feeling?" She sat up, crossing her legs.

Brianna couldn't return her smile. As it was, she was fighting to keep both vitriol and her lunch from spewing from her mouth. The things she'd allowed Fallon to do to her last night ran through her thoughts. Her body reacted, warming even as her mind rebelled.

The woman's smile changed to one of empathy. "I'm Liliana, Leo's wife. And that handsome bundle in Fallon's lap is my baby Kell."

Relief weakened her knees. She cleared her throat, dislodging the lump there. "I'm sorry." Apologizing for both the uncharitable thoughts and not remembering her.

Liliana shrugged and turned to gather up her things. The sunlight caught her hair and Brianna gasped as a memory of them in the library flitted across her mind. She narrowed her eyes, trying to chase down more of the memory.

"I spent a lot of time with you, in a library right?"

Liliana laughed. "Yes, I hate libraries, but you're obsessed with research. 'Information in hand is another tool in your arsenal.'"

Brianna smiled because, though she didn't remember Liliana, she'd often used that phrase. Fallon sat up and settled the baby in his lap and her breath caught. He was ridiculously hot, and it just wasn't fair. She licked her lips and sighed. This was why she didn't want to come to Haven. Just looking at him, she knew if he so much as hinted that he wanted her, she'd go willingly into his arms.

"Hi."

Lame.

She sighed again. "Can I sit with you guys?"

He nodded, not saying a word. His eyes did a lot of talking though, and from the looks he skimmed down her body, he wanted her as much as she wanted him. She bent to sit, surprised it was actual grass on the rooftop. She'd expected turf. She brushed through the soft tufts as she settled on their blanket. Fallon slid over to give her more space.

133

She sidled closer. Definitely a bad idea. His scent wrapped around her, and it took everything in her not to lean over and inhale. Still, …she breathed deep.

"So, what brings you out here?" Fallon cradled the baby in his arms, not looking at her.

She was struck with how natural he looked with the child. She stared for long moments, unsure of what to say. She should tell him about her lunch with Darren, and the subsequent hasty retreat, but she didn't want a lecture. She also didn't necessarily want to get into it with Liliana listening in.

"I wanted to talk with you."

Fallon studiously avoided looking at her. She rubbed her hands along her jeans.

"I saw all the children playing up here." She stuttered awkwardly.

"Yeah, they come here to soak up energy from the sun." He murmured.

"Another way Demigods fuel their body?" She asked remembering what he'd told her last night.

Fallon nodded and looked at her. A long moment passed where she got lost in his eyes. They were hazel, but there was a ring of green around the pupils that glowed brighter, the longer they stared at each other.

Liliana snorted, breaking the growing tension. "Fine, I'll leave." She gathered a towel and the baby's bag.

"You can leave the monster," Fallon told her.

She gave them both a knowing smile. "Hiding behind my baby? You should be ashamed, Uncle Fallon, but I'm not going to complain." She leaned over and kissed her son on his hair and left.

She wanted to tackle the awkwardness between them before it stretched longer, starting with the elephant in the room. "Look, about last night-"

"Don't, Brianna, you don't owe me anything."

"It was too much, too fast."

"Is that why you came to see me?"

"Everyone around me led me to believe the two of us were together. When you said it would be our first time…I'm not that woman. I don't sleep with people I don't know. That's why I balked. And yet, it feels as though we're together, why does it feel like we're together?"

He looked at her for long moments not saying anything until finally, he asked, "Are you ready for that answer?"

She pushed out a breath. She was not ready for that answer so she chickened out and changed the subject.

"I went to lunch with a member of our old Esin."

Kell shifted in his arms as Fallon growled.

"It wasn't like that." She hastily added. She sighed and lowered her head, suddenly finding the grass next to her super interesting. "I thought if I went out with him, I could question him, see if he had information about my kidnapping."

"And what did you find out?"

She shuddered at his growly tone. There was restraint in his voice, which made her curious. She lifted her head to look at him. His eyes were no longer hazel, they were copper, the color encompassing his eyes the same as it had been last night. His skin had darkened, and copper lines ran up and down his arms, there were circles in some type of pattern on his skin. She traced a line, feeling the raised whorls, her curiosity getting the better of her. The lines emitted light, pulsing with his rapid heartbeat.

135

He shuddered at her touch, his lids lowering to half-mast. So, she had not been seeing things last night when they…she shook her head as her body heated. Nope, would not be going there.

"What…" She couldn't even get out the question. Kell squirmed, his anxious cry breaking the spell.

She cleared her throat. "I'm terrible at this investigating stuff. My wheelhouse is clearly research."

He took a deep breath, his eyes capturing her. She saw his fight to restrain himself. She watched dazed, as he gradually slowed his heartbeat. The lines slowly faded along with the copper in his eyes.

"That's amazing." She whispered.

"What do you want from me, Brianna?" He turned his head and looked forward.

She sighed. "I don't know, Fallon. I just want to know what this is between us."

"And you came over to ask?"

"I actually was brought here by my guards." She admitted.

He looked up, alert. "What happened?"

"Someone followed me to the café and my meeting with Darren."

"Did you recognize them?" He shifted Kell and reached into his pocket.

"I didn't see whoever it was at all. Your guys are good."

He nodded. "Of course." He pulled out the fanciest flip phone she'd ever seen. It beeped and a small holographic image of a man at a desk appeared, hovering over the screen of his phone.

"Yes, Commander."

He turned to Brianna. "Where did you have lunch?"

"The Bag Lunch." She answered absently, her mind buzzing with questions as she stared at his phone.

He turned back to the image. "Pull up the Oras from a place called The Bag lunch, go back three hours and have it queued for me. I'll be down shortly." He closed his phone and assessed her.

"Anything else happened you want to tell me about?"

She nodded, pushing the questions to the side. "Yes, actually. I had nightmares last night, I thought maybe there would be clues in them."

He put a hand on her shoulder and she sank into the sensation. "What kind of clues?"

"Well, I was definitely held hostage at some point. I have these vague sorts of memories of being shackled to a wall."

"Any faces, location?"

"No, neither." She rubbed her temples as she tried to remember more details from her nightmare.

He hummed. "As more memories come out they could be useful. At least you're sleeping."

"Are you having trouble sleeping?"

He nodded. "I've had insomnia for some years."

Curiosity had her spinning her body to fully face him. "Why? Is your job very stressful?"

He shook his head. "I manage the security of all the Havens around the world, it's not so much stressful as wrangling."

"Are there a lot of Havens? Do you have nightmares?"

"Yes, and some nights. When I was younger I took a kind of sabbatical. Traveled the world, dabbled in magic I most likely shouldn't have."

137

"Really? That sounds like heaven." She sighed wistfully.

He laughed. "Remind me later to tell you the stories. You like to travel?"

"I think I would. I've never had the money to do so." Her shoulders slumped.

"But now you do." He reminded her.

She perked up, she'd forgotten the money she'd inherited. How could she have forgotten that? The possibilities opened before her and the fear and confusion from the last few days lightened. "You're right. Now I do."

"Eventually we have to talk about us, you know." He said softly.

She covered her face and groaned. Of course they did. She could try changing the subject again, but before long they'd need to have that conversation. "I've never been a chicken, but I swear, Fallon, the thought of you scares me. It feels so big, like something I can't control."

"You're not alone in that, Brianna. It's huge, this thing between us, I've been running since the day I met you."

Okay, he couldn't say things like that to her. He couldn't be sweet on top of hot, it did nothing to help those riotous feelings tightening her chest. To know he struggled with their 'not yet a relationship' gave her a measure of comfort.

She placed a hand on his arm, going back to his nightmares. "If you want, when you're unable to sleep, you can call me. I'm up most nights."

Surprise showed on his face before his gaze softened in wonder. It made her think she was the only person to offer.

"What if you're asleep?"

"I don't mind." She really didn't mind. It would be nice to have someone to talk to when she couldn't sleep. He probably felt the same way. "Is it okay for me to go back home? I have some more research to do."

"What are you researching?" Kell had fallen asleep, on his chest. He settled his nephew into the bassinette behind him.

"Well, I keep seeing my notes about a book I'm supposed to be looking for, but I don't, there's no reference for it."

He frowned. "We had a whole conversation about that book, you don't remember?"

She winced as her head started pounding. She shook her head. "Do you know what it's in reference to?"

"Does your head ache?" How did he

know? She nodded.

He hummed, the sound introspective.

"What?"

"It seems like every time the *Book of Divinity* is mentioned, your head aches, and you forget that conversation. I wonder if your memory loss is centered on that."

Now that was interesting. "Is it possible?"

He shrugged. "It's magic, it's unpredictable, but anything is possible. I have a few people I can ask. Do you mind seeing one of our healers while you're here?"

She bit her lip and reminded herself that she'd talked to a god the other day. Not believing in a healer, when she'd been on the end of their magic just seemed childish. She assented.

"Come then." He lifted his nephew back out of the bassinette.

She grabbed his bag and the blankets they had down and folded them. She, Brianna the skeptical was going to let someone perform magic on her. The day couldn't get any more bizarre.

Chapter 15

He led her back down the stairs and through the club. The dance floor now had tables and chairs in the middle, and there were people there talking in hushed tones, some eating, some engaged in what looked like meetings. They went through a door and down another flight of stairs. They had to be underground, and she started to get a little prickling of discomfort.

A beautiful ebony-skinned woman walked up to them as they neared the infirmary where she'd awakened and smiled. The widelegged slacks she wore paired with a silk shell top looked luxe, and obviously expensive. Her hair was jet black and pulled back into a tight braid that swayed as she walked.

"Give me my grandbaby." She said as she approached them. The woman grabbed the baby and started cooing.

"Mother, this is Brianna, Brianna, this is my mother, Sharine."

Sharine didn't look old enough to be an older sister, never mind a mother. His mother fixed her piercing whiskey-colored eyes on her and she barely stopped herself from squirming under the curious gaze.

"Well, well. You're my son's mate."

"Mother." He warned.

"Mate?" She looked between the two of them. What did his mother mean by mate?

Sharine raised a carefully kempt eyebrow. "Oh, we're still in the 'keeping secrets' stage."

"Mother," He said again, this time through gritted teeth.

"Well, pay me no mind, then," Sharine said with a smirk as she grabbed the baby bag from Brianna. "She's beautiful, Fallon." She smiled at Brianna and left.

Brianna stood there with her mouth open in shock. Fallon grabbed her arm and pulled her behind him towards the infirmary.

"Pay no attention to my mother, she has no filter and a general lack of empathy. She regularly says things to stir up trouble."

"Does that mean you want me to leave you with your secrets then?" She joked.

"For now." A smile breezed across his lips as he opened the door.

She entered the clinic and walked to the nurses' station. There was a different woman sitting behind the desk from the one who'd examined her. The woman had her hair in a high ponytail, but her hair was in braids that looked like…tree branches? It was like the woman she'd seen coming out of Xavier's office. Her eyes widened. She reminded herself they were not humans, but demigods. The countless times white women had asked to touch her hair flitted across her mind. For once, she understood the compulsion. She wanted to see if the woman's braids were actual tree branches or soft hair. She knew it was rude to ask, she hated when someone asked about her curls, but damn.

The woman smiled as they came up to her desk. "Hi, Commander, Mistress Watson. I'm Lila, what can I help you with?"

"Ooh, mistress," Brianna smirked at Fallon.

He rolled his eyes. "Do you have time to look over Brianna before she leaves to go home?

"Of course." Lila smiled and came from behind the desk. "Follow me."

They trailed her to one of the rooms surrounding the nurses' station and Lila closed the door behind them. The room was small and empty, with just bamboo mats on the floor. She looked around and frowned as there was no place to sit. Fallon sat on the floor and crossed his legs. She followed suit, and Lila kneeled directly in front of Brianna, facing her. Brianna examined the woman as Fallon explained to her about the memory thing. Lila wore a simple squarenecked, sleeveless beige dress. There were tattooed concentric circles on her shoulders disappearing into her dress. Lila hummed as she listened to Fallon, her gray eyes regarding him with a serious expression.

"I'm sorry, but, I have to ask, what manner of Demi are you?" She blurted, unable to contain her curiosity.

Lila smiled. "I'm Kira. We hail from the realm of Edin."

She turned to Fallon, realizing she didn't know what he was. "And you?"

"Cagyn, we're from Chuita."

She desperately wished for her notebook so she could take notes for research later. She hadn't seen any notes on the different types of Demi, but then she'd not been looking. Between all the children she'd seen on the rooftop, and the beautiful women around Fallon on a daily basis, she now wanted to know.

Lila closed her eyes and took a few deep breaths. She opened her eyes held out her hands, "May I?"

"Sure, can you do it and talk?" She wanted to know more about Lila.

"I cannot." Lila's serene smile never left her face.

Fallon spoke up next to Brianna. "The Kira are a healing race. They can manipulate the body's energy to help it heal itself."

143

"At least for the Demi. It doesn't work as well on human physiology." Lila murmured as she held a hand over Brianna's face. "I need your eyes closed and your body relaxed, please."

Brianna complied, but her curiosity was nowhere near assuaged. "Is that why I keep having to see healers?"

"The Demi are half-gods, thus made from the cosmos itself. We carry the Earth's energy within us to a much higher degree than humans, so we, the Kira, are able to manipulate it better."

"That's very interesting." Brianna peeked open one eye. She cursed.

"What's wrong?" Fallon asked.

"I'm mad I forgot my notebook.

Fallon smiled and shook his head.

"Eyes closed, Mistress Watson, so that I may work. Try and relax."

Brianna closed her eyes again and relaxed her body, at least until she felt the air move in front of her face. She reared back and opened her eyes. "What are you doing?"

"Sweeping your body, removing all this anxious energy you have floating around. I can't get to the state of your mind with it clogging up the way."

She narrowed her eyes and turned to Fallon. He'd pulled out his fancy device and was typing away on it. She snapped her fingers at him.

"Is this normal?"

"It is." He didn't look up from his phone.

She sighed. "Fine." She closed her eyes and tried again to relax. She thought it would be hard, but she was soon lulled into a relaxed state.

"The magic blocking your memories is weird." Lila's voice jarred her.

She blinked, waking up from the trance. "In what way?"

"The construction of the spell binding your memories is done in a rudimentary, almost childish way. Like someone who can't quite do magic."

She straightened her back and gave Fallon a smug look. Wait until she told Cassie. "That matches with who I think kidnapped me. My dad said there was hardly any magic in our old Esin."

"Is it something you can fix?" Fallon asked.

She hummed and hovered her hand above Brianna's head. "No. It's like a string that has been knotted and tangled. Only the person who tied the knots understands the way to unfurl it. Ade has assigned someone to you specifically, so I'm going to call her when we're done here. She will likely come to you and try herself."

She growled, frustrated with the lack of progress. "Will my memories come back?"

Lila tilted her head and considered her question. "Perhaps they will come back on their own. My suggestion, after Melene looks at it, is to have a Divine healer look at it."

Fallon closed his phone and put it in his pocket. "I didn't think of that."

Lila shrugged. "It can't hurt. It's their magic, they may have a better chance at it."

He nodded. "Thanks so much."

Brianna wanted to stay and ask Lila more questions about her culture, but Fallon held out his hand to help her up from the floor and shuffled her out of the infirmary before she could even form any questions. He'd guided her back up to the ground floor in less time it had taken them to get down there.

Kegan and Brian, who were leaning against the bar, straightened as they walked into the club area.

"Your guards will get you home, is that okay? I want to go check out what my men have on the person following you this afternoon."

"Sure."

He leaned down and kissed her forehead and she swayed towards him as he backed up. He smiled and cupped her cheek.

"We still need to have that talk." He whispered.

"I will look forward to it." She grabbed his wrist, wanting to touch him.

He brushed a light kiss across her lips. "I'll let you know if I find anything." He nodded to her guards and walked off, leaving her rooted to her spot.

She would play his simple kiss over and over in her mind tonight. It was nowhere near the X-rated fantasies she'd been having of him, and yet the sweet moment would have its own reel in her dreams.

"Brianna."

She turned and saw a smiling Liliana in a short-cropped black wig walking over to her. Her bikini from earlier was replaced with a simple pair of jeans and a vee neck shirt of green that matched her eyes. Her skin also looked different, not so metallic, just a normal toffee color.

"How did it go in the healing ward?" Liliana stopped in front of her.

She tilted her head, hiding her surprise. "How did you know?"

"I know everything that goes on around here."

Her guards chuckled so she assumed it was some kind of inside joke.

"Are you leaving?"

"Yeah, I have some stuff to do." She hedged, maybe Liliana would answer some questions for her. "So, since you know a lot about what goes on around here, you would know what Sharine was talking about when she called me Fallon's mate?"

"That woman lives to start stuff," Liliana mumbled under her breath.

"What does it mean?"

Liliana waved off her guards to give them privacy. "When you were in a coma, you were dying. Your life force was getting weaker every day. Fallon figured that tying you to your mate would bring you back, save you."

"What does it mean that we're mates? Like soul mates?"

Liliana nodded. "Mates are chosen for the Demi, like fate and you're Fallon's."

She mulled it over a moment. "Do I have a say in it?"

Liliana bobbed her head. "Oh, absolutely. But, when you were injured, Fallon started your mate bond to save your life. At the moment, I think he was so scared we would lose you. It was risky, for both of you, but he did it anyway."

She breathed out a shaky breath. "I don't know what to say to that. In what way is it risky?"

"There are consequences for not finishing the bond." Liliana touched her shoulder. "Just get to know him, and talk to him, the two of you can work it out."

If they were mates, it would explain a lot of her feelings for him. She was helpless to stay away from him, and even now, wanted to see him. Could that be a part of the bond he initiated? She looked at Liliana, debating asking her, but it felt too personal. It was confusing, and she'd had enough confusing things in her life at the moment.

"I won't make any promises." She told Liliana.

She needed to think about it some more before she committed to anything.

"I understand." Liliana walked her to the side door, where they'd come in through the garage. Kegan and Brian walked her over to her car and told her they would follow behind.

She and Fallon were mates.

Out of everything she'd learned while at Haven today, that one thing stood out, and scared her to pieces.

Chapter 16

Fallon punched in his code for the surveillance room, his steps impatient. He nodded at the soldiers on duty and walked back to a desk in a private alcove towards the back of the room. He sat down and queued up the Oras he'd requested and went through them.

He frowned.

He watched Brianna park her car and walked into the restaurant, but there was no one behind her. He pushed through the footage, fast-forwarding it until she left the restaurant since he couldn't see inside a human establishment. He made a mental note to see if they could get footage of any kind from inside the restaurant. He pushed until he saw her coming out the front door. She walked along the sidewalk but tensed a few moments later. Her pace picked up until Isaiah walked up to her and shuffled her into one of Haven's SUV.

He rewound the Ora and viewed it from another angle, still not seeing anyone following her. He did it twice and still came up empty. He cursed and tried another tactic. Instead of following Brianna, he watched the front of the restaurant hoping to catch sight of the male she'd gone to lunch with. He fast-forwarded through an hour and only saw humans leaving. Both the Demi and the Divine had a signature that set them apart from humans, no one with such signature left the restaurant.

He pulled out his phone and called Cassie. She answered.

"Hey, what do you know about the guy Brianna went to lunch with?"

"Ugh, he's a toady. His parents were buddy-buddy with the Oliri so he decided Brianna was going to be his wife and there was nothing she or her parents could do about it."

He scowled. "What?"

From what he knew of Esins' arranged marriages were common, but he'd never heard of anyone having to get married against their will.

"Never mind that, what does he look like?"

She sighed. "I don't quite remember. Skinny, skeletal, dark eyes, close-cropped hair, his skin was light but more ashen than a healthy brown."

"Thanks, Cass."

"Listen, Fallon."

He heard the concern and clenched the phone.

"You're going to have to get it together with Brianna."

"What does that mean?"

"No more secrets. You should tell her what you did and handle the fallout. She will want to know, and I can't keep it from her from much longer."

He sighed. "I want her to be safe."

She snorted. "Then you know nothing about Brianna. While you're trying to keep her safe, she's going to be investigating her kidnapping and trying to find that book by herself. Hell, she went out with that jackass today, who knows what other dangerous things she'll do. Trust me on this."

"Ok." He had to concede her point. Brianna herself had told him she went out with the male in order to question him. Who knew what else his mate would do as she tried to investigate.

"I'm serious, Fallon, you're going to miss out if you keep treating her like an idiot."

"Got it, Cass."

He ended the call and went back to the Oras. After one more sweep, he saw neither the guy Brianna had lunch with, nor anyone following her. He pulled out his communicator this time and called Isaiah. The soldier answered with a salute that was more sarcastic than respectful.

"Are you on shift?" He didn't bother with pleasantries.

"With your mate? No Commander."

"Get to the surveillance room now." He closed the case and went back to the Oras.

It took Isaiah only five minutes to get there. He was wearing his uniform which meant Fallon had maybe been a little too gruff. Isaiah saluted him and stood erect next to his desk.

Fallon waved. "You're not in trouble, sit."

Isaiah breathed out and sat. "I was worried."

Fallon grunted and pulled up the Ora showing Isaiah coming up behind Brianna. "What happened today?"

"Brianna was followed to the restaurant from her apartment and then that same person followed her on foot as she left the restaurant."

"Are you sure?"

Isaiah's brows furrowed. "Of course. I saw him myself."

Fallon pointed at the Oras. "There is nothing showing on the Oras."

"Commander, I don't know what to say to that. I saw him."

Instead of contradicting him, he replayed the Oras showing the area behind him and Brianna.

Isaiah cursed as he leaned forward. "What the fuck?"

Fallon pointed to two places. "There is CCTV at these spots. I want the footage."

Isaiah stood, his manner more serious. "Yes, sir."

Fallon dismissed him and went to his brother's office.

X was on the communicator when he entered. He saw the back of the screen, the Benu secretary's hands moving earnestly as they both spoke in the ancient language. Fallon waited patiently until his brother ended the transmission.

"Why do the Benu give you so much trouble?" He asked as his brother closed the file on his desk.

"Because they're snobbish pricks who feel as though service to the Amanda is below them."

He shrugged. Each race was required to serve with the Amanda. It was a part of the treaty between the Demi to keep one race for shouldering the responsibility of keeping them all safe. Xavier didn't exaggerate about the Benu. They were a snobbish race. 'Birds of a feather flock together' was a sentiment they took very seriously. They were amazing soldiers, though. And the only way their king allowed them to serve, was under a Benu liaison.

"What's the problem?"

"I think I've had a millennial full of royal problems."

"Ah, it's time for the prince to serve."

Xavier shook his head. "A mere five years as liaison and yet I have pages of needs." X waved his hand. "I'm done thinking about it, and plan to dump it on Liliana, let the princess handle it."

Fallon snorted.

"What do you need?"

"Isaiah brought Brianna to the Haven today, he says she was followed."

Xavier grunted and waved his hands for him to continue.

"The thing is, there's nothing on the Oras."

His brother sat forward. "Same as with her kidnapping?"

Fallon nodded.

"Twice now phantoms have been associated with her. What do you think of her theory?"

"That her old Esin did it?" He asked, not surprised he and his brother were on the same wavelength.

Xavier nodded. "What do we know about the Douglasville Esin?"

"As far as I know she said they were frauds. Cassandra also confirms this. And get this, I took her down to the infirmary to be checked out. Every time we've mentioned the book to her, it's been like her first time hearing about it."

"She forgot?"

"Again," Fallon confirmed.

"So, it's centered on the book."

"The facts as we have them are: Brianna was kidnapped by phantoms. According to both Rugaba and the Kira, a rudimentary, crappy spell was put over her memories. It lines up with her old Esin being frauds. Brianna's father has told me before that they barely have magic."

"So the magic they could perform was probably bastardized and that's why we're having a hard time unraveling it." Xavier hummed. "The men we sent with her to get her parents didn't see or say anything out of the ordinary?"

He grimaced. "They were the same who died so I can't ask. I'm going to her place to talk to her now."

"Rugaba talked with them." Xavier's face was pinched, his expression grim.

Fallon spared a prayer for his fallen soldiers. "What did they say?"

"They fought with two humans, and someone cast a spell at them from the van." Xavier ran a hand down his face.

"Another dead end."

Xavier nodded. "Find out anything Brianna can tell you about the Douglasville Esin. Henry and Deidre would probably know more, though. She said she left when they were teenagers right?"

Fallon nodded.

"Do you know the details around her leaving?" Xavier pressed his fingers together into a steeple, his eyes closing midway as he thought it through.

"No, nothing."

"Well, I don't like how this is panning out."

"Me either. Once I talk to her, I'll go to her parents, I just wanted to let you know where I'd be." Fallon turned to leave.

Xavier waved him out. "Let me know what you find out."

Chapter 17

Brianna was going through her notes she'd taken from the Roswell Esin's archives not understanding what she'd written. She frowned as her head started hurting. What was she looking for again? Her notes said something about hiding it in plain sight. A sharp pain went through her head and she hissed. A knock sounded, breaking the silence around the apartment and she went to open it.

Fallon stood there impossibly handsome in a pair of navy khakis and ivory cable knit sweater. Her body ached as though she hadn't just seen him a few hours ago. As he turned, a memory broke through the dark fog. She gasped.

He looked around, pushing her behind him as he entered. "What? What is it?"

"I just…I remembered you, here at my door like this talking to someone, I don't know who, I can't picture his face, but you said something about it being trashed downstairs." She squinted, trying to grasp at the memory, but it scurried away.

He put a hand over her shoulder. "Don't Brianna, it will come with time."

"But it happened?"

He nodded and with his hand on her waist, guided her away from the door and locked it behind him. He waved his hands, his lips moving, she felt a swelling in the air, her ears popped and then the room returned to normal.

"What was that?"

"I put a ward over the door."

She frowned, wanting to ask more about it, her curiosity almost demanding it, but she pushed it aside to explore the memory. "Tell me about what I just remembered."

He sighed and wiped a hand over his face. "It was the first time I got a look at you." Longing filled his eyes and he looked away and cleared his throat. "Rugaba visited you. You'd opened the *Book of Divinity*, it called to him and he summoned me to protect you." He shrugged.

"That's it? What's the *Book of Divinity*?" She grit her teeth as her head started pounding anew.

"I mean, that's not completely it, Brianna. Someone had ransacked the bookstore you'd owned for exactly twelve hours and we didn't know who. So, I posted up here, outside your door the first night and sent others in shifts in the ensuing weeks to protect you."

"Where was protection when I was being kidnapped?"

His jaw worked, moving with obvious anger. "They were killed."

She reared back, shock stealing her breath. "Someone…died trying to protect me?" She put a hand over her stomach, its roiling making her nauseous.

His throat went up and down as he swallowed and there was guilt, grief, all in his gaze before he looked away. "I didn't want you to know, but Cassie said, hiding things from you is not an option. Clearly, I've been going about you the wrong way."

She tilted her head and considered him. "What does that mean?"

He shook his head and changed the subject. "I came to talk to you about your old Esin."

"Ha, I knew it as soon as Lila examined me that I was right." She just barely managed to keep from dancing in 'I told you so'.

He growled.

"Wait, never mind, don't change the subject. Who were the guards who died?"

"I can't do twenty questions with you, Brianna. I'm knee-deep in trying to figure out who kidnapped you and trying to find the *Book of Divinity*, are you going to help me with that or not?"

She studied his face, she could push him for what he meant, but, she definitely wanted to figure out who kidnapped her. With his help, she'd get further, so she dropped it.

"What do you want to know?"

"You're convinced this Esin had you kidnapped, I have questions of my own for you and possibly Henry and Deidre."

She eyed him suspiciously. "You really do visit my parents. When they told me, I couldn't figure out why."

He gave her a sad smile. "Though I ran from you, they were my mate's parents, I wanted to be sure they wanted for nothing."

"That's so…different." She couldn't quite figure out a better word for it.

"It's part of our culture to take care of our elders." He said simply.

"They aren't yours, they're mine."

He shrugged. "There is no difference to me."

She stared at him a moment and then looked away. She loved her parents, that he cared for them without telling her, touched her. Liliana told her to talk to him, perhaps there was something to that.

157

"I need any and everything you remember about your old Esin."

She hugged herself and turned. "Do you want some coffee or anything?"

He tilted his head. "I'll take some of that fancy coffee you have."

Every time she turned around, he was showing her how well he knew her. He knew what kind of coffee she had? She thought about what Liliana said, he'd tied them together. Perhaps that was where the lust was coming from. They obviously had known each other but weren't sleeping together. Did that mean she only wanted him now because of the spell he'd put on her? Was it a spell? She didn't know how it worked, and that didn't sit well with her. She wanted to ask him, she was direct enough to normally ask him, but it felt too raw, too scary.

She busied herself at the coffee machine to stall. He grabbed a stool at the island separating the kitchen from the living room.

"Cassie and I left that place when we were fifteen. Cassie was Chosen." She cleared her throat, avoiding his gaze. "We didn't want to stick around for that."

"The Chosen are the maidens chosen to serve the gods, yes?"

She shook her head, something else their Oliri tainted. She took a deep breath. "It wasn't that way in our old Esin. It's not really my story to tell, but Elder Cedric has had multiple wives, not all voluntary, and not all survive the marriage." She shuddered and reached to open the cabinet for the coffee mugs. "Anyway, we hightailed it out of there and stayed with my aunt Sarah. She took us in when we had nowhere to go." She choked up, grief at her aunt's passing as fresh as if it happened yesterday. "You'd be better off talking to my parents."

He nodded. "Henry and Deidre will help." The certainty in his voice struck her. He spoke with an easy familiarity with her parents.

"I'll go with you." She was curious to see how he was with her parents. He spoke of them fondly.

He bobbed his head. "That's fine. We can go after coffee."

"Sure." She set a cup in front of him.

"What else do you remember about the Esin?"

She sighed and sat next to him. "I remember the solstice festivals being these big ceremonies where we would gather outside in these thin robes and sacrifice an animal at some, others…" she squirmed. "Others had events more sexual in nature."

His hands tightened on his mug. "Forced?"

She trailed her hand across the table in aimless circles. "I never paid much attention. I know the Oliri, Elder Cedric was at the top of the food chain, and what he said was law. He was a greedy, cruel man. I promised Cassie we would never live like that again."

He grunted. "Was there any magic performed?"

She sipped from her cup. "Not that I could tell. It all seemed fake to me. We were dirt poor, living in a trailer park and homeschooled."

"What did you learn in lessons?"

"We learned the basics, along with the legends about us being the true divine humans. None of which I believed. Boy, do I feel stupid now going through the Roswell's Esin's records."

He gave her a small smile. "Why didn't your parents live here with your aunt at this Esin? Why did they subject themselves to his cruelty?"

"You'll have to ask them. I don't know the answer to that, and I can't be sure I've ever asked. Up until I read my notes, I didn't even realize my aunt Sarah was a part of an Esin. I never saw it while we lived here, though we only stayed for a few years before we moved out on our own."

He finished his cup. "Come, let's go visit your parents."

159

They headed to the Roswell Esin and over to her parent's house. The drive was quiet, but it was an easy one. There was none of the awkwardness she'd expected. Fallon navigated the streets of Roswell like an expert which told her he'd visited often. He was waved through the front gate of the Esin, driving directly to her parents' home.

Deidre greeted Fallon like a son, kissing his cheek and tucking her arm in his as she guided them into the house. She was shocked at the familiarity. Her father gave him a fist bump and leaned down and kissed her cheek.

"What brings you guys by?" Henry asked as they settled into the sofa and chairs in the living room.

"I wanted some information on your old Esin." Fallon sat back and settled his arm on the back of the sofa. He didn't touch her, but she still felt the warmth from his body.

"Why did you stay there instead of being here with Aunt Sarah?" She leaned forward, to keep from leaning towards Fallon.

Henry sighed and gripped Deidre's shoulder. "It was all we'd known. My sister escaped and found the Esin here, but we didn't know any better. When Sarah left, she gave me a phone number to reach her, but we feared contacting her. As far as we were concerned, all Esins behaved in the same manner, and I didn't want to put her in any danger."

"We were so isolated out there in the woods." Deidre reached up and gripped her husband's hand. "When you and Cassie decided to leave, it was the only time I used the phone number. My fear for you outweighed any fear for ourselves."

Henry rubbed his wife's back, her tears taking Brianna back to her hasty, fearful escape from Douglasville. She and Cassie had been scared they would be caught, but more scared of what would happen to Cassie if they stayed. Her mother had called her sister-inlaw in a desperate act to give them someplace to go. Her aunt Sarah hadn't hesitated. She'd taken two teenagers she hadn't seen in years into her home and her heart. Fallon's touch on her shoulder brought her back to the present. She wiped an errant tear and focused on her parents.

"The more we investigate, the more likely it seems as if they are the ones who kidnapped Brianna."

"For what reason?" Deidre asked. "It doesn't make any sense."

"If they're not asking for money, what else could they want?" Henry demanded.

"Are you aware your daughter was guarding the *Book of Divinity*?"

Henry gaped and Deidre gripped his hand tighter. "What? Where would you have…oh my goodness. Sarah was a guardian. How did I not know that?"

"If you didn't know, is it likely the Oliri of the Douglasville Esin didn't know?"

"I don't see how Elder Cedric could've known." Henry was adamant.

"What's the *Book of Divinity*?" she asked, her head pounding.

Fallon grabbed her arm. "Don't think about that right now."

"Her memory loss stems around the book. Do you think they had enough magic to do that?"

"No way." Henry shook his head. "There was barely enough magic to interact with the Earth, never mind perform a complicated spell such as that. Esin doctrine expressly forbids using those type of spells."

"Well, Elder Cedric didn't follow most Esin edicts, I don't imagine a little thing like rules stopped him." Deidre pointed out.

"Still, the power running through the Douglasville Esin was minuscule, I can't see how." Henry stood and paced.

161

"I want to have one of your healers look over Brianna and see if they can untangle the knots around her memory."

"We don't have a healer at this Roswell Esin. But, I can talk to the Oliri here, Elder Samuel, and see if any other Esins near here have one." Deidre spoke up.

"That would be great." Fallon sat back, no more questions coming from him.

Deidre stood and rubbed her husband's back. "You two should stay for dinner."

They agreed and Brianna went off to help her mother. She had half an eye on the tasks her mother assigned her, and the other half on Fallon talking with her father. She wondered what they talked about.

"He's fine, he and your father talk all the time." Deidre put a pile of potatoes in front of her.

"They seem close." She commented, maintaining an air of nonchalance as she started washing the potatoes.

Deidre stared at her a moment. "He's a good man, well, Demi. How is it going with the two of you?"

She chopped potatoes to give herself a moment to formulate an answer. "It's been confusing not having my memory. I'm not sure where we stand."

"He's your mate." Her mother stated.

"But I don't know what that means, mom."

They worked in companionable silence for a few moments.

She broke it a moment later with a growl. "I mean, what am I supposed to do with him?"

Deidre snorted. "If I have to tell you that, daughter of mine."

Her cheeks burned. "Mom."

"Honey, just take it slowly." She paused in stirring and frowned. "Well, I guess you can't take it too slow, he initiated the bond, so there's not a lot of time."

"See, like that! I don't even know him, how do I have only a few weeks to determine whether or not I want to spend the rest of my life with him?"

Deidre hummed. "It's a valid point, my love. But, I see the way he looks at you, I watched him watch over you while you were out. The care with which he handled you. Fallon loves you. Let him show you, woo you."

Brianna sighed and looked back out into the living room. Her father and Fallon were laughing, and she smiled. It wasn't as though she felt nothing for Fallon. She'd never been as attracted to someone as she was to him.

But.

How much of that was the magic of the mating bond he'd initiated, and how much was natural?

"It will all come out in the wash, Bri. Let it go for tonight and try to get to know your mate." Her mother rubbed her shoulder.

She nodded. That's what she'd do. Let go of the worries for tonight and get to know Fallon. She was a person who knew her own mind. She'd approach it the way she did everything else.

Chapter 18

Fallon stuffed his hands in his pockets as he walked alongside his mate in the darkening evening. Dinner was fun, and afterward, Deidre had suggested the two of them take advantage of the nice weather and walk. Seeing his mate with her parents gave him another side of Brianna. One he found he liked. She joked with them, and relaxed in a way, he'd never seen. Not that he'd spent any amount of time with her in the last year before the accident.

He'd mostly seen her in the library or talking in a conference room with Liliana. Each time she'd been serious, focused. Here, she relaxed and wore an easy smile that transformed her whole aura. She'd fixed his plate at dinner and hovered over him throughout, making sure he had everything he needed. It was…his chest expanded, tightened with soft feelings he wasn't used to. She took care of him, and by the glances her parents shared, it wasn't something she did normally.

He liked it.

He liked her.

He really hadn't expected that. Did he crave her, and lust after her body? Absolutely. But he didn't expect to really enjoy being with her. He didn't feel stifled, he felt cared for. Not that his brothers didn't love him and his mother spoiled him in her way. It was different with his mate, the feeling that someone was looking out for him.

Fallon took her hand and lifted it to his lips for a kiss. She looked up at him and smiled.

Gods, she was beautiful. She'd pulled her wild curls into a bun on top her head and it left her face open, bare. He liked it, a lot.

"Tell me how the investigation is going." She said after a moment.

He rolled his neck. "I'm no closer now to finding out who kidnapped you than I was last week. We have this thing we call the Oras. It's a way we surveil all of Adro. Your kidnappers don't show up on any of the footage."

"What's Adro? What kind of footage is it?"

"Adro is what we call the Earth dimension. I imagine it's similar to the human concept of satellites in how the Oras work."

"Ok, and how accurate are they?" Her eyes narrowed, questions burning in their depths.

"We tie our magic to the Earth's magnetic energy, so it's extremely rare for them to be tampered with."

"So, they don't show up at all, as in a portion of time is missing around my kidnapping?"

He watched her face as she worked through the conundrum. He liked watching her think. It reminded him how intelligent his mate was. Even before she took over her aunt's bookstore, she'd been a researcher for a top magazine.

"No, like, my guards were fighting air before they died."

She stopped walking. "They're ghosts?"

"On the Oras anyway." He didn't believe in ghosts in the way she was thinking, so there had to be another explanation.

"I'm sorry again for your loss, but that is very fascinating." She placed a hand on his arm. "With the Esin not having magic, how do you think they managed to accomplish that?"

"Another thing I'm working on." Frustration struck him anew.

"Let me help. I'm great at research." He

smiled. "Do you do that on purpose?"

"What?" She smiled at him.

He kissed her hand. "Your offer of help? It's the second time you've offered exactly the right thing I needed."

She shrugged. "I didn't realize I was doing that."

"You fixed my plate for me, and from Henry's face, you don't do that for people." He teased, wanting her reaction.

She rolled her eyes. "That, I can't explain. Something about you makes me want to take care of you. It's driving the modern woman in me crazy, let me tell you."

He laughed and pulled her into a hug. She stared up at him, her eyes swirling with heat and joy.

"You don't do that a lot. I'm not sure how I know that, but…" she shrugged.

He smiled and kissed her forehead. "What?"

"Laugh."

He sighed. "I smile all the time, but you make me genuinely happy, Brianna. Which, is new."

"Tell me about your travels." She tugged his hand to start walking again.

"I needed to get out of the house. I'm sure you can understand that."

She nodded.

"I visited a lot of places looking to expand my knowledge of magic."

"Why?"

He frowned and thought about it. He hadn't had a reason, only that he'd wanted to be powerful, more powerful than he'd felt at home in the midst of his parents' turmoil. "It seemed like the thing to do."

She hummed. "That's an evasion, but I'll let it slide."

He chuckled. "Yeah, heavy stuff."

"What's the most interesting thing that happened while you traveled?"

He grimaced, deciding to tell his mate something that he hadn't even told his brothers. "Well, I made a deal with Azra in order to get some precog abilities."

"Azra, Azra..." she mumbled, her brows furrowing as she went through the Rolodex she kept in her head. Her eyes widened after a moment. "Hell god? You made a deal with the devil?"

"Firstly, Azreal is not exactly hell, as humans envision it." He defended.

"I have to hear this. What was the deal?"

"Well, this stays between us." He warned.

She crossed her chest. "I promise." There was a twinkle in her eye that he really liked.

He pulled a coin from his pocket and handed it to her. She turned it over and frowned at the two-headed coin a moment before handing it back. He flipped it around his fingers, toying with it.

"I promised to do favors for him in exchange for the ability to see into the future."

"And how did that work out?"

167

He groaned. "Azra is a trickster, dealing with him is rightfully scary. I got the power of precognition, but it's vague, damn near useless, but Azra has a servant he can call on at any time."

A look of understanding crossed her face. "The two-sided coin."

He nodded.

"Has he ever asked you to do anything scary?"

"Surprisingly no. The tasks have been fairly innocuous. He can't visit this realm, so he has his servants do things he can't physically do."

"How did you make the deal if he wasn't here?"

"Through his oracle."

He'd made his original deal through Azra's oracle, but that same evening, the god had visited him in a dream. It was the start of his many nightmares, that tiny glimpse he'd gotten into Azreal. Fallon shook his head at his youthful arrogance and decided that was enough talk about hell gods.

They turned around and walked back to her parents' house, both of them avoiding talking about their relationship. Still, they'd found plenty of things to talk about. He enjoyed spending time with her.

Deidre met them at the front door. "Nice walk?"

"Yes, mom." Brianna rolled her eyes when Deidre turned her back.

He smiled at her and rubbed a hand down her back.

"Fallon, I made up the guest room for you."

"Thank you, Deidre." He leaned over and kissed her cheek.

They separated to take their showers and get ready for bed. He came out of his room to get a drink of water and ran into his mate coming out of the hallway bathroom. Her hair was wrapped in a scarf, her face clear of makeup and he wanted her more than anything.

His eye twitched, a dull headache forming as a vision overcame him. In it, he saw his mate as she was now, a scarf over her head. But this time she wore a nightgown and smiled from his kitchen. He blinked and it was gone, but the warm feeling lingered. He wanted, no needed that vision to come true. He very much wanted the intimacy of his mate, comfortable and relaxed in his space. He wanted to wake up next to her every morning.

He leaned down, unable to help himself. He gave her time to back away, and when she didn't, he slanted his lips over hers and kissed her. She stood on her tiptoes and kissed him back. His body came alive, his magic flaring, pheromones wafting from his skin. His mate sighed and he deepened the kiss. Her nails dug into his arms and her mewl of need nearly made him forget where he was. He pulled back from the kiss reluctantly.

She gave him a dazed smile. "Well then."

He laughed, enjoying this silly side of her. His gaze racked her body in the tank top and tiny shorts she wore.

"What's the scarf for?" He toyed with the silk bow tied in the front.

"To protect my hair, do Demigods not need to protect their hair?" She joked.

He smiled, and using his magic, changed his hair from the short-cropped style he wore normally, to the long black strands of hair he wore in his Cagyn form. Her eyes widened, and she smiled.

"Holy shit, that's cool."

He chuckled and kissed her lips. "To answer your question, no, we don't need to protect our hair."

"You know I have a ton of questions now." Her eyes were bright as she ran her fingers through his hair.

He skimmed a finger down her cheek. "You're beautiful, you know that, right?"

She ducked her head, the shy act charming for someone as brash as Brianna. He leaned down and kissed her again.

169

"I wish I was sleeping with you." He dropped a small kiss to her nose.

"I bet." She snorted.

He rubbed their cheeks together and closed his eyes, reveling in the feel of her skin against his. "Just sleep, *ife*, I want the comfort of your body against mine." He whispered.

Her scent deepened and she inhaled against his cheek. He knew his pheromones were all over the place, but it wasn't something he could help around her.

"You always smell so amazing," she murmured. She pulled back and cupped his cheek, looking into his eyes. "If you promise to behave, I don't think my parents will mind us sleeping in the same room."

His beast bucked, his magic flaring. She traced the whorls on his arm as his human skin wavered. He tamped down on his power. "I promise."

It wouldn't be an easy promise to keep, but he would do anything to sleep in the comfort of his mate. The nights he'd lain awake worried about her didn't count. Even the night he'd held her skin to skin wouldn't compare to having her alive and well in his arms. She grabbed his hand and pulled him along the hall to the small guest bedroom. It was a queen-sized bed, so it would be a tight fit, which suited him well. They settled into bed, and he pulled her back into his chest, spooning her body.

She sighed and snuggled closer. "This feels amazing." She kissed his hand and before long her breathing deepened.

He stayed up a while longer, reveling in the feel of Brianna in his arms. He'd been stupid to deny them this. Tahir was right in his admonishment of him. He'd wasted time, and he would no longer do that. He kissed her neck and settled down to sleep.

Chapter 19

A pile of work greeted Fallon as he sat at his desk the next morning. He had to smile though, because this morning, he was actually equipped to tackle it. He'd slept better than he had in years, and he knew lying next to Brianna was the reason. Last night Henry had suggested taking Brianna out on dates to further their relationship. Not that he knew anything about dating a human, but for his mate, he would try. He'd left her at the Esin this morning because she wanted to use their library. She'd probably grumble at a phone call distracting her, but even though he'd just left her, he wanted to hear her voice.

She answered, her voice distracted. "What?"

He laughed. "What are you doing?"

"Knee-deep in research about memory spells." She sighed.

"Anything?"

"Nothing useful, actually. Seems dad was right, it's considered taboo to mess with someone's memory. There are some pretty damning things about you guys doing so, though." She teased.

He grunted. They had spells to erase memories and he used them regularly to keep the Havens hidden and safe. He didn't think his mate would want to hear that.

"You just left here a second ago, why are you calling?" she asked changing the subject.

"I wanted to ask you out."

She paused, it was quiet for a moment, only her breathing over the line. "Like on a date?"

"Do you have an objection to that? I'd like to get to know you." He held his breath as he waited on her answer.

"Well, no, I, yes, yes, I'd love that." She stuttered.

"Perfect. I'm on duty tonight at the club, but can we do tomorrow?"

"Sure." She sounded happy and that made him happy.

"What's your favorite restaurant?"

"I'm not picky. I like food."

He laughed again. "Ok, I'll see you tomorrow night, at eight o'clock?"

"Yes." She ended the call and he smiled.

He made a mental note to ask Liliana about places to take Brianna on a date. His father walked into his office without knocking as he started organizing his work.

"Father." He sat back in his chair and watched Ranolph with a leery gaze.

"What's going on with your mate and her old Esin?"

He paused a beat before answering. His father didn't do much without a motive. He wondered what his angle was. "We haven't figured out who exactly kidnapped her. We suspect her old Esin for now, but there is no concrete proof. We won't make any moves without absolute certainty."

"Tensions between the Divine and Demi are always precarious, it would need to be irrefutable proof. Anything I can do to help?"

He remembered the conversation with the Kira the other day in the infirmary. "Coincidentally, do you know any Esins that have healers? The local Esin doesn't and they were going to look around. If you know where to look, it could go faster."

Ranolph sat and crossed his leg over his knee. "They don't practice their magic as they should, the years have seen them breed their power away."

Fallon sighed inwardly, not wanting to hear the 'breed with your own kind' spiel his father was likely to launch into. That probably explained why he'd come down to Fallon's office. Ranolph likely wanted to probe his mating to a human. For a moment fear seized him. His father was still head of their household. Since Fallon had not completed the mating, technically Ranolph still had time to petition his mating with the Eminzu.

The Eminzu were a council of their ancestors, the counterpart of what they did in the Amanda. The family council picked their mates, and their main motivation was making sure the Demi stayed strong. Mating to humans was rare, and he imagined his father would use that fact to petition his mate. In his case, though, his mate was both a Divine and a Kokoro soul. She would add power to their family line, and he was hoping that distinction would keep his father off his back.

"I had some trepidation when I found out your mate was human."

Maybe it wouldn't. "She's Divine, father."

Ranolph waved away his words. "I'm just saying, our lineage."

"Father." He interrupted, not wanting to hear it. "The Eminzu have marked us as mates, clearly the fates disagree with you."

Ranolph grunted and looked around Fallon's office.

"Is that why you came down here, to see if I wanted you to petition my mating?"

173

"Well, you're not making plans for the *di êjê*, nor have you completed the bond. I wondered."

Fallon shook his head. "It's complicated with Brianna, and I have my own issues. I'll handle it on my own time." Ranolph sighed but dropped it. "California, maybe."

He frowned, not knowing what his father meant.

"A Divine healer, there is one in California I think, one for sure in Arizona though. They didn't breed with Neanderthals, but with the first peoples. They have more magic and power in the Esins there."

"Thank you." He pulled out his communicator and sent a message out to Ade. The Kira would take the necessary steps to get a healer here. He looked over to his father once he'd sent the message.

"Is there anything else you wanted?"

"No, just checking in."

There was a knock on the door and Leo peeked his head in. He saw their father and his jaw clenched.

Ranolph stood. "How is Kell?"

Leo didn't answer, instead, staring at his father. Fallon hurt for his brother and stood to break the awkward silence.

Ranolph held up his hand towards Fallon. "He doesn't need you to rescue him, Fallon."

Leo growled. "Far be it for my brother to show concern for me. What should he do instead *baba*, perhaps use my pain for some ambition he harbors."

Fallon threw his head back and stared at the ceiling. It was in his nature to go in and smooth ruffled feathers. Seeing Leo hurt made him anxious. Yet, he didn't want to be in the middle of this. It was one of the reasons he'd run so far for so long. He was tired of mediating family fights.

"Leonalph, you cannot still be angry about a centuries-old misunderstanding."

"Seriously, *baba*," Fallon said disgusted that his father would reduce his brother's concern to a misunderstanding. Their father had essentially pimped out their mother for power and Leo had been the result. His brother was rightfully upset. Far be it for Ranolph to apologize or take accountability for it.

"Stay out of this, Fallon. You've coddled him his whole life, surely he can stand on his own for a few minutes."

"I see we're no longer pretending remorse." Leo spit out.

Fallon sighed and massaged his temples, already a stress headache forming.

"My only concern is the security of this family. All of you are where you are today because I maneuvered with the best of them. I'm sorry if in this one instance it hurt your feelings."

"You let me think my mother was a whore, and you let me treat her like shit my whole life." Leo slammed his hand against the door jamb.

"I can't make you do anything. You need to take accountability for the way you treated Sharine."

Leo raised his chin. "I have, and I have made amends with my mother."

"Then why are we still talking about this. It's over." Ranolph said it in a tone that lent finality to the conversation.

Fallon crossed his arms, obviously, their father knew little about his sons. Leo was every bit his mother's son, in that he didn't let shit go until he was good and ready.

175

"When will you allow me to see my grandson?" Their father demanded.

"He has to report to Legba on his eighth birthday for his formal acceptance of the crown prince title. Perhaps you will see him when his other grandfather does."

Ranolph straightened, anger making his magic waver. "You would be so spiteful?"

"I'm not letting you manipulate my family any longer. You can take us off your chessboard." Leo's face was set in stone.

"Leo." Ranolph closed his hands into a fist.

"Fallon, I'll come back when you're not busy." His brother said and shut the door, thankfully not slamming it.

Their father swung around to him. "You have to talk to him. You're the only one he listens to."

"Perhaps because I raised him while his parents took their anger out on each other." He commented. He wouldn't be putting himself in the middle of their fight, and nothing his father could say would change that.

Ranolph made a disgusted sound. "Not you too? You have a problem with the way I raised my family?"

Fallon snorted. "Raised your family? That's rich, *baba*. I have things to do if there's nothing else?" He held his hand out towards the door.

Ranolph stormed out and Fallon flinched as he slammed the door. He sat back down and let out a breath. He hated the tension in his family and hated being put in the middle even worse. He should've left, but unfortunately what his father said was true. He'd coddled Leo, had since he'd first held him in his arms. Well, there had been resentment, but eventually, he couldn't resist his brother's charm.

Age didn't stop the instinct, no matter how many centuries had passed. He scrubbed his face with his hands, breathing to calm his body. A beep from his phone had him peeking through his fingers. It was a message from Brianna.

Not sure if I told you, but I enjoyed cuddling with you.

He smiled. A simple text message from his mate had the tension leaving his shoulders.

I did as well, and I look forward to our date.

Ditto. Was her answer.

He pocketed his phone and got back to work.

Brianna put her phone back on the table and went back to the tome she was reading. She'd been in the library since he'd left her this morning. All the talk about the Douglasville Esin had brought up questions and she was hoping to get the answers from the many books currently surrounding her. The library was well organized, books sectioned off according to its content. Most of the books in there were journals and personal accounts of the Divine. But there was a section dedicated solely to spells, their history, and results. It was where she was currently posted, with books spread around her on the table. She was doing as she'd told Fallon, and searching through any mention of memory spells. The last time she'd been there, she'd been overwhelmed with the sheer amount of books. Today, she had a purpose, and that made her focused.

She smiled and looked back at her phone. She had enjoyed sleeping with him. She'd slept better than she had in a while and attributed it to being enfolded in his arms. He was different than what she'd expected. At every turn, she saw a different side of both he and the Demi. She was eager to see where their relationship went, and that surprised her. She expected her cynicism to keep her from putting too much stock in their relationship, but she would take her mother's advice and take it a day at a time.

She went back to the book she was reading and flipped to another page. It made no sense to keep reading through the reasons why the Divine didn't do memory spells. That would be of no help to her. Her eyes widened when she saw the text on the next page. It was about curses affecting personal magic use. Intrigued, she kept reading. Fallon told her and Cassie that people in Haven were staring because they could see their magic. She was supposed to ask him about it and forgot. Did she have magic?

If she could suspend belief about everything else, surely, it was worth a try. She read through the instructions for testing personal magic. She followed it to the letter and held her hand out. According to the page, there would be a light hovering…

Oh God! It worked.

She moved her hand around and watched as a green light danced along the skin on the back of her hand. She had magic, real magic. Her heart thudded and she extinguished the light. The page talked about Divine being blessed with magic, not needing the use of spells. She flipped the page and stared, agog. It was a list of simple magic she should be able to perform if her magic had not been tampered with. After an hour of practicing and reading, she was able to shift the books around on her table.

Ecstatic, she did a small fist pump.

Then she grimaced.

She owed a few people some apologies. Namely her best friend. She cringed to think about how adamant she'd been just days ago about magic not existing.

She looked up as someone cleared their throat near the table. It was a pretty woman, wearing a simple pair of slacks and a white shirt. Her hair was up into a no-nonsense bun, her brown skin unadorned by makeup. Brianna gave her a polite smile.

"Brianna, hi, I haven't seen you in months. How's it going?"

She blinked and closed the book she was reading, not sure if she should've been playing with magic in the library. "You know me?"

The woman frowned and then looked down at the books she'd pulled. "Why are you looking at curses? My goodness, did something happen?"

She shrugged, unsure how much she was allowed to tell the woman. "I was in an accident, lost some memories surrounding it."

The woman made a sympathetic sound. "I'm Emilia, we've talked many times when you've come to the library." She put her hands on her hips and looked at the table again. She grabbed the book Brianna was looking through. "Come with me."

She walked Brianna to a small conference room tucked into the back of the library. There was a table with books neatly stacked, notepads and pencils in a neat little row like she kept on her desk at home. Emilia went to a small cabinet and pulled out a pair of gloves and passed them to her.

"This is where you spent the majority of your time. I left the books you normally referenced on the table." Emilia waved over to the table.

"I wonder why the last librarian didn't show me this room." Her eyes scrutinized the small room anxious for something to trigger a memory.

"Well, did you tell her you'd lost your memory?"

That was a good point. She had not. She donned the gloves. "What was I researching?"

Emilia smiled. "Oh, well, it varied. Some days it was spells."

Though she didn't remember it, it was true to her character. She'd spent years researching and fact-checking stories for the magazine where she worked. With everything Xavier and Fallon had told her about her past year, her default coping mechanism would've been research. She'd want to know everything she could about her new circumstances. So, it made sense she'd research a little bit of everything.

179

"Like what kind of spells?" She sat at the table and pulled some of the books over.

Emilia brought her over the book of curses she'd been reading in the other room. "You were looking at voids, how to make them, how to close them. Hiding places." Emilia smiled.

"What? Why would I want to know that?"

Emilia shook her head. "Well, honestly, Brianna, I couldn't make rhyme or reason why you did a lot of things. You're a secretive person, even after a year here, you didn't really trust anyone."

She frowned, she wanted to deny that, but she wasn't one to lie outright. Instead, she just shrugged.

Emilia stood over her. "I understand where it stemmed. From what you told me, your first Esin was horrible, it would be hard for you to trust."

The woman was so sweet that Brianna almost felt guilty for her lack of trust.

Almost.

"So, anyway. You also researched general history. You were interested in the Great War, you researched what we had on the Demi so you could compare it to what they had. Between the two of us, we even were able to update some of our information on the Demi."

She was stunned. "So we were working together?"

"On that one thing. Secretive, as I said." Emilia's smile was infectious.

She grinned. "I was a pain in the ass is what you're saying."

Emilia laughed. "Yes, and no. We don't get many visitors, so every time you came by was a treat for us."

"Us, there are more than the two of you I've met so far?"

She nodded. "Of course. You were known to us all, so if you come back and I'm not here, anyone will be able to help you."

"Anything else I researched?" She was anxious to peer through the notebooks on the desk.

"Well, I made you a section with the books you looked at most often. I'll add this one with the curses to it, so you have it next time you come."

"Thank you so much," she said heartfelt. Emilia probably had more important things to do than help her.

"No problem. I'm right at the front if you need anything."

"Can you refresh my memory about any rules you have?"

"Oh, of course. Gloves at all times, nothing leaves the library, you may take notes, but I'll have to read them before you leave to make sure nothing harmful leaves the library."

"By harmful you mean?"

"Any spell that can do harm to humans specifically, or that would disrupt the Earth in any way."

She looked at the pile of notebooks presently on the table. "These contain harmful material?"

"Not necessarily. Sometimes if you didn't have time to go through the song and dance of checking, you'd just leave your notebook."

She narrowed her eyes. That sounded a little unlike her, but she let it go. "I can handle that." She rubbed her hands together, anxious to get started.

She opened the book on curses again. Air stirred in front of her and she looked up. Her eyes widened and she slammed the book back shut as the god, Rugaba, popped into the library in front of them.

"My lord." Emilia curtseyed next to her. "How can I be of service?"

"I need for nothing, librarian, you may carry on with your duties." He didn't even spare her a glance.

Emilia blushed and went back to her desk.

"My lord?" She asked, narrowing her eyes.

"I am a god, Brianna, little g, but all the same." He turned over one of the books she had on the table. "What are you researching now?"

She paused at the question. It intimated that he too had knowledge of her movements and habits. She couldn't get over the fact that she was on somewhat intimate terms with a god. Her head spun.

"Magic."

"To what purpose?"

"I was hoping maybe to find a spell to get my memory back."

He sat back, an impressed look on his face. "And what have you found?"

"Nothing useful."

"Have you given thought to where you hid the book?"

She grimaced as a sharp pain struck. "What book?"

He hummed. "That's problematic, Brianna." He drummed his fingers on the table and stared at her. She squirmed and lowered her eyes.

"May I?" He asked, holding his hand out.

She nodded, unsure what he wanted to do. He placed his hand against her forehead, the same as before. She felt the warming sensation as he held his hand there with his eyes closed. A moment later he opened them, and they were all black with pinpricks of light, like stars where his pupils should've been. He removed his hand and sat back, his eyes soon changing back to a dark brown.

"It's a spell as I suspected. It's confusing to me why I am unable to fully dismantle it. Have any of your memories returned since I last saw you."

She shrugged. "I don't think so."

He nodded and left. She blinked and sat for a moment confused, then went back to the book she was reading. There was no use remarking on the strangeness of her life anymore. Gods popping in and out, magic spells and Esins. She'd fallen down the proverbial rabbit hole, and she couldn't work up any concern over it. She lifted her head and frowned. That in and of itself should be concerning. But, she raised her hand and manifested the green light again.

She could do magic.

She smiled. As far as she was concerned, that was cool as hell and made up for a lot of the other weirdness.

Chapter 20

Brianna adjusted the towel on her chest to keep it from slipping as she braided her wet hair down her back. The curls were springing around the other side of her face as she tied off the finished braid on one side. She was standing over her mirrored dresser reading through the notes she'd taken in the library. She had spent a good portion of her day teaching herself to use her magic. After a few hours of that, she'd turned to the notebooks she'd left on the table and some of her older notations had drawn her attention.

Once she'd started reading about the Demi and their different dimensions she'd been hooked. There were some artist renderings of places that looked amazing. She should ask Fallon if he could take her to any of those places. She looked over at her phone on the nightstand. Tying off her second braid she walked over and sat on the edge of the bed. She debated a moment but decided to see if he was awake.

Are you up?

She held her breath, not sure if she wanted him to answer the phone or not. It beeped moments later.

I am. Another nightmare?

No, I haven't even attempted to sleep yet.

Her phone buzzed with an incoming call a moment later. She smiled as a silly picture of him flashed across her screen. When did he have time to program it into her phone? She answered.

"What are you doing up so late?" His deep voice soothed her and fired her up at the same time.

"Reading my notes from the library." He

hummed. "Come to the window."

Her heart tripped a little and she rushed to the big windows in the living room. He stood on the street below and waved.

"What are you doing here?"

He chuckled. "I found myself wandering your street."

She narrowed her eyes. And he laughed.

"I can almost feel your suspicion from down here. Come take a walk with me."

"Okay." It popped out of her mouth before she had a chance to overthink.

She rushed around looking for something to wear and then decided to just be herself. She put on a pair of tight jeans and a sweatshirt with slides.

She grabbed her keys with her mace on it and rushed out the door. He was there, as she exited the building, looking amazingly handsome, but relaxed. Also in jeans and a sweatshirt. It struck her as odd because the last few times she'd seen him, he'd been dressed and put together. He held out his hand and she happily grabbed it.

His touch sent her body reeling and she floated next to him as they walked down her street in silence. Streetlights were on, up and down the street, so it wasn't completely dark, but still, she stepped a little closer to him.

"I thought you had to work tonight."

He chuckled "I snuck out to see you."

She warmed. "You're gonna get in trouble."

"My brother is the boss, and I trust my staff, I'll be fine. Any luck with your notes?"

She shrugged. "The librarian, Emilia, was really helpful. She'd kept the books I used the most in my own little section."

"Did anything jog your memory?"

"Unfortunately no, I researched a lot of history, some spell work, but nothing that brought back memories. There is no mention at all about the Oras that you were talking about, so I think I'll have to tackle that problem in the Haven library."

185

"There aren't many Demi outside of the Amanda who know about the Oras, and the Divine don't know at all so that doesn't surprise me."

That he'd told her showed her he trusted her. She held the pleasure of that to her chest. "I had another visit from Rugaba."

"And yet there are no scorch marks." He remarked.

"Is he mean?"

Fallon snorted. "Not mean, but human empathy is not something from which the gods suffer."

She shrugged. She was trying to work around to ask him some of the questions she had on mating. There was not anything in her notes about it which sort of led her to believe he didn't tell her they were mates.

"I see your mind spinning. Care to share?"

"I spent a better part of the day researching the Demi. I was drawn in."

"Anything interesting?" His grip on her hand tightened.

"Nothing on the subject I was looking for."

"Which is?" He prodded.

"Mating." She said quietly.

He hummed and pulled her hand up for a kiss. She was starting to recognize it as his way of stalling. "What questions did you have about it?"

"Did we do this before?" She was not opposed to stalling herself.

He looked ahead and she wondered if he wouldn't answer. He sighed and rubbed his thumb along her knuckles. "I made a lot of stupid decisions in my life, Brianna, and not doing this, this getting to know you, with you. That's one which weighs heavily on me."

"What changed?"

She didn't understand much about mating, but from what Liliana told her, Fallon had bound them together in order to save her life. She was still deciding how she felt about it. On the one hand, she valued her life and her second chance at it. But on the other hand, were these feelings they had because he'd bound them together, even partially?

"Liliana let slip what you did to save me."

"Let slip, huh?" He murmured but didn't elaborate.

"What do you have to say to that?"

He shrugged. "I couldn't sit back and allow you to die, Brianna."

She frowned, not sure his answer was all that flattering. "So I'm not your mate, and you bonded us only to save me?"

"You are my mate."

"No equivocations on that?"

"I kept stalling, not quite ready to commit. I had decided to stop denying myself our mating and was coming to talk to you. That's how we found out relatively quickly you were missing. Not that it did any bit of good." His grip tightened on her hands.

Her heart dropped. "So you only bonded us to save me?" She worked to keep the impatience out of her voice.

"I'm getting to that." He said, absently. "When I realized someone had taken you from me. I don't think despondent is even a strong enough word. I had known you were my mate the moment I laid eyes on you and knowing I'd let you slip away because I wasn't ready. It was..." He shuddered.

Sympathy for him choked her up. But also a little resentment. Had he claimed her when her memories were intact, what could they have had? She didn't know since she didn't know how she'd felt about him.

"So these feelings I have for you are because you bonded us together?"

187

He stopped their progress and turned her to face him. His face was hard, his eyes desperate. "We are fated to be together, no amount of magic would change your feelings for me if there were none. You are mine."

Her heart thudded, as he stepped closer, crowding her space. The heat from his body wrapped around her as he tipped up her chin. His eyes were copper, his voice deeper as he demanded, "tell me you understand that?"

She nodded and cleared her throat. "Liliana tells me that you took great risk binding us together."

He kissed her forehead and brought her into his chest for a hug, but said nothing.

"What happens if we're not bonded before next month?" Her words were muffled into his chest.

She inhaled his scent and closed her eyes as it seemed to warm her from the inside. His mirthless chuckle vibrated against her cheek.

He stepped back and she shivered as the cold of the night surrounded her again. He drew her against his side.

"Celibacy for me, I'm not sure what the result would be for a human, but our women become sterile, unable to have any children."

Her heart lurched. She didn't want kids yet, but someday she hoped to. She mourned a little bit at the thought of not having them. "Just celibacy? That hardly seems fair."

"Right, meaning I wouldn't be able to pleasure anyone or myself. A completely useless tool."

She sucked in a breath. That seemed cruel.

"I'm told the urges are still there. I can't imagine…Well." He stopped talking, and she knew it was to keep from pressuring her.

They walked along in silence until they circled back to her apartment. She stood in front of him studying his face in the moonlight.

"Thank you for this. For allowing me to know you."

He nodded and leaned down. She had time to back away, to stave off his kiss, but she didn't want to. Instead, she stood on her toes and met him halfway. His kisses had a way of completely making her forget herself. She moaned, wanting him more than anything she could ever remember wanting. Was his magic the only reason?

He pulled from their kiss. "I'm looking forward to our date tomorrow night." His deep voice rumbled and she wanted to roll around in the sound. He was potent.

"Me too." She said softly. She stood on her toes and kissed him again. She put her hands under his sweatshirt, loving the feel of his warm skin.

"Don't start nothing, *ife*." He growled and nibbled her bottom lip.

"I think I should sample the milk before I have to buy the cow." She kissed the corner of his lip.

He threw his head back and laughed, hugging her tighter to him. "You're funny, do you know that?"

"I promise you're the only person who finds me funny." She smiled as the joy on his face made her happy.

"Good night, Brianna." He whispered, dropping a final kiss to her forehead.

She waved and walked back up to her apartment. She waved again from the living room window. Fallon waved back and she watched him walk away into the darkness. He stopped and talked to her guards, and she watched until he disappeared from her view. He said they were fated, that their bond didn't give her feelings not already there. She believed him, trusted him even, which was rare for her. That told her more than his words did.

Chapter 21

Fallon stood at Brianna's door and willed his body under control. He'd barely been able to get through any work thinking about her. He'd been given a pep talk by Liliana, but he was still nervous. The Demi didn't date. They had a lot of sex, but dating was superfluous since they knew when they met their mates. Liliana told him to be himself, which, was generic, but he gave his sister in law props for trying. He took a deep breath and knocked on the door.

She answered and his heart rate tripled. She looked beautiful. She wore a wine-colored dress that hugged every curve all the way down to her ankles. The fabric looked soft and his fingers itched to touch it, and her. She wore her hair up in a bun, with tendrils curling around her face. Her dark eyes looked sooty, bigger with the makeup she wore. She smiled at him and he couldn't resist. He leaned down and snagged a kiss. She moaned and tilted her head. She wore heels that brought her up to right under his chin, making it easier to deepen their kiss.

She pulled back. "I'm glad to see you, too."

He smiled. She turned to lock the door and he damn near swallowed his tongue. Her ass looked amazing in the dress. How he was supposed to get through dinner? She handed him her coat and he helped her into it. They walked downstairs and through the café. The quiet between them was loaded. The bookstore was nearly empty, with it closing in another thirty minutes. Brianna waved at the two ladies working as they neared the door. He guided her with a hand on the small of her back, unwilling to relinquish his touch. He wanted her out of that dress, and flat on her back, no bent over on the edge of the bed, or, goddess, on the kitchen counter, legs splayed for him. He groaned, unable to get the images out of his head. A male stepped in front of them and he growled, the sound carrying in the empty cafe.

"Darren." Brianna sounded surprised. "What are you doing here?"

He looked at Fallon and looked away nervously. This was Darren, the guy he couldn't see on the Oras. He was as Cassie described, gaunt, his skin ashen. His eyes were sunken and he looked to be sweating in his coat. Fallon frowned and brought Brianna closer.

"I didn't realize you were busy."

"Well, you didn't call ahead, so…" Brianna tilted her head and raised a brow. "I have to go, have a great night."

She grabbed Fallon's hand and led him from the bookstore. They walked to his car parked on the street. He escorted her to the passenger side of the car and then came back and got in.

"Nice car." She wiggled in the seat.

"So that was Darren." He looked back at the bookstore.

She rolled her eyes. "Yes, I don't know what he was thinking. Just ignore him."

He thought about it but decided he wouldn't be ignoring him. Something about him raised his hackles. "No can do, *ife*. Seeing him in person makes me want more information on him."

"I don't want to talk about him on our date though." She touched his shoulder to bring his attention back to her.

He stared at her, falling into her gaze. "Very well then." He started the car.

"Where are you taking me?"

"This place Liliana told me about."

She didn't say anything to that and turned and watched out the window. He thought back on Darren. He would investigate him a little harder when he got back to Haven. There were a lot of factors that made him suspicious, jealousy being one he easily admitted to. He wanted to know who the male hanging around his mate was.

He took them to a quiet Spanish restaurant Lilliana recommended and from the smells emanating, the food would be good. He gave them his name at the front and they were shown to their table. It was a quiet booth near the back and he was happy. It gave him a full view of the room. Brianna sat next to him in the booth. A waitress came and dropped glasses of water off and a bowl of tortilla chips.

"How was your day?" Brianna turned to face him.

"I spent it anxious to get to you." He admitted.

Her eyes softened and her lips parted on a sigh. "That was…wow."

"How about you?"

"I spent it researching of course, oh and playing with magic."

He knew it wouldn't have taken her long to start. "How did it go?"

Her eyes brightened. "Well, I didn't have to use any spells or anything. Some of the texts walked me through using the innate magic I have."

She took a sip of the water at the table. "I can't even believe I'm talking about stuff like this."

He smiled and grabbed a chip from the bowl. "I knew it wouldn't take you long."

She inclined her head. "It's all pretty exciting."

The waitress came back and took their order. When she left, he leaned and kissed his mate.

"I like kissing you." He told her, tracing her bottom lip with his thumb.

"You should definitely do it often." She said smiling. "So, I have questions."

He leaned back and put his arm around the back of the booth. "You always have questions. Fire away."

She smirked. "Well, the other day, right before I texted you, I could feel you. You were anxious, is that normal?"

He thought about it. "This early in the bonding process. Not necessarily, but stronger emotions do travel across the bond."

"Why were you so anxious?"

He knew she would ask, but he cringed all the same. He hated talking about his family. "My father and Leo are fighting and I always seem to get thrust into the middle of it."

She rubbed his thigh. "I'm sorry. I've never had siblings, so I don't quite know how that feels."

He leaned down and inhaled in the skin of her shoulder, exposed from a cutout in her dress. "Your text message was timely, so you helped even if you didn't know."

She gripped his chin and brought him close for a kiss. "I like knowing that."

His body heated and he put an iron grip on his magic. His mate made him forget where he was. Their dinner came quickly enough. They didn't talk much, but the tension between them rose as time passed. He asked for the check before they were done eating. He wanted nothing stopping him from leaving.

Brianna was anxious to leave herself. Fallon had been the perfect gentleman throughout dinner and she was over it. She grabbed his hand as they got up to leave. He pulled her hand up and kissed her knuckles. He did that a lot, and she loved it. He drove them back to her place. Tension coated the car. She squirmed in her seat, her body needy, restless. He walked her to her front door and she unlocked it.

She paused with her hand on the knob and turned back to him. "Do you want to come in for coffee?"

He leaned down and sipped at her lips. "Not for coffee, no."

Her knees went weak. "I didn't actually plan on making coffee." She whispered.

He growled, and the sound drew her nipples tight. She loved when he made that sound. He had so many different growls depending on how he felt, but this particular growl only came out when he was turned on. She opened the door and let them in. Cassie had left yesterday, so she was in the apartment alone.

He paused her at the front entrance. "Stay here a moment." He whispered, nibbling a trail from her ear down to the crook of her neck.

He turned and put a spell at the door and then walked through her apartment to make sure it was empty. When he came back she was holding her heels in her hand.

"That was time we could've spent having sex, you know."

He smiled and stalked towards her. Her stomach did a slow flip, and her clit started throbbing. "Trust me when I tell you, sex between us will always take longer than that."

He grabbed her around the waist and lifted her until their mouths were at the same height. He then kissed her. It was unlike any of his other kisses. It was the kiss of a man who knew he wouldn't have to stop. A confident plundering of her mouth. She wrapped her legs around his waist, impatient to feel him. Her head swam as his tongue danced with hers. She dropped the shoes onto the floor and linked her hands behind his neck.

He walked them back into her room. She would ask him later how he found her room with only a sliver of light coming from beneath the curtains covering her windows. She sighed as he kissed down her neck.

"I want you out of this dress, Brianna." He whispered.

She untangled her legs from around his back and put them on the floor. She had her dress up and over her head in one motion, her body aching with need. She stood in front of him in only a black lace thong. His eyes lit, the whorls on his arms appearing, filling her room with copper light.

"I have no control near you." His voice rumbled, the deep timbre sending shivers down her spine.

The smell of his cologne filled the room and made her head spin with lust. She stepped back into his arms. Her hands moved, clutching his shirt.

"Your turn." She ripped the buttons on his shirt open.

His chest was like marble. She ran her palms down, loving how velvet his skin felt. She was unhooking his belt when all his clothes disappeared. Her eyes widened and she stepped back.

"How did you do that?"

"Magic, *ife*." He murmured, closing the distance between them.

Her heart thundered as his hungry gaze swept her body. Her knees hit the bottom of her bed. She sat down and he towered over her.

"I want you to spread for me. Can you do that?"

She nodded, her mouth dry. She scrambled on top of the bed and spread her legs. He growled and like a dark panther, crawled over her body. Her breath came out in hard pants as he lowered his head, kissing a trail up her thighs.

"Do you have any idea how long I've wanted to taste you?"

She shook her head, feeling the wetness flow from her center. He lifted his head and gave her a smile that made her feel vulnerable and needy all at the same time. He lowered his head and the first swipe of his tongue had her throwing her head back. He devoured her, alternating between licking and nipping at her. When his lips wrapped around her clit, her back left the bed and her hands held his head in place. The orgasm surprised her with its intensity.

Before she came down from the high, he was wrapping in his cock in a condom, lifting her hips, and plunging into her. It took him a couple of strokes to fight through her clenching channel, but when he did… she sighed into his mouth. He kissed her, his tongue mimicking his every stroke. He filled her, his strokes stoking the heat between them. Magic danced in the air, his and hers, she actually felt it. His skin glowed, the light encompassing her. He didn't hurry, his movements were unrushed as he took over her mind and body.

"Come for me, *ife*," he whispered.

She raked her nails over his back and he growled, his strokes speeding up. She complied, unable to stop the orgasm building in her core. Her body seemed to explode, light flashed behind her closed lids. He shouted a moment later, and she felt the warmth of his release. He scooped her up and turned, pulling her on top of him. She couldn't have kept her eyes open if she wanted to. Between his heated body, and her sated one, she managed to kiss him and mumbled for him to stay before she fell asleep.

Chapter 22

Fallon rolled over and cursed as his communicator beeped for the third time. He was pretty much going to slap around whoever it was calling him over and over. He ran his hand over the empty side of the bed, remembering his mate rising a couple of hours or so ago. He peeked open an eye and cursed anew when Ade's image hovered over his communicator. He grabbed it.

"Yeah."

"Your Divine healer is here." Ade's voice was blank, his face uncomfortable.

"What's happened?"

The Kira cut his eyes to the left. "How soon can you come in?" He asked instead of answering.

Fallon sighed. "Let me gather my mate, give us an hour."

"Fine." Ade cut off the call, his image disappearing and leaving the room dark again.

He laid flat on his back for a moment, knowing he'd have to go in and soothe ruffled feathers. The Kira was clearly irritated, which meant, either, he and the healer weren't getting along, or someone was committing a serious enough breach of protocol to make the male uncomfortable. He rolled out of the bed and made use of his mate's shower.

He followed his nose to the kitchen when he was done, where he found her humming over a waffle iron. He smiled, as he remembered an earlier conversation he'd had with her mother. According to Deidre, Brianna didn't like cooking, yet his mate was making him breakfast. He walked up behind her and put his hands around her waist.

"Your mother is under the impression that you aren't domestic." He kissed her shoulder.

"It's just waffles." She turned and wrapped her arms around his neck with a frown. "Besides, something about you makes me want to take care of you."

He was touched and speechless. He leaned into her neck and inhaled her scent. "The divine healer from Arizona is here to take a look at you."

"Here?" She pulled back.

"At the Haven." He clarified.

"Oh, ok." She turned and took the waffle from the iron. "I'm anxious to get my memory back."

He nodded and grabbed a waffle from the pile she'd already made on a platter. "I can imagine."

"You eat, I'll go get dressed."

He grabbed her arm as she tried to pass him. "Have you eaten?"

She looked sheepish. "An hour ago. I couldn't wait for you to wake up."

He released her and turned to watch her walk away. The shorts she wore made her legs stretch on forever. Memories of those legs wrapped around his waist played through his mind. Gods, the woman easily distracted him. He grabbed another waffle and wolfed it down as he waited on her to get dressed. She came out by his fourth waffle, in a pair of jeans that looked painted on, and a sweater. She walked to him and kissed his cheek.

"The look in your eyes as you saw me does a lot for my ego." She smiled.

"You're beautiful, and smoking hot in these jeans." He kissed her lips lightly and pulled back before he got carried away.

She didn't live far from the Haven, so they made it under the hour he'd asked Ade for. If the Kira's face was anything to go by, it still wasn't soon enough. The other Kira in the infirmary sat behind their desks, their faces serene, so the problem had to be between the two males.

"Commander." Ade greeted him.

Fallon frowned, Ade was never formal with him. "Where is he?"

"We've put him in a room. I tired of answering questions. Mistress Watson." Ade greeted his mate. "Follow me, please."

Brianna gave him a shrug and walked behind Ade. He took them to a room with an examination table. Brianna sucked her teeth.

"Y'all made me sit on the floor while this was here?" She whispered.

He rolled his eyes.

The Divine eyed them as they filed in. The male was elderly, his long gray hair tied in a queue at the bottom of his head. His gray eyes raked over them curiously.

"Commander, this is Achak, from the Phoenix Esin. Achak, this is Commander Tegan, and his mate Mistress Watson."

"Call me Brianna." She quickly insisted.

"Sure." They all shook hands and Achak indicated for Brianna to climb atop the examination table.

She sat and Achak placed his hand on her forehead and closed his eyes. Brianna's eyes darted to him. He shrugged and crossed his arms over his chest to wait the male out.

Achak cleared his throat. "There are a couple of different spells over you. They're meshed together as one by someone who must not have known but the most basic fundamentals of magic."

"Explain." Ade stepped closer to Brianna.

"Well, the spells are not necessarily for erasing memories, but for hiding physical things. I assume whoever rendered the spell wanted to obfuscate her knowledge of something specific. A seasoned magic-user would've assumed it wouldn't work."

"So they got lucky?"

"There is a cleverness to it, but instead of going in with purpose and precision, they wiped out everything."

"Can you undo it?" Ade asked.

"I can try and unwind the spell, maybe split it apart into each individual spell." Achak didn't look confident it would work.

"Will it dissipate without you doing anything?" Brianna asked.

"I believe eventually it will. You, yourself are pretty powerful, eventually, your magic will… dislodge the foreign magic."

Brianna straightened and got the look in her eyes he recognized. "Is there anything I can do to speed it along?"

Achak put his hand to his chin. "It has bound your magic, so if I can first undo that, you will probably recover faster."

She opened her mouth.

He interrupted, knowing his mate well enough to know she wanted to interview the healer. "Bri, perhaps we can work on that first, and then you question Achak to your heart's content when we're done?"

"So it is a Divine trait." Ade mused.

"A trait most intellectuals carry, the Kira included." He gave Ade a chastising look.

The Kira gave him a sheepish smile. "Indeed."

Brianna sighed. "Fine. Mr. Achak, are you leaving directly after? Can I get coffee with you?"

Achak looked at Ade. "Perhaps the three of us?"

It was Ade's turn to sigh. "Of course."

"Yay!" Brianna wiggled on the table. "Let's get on with it then."

Brianna squirmed again, anxious to see what happened when Achak removed whatever block was over her magic. It was weird to think about having magic when days ago she'd been so rude about not believing in it. The experiments with using it over the past couple of days had been interesting though, so she was ready to see the difference in her magic. Achak placed his hand back on her forehead, but instead of working silently, this time he chanted. She felt him gather magic from the room and couldn't help but smile. It was cool to witness. The room went topsy-turvey and for a second swam in and out of focus. She braced her hands on the table to keep from tipping over, that's how hard vertigo struck her. Fallon stepped forward in alarm, but then Achak removed his hand and the room righted.

"What was that?" Fallon demanded.

She held up her hand to let him know she was fine. "Just a little dizzy." She gasped as her chest heated and magic filled her.

"What's happening?"

Achak frowned. "You have a lot more magic than I anticipated. How have you not been taught to use it?"

"She was getting training prior to her accident," Fallon answered.

She shrugged, having no answer. With her memory gone, she couldn't confirm or deny Fallon's claim.

"How do you feel?" Ade asked.

She closed her eyes and tried to remember something beyond what she already knew. Nothing came to her. She shook her head.

"I don't, I still don't really remember anything."

Ade stood over and swept her form. "There is still something blocking those memories."

Achak shrugged. "As I said, the spell was done differently than anything I've ever seen. I would guess they wanted you to forget one thing, and it instead took more memories than they bargained for. It's the very reason we don't tamper with memories."

"So the spell around the book is not gone?" Fallon asked.

The healer looked sharp. "What book?"

Ade waved away his question. "Were you able to dismantle the spell at all?"

"Some." Was his answer.

"Do you think with more time, it will help?" Fallon asked. His fists were clenched at his sides and she felt his worry for her.

Wonder filled her as she realized she felt more than just his worry. While vague, she got a general sense of his emotions. It was awesome. Could he feel the same from her?

Achak shrugged. "It won't hurt to try."

Brianna winced as her head started to pound. Ade looked at her and touched a hand to her head. The headache disappeared and she sighed in relief and thanked him. She glanced at Fallon and smiled at the scowl on his face. Her brows furrowed as a memory of his scowl was triggered. She closed her eyes to chase it down. She remembered going to him, frustrated about something…her parents. She gasped and popped her eyes open.

"What's wrong, *ife*?" He asked rushing to her side.

She shook her head. "I'll tell you later."

"Then, let's get you out of here." Fallon helped her from the table.

"Well, I wanted to talk to Mr. Achak."

"Later, love. Achak has traveled all day. Perhaps tomorrow." She growled.

"Your mate has a point, Brianna." Ade looked her over. "Besides, though you did nothing physical, the spell work can take a toll on you. You should rest."

"I just woke up. Surely sitting for coffee won't-"

"*Ife*," Fallon growled.

She sighed, "Fine." She agreed, his anxiousness bombarding her.

He led her from the room before she could get another word in.

"That was rude." She grumbled. He stopped her in the middle of a hallway.

"It would've been ruder had I taken you in the infirmary." He leaned over her and kissed her.

Did his words both set her on fire and make her mad? Yes, yes they did. He moaned into her mouth and nibbled on her lip. He pulled back from her and grabbed her hand again.

203

“Where are we going?” She asked, hustling after him.

“My room.”

Chapter 23

His bedroom was bigger than hers, the massive bed giving them plenty of room to roll around on. Not that they did. He'd barely let her get through the door before he was on her. They eventually made it back to the bedroom.

"What was that about?" She propped her head in her palm.

"It's the frenzy. Every day we near the new moon, it will get harder for us to be separated." He pulled her closer to him, nibbling on her shoulder.

"Is that true, or are you making it up?" She tilted her head to give him access to her neck.

"It's true, I promise. Also, your magic flared once Achak worked his spell. It called to me." He ran his hand up her stomach, stopping to cup her breast.

"What time is it?" She asked, looking around for a clock.

"Who cares?" He murmured, moving the sheet covering her down to her stomach.

She pushed him off. "I care, I have stuff to do."

"What will you do?"

She bit her lip. "Well, to be honest, I want to practice magic." He snorted.

She punched his arm. "Don't be like that. Now that he unlocked my magic, I want to see what the difference is."

He came up on his elbow. "That reminds me, what did you remember in the infirmary?"

She smiled and ducked her head. "You."

He frowned. "We didn't, we weren't "together" prior."

She shook her head. "It's not clear, but, I remember coming to you upset about my parents. You helped me save them."

Gratitude filled her, along with a sense of wonder. He said he'd avoided her, and yet, she'd come to him when she needed help. It meant a lot to her and cleared some of the doubts she'd had about them. She trusted him prior to her accident. That meant a lot to her.

"If it's in me to do, *ife*, I'll do anything for you."

Her heart melted, a little, okay a lot. She leaned over and kissed him. Their tongues danced and her body came alive, acting as though they weren't lying in bed having just slept together a few minutes ago.

"I want you to come back tonight. It's sensual night, and I want to spend it with my mate." He nibbled her bottom lip.

She thought about the last time she was there. How her body had come alive. "I don't know how I feel about your sensual nights. The magic is akin to someone being drunk and not knowing what they are doing."

"Wrong." He kissed her nose. "The magic doesn't force anyone to do anything. If the person is not attracted, they aren't magically attracted. It's their choice whether or not to leave with that person. Are they super horny? Yes. Are their inhibitions lowered? Yes, but it's not a situation where they would do something they wouldn't normally do. It lowers inhibitions only to the point where the lust is pure and untainted. But, a prude won't magically leave and have sex with a stranger. Clearly, you had the presence of mind to stop."

She rubbed his arms, conceding his point. She was able to stop the moment she realized they'd never slept together despite how attracted she was to him.

"The kind of people we let into Haven are adults. They know what they want, they know their limits. My guys don't let women who look too intoxicated leave with strangers."

She felt bad for what she'd said. Just because she'd damn near hiked her skirt up in a club didn't make him the bad guy. She kissed him again. "I'm sorry, and yes, I'd love to come. I have to go, though, plus all my clothes are at home."

"Fine, I guess I can wait a few hours." He helped her out of bed.

She swatted his hands away as she got dressed, laughing because he wouldn't let her get dressed in peace. She prodded him out of his apartment door and followed him back through the extensive corridors Haven seemed to be full of. It wasn't until they were on the ground floor, she recognized where she was. He walked her to the garage, kissing her and handing her his keys.

"Do not drive crazy in my car." He ordered.

She grinned and snatched the keys from him. "I'll think about it."

She rolled her eyes when the passenger door opened and Isaiah got in. Michel hopped into the back seat, neither of them saying anything. She sighed.

"Seriously."

"Commander's orders," Isaiah said, buckling his seatbelt.

She pulled out of the garage and floored it, taking petty pleasure in Isaiah gripping the door frame.

"You're a lunatic." He grumbled when she parked the car on her street twenty minutes later.

"Sorry about that." She lied.

He shook his head and he and Michel got out of the car. She hit the alarm and turned around to say something. They were gone. Into thin air. It was definitely a skill. Fallon was right in that his men were trained well. She shook her head and headed upstairs to her apartment. She needed to shower, then get some research in before she had to be back at Haven. As she passed her library a memory surfaced.

There was a safe in there.

She rushed into the office, going into the corner near her desk as if compelled. She moved a small, three shelf bookcase aside and removed the throw rug. There, built into the floor was a safe. She pressed the combination, not even registering the numbers until she heard a click. It was obviously something she did often.

It worked!

She did an excited dance and opened it. Inside was a brown leather book bag. She frowned. Why would she lock it up? It was something she'd carried for as long as she could remember. She took it everywhere. Unless… could the book be in it? She ripped it open and stuck her hand in. There were more notebooks, but nothing that would be a spellbook. She stood straight. She remembered the book! Her head started a dull throb, but she smiled. She remembered that she was supposed to be looking for a book. She pumped her fist in excitement. It was the first sign that her memories were returning. She couldn't wait to get back and tell Fallon.

Chapter 24

Fallon rushed through the hallway to get to the garage. He was supposed to meet Brianna in a few minutes and he was anxious. He'd gone over his security checks earlier with a fine-tooth comb. He wanted to be sure nothing would get in the way of his night with his mate. He heard shouting as he reached the main deck. He cursed as he recognized the voices. Sure enough, he rounded the corner to find his parents, yelling at each other in the hallway.

"What's going on?" He shouldn't have asked, he should've kept walking and stayed out of it. And yet, habit had him marching over to them to intervene.

"Your father thinks I should give up the tentative bond I have with my son to sneak and let him see my grandson."

"He is my grandson too," Randolph shouted.

"But he's not," Sharine said, a nasty smile on her face. "Remember, you asked me to fuck your best friend."

"Mother." He said sternly, grabbing her by the arm and shuffling them both into an empty office. "Must the two you spread our business to the world."

"He's impossible."

"And you're a bitch."

"So long as I'm no longer your bitch," she spat.

Fallon rubbed his temples, a headache brewing. "Father, Leo has asked that you not see Kell. Why go behind his back? He already distrusts you."

"The boy should know me." He demanded.

"How does it feel?" Sharine taunted.

"*Iya*, please."

"Were it up to me, you would never see my grandson." With that, his mother stormed out and slammed the door.

"You have to stop this."

"Stop what, trying to see my family?"

"First, quit making an ass of this family in the hallways of the place where we have to work. As I recall, scenes were for undisciplined trash."

Ranolph growled. "Have you talked to him as I asked you?"

"Have you genuinely apologized to Leo?"

Ranolph turned his head.

"You can't ask me to stay out of it but to also advocate for you. Your actions had consequences, now you have to live with them."

Ranolph said nothing and walked out of the office. Fallon let out a breath and wiped a hand across his face. He was tired of being the peacekeeper. He desperately needed to see his mate. He walked out of the hallway, intending to meet her in the garage but he found her waiting at the bar, a pair of tight jeans molded to her curves. He wanted to skim those curves with his hands. She had on a red sweater that hung off one shoulder and a backpack slung over the other. Which meant she was spending the night.

His beast reared up in excitement. After two nights of sleeping with her, he was hooked. Having her in his arms had calmed the majority of his nightmares and he'd awakened, much more peaceful than he had in years. He tamped down his power. She traced his arms when he got to her which meant that he wasn't hiding his magic as much as he thought he was.

"What's wrong?" She cupped his cheek, her eyes roaming his face.

He got close and leaned over. "Family crap."

"Want to talk about it?"

He sighed. "Playing referee, again."

She hummed and stood on her toes and kissed him. "So making a deal with the devil is easier than dealing with your family?" He laughed, tension leeching from him. "It was not the devil."

"If you say so." She smirked. "I brought clothes to change into, let's go to your room."

"I don't know that I can trust myself in a room alone with you." He growled.

Her scent deepened, and he wanted to wallow in it. He kissed her, and the bartender cleared his throat. They needed to get out of the way.

"Let's go." She grabbed his hand and he led them back down to his room.

Brianna put on the finishing touches to her makeup and tugged down on the dress she wore. Since she wouldn't need to walk out in the cold, the off the shoulder dress would be fine. She loved the way it fit. Cassie had helped her pick it out when they went shopping. She'd bought a few items she'd stuffed in her backpack for later tonight as well. She didn't let him look in her bag and kept him out of the bathroom as she dressed.

"You like?" She spun a circle as she walked from the bathroom.

211

"Goddess, the way you fill out that dress," he whispered. He was his usual sexy self. He wore all black, his slacks tailored to perfection and the dress shirt clinging to his chest.

He walked to her and she took a step back. "Nope. Date first, hanky panky after."

He frowned. "Hanky panky?"

"The sex."

He snickered and grabbed her hand, leading her up to the club level. She pushed down on her panic as they traveled through the corridors leading from the room. The tunnels back here were a lot wider than the ones in the infirmary wing and she was happy. She didn't feel nearly as claustrophobic. She didn't know where the claustrophobia came from, she'd never been that way before. But for some reason, being down in the tunnels below Haven triggered it.

They entered the club and the music was loud. Red lights painted the writhing bodies on the dance floor. The lust hit her, and it was like the first time she'd come there. This time, she reveled in and let her guard down.

He growled next to her. "You're a lot more open than before."

She smiled at him and dragged him to the dance floor. She started moving her hips and the look on his face was worth every second she would have to dance in the wedged heels she wore. He moved behind her, his movements graceful, sensual. Damn the magic around them, she fell under his spell. His hands skimmed down the side of her body and she lifted her hands to hook around his neck.

He smelled amazing. She would have to ask him what kind of cologne he wore. It wrapped around her, drowning her senses in the scent. He grabbed her hand and turned her around, pulling her back into his chest. He kissed down her neck, his fingers moving along the bottom of her skirt.

She looked around, wondering if anyone saw them. What she saw on the dance floor further sped her heartbeat. She wouldn't say she was a voyeur, but seeing the carnal sight of the others around her did turn her on.

He groaned. "What are you thinking about, I swear your lust just spiked." He nuzzled into her neck.

While he traced along her skin, he never once crossed her personal boundary. He didn't lift her skirt, or expose her in the way some of the women on the floor was.

"Because you are mine." He growled in her ear. "No one will see what is mine alone.

Had he read her mind? His words brought her further under his spell. She had to admit, it made her love him a little. The song changed, the lights deepened to an almost maroon and her skin came alive. Fallon licked up her neck, his teeth tracing her skin.

"Feel that, *ife*?"

She nodded and threw her head back as her body loosened, her womb tightened. Her magic seemed to surround them both, jacking up her senses. She knew she had magic, and she'd been practicing with it, but to feel it now as its own entity…it was overwhelming, but in the best way. They swayed together through two songs, their tempo speeding and slowing when the music did. Her body loosened with each song. Her eyes closed and she threw her head back onto his shoulder, the music carrying her away.

"There it is, give me more, *mi okan*."

She turned around and kissed him. He pulled back and whispered in her ear all the things he wanted to do to her when they got back to his room and she swayed, needing to feel him.

"I need you," she whispered.

"How, *ife*? Tell me, what you need."

"I want you inside me." She bit his ear lobe, enjoying the way his erection flexed against her stomach.

213

His hand reached under her skirt and she didn't stop him, didn't even think of it. He brushed his finger over her clit.

"I want you to come, here, now." He ordered. He put his knee between her legs and she rode his leg. "Say yes, *mi okan*."

"Yes," she whispered.

He growled and kissed her, moving her hips to the rhythm of the song. She was breathing hard by the time he'd pulled back from their kiss. She felt the release barreling down on her and she bit her lip to trap her moans.

He smiled and hovered over her mouth. "Give it to me, *ife*. Feed me."

His whispered plea set her off and she gasped. He hovered over her mouth and she felt the energy leave her body and move into his, some of it cycling back to her, feeding her orgasm. It was…she couldn't describe it. Her orgasm prolonged and her body was like liquid by the time he'd finished. She opened her eyes, speared by his copper eyes, he didn't quite glow like last time, but he seemed bigger, more powerful. It was a heady feeling, knowing she gave him energy, life. To know she provided for him made her proud. He kissed her, brought her down from her own high.

"Shit," he whispered in her ear. "We're leaving now."

He lifted her in his arms and marched toward the back door.

She laughed. "We just got here."

"Don't care, need to be inside you."

Was it possible for her to actually go up in flames? There was a bouncer at the door who lifted an eyebrow at them. He moved in front of them.

"*Ife*, you have to let him know you're leaving with me of your own volition."

She felt delicious, her body languid, her spirits high. It was almost like being drunk, without any of the icky feeling. She giggled. "You're going to have to tell me what that word means, you keep calling me that."

She let her head fall back, enjoying the weightless feeling of him carrying her. The door opened, and someone came out, the lust from the club leaked out into the hallway and that quickly her body wound up again.

"Damn," Fallon murmured, his hands gripping her tightly. "*Ife*." He prodded.

"Are you going to stop us, if I don't say it?" She addressed the bouncer.

He smiled. "I am."

She laughed, enjoying Fallon's frustrated growl. "Then move aside sir and allow him to ravish me."

The bouncer moved to the side and Fallon carried her down the hallway. It wasn't even ten steps before he opened a door to a darkened room and deposited her on an empty desk.

"Need you now." He hissed as he kneeled in front of her.

He opened her legs, and propped her feet on his shoulders, his head dipping to taste her. She arched her back, biting her lip to trap her needy pleas. He growled and lifted, wrapping her legs around his waist. He had his erection out and pressing inside her seconds later. She could barely make out his shape in the dark and it added to the moment.

"I had to taste you." He murmured surging forward, stretching her channel.

"Fuck me," Brianna demanded, lifting her hips.

"My pleasure." He kissed her, his hips driving him deeper into her. He hit a spot that had her seeing colors, her body thrown instantly into orgasm.

He hovered over her mouth, and remembering the first time, she opened hers, this time actively feeding magic into him. He moaned, his release driving the magic higher, burning brighter. He glowed, the whorls on his arms coming to life. The room lit with an amber light.

She stared at him, her eyes hooded, drunk off the power flowing between them. Usually, he cut off the power exchange when he was done feeding, but he was enjoying the closeness with his mate. Her mind was open to him. He saw the block over her memories, but whatever magic it was, it didn't touch her spirit. Her strength and compassion were there for him to read, and honest love, purer than anything he'd felt wrapped around him. He loved his mate, and he saw the beginning threads of it in her. Until their bond was completed, this was as close as he would get to feel with Brianna. He looked forward to their bond. Being inside her, feeling her love and lust for him, was heady.

He cooled down their magic, containing it as best as he could. Brianna's magic drew back inside her easily, but his beast was harder to tame. He still wanted his mate. The frenzy rode him hard. He looked around the abandoned office and realized there were pictures on the desk.

"Shit." He murmured.

"What?" Her voice was sleepy, sated.

"This office is not occupied currently, but it's definitely not abandoned." He lifted her and used his magic to clean her off.

She giggled a moment before it turned into full belly laughs. "Do you mean we just had sex on someone's desk?"

Her laughter was contagious. He laughed harder than he had in years, the two of them sprawled across another person's desk.

She wiped tears from her eyes and shuffled off. "Oh my God, we shouldn't be laughing."

He said a quick spell to put it back the way it was when they arrived. Not that anyone who worked at Haven wouldn't know there was magic performed in their office. He shook his head. He hoped he wouldn't end up in his brother's office explaining it.

"Let's get out of here." Brianna tugged his hand, snickering the whole time.

Chapter 25

He grumbled as he shuffled into his kitchen the next morning. Granted it was closer to ten a.m., but it was really unnecessary the way his mate woke early. He'd have to break her of that habit. He'd been looking forward to morning sex, and she was not cooperating. He nearly forgave her though when he smelled the coffee.

"Why do you wake up so early?" He kissed her forehead.

"I've always been an early riser." She handed him a coffee cup "You don't have foodstuff in your fridge."

He sighed at his first sip. "Just call down to the kitchens and order what you want. They'll bring it down."

"Ooh, you have room service in this place." She did a dance.

He laughed and showed her how to use the comms pad. He sipped at his coffee, smiling as Brianna joked around with the kitchen attendant. Her hands moved in an animated pattern as she described the omelet she wanted. She ordered enough food for the two of them and ended the call. He pulled her into his lap.

She wrapped her arms around his neck. "I wanted to ask you about last night."

He hummed, nuzzling into her neck.

"That guy really wouldn't have let you carry me from there?"

He set his mug on the table in front of him. "Not carry you, no. He wouldn't have stopped us had you been walking."

"Really? That's reassuring."

"It didn't always use to be that way, it was one of the first things I changed when I took over the head of security position. We're Demigods, after centuries of life, some tend to look at humans as simple prey." He ran a hand over her headscarf.

"You're a good man." She murmured, dropping a chaste kiss to his lips.

"I'm not a man, *ife*. Remember that." He warned.

"And what does that mean?"

"What?"

"Ee-fay." She sounded out the word.

He smiled at her pronunciation. "It means love."

Wonder crossed her face and she kissed him. There was a knock on the door.

"That was fast." She stood and walked towards the door.

"I'm an officer, darling." He called after her.

She answered the door and brought in their food. They ate and discussed their schedule.

"I want Achak to look over you again before you leave."

She nodded. "That's fine, I want to visit the library here, is that okay?"

"Of course, *ife*. I'll walk you down."

She frowned. "There are lower levels?"

He would've smiled, but he felt her discomfort. "It's not too bad. Plus, imagine all the information down there."

She perked up. "Maybe they have spells here I can use since you guys have no qualms about messing with memory."

"Our spells won't work for you. Not only are they in another language, but they also use a different essence than the divine spells."

"What?" Her brows lowered, and her eyes darted, a sign he knew signaled her interest and would likely resort in a million questions.

He stood and gathered their dishes. "We are of the gods, *ife*. Different cosmic makeup."

She frowned. "I didn't think of that. Still, I'll go look around."

"I would expect no different." He kissed her forehead. "Come, I'll escort you there."

She stood, and looked down at her pajamas. "Give me a few moments."

She darted from the room and he perused his comms tablet until she came around the corner a half-hour later, dressed and smelling amazing. He led them from his apartment, heading towards the lower levels.

"How will I find my way back?" She asked minutes later as he led her to down a sloping hallway.

He shrugged. "Whoever is on duty won't be far from you. They'll lead you to my office when you're done."

She nodded, her curious gaze roaming the hallways as they traveled to the library. He led her in minutes later.

"Commander Fallon." The archivist greeted as they walked in.

"Penny." Fallon released Brianna's hand and lifted the oft grumpy archivist. He kissed her cheek. "How is my favorite archivist?"

Penny snorted. "Put me down, you brute."

Fallon smiled. "How was your trip?"

"It was very much needed and appreciated. The primal source south of the equator is magnificent. I should move to the African Haven."

"Who would I pester for information if you do that?"

"So true." She smiled at his mate. "Brianna, I heard about your memory. I wondered when you would make it down here."

The woman looked familiar and Brianna unclenched her hands, and relaxed. She hated to admit jealousy had her irritated at the way Fallon greeted the woman. She looked around and the ghosts of memories hovered right on the edge of her consciousness, but nothing tangible she could grab on to. It was more than before and she wondered if the healing was working.

"Today's the first time I've had time to come down." Brianna offered.

Penny nodded as though it made sense.

Fallon leaned down and kissed her forehead. "I'll leave you in the archivist's capable hands."

She watched him leave, loving the way he filled out the black cargo pants he wore. She turned back to Penny.

"So, what was I researching down here?"

"It varied. Some days it was information on the Demi, or the Divine and the Great War. I think you were more fascinated with the different accountings of the same events."

It matched what Emilia from the Divine library had told her. She thought about her conversation with Fallon the other night. "Can you explain Kokoro souls to me?"

"Do you remember Ofeeree?" Penny asked.

She nodded, seeing her notes on the evil being that had unleashed hell on Demi during the Great War.

"Well, there were three souls responsible for what we all knew would be his final resting place. They were responsible for both binding his body and power, and hiding him where his followers couldn't find him."

"And the souls were reborn?"

Penny frowned. "In theory, Oya, the goddess of the afterlife would release the souls to be born again if he came close to escaping his prison."

Full body chills racked her. Penny had no clue that she was a Kokoro soul, which meant, no one outside of Fallon and his brothers knew. Did it mean an entity her notebooks described as the ultimate evil was in danger of being released? She would have to ask Fallon whether or not they would warn others and what they were doing about it. Her position as a Divine in a Demi space rested heavy on her shoulders as she thought about it.

"What would the souls do to stop him from escaping?"

"Well, they each had separate jobs so to speak." Penny sat on the edge of a table. "There is scant information on them, to be honest. Commander Leonalph was down here seeking information about that same thing last year. Strange that you would ask now."

"Well, there was a note about it in my notebook, so I was curious." She lied.

Penny nodded. "The first two are intertwined in a way. Ofeeree is locked in a location no one knows or can access. One soul will know the location, but it won't be the same person that has access to his hiding place. Only one of them will be able to even get to that location. The other person, and it more than likely will be someone human, a Divine to be specific, I suspect. They would know the spell to bind him again."

She clenched her hands in front of her and forced her body still as a shudder went through her.

"Why a Divine?" She managed to get out after swallowing several times.

"A Divine person was responsible for the spell that bound him to begin with, so likely only a Divine will have the knowledge to do it again." Penny shrugged. "It's all speculation, as I said, the information on the Kokoro is hard to track down and even harder to understand when it's found."

Brianna decided to change the subject, already scared enough to last the rest of her life. "I saw some information about the different realms of the Demi, can you explain how they work."

"Towards the end of the Great War, the Demi were given the different realms to escape the carnage of the war. The dimensions are sort of stacked on top of each other, with the power of the primal source lessening with each layer."

"Harsh. How did they decide who could be closer to the 'primal source'?" She made a mental note to research that as soon as she was done talking with the archivist.

Penny laughed. "That's a whole separate animal and you'll have to ply me with a drink to even go into it."

Brianna smiled. "So, can humans visit these realms?"

"There is nothing stopping them, save not having access."

223

"So if someone stumbled onto a portal they could get there?" Her interest peaked.

Penny raised a hand. "I see your mind working. In theory, they could. No, I will not be going into detail about where they are and hypotheticals to get humans through our portals."

Brianna had to laugh. Clearly, the woman knew her well. "I mean, you can see how I would have questions."

Penny shook her head and stood, her face amused. "Were it not for your complete reverence of information and history I would find you most annoying."

Brianna laughed harder. "Why is the library so empty?"

The archivist raised her brow. "We are more than a library, young lady."

Brianna looked around at all the books on shelves.

Penny snorted. "Okay, but more like your library of congress, or law library. I only get visitors when there is trouble and someone needs a bit of history to help them out. Your mate frequently visits for the history and origins of different spells."

Brianna narrowed her eyes at the mention of Fallon.

"You two are a perfect match in that, I think," Penny remarked. "Well, I have work to do, of course, Brianna. The books are at your disposal. If you need anything else, just shout for me, I'll be on the other side of the stacks."

Chapter 26

Brianna looked up as someone sat down. She squinted at the intruder, wondering how much time had passed since she'd been down in the library exploring. A lot of the books were in a language she couldn't read, so she'd focused on those she could. She blinked in surprise as she realized it was Fallon's mother.

Bangles covered her arm from wrist to elbow, the sound tinkling as his mother pushed the heavy fall of black hair behind her shoulder. It was parted down the middle with a couple of small braids tied to keep it off her face. She wore an emerald color blazer that set off her dark skin beautifully. There was no shirt beneath the blazer, and every time the woman adjusted, she flashed a hint of cleavage. The woman's smell reached out to her and she leaned forward.

"You smell amazing." She blurted.

His mother smiled sheepishly and after a moment, the perfume wasn't as strong. "Hi, Brianna."

"You're Fallon's mother, Sharine, right?" His mother's face lit with pleasure at her remembering. She thought about what Liliana and Fallon said about the woman. "You've come to start some shit?"

Said with a smile, Sharine didn't take offense, instead, her eyes glowed with amusement. "Who me?" She put a hand to her chest. "Okay, maybe just a little."

Brianna laughed, liking the woman's frankness.

"So, you and my son are getting along well?"

She thought about last night, the magic they'd exchanged, and the way they laughed together. She had fun with him, and he made her burn with a passion she didn't think was possible. She blushed as she caught his mother's gaze.

"Yes, we are."

"How do you feel about visits from your mother-in-law?" Sharine got a wistful look on her face.

"Depends on how my mother-in-law plans on treating me."

Sharine smiled and grabbed her hand. "Well, I don't want both my daughters cringing when they see me."

"Ha! So you did come down here to start shit. Am I going through the 'are you good enough for my son' portion of dating?"

Sharine snorted. "You're mated, if the Eminzu chose you for my son, you are good enough."

Brianna smiled, liking the thought of that.

"Do you want kids?" Sharine leaned one elbow on the table and dropped her chin into her palm.

Brianna narrowed her eyes. "Yes, eventually."

"How many?"

"Depends on how bad the first one hurts."

Sharine snickered, and the sound charmed her. She leaned forward again trying to track her elusive smell.

"I like a blunt female," Sharine said, waggling her eyebrows.

"Are you going to meddle?"

"Of course, duh." Sharine sat back in her chair with a mischievous smile that reminded her of Fallon.

Brianna laughed again, really liking Sharine's honesty. "Why does Liliana have beef with you?"

"Beef?" She frowned, not understanding.

"A grievance." Brianna supplied.

"Oh." Her face cleared. "Well, I may have ruined her wedding reception a bit."

Oh, that sounded messy, and she absolutely wanted to hear the story behind it. "A bit?" She put aside the book she'd been reading. "Do tell."

Sharine shook her head. "Leo's biological father is different than Fallon's, long story, but he's the king of the Eshu."

"Legba right?" She remembered.

Sharine nodded. "The queen tried to kill Leo when he was a child because she couldn't have an heir. I took exception to that."

"Rightfully," Brianna said, getting mad on Sharine's behalf.

"Thank you! Well, of course, because of Leonalph's station he had to have a royal wedding."

Brianna squelched a giggle and leaned forward. "Oh God, did you fight the queen? Tell me you bitch slapped her."

"No." she pouted. "I promised Fallon I wouldn't get physical."

"Bummer."

Sharine eyes lit, literally, the hazel turning to gold and glowing. She laughed, a belly laugh that made Brianna join her. "According to my sons, the arguing was bad enough."

"But you and Liliana get along now, right? I like her." Though she'd only had a brief conversation with Fallon's sister in law, she'd liked her.

227

Sharine waved away her concern. "I do too, she's a tough female. I like her for Leonalph. We get along now, but not everyone likes my bluntness."

She understood that. It was the reason she didn't have many friends. "Did I pass the test?"

Sharine smiled. "With flying colors. Fallon has been happier lately, sleeping, thank you for that." She got a sly smile. "You know, I didn't get to help plan Liliana's wedding."

Brianna raised a brow. "We're planning weddings now?"

"There are only a few weeks left before you have to seal the bond on your mating. We should plan the reception for the mating ceremony, and then whatever humans do for a wedding."

She leaned back and crossed her arms, thinking about the big step Sharine was proposing. "First answer me this, do you know why Fallon took so long initiate our bond?"

Sharine's smile dropped but she didn't avert her eyes. "I think his father and I are to blame for that."

"In what way?"

His mother sighed. "Fallon was right. You ask a lot of questions."

Brianna shrugged, not offended by the truth.

"Well, we've had what could only be called a contentious mating."

"Contentious?"

"That long story I was talking about," Sharine said, looking away a moment. "Well, Fallon was left to clean up after the fall out from our arguments. He's a peacemaker by nature. So he would shuffle behind us smoothing ruffled feathers, making sure everyone was taken care of. I think it's made him shy away from the thought of having a mate."

She put the puzzle pieces together from what Fallon told her and what his mother was saying. "The thought of one more person to care for made him gun shy?"

Sharine looked relieved. "Exactly. From what I can tell, and what I hear, that won't be you."

She crossed her arms and considered the commitment she'd be making being mated to someone like Fallon. He was leery of the commitment, yet, even as he ran, when she'd needed help he was there for her. Even as he'd run from her, he set up protections and was still taking care of her parents. In all the years she'd dated, not one man came close to making her feel as secure as Fallon did. Certainly, none of them had turned her on as much as he did. She made a decision.

"If we're going to plan a wedding my mother will have to be involved, oh and my best friend."

Sharine smiled, and again, she found herself drawn to his mother. The two of them loved Fallon, and she found comfort in that.

Chapter 27

Fallon opened the door to his mate's apartment, palming the key she'd given to him before she left Haven. He thought it a good sign that she entrusted him with a key to her apartment. He knew Brianna didn't easily give her trust. He remembered when she'd finally come to him months ago to help her parents. She'd been distraught, no trace of her normal confidence as she explained her problem. Their Oliri was holding her parents hostage and he'd asked for money. She had the money, but she'd rightly suspected the male wouldn't release them even if she'd paid the ransom. He wanted to go himself with her, but Xavier had nixed it, concerned having someone high ranking from the Amanda storming into an Esin would cause friction.

He'd argued until he and Xavier had come to a compromise. He waited in a hotel near the Douglasville Esin, needing to be there for his mate, even if he'd not claimed her. It was a long night. He paced the floor until the group had come back with her parents terrified of the consequences of them leaving. He shook away the memory, walking into the kitchen.

"It smells amazing. Here you go, cooking for me again. If we were at Haven, someone could do this for us." He kissed the side of her neck.

She smiled. "I like cooking for you. How was your day?"

He sat at the island. "Frustrating. Still no lead on the person who kidnapped you. Also, your friend Darren? Doesn't show up on the Oras, I wasn't sure after the lunch you had with him. But, it's official." He'd rooted around the Oras searching for Darren. He'd checked the night they'd gone out on their date and the male hadn't shown up at all.

She whipped around. "Like the others who kidnapped me?"

He stared at her. She was beautiful with her eyes lit with excitement and curiosity.

"You know what that means?"

He nodded, loving the smug look on her face.

"I was right, it has to be my old Esin."

"Well, does that mean your friend is still in contact with them?"

"Maybe, you should have him followed to figure it out."

She'd surprised him. Once again he lamented getting to know her before she'd lost her memory. "Do you know where he lives, I haven't been able to find out."

She shook her head. "I've avoided him, to be honest. But, you know, I can call him and have him meet me somewhere. You can follow him from there."

"I like the way you think, Ms. Watson."

She gave him a little curtsey.

"Come here." He beckoned.

She turned off the stove and went into his lap. She buried her head into his neck. "You always smell so amazing."

"There is so much I don't know about you." He mused.

"Well, that comes from avoiding your mate for a year." She chided.

He smiled. "Are you now embracing being my mate?"

She shrugged. "I'm a pretty upfront person. I follow my instincts and once I make a decision I stick to it." She touched her temple.

"And have you made the decision about our mating?"

"I even made wedding plans with your mother today." She dropped small kisses along the bridge of his nose.

"Wait what?" He reared back. "You talked to my mother?"

"For a while. I like her."

Now he was really confused. "You like my mother?"

"Is that so hard to believe? You like your mother, right?" She burrowed her head into the crook of his neck.

"I love my mother, it's just, she's a lot."

"Well, I like her."

Well, damn. "What kind of plans did you make?"

"Nothing important, but we did make a date to meet with my mother and Cassie to really plan it. Do you realize we'll have to do two separate ceremonies?" She stood and went back to finishing dinner. "We have to have the actual bonding ceremony first. Your mother said it had to be done on Chuita, which I'm very excited about. And then, we'd probably have to have a Divine ceremony. I don't know about that one yet, though. Since we haven't really left a lot of time to plan everything, she said it will have to be a smaller reception than she'd like."

He snorted, knowing his mother, small could mean anywhere from two to three hundred people. He decided to leave it to his mother to break that bit of news to his mate.

"I'm so excited about traveling to another realm." She smiled at him. "She said you would describe the actual ceremony."

He watched her move around the kitchen, missing some of her chatter as she talked about the meeting with his mother. He was madly in love with his mate and was mad that it had taken him so long to see it. She was his and had he quit running scared months ago, they could've had this sooner. He understood what Leo meant when he said everything would come together once he accepted his mate.

She stared at him.

"What?"

"Are you listening?"

"Well, you're prancing around the kitchen in yoga pants, so I may have missed a few things."

Her eyes softened as she smiled and put his plate on the table. She leaned down and kissed his forehead. He loved the way she took care of him.

"But, yes. I heard you. You went out to lunch with Achak and Ade. What else did you find out today?"

She snapped her fingers. "The Kokoro souls. No one knows they've been reborn?"

He dropped his fork and sighed. "Rugaba has instructed us to keep it under wraps. If word got out more than it has, he's afraid someone will try to free Ofeeree."

Real fear flitted across his mate's face. "How would they do that?"

"That's not something we need to discuss or even think about just yet, *ife*." He knew she was scared because instead of insisting on answers, Brianna simply nodded and let the subject drop.

They ate dinner, talking of other mundane things. That night he held his mate tight while she slept, happy she'd not insisted on details about how the Kokoro souls would be used to free Ofeeree. Leo said he had nightmares about the thought of Liliana being subjected to the torture required to free the knowledge locked in her soul. He shuddered and leaned down to inhale Brianna's scent. It grounded him and brought home the responsibility he had to protect her. He prayed for the strength to do it.

His communicator woke him hours later. He, of course, reached next to him to find his mate missing. So she was awake and out of bed. The waking early madness had to stop. He already knew she would ignore his complaint about it. He checked his communicator and found a message from Isaiah. They caught Darren sneaking around Brianna's building and Isaiah wanted him to know that he'd sent Michel to follow him. He rubbed his hands together, happy to finally have something go right. He shot off a message to the roster Commander on duty to replace Michel with a fresh set of guards. He'd keep an eye on the male and see what information they could glean from him. Satisfied, he sent a message to Isaiah.

He got up, clothed his nude body in a pair of jeans and a simple button-down and went in search of his wayward mate. He found her in her office typing away at her computer. He leaned against the door jamb. "Any luck with your passwords?"

233

"No." She blew a raspberry and kept typing. "I'm jotting down what we talked about last night and then I'm going back to the Roswell Esin to see if I can find a reason we can't see Darren on those Ora thingys."

"Where would you look?" He asked, curious since she'd already told him there was no mention of the Oras in the Esin's documents.

"Well, I need to first research the primal source, I think. You said that powers the Oras. There could be something specific to the people of the Douglasville Esin that makes them invisible to the primal source. Maybe a spell or something."

"It's not the whole Esin. You and your parents show up on the Oras. So does Cassie."

That got her attention. She swiveled in the chair. "Have you tried to find anyone else from Douglasville?"

Now that she'd mentioned it, he hadn't. "I'll check when I get in. Give me the coordinates and I can take a look."

"You won't necessarily know if anyone shows up that way." She mused aloud. "Maybe it's only a few people." She stood. "Do you think they are the only Esin that way?"

He shrugged. "I've never encountered it before."

She rubbed her hands together. "Well, I'm off. Do you want me to make you breakfast?"

He shook his head. "No, I'm going to head in. They found Darren wandering around outside, so we have a tail on him. I'm going to see what I can find out about his movements."

She shuddered. "That's creepy. I'm going to carry my taser today."

He snorted.

"What? I'm a practical woman." She walked to him and tilted her face up for a kiss.

He dropped a kiss to her lips. "That you are, beautiful."

"Do you have duty tonight?"

"No, want me to come over, or do you want to go out?"

She tucked her hands between his arms and linked them behind his back. "Let's stay in."

He kissed her deeply. There was a knock on the door. She frowned.

"Who's that?" They walked around to the front door.

"I don't like that Darren is hanging around, so I asked your guards to be visible for now, until we can figure him out."

She growled.

"Practical woman, remember?" He wagged his finger at her.

She clicked her teeth. "You're right. Fine."

She kissed him and walked out with Isaiah. That had gone a lot better than he thought it would. He smiled and locked her door, warding her apartment and heading back to Haven.

Chapter 28

The library was blessedly empty when she entered the door. She was still processing the fact that Darren was skulking around her apartment. It wasn't as though she had given him any hint she was interested in him. She'd told him in no uncertain tones before she left Douglasville that she would never be with him. Even after their lunch, she'd avoided his calls. The last time she'd seen him was the night of her date with Fallon. Ghosting him was obviously not the answer. She'd need to be more direct. Next time he called, she'd tell him to leave her alone.

She shook her head, she was done thinking about him for now. Though, she was happy she'd packed her Taser. She didn't relish being kidnapped again. The next person to try would have a fight on their hands.

Emilia came around the corner and smiled. That smile dropped when she spotted Isaiah behind her. The librarian frowned.

"This is my friend Isaiah. He's not going to touch anything, he's just my shadow today." She hurried to soothe the woman.

She didn't know how politics between the Divine and the Demi worked. She didn't know if he would be barred from entering the library or not, so she put on her most charming smile.

Emilia blinked and turned her focus back to her. "Oh, is there something wrong?"

"Nothing I can't handle." She kept walking not giving Emilia time to protest. "We'll just sit back here quietly."

The librarian wanted to say something, her mouth opened and closed as she decided what. "Okay."

Brianna gave her a bright smile. "Great!"

She grabbed Isaiah's hand and dragged him to the back room where her stuff was set up. She dropped her bag in the chair across from where she would sit. She pointed to a chair along the wall next to her and Isaiah plopped into it without a word.

Isaiah pulled out a tablet and was quietly working as she picked a history book and started reading. She was happy he wouldn't be chatting and disturbing her while she read. She soon lost herself in the research. Emilia came in every now and then and peered at them, but left them undisturbed. Soon she came upon an entry about the time before the Great War.

She frowned. She hadn't thought to check records before the war. The entry was about an angered god, and an Oliri cast out who had been cursed. She frowned and stood. She went to Emilia at the front desk.

"Hey, do you have any records before the Great War?"

"Anything in particular?"

She rubbed her forehead. "Well, there is some mention of an Oliri being cast out. It references him as the reason the Divine's lifespan was shortened?"

Emilia's brows furrowed as she thought. "Let's see."

She followed behind her as she walked over to a reference section towards the front. The librarian pulled a ladder over and went up. A few moments later she brought down a huge tome.

"Here is a journal of record keepers before the war. Once one died, they passed it down until the pages were full and they moved to another. This one is about four hundred years prior to the war."

They went back to the back room and put it on the table. Emilia was careful as she opened the book. It was old but the pages were still supple.

She leaned closer for a better look. "I wonder how they preserve the books this well."

"There are spells to do so." Emilia bragged as she straightened. "Let me know if you need anything else."

"Thanks." She was already skimming the writing, trying to find a place to start.

It took her nearly an hour until she found mention of a cursed Oliri. She slowed her skimming to read it thoroughly. It took her a while to find another reference. This one toward the beginning of the skirmish. The Divine used to live for centuries, at least four hundred years before they died. It noted that their progeny lived longer, stayed younger. The writer wondered if the gods could be convinced to prolong their life and youth as such. One Oliri raised the point that they should do a human sacrifice.

She made a disgusted sound and kept reading. They chose a princess, a Kira princess because that race had a lot of power. They kidnapped her in the middle of the night and the priest killed her and sacrificed her to Rugaba as the sun was rising.

"Holy shit." She whispered.

He got furious because it was his daughter. He shortened the life of the Divine and the actual priest who did it. Rugaba nulled the Oliri and cursed his whole line.

"Anyone born from the line would not be able to be seen in his presence." She read aloud. "Holy shit." She said again. "We gotta go." She told Isaiah.

She glanced towards the door of the conference room, to be sure Emilia didn't come in. She pulled out her phone and started snapping shots of the pages. It was risky, especially with Emilia already suspicious about Isaiah. Her hands were shaking as she turned the page and took pictures of the other reference as well. She sent them to her email address, then deleted them from her phone.

"Let's go." She whispered to Isaiah.

She gathered up the book and took it back to the front desk. Emilia looked up from what she was doing and smiled.

"I'm done for today." She covered her nervousness with a cheery smile.

"Okay, do you have any notes?"

"None today." She waved and forced her body to take slow steps.

Once outside they rushed to the car. Isaiah started the ignition and glanced over to her. "What's up?"

"I think I figured out why my kidnappers aren't showing up on the Oras."

Isaiah's eyebrows winged high. "You're good."

"We'll see." She murmured, turning to glance at the library. Emilia stood at the door watching them leave.

Had she given them away? She shook her head, no way to know until the next time she tried to come to the library. Isaiah cursed and slowed the car as they reached the front gate of the Esin community.

Darren was standing in front of a car, blocking their way.

"Stay in the car," Isaiah ordered as he opened the door.

She stayed, but she pulled her Taser out of her backpack and gripped the doorknob. Isaiah barely stepped from the car, one foot still inside when he flinched, staggering back as a wave of magic rippled across his body. Isaiah's form changed, his hair spilling to his waist in different hues of blue.

239

His body got taller and thicker and he braced his hands on the car. Real fear ignited as she thought about the other guards who'd died when she'd been kidnapped. She gripped her Taser tighter and pushed her door open.

"Stay in the car, Brianna!" Isaiah shouted through clenched teeth.

No way was she letting him die for her. Darren's attention turned to her. He looked terrible, worse than he had when she'd seen him just days ago. Michel materialized from behind the guard's shack, rushing to Isaiah as he dropped to the ground. Darren turned to her and lifted his hands. Screw waiting around for a spell, she fired off her Taser at his crotch.

His scream of pain drowned out her thumping heartbeat. He bent over and she rounded the car to help Michel with Isaiah. They lifted Isaiah and stuffed him into the back seat of the SUV. They both turned their head at the sound of a car peeling wheels. Michel cursed as Darren sped away.

"Into the car, Brianna, we need to get him to a healer," Michel ordered.

She ran on the other side, snapping her seatbelt as Michel jerked the car in drive. "What happened?" She looked back at Isaiah in the back seat.

"Spell of some kind." Michel's face was a fierce mask of concentration.

She pulled out her phone and called Fallon.

"*Ife*." His voice was worried.

"Darren tried to attack us. He hit Isiah with something. We need a Kira."

He cursed in another language. "I'll have someone here waiting for him. How bad?"

She turned and gave Isaiah another glance. "Bad."

"Come home, *ife*." He ended the call and she threw her phone back into her backpack.

Isaiah was slowly getting quieter, his breathing labored as they rode on. Michel was speeding down the highway, swerving through cars until he jerked to a stop in front of Haven minutes later. There was a Kira there, who opened the door as soon as the car stopped. He and Michel unloaded an unconscious Isaiah.

She jumped out of her seat and ran after them. Fallon grabbed her as she passed him, lifting her and hugging her tight.

"The healer has him, he'll be okay." He murmured as she fought his hold.

"I don't want another guard to die for me." She whispered, distraught.

Fallon put her down and stepped back to examine her. "Are you sure you're alright?"

"I swear, I'm fine." She glanced over in the direction where the men had taken Isaiah.

He pulled her into the club, headed downstairs, but instead of heading towards the infirmary, she recognized the way to his brother's office. "Isaiah will be fine. The infirmary will call us as soon as they know something."

She nodded, adrenaline still coursing through her body.

Fallon stopped halfway and looked over her again, fear transforming his face. He pulled her into a hug. "Goddess, *ife*, it scared at least ten years off my life when I felt your fear through our link."

It reassured her that he was able to feel her. She tiptoed and kissed him softly. "I'm ok."

He cleared his throat. "Come, Xavier is waiting to hear what happened."

241

She followed dutifully behind him, everything in a haze. She wanted to know about Isaiah, and she also needed a moment in a quiet place to calm her nerves. She'd give Xavier the information he needed, then she'd ask her mate to take her to his apartment.

They entered his brother's office and Xavier was pacing in front of his desk. He whipped around as they came in. "Is she okay?"

"She is standing here." She said wearily.

His gaze raked over her and he actually looked concerned. She couldn't argue with him when he was genuinely worried. She nodded that she was okay.

"What happened?" Xavier asked.

The door burst open. A man stumbled into the door, his face worried. "I heard, is Brianna okay, what do we know?" He saw her standing next to Fallon and sighed in relief. "You look only a little ruffled, what happened?"

"She was just about to tell us. Close the door, Leo," Xavier ordered, walking around to sit in his desk with a hard sigh.

It had to be Fallon's other brother. He didn't necessarily favor the other two, but he had enough of Sharine in him that she recognized. It was her first time meeting him in person...at least since her memory had been lost. She blinked. And looked to the door. When no one burst in, she sat in the chair in front of Xavier's desk and told them what happened.

Fallon lifted her out of the chair, sat and then pulled her into his lap. "How did you get away?" he asked.

"I tased him in the nuts." She leaned her head onto Fallon's shoulder, taking comfort in being in his lap.

Leo choked. "What?"

Xavier and Leo both stared at her, alarm on their faces.

"I tased him. He hit Isaiah with some kind of spell before he could even get out of the car good." She took a deep breath and sat up.

"You tased him?" Xavier asked, stunned.

"In the nuts." Leo started laughing.

Xavier put his head on the desk and sighed. "I can't even…Brianna, did it occur to you to allow your guards to do their job."

"How? Isaiah was down and Michel rushed over to help him."

Xavier turned a sharp eye to Fallon. "I thought you had someone on that Darren guy?"

"Michel was watching Darren while the other soldiers I sent were searching his house." Fallon gripped her waist tightly as he sighed.

"I clearly took care of myself." She reminded them.

"Yeah, clearly," Leo commented with a smile.

Fallon glowered at his brother, before turning his gaze back to her. Was he mad she'd taken care of herself? He didn't seem angry.

"X, let it go, my mate did what she had to do to get away." She faced Xavier. "Are you always fussing at me like this?"

"Always." Leo supplied.

"Hmph." She narrowed her eyes at him as he rolled his.

"You're a frustrating female." He mumbled.

"X doesn't like anyone disobeying his orders. You make it a habit to do so." Fallon told her. "But we're not talking about that now." He warned them both.

"Fine." She leaned over and opened her backpack, taking out her phone. "Before I was attacked, we were on our way here. I found out something." She pulled up her emails.

She showed them the pictures she took of the ancient text. She passed it to Xavier who read it, his face darkening. "I remember the tales about this." He passed the phone to Leo who read and passed it back to Fallon.

Fallon shook his head. "Princess Iliya's death."

"Murder." Xavier corrected grimly. "What does that have to do with now?"

"Well, Rugaba made the descendants from that line Null. Meaning they couldn't be seen under the sun. Our Oliri never went outside during the day time. He could go out around sunset, but he would burn easily. What if that's why they don't show up on the Oras? Rugaba stripped that line of the very energy needed for the Oras to read them."

Fallon was stunned, but pride glowed on his face as he gaped at her.

"Well damn, Brianna," Leo said, impressed.

"That doesn't answer the question about why they want you." Xavier leaned back in his chair.

"Or what we can do to them," Fallon commented.

"Do we tell Rugaba about this?" She asked

"Shit." Leo blew out a rough breath.

"I don't know, actually. Let's hold off for now." Xavier looked at Fallon. "Fallon, have the guards searching Darren's place stay on him once he gets back home. Brianna, I want you to stay here."

"No, I'm taking her home. I'm not waiting around for someone to take her again." Fallon declared.

Xavier opened his mouth to argue but closed it at his brother's feral growl. She stared at Fallon for long moments then nodded. Xavier and Leo exchanged shocked glances.

"You're not arguing?" Xavier asked.

"Hey, I'm not stupid, I don't want to be kidnapped again. Duh. Do you think Cassie is in danger?"

"Cassie is at the Esin, she's fine," Fallon assured her.

"Cassie lives at the Esin and she didn't tell me?" She frowned.

"No, we pulled her in when you were on your way back here," Xavier said.

She breathed a sigh of relief.

"We're leaving. Call me if you need me." Fallon stood, holding her in his arms a moment before he put her down.

She waved at his brothers as they left, her heart pounding for a different reason. She was going to visit a Demi realm. Her breath caught as they entered an open chamber, the ceilings were at least ten feet high. There were people milling about, standing in lines, at what looked like a check-in station. There were all shapes, sizes, and colors of people, and Fallon slowed as she turned her head from left to right, her mouth agape. He went into a side corridor where the crowd thinned to one or two soldiers in uniform until they reached a blank wall.

She wanted to ask questions, but his face was ferocious, intense as he concentrated on the wall in front of them. He waved his hands, muttered and a grid appeared on the wall. There were symbols in each square of the grid. His hands' movements were intricate as he weaved the floating letters into place. He moved them around until he formed a word. It made her realized, there would be no humans stumbling on a portal and going inside. It glowed and a moment later the wall disappeared and she could see another place. It looked like an airport.

He looked at her. "Trust me?"

"Yes." She said, excited to go through.

Chapter 29

He walked them through and she felt a shift in her body. A bright light blinded her for a moment until he stopped her. She took a deep breath and smiled in surprise as heated, damp air entered her lungs. She opened her eyes and looked around in awe. Everything was lush, green plants in every corner, the windows letting in bright light.

He walked her through and they skipped the long line waiting at some kind of counter.

"What is this place?"

"The portal station of my homeland, Chuita." He answered.

"So like an airport?"

He smiled and kept walking. They got outside and there was a guy waiting in front of a jeep. The guy was very tall, nearly seven feet, his skin black, like the actual color. There were amber lines running throughout his skin with raised whorls pulsing as he leaned against the jeep. He wore fatigues in a green that matched the scenery. Fallon held out his hand and the guy tossed keys to him and walked away.

Fallon lifted her up into the jeep and walked around the front. He pulled out of the station and started driving. He merged into traffic on a dirt road leading from the portal station. They turned off onto a smaller, winding road that took them directly into a jungle.

Her mind was spinning, her eyes wanting to absorb everything she was seeing. She was in a new dimension, one humans didn't even know existed. She wanted her notebook, and a few hours to look around. Her breath fogged the window as she pasted her face to it. Her body rocked and jostled with the jeep as they went deeper into the rainforest of Chuita.

"That guy had the little whorls on his arms like you, is that how you look when you're not passing for human?" She turned to face him, fascinated by the thought of his other form.

"Certainly more handsome." he joked.

She smiled. "Can all Demi change forms?"

"All have a base form and their human skin. Cagyns, which is what I am, can change into any creature from whom we have essence."

She wrinkled her nose. "Essence?"

"Like hair or any biomaterial."

She frowned. "Really? Just hair or skin from anything and you can become that…thing?"

"Any living being. It's why we're so feared. We can be and pass as anyone. It's one of the reasons our race dominate the Amanda."

That was equally fascinating and scary. He'd spent nearly every moment she'd seen him in human form, what did that mean for him? "Do you expend magic to keep your human form?"

He nodded, not taking his eyes off the jungle road they were traversing.

"You don't have to do that around me. I want you able to relax."

He smiled absently but said nothing.

The road turned to cobblestone as they passed through a small city. Elegant whitewashed structures surrounded them on either side, colorful awnings on some announcing them as shops. There were Cagyn eating in outdoor cafes, and women chatting as they walked along the sidewalk. The whole place resembled a resort town and it was all alien to her, a small-town Georgia girl. The further they got from the portal station, she saw his shoulders lose their tension.

She put a hand on his shoulder. "You seem lighter here."

Fallon turned to her and smiled. "It will be harder for someone to kill you here."

She raised an eyebrow at his blunt words. "I imagine Xavier won't let anyone from the Douglasville Esin through Haven to get to the portal."

"Yes, and now my beast knows that, so I can relax."

She smiled and ran a hand over his head. He smiled and continued driving. She watched out the window as the rainforest passed. She'd read about Chiuta in the library and was fascinated by the realm, knowing his race was from there.

"I want to show you something." He broke the amiable silence between them.

He drove through a small path, and they bumped along, large leaves slapping against the side of the jeep. The path looked just barely big enough for them to fit through. She held on as they bumped through, and around a mountain. Her breath caught as they came out to a clearing, and a cliff. The ocean was spread before them, crystal clear, reflecting the sun that held a pinkish hue.

She gasped, wanting very much to jump into that water. "It's beautiful."

He pointed further up the hill. Overlooking the beach was an outcropping and a large beautiful mansion.

Her eyes widened. "Is that your place?"

"The family home. We all stay here when we're in this realm." "I can't wait to see the views from there." She said wistfully.

He smiled at her and reversed from the spot and continued upward. They pulled into a garage ten minutes later. He got out of the car and walked over and opened her door. She usually got out of the car, but something in her paused until he came around and let her out. She wasn't usually so submissive, but seeing the pleased look on his face as he helped her down from the jeep was worth it.

He led her into a spacious house. They walked through a mudroom, and into a large kitchen. Terracotta colored tiles stretched throughout the length of the open plan. A large brick arch separated the kitchen from the living room and she gaped at the beautiful mosaic tile that ran along the walls in the kitchen. There was an oversized fireplace in the living room with a fuzzy rug laid in front of it. The whole place was decadent. It was like a Spanish villa, all tile and big giant windows letting in a breeze. She'd left Haven in fear, and here she stood in a mansion on a tropical vacation. She couldn't wait to explore.

Fallon took a deep breath and set the remote for the jeep on the kitchen counter. His mate walked in a circle, observing the house, her face flushed with excitement. He tried to remind himself that she was safe, that nothing and no one could get to her in this realm but still, his beast bucked at him, anxious. He wouldn't be leaving this realm without bonding with Brianna.

He dragged her to him as she passed him in her exploration, hugging her tight, and breathing in her scent for endless moments while he got his beast under control. His human skin wavered as he took a shuddering breath. That she didn't protest told him how much she too needed it. He took a final deep breath and separated enough to look down on her face.

"A shower, and then dinner?" he rained kisses across her face.

"Sounds good." She sighed and tiptoed, joining their lips.

He devoured her mouth and lifted her until her legs wrapped around his waist. He used his magic to start the shower in his room wanting it warm by the time they arrived. He guided her down the hallway into his room and the adjoining bathroom.

Steam had built up in the bathroom, warming it. He was glad for the size of the shower stall as he walked into it, his mate still tangled around his body. He didn't release her mouth, needing to taste her. He separated long enough to whisper a spell to remove their clothes. He braced her against the tile a moment later and entered her.

She pulled back from their kiss and looked down at her naked body. "How did you do that?"

"Magic, *ife*." He moved his hips, surging into her.

She threw her head back and sighed. "I like your magic, a lot."

He gripped her neck with his teeth, wanting, no needing, to assert his dominance over Brianna. He growled and pushed his hips into her faster, getting lost in the feel of her. His beast was riding him, worry for her at the forefront of his mind. Her brown skin glistened in the water, he bent over and sipped at the water on her shoulder.

"Kiss me." She demanded.

His pheromones were in the air, the magic of it making him drunk. His mate's magic glittered around her and drew him in. Their moans echoed around the glass enclosure turning him on further. He loved the little pants she made when he hit a certain spot. Her pussy clenched around him and he exploded with her. He didn't want to leave her body. He slowed his strokes to lazy ones that dragged out their orgasm. She sighed into his mouth, kissing him sweetly. Gods, he loved this woman. She ran her teeth along his neck and he jerked, his cock hardening. He took her again, panting as they both came.

He let her legs down and grabbed the sea sponge and soap and washed their bodies. She gave him a sweet smile as he sat her on the sink and dried her off. She groaned as she caught sight of her hair in the mirror.

251

She stretched out a chunk of her curling hair. "Ugh, this will take forever to dry."

Curiosity had him playing with the springy curls. "What do you normally do with it at home?"

"I have to moisturize it, then twist it." She grumbled.

He was pretty sure he could do it with magic, but he wanted an intimate moment with her. He looked below the sink and rifled through all the oils his mother bought for him on her trips to the market. He scented through them and picked out the one he liked the most.

"My mother is always buying us oils when she goes to the market. Would you like to try one?"

She grabbed and wafted it under her nose. Her eyes closed. "This smells amazing."

"What else do you need?"

He conjured a big tooth comb per her instructions and lifted her from the sink. He sat her on the padded bench in front of a wide mirror. "Tell me what to do."

She walked him through parting her hair and combing the oil through the strands. She closed her eyes and moaned. He liked doing it for her and enjoyed the lazy smile on her face. Once he was done, he told her he would go cook while she twisted her hair. She came out as he was finishing their dinner with a scarf wrapped around her hair and a giant shirt he'd conjured and told her was his. She was adorable, and having her in his family home did something for him. It brought back the vision he'd had of her in her parents' home. He smiled. His beast was content, sated, his magic flowing through his body to overfill. He realized how dangerous it had been for him to run around not at full power. It could be why so many infractions had happened last year at Haven. With his magic near depletion, he'd missed a lot, he wouldn't make the same mistake. He was surprised his brothers hadn't noticed earlier.

"Do you want to eat on the balcony?"

A large smile lit her face. "Yes, please."

He placed the dinner on the small table on the balcony. They ate overlooking the ocean, its sounds lulling them both. His mate smiled at him and tucked her feet under her. They ate dinner and conversation flowed between them. Both of them avoiding talking about what happened earlier. He'd been working on her case since she'd been dumped at Haven and he needed a break. He would take that break with his mate, in a place he personally knew was secure. They could talk about unsavory things later.

Chapter 30

Brianna tinkered around the giant kitchen humming to herself, Fallon's t-shirt hanging from her shoulder. It reached her mid-thigh, and he loved the way it looked on her. The front door chimed a warning that someone approached a moment before Sharine, wheeling a small suitcase, came in. She smiled when she saw Brianna.

"Are you cooking breakfast for my son?"

Brianna smiled. "Good morning, Sharine."

Sharine kissed her on the cheek. "I like you taking care of Fallon. I brought you some clothes that Cassandra said you'd want and some of your toiletries."

Brianna's face lit. "Thank you! We rushed out yesterday, I didn't even think about it until this morning.

He watched them interact from the hallway, enjoying the sight of his two favorite women getting along. Magic floated around Brianna in a lazy fashion, showing her lack of control of it. He frowned. He'd need to do something about that soon, at least until she got her memory back. He knew she'd learned to use and harness it prior to the memory loss. He imagined all that wild magic during their *di êjê* and had to adjust the growing erection in his pants.

Every day they were closer to the deadline to complete their mating. Soon, their bodies would go into a frenzy to force the issue. He found himself looking forward to that.

"Fallon let me use some kind of oil you bought for him. I put it in my hair and it smells wonderful and this morning my hair still feels like a cloud." Brianna's voice broke into his musings. She pulled at the deep waves framing her face and falling to her shoulders.

"I can take you to the market below and get you some," Sharine promised, fixing her a glass of juice.

"I'd love that."

His mother spotted him as she went to sit. "You could have conjured her some clothing, son."

He walked over and kissed his mother on the cheek. "I like my mate naked, but I thank you for bringing her something personal from home, *Iya*."

Sharine put her glass on the table and turned to give him a hug. He savored the comfort from his mother, happy that she was slowly getting back to the woman he knew from his early childhood.

Brianna smiled at them and turned her cheek up for a kiss when he walked over to her. He snuggled up to her back and kissed her neck.

"Sit." She ordered, pointing to the table they sat at last night. "I have breakfast done. I didn't recognize much in your refrigerator, but I figured out eggs and made you an omelet. And there is fruit here that I don't think was there yesterday."

Sharine chuckled. "The staff here is very good at staying hidden." She took plates out.

He grabbed the platter of fruit and followed her. When they were all settled around the table, Sharine speared him with a look. "Since you're here, have you decided to do the mating ceremony?"

Fallon sighed, not wanting to pressure Brianna. "I didn't like the way things were escalating on Adro. I'd like to have the *di êjê* done while we're here." He looked at his mate. Had she been taken, his tie to her would have helped find her a little easier.

She frowned, her fork hovering over her plate. "What's a di edge?" She frowned at her pronunciation of the word.

"It's the bonding ceremony, roughly translates as the blood bond." He said carefully.

She grimaced. "What does it entail?"

He dragged her chair around the table until their legs met, happy she'd agreed to mate with him. He leaned over until he was a hairsbreadth away.

"We exchange blood."

255

"Ugh, no."

His lips quirked into a small smile. He lifted her from her chair and made her straddle his hips. His scent rose up and blanketed her. She took a deep breath.

"God, you smell amazing."

He nibbled along her neck and found the spot where he'd put his bite. He had a hard time remembering his mother was at the table. "A little bite here, *ife*, a little blood and we'll be bonded for the rest of our lives."

He gripped her chin with his thumb and forefinger, bringing her head down for a kiss. "That's not so bad is it?" He asked hovering over her lips.

She sighed, the scent of her lust driving his frenzy higher. She shook her head.

"Brianna you're going to spoil him if you agree with everything he asks." Sharine joked on the other side of the table.

He sighed. Goddess, that woman lived to start up shit. "*Iya*, really?"

Brianna laughed and settled her head on his shoulder a moment before she pushed off him and sat back in her chair. She moved it away from him and pointed a warning finger at him.

"You're doing something to me with your smell."

Sharine snorted. "The Cagyn have pheromones we wield to make people...compliant."

Brianna's mouth dropped open. "Seriously? Is that why you both smell so good?"

"Notice how much better we smell when we're trying to talk you into something," Sharine smirked into her teacup.

"*Iya.*" Fallon groaned. "Will you leave me nothing to make my mating easier?"

Sharine laughed and Brianna shook her head.

"So back to the *di êjê,*" Sharine said.

"What will we have to do?"

"Well, it should definitely be on the family beach. I know the best location. I have the shaman lined up, we're just waiting on the two of you to decide what you'll do."

"We're doing it," Brianna announced with no hesitation.

His stomach did a slow turn, and he wished his mother wasn't there so he could show his mate how much her words meant.

"Can my parents attend?" She asked, spearing a piece of fruit.

Fallon cleared his throat. "Well, Cagyn ceremonies are different."

"Different how?" She turned to him and he squirmed.

"The ceremony itself is just the two of us. The reception is where the family congratulates the newly mated couple." He answered.

That didn't seem so bad. Why was he nervous? "So just you and I and a shaman?"

He nodded.

"Oh. Ok." She looked between the two of them as they exchanged a look.

"It will be done at midnight," Sharine said, her voice even, careful.

"Why midnight?"

Fallon's eyes speared her. "It's believed the veil between the spirit world and that of the world we inhabit is thinner starting at midnight. It's said midnight allows you to align and bond, your body, your spirit, and your soul all at the same time."

"That's beautiful." The sentiment was romantic.

"It's…the ceremony is beautiful," Sharine whispered. "It's the closest you will ever be with your mate."

"*Iya*," Fallon whispered. He grabbed his mother's hand. She clutched his hand a moment before releasing it and taking a deep breath.

She blinked, clearing her misty eyes. "I'll give you two an hour between the ceremony and the reception."

"For pictures?"

Sharine snorted. "One hour, Fallon Tegan, you're to have your mate at the bride suite ready to don her gown."

Wait. "I won't need a gown for the ceremony?"

"Tuh." Sharine stood and gathered their dishes. "You explain to your mate in explicit detail, what's to happen."

She turned back to Fallon. He sighed. "Explicit detail, your mom said, no omission, Fallon," Brianna warned.

"I'll need a drink for this." He stood and scrambled in his cabinets. He came back with an expensive-looking bottle of some type of whiskey and two tumblers.

"No, thank you, I don't drink anything that hard, especially not this early in the morning." She smiled at his grimace and rested her chin in her hand with her elbow on the table. "Come on, buck up and tell me and then I want to go down to that beach."

"Well, firstly, it will just be the three of us, on water's edge. We start the ceremony shoeless, in ceremonial robes."

She narrowed her eyes, almost knowing where this was going. She straightened. "We're going to have to be naked aren't we?"

He nodded.

"Nope. Next."

"Not, nope. There is a very spiritual significance of us being nude, *ife*, it's not something you can just nope."

She growled. "No way is my big ass standing in the middle of a beach naked, nope, not going to happen."

He stood over her, leaning down into her space. His breath smelled like honeyed cider as he hovered over her lips. "I like the size of your ass, and you will. I'll make sure you're relaxed enough to do it."

"With magic Cagyn pheromones?" she joked, getting drunk off his nearness.

He laughed and nibbled on her lip. "Let's get dressed and play in the water for a while."

"I hope there is a swimsuit in my bag."

"What kind of suit would you like?"

She thought about Sharine saying he could conjure her some clothes. She perked up. "A one piece."

"Done." He straightened, his fingers moving as he murmured. A bright yellow one-piece swimsuit appeared on her body underneath the t-shirt she wore.

She lifted the shirt and gaped.

"I was right, your skin looks fantastic in that color."

She narrowed her eyes. "Your mother wasn't just talking. You could've conjured me some clothes at any point last night." She'd slept in his large shirt and nothing else.

He smiled and leaned down, kissing her. She loved kissing him and let him get away with distracting her.

"You'll be able to do the same, once you learn." He promised.

She hummed, actually liking the idea of that. "Are you going to relax enough to go in your Cagyn form?"

He growled. "I don't know if you can handle me in my base form."

"So you letting your whorls show is not you in your base form." She traced his arms.

He shook his head.

"What happens?" Imagining the soldier she'd seen yesterday.

"My hair grows, my body, in all places." He waggled his eyebrows.

Her eyes widened and she instinctively opened her legs. How much would he grow? Would it be impolite to do a package check once he got into his base form? He growled as though he knew the direction of her thoughts. She liked the sound. He made it a lot when he was turned on.

"Beach first." He murmured, "Then don't expect to leave our bedroom."

Her stomach flipped and fluttered. Perhaps they could skip the beach altogether. She considered, then decided she'd get to play with him later. The closest she'd been to a beach was Lake Lanier in Atlanta, she was looking forward to seeing the water and black sand.

"Deal." She said, pecking him on the cheek. She backed away. "Now, you change, I want to see your base form."

He sighed. "Okay, but I need you to be as calm as possible. Any hint of you running will send me scurrying after you."

She swallowed and nodded. Wait, "Why?"

"We have a predatory nature, the beast as we call it."

She frowned. "Is it separate from you?"

"No, it's just, in our base form, we are more aggressive, more animal n our thoughts. It takes a lot to suppress it."

"So, you don't turn into an actual beast?" She perhaps should be scared, but she trusted him not to hurt her.

He shook his head. "No, actual beast, no. But, when we let nature ake over, there is scant reasoning or human-like thoughts." He warned.

She shrugged. "So, no running. Got it."

He breathed deep and she watched as his skin gradually darkened, and he grew taller. He was a full foot taller than her when he was done. His hair reached his shoulders, pitch black and silky. His eyes were still his eyes, but the green ring around his irises glowed every time they caught the light. He was beautiful, fierce, and her body tightened with need. Maybe they wouldn't make it to the beach.

He smiled, and she saw a hint of fangs. "In this form, I'm much more connected to you, and your thoughts are…" He took a deep breath and closed his eyes as though savoring something.

It was hot.

"Beach first, mate, I can feel your excitement for it." He lifted her from the chair.

He was right. She was excited to see the beach, but the thought of running her hands over all that ebony skin, and playing in his hair… That made her an entirely different kind of excited. He kissed her, his tongue tracing the seam of her lips. She let him in, sucking on his tongue.

"Beach first." He whispered.

Right. Beach first.

Chapter 31

The weather was beautiful, the moist air blowing around them with the wind as they reached the beach. The black sand was warm beneath their feet as they looked around for a place to put their blanket and basket.

"There aren't any people here." She commented.

He pointed, and down the beach a ways were other beachgoers.

"This beach is private?" There was a mischievous glint in her eye.

"It is."

She nodded and took off the cover-up she'd insisted she needed. She told him it wasn't proper to walk around in just a swimsuit. Humans had weird hang-ups about nudity and their bodies, so he'd made the flimsy dress to appease her sense of propriety.

He stared at her body as she bent over to fold her cover-up and place it on their towel. He was right, his mate looked amazing in yellow. She'd asked him to come to the beach in his Cagyn form, and he was having a hard time with the concept of patience. Seeing her in the suit, and the stretch of her long, thick legs... He growled.

She turned at the sound and walked up to him. Her head barely reached his chest in this form, and it was a huge turn on. Brianna in a submissive position was something he liked a lot more than she'd probably want to know. She skimmed her fingers across his arms. His magic flared, his light pulsing with his increasing heartbeat. Her magic responded, dancing around her aura. It was beautiful to see.

"If you plan to swim, my gorgeous human, I would suggest you go now."

Her eyes widened and she raised her hands and ran them through his hair. "I like your hair a lot." His beast was pleased. "Will you leave it loose?"

"Of course." He would agree to anything she asked. Unable to stop himself from tasting her mouth, he kissed her.

She moaned and then back away. She gave him a mischievous smile that heated his blood and turned. She ran to the water and squealed when the cold waves slapped against her knees. He gave chase, unable to stop himself, not that he wanted to. He scooped her up as she tried to run into the rushing waves. She laughed and wrapped her arms around his shoulder. He took them out far enough where she could float while he stood. She bobbed around him as the waves rushed to the shore.

"This is amazing." Her breathy voice was a sound he wanted to hear for the rest of his life.

They spent the whole day at the beach, alternating between making love and nibbling on the food they'd stashed in a basket. He liked spending time with his mate and was happy he'd brought her home. Dusk was settling around them, the pink sun dipping below their horizon. His mate was sprawled across his chest, her skin tasting of saltwater and sunshine. He wouldn't change a single thing about their day.

He fumbled with his coin as they traversed the stairs back up to the house. His head throbbed and he grabbed the railing of the stairs as a vision of his mate laughing with him in a café flashed through his mind. He frowned not recognizing the place. She looked back at him with a question and he held up the coin.

"Anything interesting?" Her smile was sweet, and one of his favorite things about Brianna.

"Nope, mundane."

She shrugged. "Bummer."

Sharine had the patio table set, dinner awaiting them on heated trays when they reached the top of the stairs.

They took separate showers because she didn't trust him or herself for that matter. She hadn't been able to keep her hands off him at the beach. She should be sated, but every time she glanced at him, her body warmed. She told him to find another bathroom and she'd meet him at the dinner table.

She rushed through her shower, slathering conditioner in her hair and pulling it up into a bun. She slid into a tank top and comfortable wide-legged trousers. The tank top was silky, the feel of the fabric decadent against her skin. It was casual but still decent enough for dinner at home.

Sharine was sipping wine, scrolling through a fancy tablet when she came to the table. Fallon came out of the bathroom, his hair still wet and falling down around his shoulders. She licked her lips and stared. Sharine cleared her throat. She gave his mother a sheepish smile. He came up behind her and nuzzled into her neck before sitting across from Sharine.

"I wanted to show you pictures of the reception hall, Brianna." Sharine spun the tablet to her and she leaned over the table.

Fallon made a low sound in his throat that beaded her nipples. She realized the view she was giving him as her tank top dipped low. She lifted the tablet and sat in the chair next to him, making the mistake of looking at him. His eyes were completely copper, and they stared at her with an intensity that made her body flush. Sharine clucked her teeth and reached over to take the tablet.

"The place can certainly hold everyone, so it's ideal. Do you like it?" Sharine prodded her, holding up the tablet.

She reluctantly looked back at the pictures displayed. The place was beautiful. It looked like a temple, with columns and beautiful murals. She nodded. She didn't care where the reception was.

"Will the reception be big? I know it's last minute."

Sharine bobbed her head side to side, considering her question. "Not too big. There is family here, mine and Ranolph's which should make for an interesting time. Then some of the higher ranking Amanda because Fallon is an officer."

She fixed her plate and Sharine steadily listed off people that needed to be invited. She was realizing Sharine's 'not too big' and hers differed greatly.

"How many people do you need to invite?" Sharine asked a few moments later.

She grimaced. "Three people."

They both paused eating and stared.

She shrugged. "I don't know if I kept in touch with any of my other coworkers, and I quite frankly don't feel like explaining this to anyone else. So, yeah, just my mother and father and Cassie."

Fallon went back to eating, devouring his food. He even ate differently in his Cagyn form. It was fascinating to see.

"Will there be dancing?" She loved to dance, and looked forward to dancing with Fallon.

If she had to have anything at the reception, that would be her only request. She took the bigger pieces of meat from her plate and put them on

Fallon's plate as she waited on Sharine's answer. She grabbed the smaller ones from the dish and replaced the ones she'd given to Fallon on her plate.

It took Sharine a moment to answer so she looked up. His mother's eyes were teary before Sharine cleared her throat. "Umm, yeah, if that's what you wish."

Fallon finished his plate and turned in his chair putting his legs on either side of hers. He nibbled on her shoulder, and she rolled her eyes. She speared a piece of steak and offered it to him. He ate it, a satisfied smile on his face.

Fallon couldn't remember a time when he'd felt so content. He'd tuned out the planning between the two women, and focused on Brianna. He loved to watch her mind work. His mate continued to eat, giving him more from her plate until he put his hand on hers.

"Enough, you need to eat as well." Still, he was pleased and didn't think she realized the significance of feeding him from her plate.

She snorted. "Trust me, I don't miss meals."

"I had the cook prepare dessert for tonight, so save room for that," Sharine said before steering the conversation back to the reception.

It was the only part of the whole process his mother would have any input in, so he understood her excitement. Especially since she'd had no part of planning Leo's mating or reception. He tuned them out again, dropping light kisses along Brianna's skin. She smelled amazing, sweet, yet with a smoky sensuality. The Eminzu couldn't have picked a better mate for him if they'd tried. Brianna was everything in a mate he'd never known he wanted.

She challenged him, cared for him, and supported him. He planned on making up for his mistake of delaying their mating. He'd spend the rest of their life making sure Brianna felt loved, and wanted. Though she didn't remember his rejection, once her memory returned, he knew it would weigh on her. He would make sure she had no doubts about them.

The new moon was a few days away, and the frenzy was riding him hard. Especially in his Cagyn form. He moved her chair closer to him and nuzzled into her neck.

"Fallon." His mother said, in exasperation. "Can you not give us a few minutes to plan?"

"*Iya*, I'm taking my mate to bed. I will give you all day tomorrow to plan." He announced.

Brianna squealed when he lifted her out of her chair. She slapped at his back laughing. 'I want desert, you oaf."

He grabbed the decadent cake displayed on the table as he passed it, his mate laughing with her head hanging over his back. His mother cursed at him and he realized he'd never been happier.

Chapter 32

The next morning when he awoke, the house was full. There were women everywhere, including his grandmother, aunt, and some cousins. There were samples scattered on the coffee table. The varying level of magic from the women surrounded them and added to the atmosphere in the house. It felt bubbly, with literal excitement in the air. They all waved as he shuffled into the kitchen, groggy.

"Breakfast is in the warmer, babe," Brianna called out to him as he passed.

He nodded and waved to the full room.

"You cooked?" Cassie said loudly.

"Yes, I cooked," Brianna said defensively.

Deidre laughed. "You should've seen her at the house, Cassie. She actually fixed Fallon's plate."

His mother sighed. "She was feeding him from her plate last night. It was quite beautiful."

The fact that the women were talking about him as though he wasn't ten feet away should've made him upset. He was too busy eavesdropping to be offended.

"Oh my lord, you actually love him." Cassie gasped.

Brianna laughed. "Stop it, and yes."

That perked him up. He fixed his breakfast and ate it standing over the sink, listening to the chatter of the women. They ooh and aahed over place settings and decorations and his mate looked comfortable and content. He contemplated his mother as she interacted with the other women. She was vibrant, hints of her old self present as she joked with the ladies. From the first interaction with Brianna, Sharine had never used her normal acerbic tone when speaking with his mate. She was more like she'd been before the troubles in her mating and bitterness took over. He was happy, relieved to witness the change.

His phone beeped, taking him from his musings. It was his brother. He walked out onto the patio to take the call.

He flipped it open and a tiny hologram of his brother sitting at his desk sprung up. "Yeah."

"Your men lost Darren." Xavier scowled.

He cursed. "They didn't tell me."

"I'm trying to give you time with your mate, so I had them report to Leo." Xavier crossed his arms over his chest and leaned back in his chair. "He never went back to his apartment after attacking Brianna."

"Did they find anything in there?"

Xavier shuffled through screens on his computer and pulled up a report. "He's living with a female. I'll message you the picture. Maybe show it to Brianna and see if she knows who it is."

"Sure. He's null, so finding him on the Oras will be impossible, perhaps we can find the female." He ran a hand through his hair, his good mood souring.

"We're looking into this nulled angle Brianna found. Rugaba is being less than forthcoming about the whole thing."

"What's our next move? A part of me is content to keep my mate here, in Chuita, damn everything else.

Xavier grunted. "I wouldn't blame you if you did, but I want that book found and secured, so don't get comfortable there. The healers here want to see her again also, and they're being persistent. Ade is curious and this divine healer he found is worse than Brianna with the questions. I've banned him from my office."

Fallon laughed at his brother's grumpy tone. "We're going to do the *di êjê* before we come back to Adro."

"I had to approve a couple of Divine to go through the portal. I assumed they've descended on the house for the purpose of planning your reception."

And how. He glanced back into the living room to see the women laughing. "*Iya* is supposed to give me the details once they've figured it out."

"I'm sure I'll find out everything once you have. How is your mate?"

He glanced at Brianna, her magic glowing around her. "She fits here. I like it."

Xavier shrugged. "I'm happy for you, Fallon. Though your mate gets on my nerves, she works for you."

He looked out at the ocean. "I'm finding that out." He sighed, hating that he'd have to disturb Brianna with talk of her kidnapping. "Send me over that picture and I'll see what Brianna knows."

Xavier nodded. "I'll keep you posted in case anything happens here."

"Wait, Isaiah, how is he? Brianna will ask."

"He's better, though nowhere near one hundred percent. Whatever spell he was hit with was weak enough for the healers to mitigate some of the damage."

Fallon sighed. "Thanks, X."

His brother ended the call, the image of him disappearing.

Moments later his communicator beeped, a single picture coming up on the screen. He narrowed his eyes. He didn't recognize the woman, and he'd not seen her around his mate, but that didn't mean anything. He walked back into the room and caught Brianna's eyes as she looked up. He inclined his head towards the hallway.

Her smile dropped and regret was a knot in his stomach. He loved the way her magic looked when she was happy.

Brianna wiped her suddenly sweaty hands on her pants leg and excused herself from the group. Fallon's face was serious as she met him in the hallway.

"What's happened?"

She didn't want to hear it. She wanted to continue planning this reception and pretending bad things wouldn't happen to her in this paradise. Fallon cupped her cheek and kissed her softly. "I'm sorry to even have to talk about this, *ife*." She nodded. She was sorry too.

"Darren's gone off the grid again." He told her.

Her stomach dropped and she wrapped her arms around her waist. She wasn't worried he could get at her here in Chuita, but her glance strayed to her mother and Cassie. Nothing was stopping him from attacking either of them. Fallon followed the direction of her gaze.

"They'll both have guards. Don't worry, *mi okan*." He promised.

His words reassured her. She turned back to him. He was holding his phone out to her, and a picture of a framed picture was displayed on it. "Do you know this female?"

She squinted at the image. "That's the librarian, Emilia. The one at the Roswell Esin's library. Why do you have a picture of her?"

Fallon looked grim but started typing on the phone. "Darren was staying with her. My guys found pictures of them together."

Shock had her speechless. Darren and Emilia, together? "How would they have even met?"

Fallon shrugged, typing away at his phone. "I sent a message off to X. He'll find out all he can about her."

She thought back to a couple of days ago when Darren had attacked them. "That's how he knew where we were." She whispered.

"When you were attacked?" He pulled her into his arms, his heat soaking into her body.

271

She was thankful for the comfort. She thought she was safe on her parent's Esin's land. To know Emilia could've helped kidnap her at any moment. She shuddered.

"She must have called him as we were leaving the library." He cursed and gripped her tighter.

"Oh God, I have to warn my mother, she'll be at the Esin with her."

"Calm yourself, *ife*." He kissed her temple. "I'll take care of everything."

She nodded, trusting him. She looked back at her mother and Cassie, fear stealing her good mood. Thinking of her attack had her thoughts on Isaiah.

"How is Isaiah?"

"X says he's recovering, they got to him in time." He kissed her forehead.

"My mother wants us to have an Esin ceremony, will it be safe?"

His brows furrowed as he thought it over. The light of his whorls flared and he gripped her tighter. "X will know something soon about this Emilia and we'll be able to have our ceremony."

She sighed. "God, I just want this to be over."

He kissed the top of her hair. "I too, love. In the meantime, try to put it out of your head."

That was easier said than done. He smiled at her incredulous look.

"Try, *ife*." He turned her body and pat her butt towards the living room.

She glared at him before complying.

Chapter 33

For the most part, Brianna had taken Fallon's advice. She'd tried really hard to put Darren and Emilia and the attack from her mind. She woke up this morning to find Sharine and her mother up, waiting for her. Fallon's mother was anxious for them to find a dress. The new moon was in a couple of days, so she understood the urgency. Their mating had to be completed by midnight of the new moon, and Sharine was antsy about the lack of time she had to plan the reception.

Between her and Cassie, it had taken an hour for them to get up, showered and dressed. The four of them took a jeep into the local market. She was excited to see more of Chuita. Her eyes absorbed everything as she looked out the window. Everything was lush, a vibrant green as they drove through the winding dirt roads of the realm. Trees towered over their jeep and formed a canopy that should've made their route dark, but sunlight pushed through the flora, giving everything a bright and cheerful glow. She caught a glimpse of a river winding through the thick vegetation adding to the moisture that thickened the air.

She squinted for a fleeting look at the stone mansions scattered high on the hills jutting from the forests. A cacophony of animal noises raised as they crossed over the river she'd seen earlier. She smiled, the place was beautiful, exotic. They'd passed jeeps identical to theirs as they drove, and she fought not to gape at the riders for a further glimpse of Chuita's residents.

273

The trip didn't take more than twenty minutes. The jeep left the narrow jungle roads and soon rode on a tightly packed clay road that turned to cobblestones, rocking their vehicle as they neared the market. Sharine passed the keys to a valet person who stood at a stone arch that was the entrance to the outdoor market. The valet spoke, but his voice was lost in the rush of sounds surrounding Brianna.

The clamor of voices and sensations flowed around Brianna, Cassie, Deidre, and Sharine as they entered the marketplace grounds. Numbers, foreign-sounding languages and grunts signaled business was in full swing all around them. A silk-like canopy floated above the grounds acting as a prism, casting light of all shades and hues over the market. Vendors not actively haggling a sale were calling out to passersby showing textiles, trinkets, foods, and fresh produce. Those participating in the back and forth of haggling were almost dancing with activity, lowering hands to decrease a price, waving away counteroffers, and working toward a reasonable middle ground.

The smells wafting in the air sent Brianna's senses into overdrive from the most tantalizing perfumes to the most delicious smelling bread and fried meats. Sweet-smelling pastries and candies called to her, their temptation one she forced herself to resist. She had a dress to try on. The last thing she wanted to do was go into a dress shop with sticky fingers, and guilt over the empty calories. She shook her head to regain her senses as she started to follow Sharine through the labyrinth of vendors and shoppers. She smiled at the different people milling around, her mind formulating questions she'd ask Fallon later.

Vendors familiar with Sharine called her by name, requesting the honor of her presence before leaving the market. They had special wares saved just for her pleasure, they all claimed. Sharine's steps were fast as they moved through the throngs of shoppers, headed to see a woman about a dress. Most parted the way, though, staring as they passed. In her full Cagyn form, Sharine was a little over six feet tall and was certainly beautiful enough to command attention. Her hair was flowing behind her, gold bangles up and down her arms and a long skirt with a midriff-baring top. She looked sexy. Was it weird to think of one's mother-in-law as sexy?

Cassie wore a flower-patterned romper that showed off her long legs and her mother wore a sundress in a teal color that set off her brown skin. She herself wore a linen button-down shirt in denim color, tucked into a pencil skirt of a matching color. They made a striking picture, but still, she felt a little self-conscious. She'd started to change into jeans when she'd seen the way the skirt clung to her hips, but Fallon had come out of the bathroom still groggy, and his eyes had nearly left his skull. With that type of appreciation, she'd left the house feeling good.

At least until the stares. She tugged down on her skirt as their group garnered more stares. Men and women of different races followed her with their eyes taking in her curves as she walked through the plaza. None stepped forward or said anything and she could only assume her mother-in-law was the reason.

She must've spoken aloud because Sharine waved her hand in impatience. "You're exotic here. Revel in it, no one will disrespect you while you're with me."

She sighed.

"I know a tailor who will have your gown made in time." Sharine continued on, ambivalent to the attention they garnered.

She frowned. "If they use magic to make it, why wouldn't it be made on time?"

Sharine sighed. "It's an art, my dear. Overall, the dress will be conjured to our specifications, which will take a while. That is why we got such an early start."

She groaned and Sharine smiled. "Once the dress is conjured, each dressmaker likes to add handmade touches to make it uniquely theirs."

The bamboo matting under their feet turned to cobblestones as they entered what looked like a shopping center. Conversation paused as they passed.

275

"Ignore it. Your divine magic is like a halo around you all, of course you stand out."

"Is that what it is?" Deidre asked, her face equal parts nervous and excited.

Brianna was just relieved to know it wasn't just because they were human.

"There hasn't been any Divine in our realm in…" Sharine paused. "Goddess, centuries."

She gaped.

Sharine opened a glass door in front of them and she sighed in relief as cool air from the shop rushed over them. The shop owner smiled as they came in.

As they fully entered the shop, the owner waved her hand masking the windows from the outside to allow them privacy. The small parlor was welcoming, the front quaint, and similar to many boutiques Cassie had dragged her to over the years. A set of fine wicker seats surrounded a knee-high table with several books of fabric swatches and embroidery samples open for customers to peruse. The aroma of jasmine filled the room emanating from an incense holder sitting on the cabinet holding jewels and stones and laces of differing sizes and colors.

Behind the display case was a wall of images of the shopkeeper and past clients in an assortment of formal gowns for all imaginable occasions. Brianna's eye roamed the images in awe of the beautiful garments.

"Sharine! What a nice surprise." A slender woman, her hair in an intricate braid atop her head came from around the counter. She wore a flowy gown that moved around as she escorted them to a back room.

"I know it's last minute Kiara, but I need a gown for my daughter's reception."

Kiara turned and her sharp eye went over Brianna. "Which of your handsome sons has finally met their mate?"

"Fallon," Sharine said proudly.

Kiara indicated she stand on a short dais in front of three mirrors. To say she was self-conscious was an understatement.

"Well, she's certainly beautiful. I have the perfect idea to flatter those curves."

Brianna released the breath she was holding, shocked the woman didn't have something despairing to say about her size.

"Shall we get started then?" Sharine asked, sitting in a high, white, winged-back chair behind her.

Her mother and Cassie settled in a small divan next to her, their faces excited.

The woman stood still for a moment muttering, and before long a garment appeared on her. She gasped. Again, she was surprised. She'd expected the woman to swath her in fabric. Instead, she wore a mermaid gown that fit her like a second skin. It tucked in her waist and made her look voluptuous. The top was scooped, and off the shoulder, the sleeves three-quarters lace. She felt beautiful. She swallowed the lump in her throat.

Using magic, the woman made changes here and there, adding crystals, then sapphires, which Sharine promptly downvoted. After nearly an hour of back and forth between the five of them, they had a gown that she loved. The tailor promised to deliver it after final touches. They left and Sharine linked their arms together as they went back the way they'd come through the open-air market.

"I think shopping is in order," Sharine announced.

They walked to a stall she could smell from at least fifty feet away. She took a deep breath as entered his brightly colored tent. There were bottles of different sizes, shapes, and colors. She could spend hours in there. She smelled and fell in love with a few. Getting help from the shopkeeper,

277

she picked up the oil he suggested was best for hair. She bought gifts for her mother and Cassie despite their protests and when she went to pay, the shopkeeper waved her away.

"The Tegans have an account here, Mistress." He said with a smile, boxing up her purchases.

"Yes, but that won't stop me from negotiating the price," Sharine announced as she placed her own purchases on the counter.

She wanted to argue that she'd pay for her own things, but, one: she didn't have whatever currency they used, and two: Sharine had started negotiating in earnest. She couldn't get a word in edgewise. Both Sharine and the shopkeeper were smiling by the time they were done, so she assumed it went well. She opened her mouth to protest Sharine buying her things, but Sharine held up a hand.

"Don't bother arguing. We have centuries of wealth, and besides, let Fallon spoil you a bit."

"Still, thank you." She held up her bags.

They spent another hour window shopping. She'd expected to get bored, but spending the day with her mother was something she didn't think she'd get to experience again. She linked her arms with Deidre and rested her head on her shoulder as they watched, giggling at Sharine haggling with a baker. Her soon to be mother-in-law turned and beamed at them, victorious in her purchase.

"I messaged my son. I'm sure he's awake by now. He's going to meet us at the restaurant for lunch."

They walked further through the market and passed a white stone archway. On the other side, the streets were once again cobblestone, and whitewashed buildings lined the walkway. She was fascinated by it all. Sharine guided her into an arched doorway, and she breathed a sigh of relief at the cool air. The interior was bright, the walls a beautiful clay color.

Brightly colored tapestries hung from the ceiling, matching the fabric of the heavily cushioned chairs at each table. They were escorted to a table and she sank gratefully into the upholstered chair. They'd walked a lot today, and she was tired.

She was looking through the menu when she felt Fallon enter the restaurant. If asked, she would never be able to say how she knew, but she just did. It was as though her whole being amped up, energy flooding her body. Her skin came alive, sensitive to even the small breeze from the restaurant's air conditioning.

She looked up from her menu and spotted him at the door and her body went into nuclear meltdown mode. He was in Cagyn form and she was quite…excited about it. He'd stayed in his base form since he'd changed yesterday, and she swore every hour he got hotter. His black hair was loose around his face and fell to his shoulders. He wore a linen shirt that was open mid-chest and a pair of pants that were blue and reached only to his calf. They were wide-legged, loose, but somehow still managed to make his body look powerful.

The men all over the market wore the same type of clothes to a varying degree, but no one filled it out quite as he did. His ebony colored skin glowed, the copper lines pulsing as he saw her. Her breath caught and her mouth dropped open. How could he be so gorgeous? He walked through the crowded restaurant taking up more space than anyone there.

When he reached their table, he leaned down over her.

"Mate." He growled and hovered over her mouth a moment before she closed the distance.

The kiss they shared was more than likely not polite in the fancy setting, but she found she didn't care. She let her hands play in his hair and he broke the kiss, nuzzling into her neck.

"I never realized having my mate play in my hair would be such a sensual thing." He whispered in her ear.

279

She squirmed in her seat as moisture gathered between her thighs. Really, it was inconvenient how turned on he made her. At least in public. His scent surrounded her, and she wanted to rub her body along his like a cat begging to be petted.

"Good Lord," Cassie muttered.

Sharine cleared her throat. "Enough you two. Fallon, shame on you for enticing your mate with your base form in public."

Fallon smiled at his mother and sat down next to Brianna. He pulled her chair closer and put his arm around the back of it. "I don't know what I was thinking so close to the new moon." His face showed no remorse. He grabbed her hand and brought it up to his lips. "Did you find a dress, *ife*?

She nodded. "It's beautiful." She whispered, her mouth dry.

He leaned over and kissed her right under her ear. "How long do I have to let you stay in it before we—"

She cut him off before his words set her closer to flame. "Fallon, our mothers are at this table."

"A very public table, I might add." Deidre admonished, not taking her eyes off the menu.

"The two of you are likely to catch this whole place on fire if you keep it up." Sharine snickered.

"Seriously," Cassie chimed in. "It's obscene and I'm very jealous."

"*Iya,* " Fallon growled.

Brianna saw the mischief dancing in Sharine and Cassie's eyes and laughed. Fallon nipped her ear.

"Don't encourage them." He sat back in his chair, a mock pout on his face.

She laughed louder and covered her mouth when gazes turned to their table. "Behave. Do I need to move to the other side of the table?"

He snorted. "You'll need to move to the other side of this realm if you expect me to keep my hands off you."

"Well, damn." Cassie used her menu to fan her face.

His mate's lids dropped and she took a shuddering breath. Heat radiated from her body, and the scent of her arousal rose. His mother was right. It was not a good idea letting his beast out with the bonding period nearly over. Until they secured their bond, the frenzy would get worse, hotter, almost making it impossible for the couple to be apart. He'd spent the time they'd been away shopping, running in the jungle to give his beast a release. It hadn't helped. He'd come from his run wilder than ever and aching to reach his mate. He'd promised his mother that he'd meet them for lunch after their shopping and he was regretting it. He wanted Brianna alone, and on top of him, riding him so he could watch her face as she took every inch of him.

Brianna joined their hands together and picked up her menu with the other hand. He watched as she bit her lip considering the options. Her hair was braided, but tiny springy curls framed her face, some sticking to her neck he was sure from the heat outside. He looked down at the small bags she'd put on the floor next to her seat. He'd expected to see more bags.

"Did you enjoy shopping, *ife*?"

She frowned her nose. "Not normally, but I enjoyed myself today. Watching your mother haggle and throw her weight around was amusing."

Sharine huffed. "I do not throw my weight around. It's part of the song and dance, dear."

The women talked over their excursion and he tuned them out, unable to keep from touching Brianna. His mother flagged down the waiter and he growled when the male turned his attention to his mate.

Brianna rubbed her hand down his arm. "Excuse you," she chided him.

He should probably feel some contrition, but he wanted the male gone from his mate's side. His fierce frown had the waiter backing up. Sharine ordered for them all, and then in the ancient language asked that a female waiter be sent to take care of them.

"Their *di êjê* is in a couple of days," she said in English.

The male's face cleared. "Oh, of course. We'll stay out of the way then."

Brianna turned to him. "What does that mean?"

"The closer to the *di êjê*, the more…possessive we'll be."

She snorted. "I'm not a Neanderthal, so I don't foresee that being an issue with me."

He growled and his magic flared, his pheromones encapsulating his mate. She leaned towards him. "No fair, Fallon." She murmured, bringing his head down for a kiss.

"I can't help it." He said when they parted. "Your defiance is a heady thing, but it brings out my natural instincts to subdue my prey."

"I'm prey?" She gripped his chin.

"In that, I would love to chase you down and fuck you? Yes." He leaned over and whispered in her ear.

Her breath shuddered, and her lids lowered. "Behave."

"It would help me behave if you were a little more submissive," he purred, raking his teeth down her neck.

She hissed. "There is no way we're making it through this lunch," she whispered.

He growled and backed up, standing. "*Iya.*"

Sharine waved them off. "Go. I'll have lunch sent to you and the three of us will sightsee, and visit friends."

Brianna leaned down and kissed her mother and best friend goodbye. She grabbed his hand and he pulled her close to his side.

He rushed his mate from the restaurant, grabbing his keys from the valet. They didn't quite make it to their house. He pulled over and dragged her across the seat. She straddled his legs, and he was so happy he'd worn the traditional pants. There was a button in the crotch that freed his erection. He ripped her panties and was inside her within seconds.

She threw her head back and moaned, leaving the column of her neck open. He ached to bite her. As her heat enveloped his cock, he didn't even trust himself to kiss her there. She whispered his name as she flexed around him, and he didn't think he'd last. She opened her eyes and they widened. He knew his teeth had descended.

She reached over and touched them, her face fascinated. "Is this you, out of control?"

He shook his head. "I have enough control left to keep myself from finishing our bond and dragging you off to myself until I get my fill."

He lifted his hips, hitting a spot deep within her.

"Yes," she hissed. "Right there." She leaned over and licked at his lips.

He opened his mouth and let her in. Their kiss was as frantic as his strokes had become. Her walls fluttered, her breath hitched.

"Almost there," she panted.

"Come for me, *ife.*" He scraped his nails down her back and that did it. She leaned over his neck and bit him right below his ear. He exploded, his magic blinding him.

"I love you," she moaned.

283

It stopped his heart.

"*Ife*." He whispered. "I love you more than anything."

He brought her head to him sealing their lips together. He didn't taste blood, so she didn't break the skin. He told himself to be patient that he would have her bond in a few days' time, but he was still a little disappointed.

She looked around, as though waking from her trance. "Did we really just have sex in the bushes?"

He snickered. "We are in a transport vehicle, madam. We have some class."

She burst out in a fit of giggles. "Do we though?"

She shifted, he was still inside her and damn if he didn't get hard again. Her eyes widened. "You cannot possibly."

"*Ife*, this near to our *di êjê*, we're likely to be fucking every ten minutes." He warned.

Goosebumps raised on her arms, and her magic sparkled around her. It was beautiful to see. He didn't think she realized how much magic she had. It certainly increased each day they were together.

She lifted her hips and slid back down at a leisurely pace. "We should probably go home for round two?"

He gripped her hips and lifted his own. "You think so?"

It was a rhetorical question, there was no way he was stopping anytime soon. With their initial frenzy over, he retracted his teeth, able to control himself a little more.

"Maybe round three." Her husky voice washed over him.

"Yes, definitely round three because I need to have you naked underneath me. I also need to taste you." He reached down and plucked at her clitoris.

She moaned. "Oh, God. We can save that for round four."

"Round four? You're going to wear me out."

"You can recover your strength while you eat me out."

Goddess, that was…he lifted his hips, his pace increasing as her words lit him on fire. She came, gripping him tightly, dragging him into another orgasm. Their harsh breathing echoed around the transport vehicle. Driving was out of the question, as his body was as pliable as wet clay. He pulled out the navigation system and hit the button for home. The vehicle started, and they started moving.

She squealed and looked around. "What is happening?"

He nibbled her neck. "We're going home." He said lazily.

"You're not, who's driving?"

"They're self-driving." He closed his eyes and rested his head back on the headrest. He didn't bother trying to pull out of his mate's body, not when his body was still craving her as though he hadn't just had her.

"What?" She got that curious look on her face he was coming to know.

He kissed her lips to hopefully stall the million and one questions she would ask. She gave him a drowsy smile. "I'm too sated to answer a hundred engineering questions, *mi okan.*"

She huffed out a breath. "Fine," she pouted.

He kissed the pout from her lips and she settled her head on his shoulder.

"Shower before round three," she said around a yawn.

He rubbed her back, content, a foreign feeling for him. One he only got when he was with this mate. He liked it…a lot.

An hour later they lay in bed, her body sore in the best way. She traced the whorls on his arms. "I love these. Every Cagyn has them?

He nodded, his eyes closed as he lay back on the headboard.

"And the light?"

He chuckled. "Yes, my love."

"What causes the light?" She persisted.

"We call them power lines. They cover our skin, carrying our magic throughout our bodies in a fluid manner, allowing us to transform."

"Very interesting." She intertwined her fingers in his and raised his arm. She traced the tattooed band around his wrist. "And this?"

His eyes opened, and he speared her with a heated look. "It's a mating mark. Shows everyone that we're mated."

She returned her gaze to his wrist, knowing if she stared at him any longer, she'd be in trouble. She used her finger to go over the writing on the inside of the band. "What's this say?"

He hummed and rolled over to nuzzle into her neck. "It's Sanskrit, it has my name and my family name."

"And this underneath?" He showed no frustration at her incessant questions which she totally marked in his favor.

"Yours."

She smiled, loving the thought of that. Did it make her a tiny bit possessive, yes, yes it did. "Will I get one?"

"Humans are different, so I'm not sure. I hope so if not, I'll have to mark you in other ways." He growled and nipped her neck.

Heat moved through her body, it coming alive despite the fact that they'd spent the entire afternoon going at it like bunnies. As though he knew her body's reaction, his erection bumped into her hip.

"You're feeding me before you get any more sex." She grumbled, probably meaning it.

Chapter 34

Brianna sat on water's edge, her fingers playing in the black sand. The damp air pressed against her skin and should've felt stifling, but a breeze drifted in off the water and she sighed in pleasure. It was beautiful here, and she felt at home. It was a foreign feeling for her. Not that she hadn't made Atlanta her home, but this felt right. It had been two days since her trip to the market, and they were filled with Sharine and her planning the reception. Tonight was the new moon and the night of her *di êjê*.

She was nervous, and yet, calmer than she thought she'd be.

"Tsk, tsk, Brianna. All my lessons and you're sitting here with your power floating around you all untamed and chaotic."

She whipped her up her head and squinted at the tall male standing next to her. He was a Kira, that much she recognized. She sighed.

"Someone else I've forgotten." She grumbled.

"May I sit?" His voice was deep, amusement threaded throughout it.

She looked around wondering why he was on the private beach and how he'd gotten there.

"Don't worry, your guards let me pass." He reassured.

"Guards." She muttered under her breath. She should've known Fallon would have people watching her. She waved next to her for him to sit. "You're a Kira."

"I am. And you're Brianna, a human. This place agrees with you." He commented.

"I was just making that observation myself. What makes you say that, strange Kira?"

He laughed. "I'm sorry, I'm Tahir, a friend of Fallon's, and even a friend to you."

She clasped his extended hand. "It's nice to meet a friend of mine, Tahir. Back to my question."

He smiled and she was struck by how handsome he was. "Your magic is sparkling around you."

She frowned. "I used to be so skeptical of the idea of magic, and you're like, the second or third person who's said something to me about it."

"As a Kokoro soul, you have more magic than most. It was one of the reasons I agreed to help you learn to use it."

She was surprised. From what she read, the Kira were selective with whom they passed along their wisdom. "Really?"

"Fallon and I are as close as brothers. I traveled with him for a while, the two of us learning new magic. When he asked me to help you, I was honored."

"Did I know?"

"About?"

She sighed and traced the sand around her. "He asked you for what I'm assuming is a big favor. Did I know he'd done that for me?" She studied Tahir's face, waiting for the answer.

289

"I don't have an answer for that. It wouldn't surprise me if you didn't know. Fallon isn't the type to brag. He usually does what he does in the background, making life easier for those around him."

"I'm finding that out about him." She murmured, resting her chin onto her raised knees.

An easy silence fell between them. He was a serene person. Tranquil as they sat, unhurried in his manner. She observed him, her curious gaze cataloging all the differences between him and Fallon.

"What do the rings on your shoulders mean? I've seen them on all the healers I've come across."

His teeth were straight and white as he smiled. "I was wondering how long it would take you to ask questions."

She rolled her eyes, clearly, he knew her well. "Are you going to answer?"

"We are of the forests that cover the peaceful valleys of Edin. Much like the trees that inhabit the forest, our rings denote our age and ranking."

She spun in the sand to face him. "So like if I count them, I'd know your age?"

"I don't know that it's quite that simple. But to another Kira, it's easy to discern."

"So you're like, treefolk. That would explain your hair." She squinted. "And your stillness."

Tahir laughed, the joyous sound making her smile.

"Did you come for the *di êjê*?"

He smiled at her again. "I did. I was happy to hear Fallon would be completing the mating."

She opened her mouth to say something when a dark growl sounded behind them. It was completely different from Fallon's turned on growl. This sound, for a small moment, made her wary.

Tahir's brow raised and merriment danced in his eyes. "Uhoh. Your mate has found us."

Fallon stomped across the sand and grabbed her up, turning to put her behind him and keep her away from Tahir.

She slapped at his arm. "Watch how you handle me, jackass."

He growled and leaned down as if to kiss her. She put her hand over his face. "I don't think so. I don't respond to that type of stuff."

She just had to remind her body of that, because damn if her nipples weren't standing out begging to be touched. He reared back in surprise. Tahir started laughing and Fallon turned and snarled.

"Frenzy giving you a hard time, brother?"

Brianna extricated her body from his arms. "Tahir, I'm going up to make breakfast, would you like to join us?"

Tahir stood and brushed the sand from the long pants he wore. "Your mate has better manners than you, Fallon." Tahir slapped him on the back.

Fallon had said nothing in the whole time he'd come down, outside of his growls. She gathered her towel and blew out a raspberry when a long caftan appeared on her body. Tahir laughed louder and she shook her head.

"You're lucky I love you, you Neanderthal."

He walked up to her and wrapped his arms around her from behind. His pheromones were working overtime, and his scent enveloped her. "It's the frenzy, I'm not normally this possessive, I promise." His voice was deep, the timbre drawing her body in a maelstrom of heat.

291

"Don't think you can come sweet talk your way into me excusing your behavior." She warned him, even as she was falling for his sweet-talking.

"I'm sorry, *ife*. You don't show me enough submission as far as I am concerned."

She snorted. "If that's what you're looking for in a mate, you're fucked."

"I want only you."

"Then act like you have some sense." She scolded and sauntered off.

He watched her walk. Despite the caftan, her ass swayed in a way that made him want to take her down into the sand. Tahir walked up on him. "You got it bad."

Fallon grunted.

"For what it's worth, I like her."

"Of course you would, she calls me on my shit more than you." He grumbled.

"You need it more than most. Are you ready for tonight?"

He growled, he was more than ready. It had taken everything in him not to attack his best friend when he'd come down on the beach and saw him sitting next to his mate. Knowing he would be bonded to her in a few hours' time had him anxious, jumpy even. He couldn't wait.

The house was full by the time he and Tahir made it to the top of the stairs. He opened the sliding door and the smell of cooked food greeted them, along with the sounds of his brothers. He smiled when he heard Kell's gurgling.

"Full house," Tahir commented.

He sighed. He'd hoped to have a few hours of his mate to himself before the family descended. As it was, he'd spent the last two days on his best behavior since her mother and Cassie had been staying with them. That was the reason he'd been so irritated when he'd come upon his best friend talking to his mate.

Yeah, that was the reason.

Breakfast was a noisy affair, and he had fun. He liked how Brianna fit in. Everyone was getting along and that was really all he could've asked for.

Hours later he was on the balcony outside of their bedroom, looking down on the beach. It was close to midnight, and he was anticipating joining with his mate. His father knocked on the glass before sliding the doors open and joining him outside. Randolph had arrived with Henry right as they were done with breakfast. Brianna had been sequestered with the women soon after their fathers had arrived. He knew there was a whole host of things she had to do prior to the ceremony, but he missed her.

"Cutting it close." His father commented.

Fallon swallowed his sigh. "I know."

"She's powerful, your mate, I hadn't realized that." Ranolph leaned on the guard rail next to him.

"Does that change things for you?" Not as though he needed the answer. He knew his father well enough to know what the answer was.

Ranolph shrugged. "I'd be lying if I said it didn't. But don't worry, I won't use your mate for my own ambitions." The bitterness in his father's tone told him Ranolph was regurgitating an argument he'd had with Leo.

He snorted. "As if you could."

He wasn't worried about his father using Brianna in any way without her consent. He smiled and relaxed as he thought about it. His mate was strong and strong-willed. He wouldn't have to worry about his parents

293

running over her. There would be no mediating between them. Brianna handled problems herself.

Gods, that was a huge weight off his shoulders. He wanted to laugh.

"The *di êjê* is special, enjoy it." His father cleared his throat. "I'll give you the same advice I gave Leonalph. Treat your mate well."

Fallon nodded and planned to take that advice to heart. He loved Brianna and had no plans to mistreat his mate.

His brothers crowded onto the balcony.

"It's time, Fallon." Leo passed a heavily embroidered robe to him.

Xavier nodded at him and clasped his shoulder. He stared at the garment in his brother's hand for a moment, burning the sight and occasion into his memory. He wanted, centuries from now to remember the feelings from his *di êjê*. He grabbed it and headed for the bathroom to start his preparations. When he came out, Tahir was the only one waiting in the room for him. He was sitting in the middle of the floor with his legs crossed. He sat in front of him, adjusting his robe.

"You're making the right decision." Tahir smiled.

The nerves gathering in his chest settled. "I know."

Tahir nodded. "Close your eyes, let me give you a quick sweep."

Grateful, he did as he was bid. He breathed deep, trying to calm his rioting body. Wind from Tahir's hands brushed his face and he sighed. Tahir touched his shoulder to let him know he was done. He opened his eyes to find his best friend with his hand out to help him up.

"You went under quicker than normal, Brianna is good for you."

He smiled and grabbed his hand. "I'm lucky to have her."

Tahir walked him out. He passed his family in the living room, waving as he passed and walked towards the back of the house and the wooden stairs that would lead him to the beach. His steps were lighter, his beast anxious, yet not pushing against his body. He traversed the weather-worn wood, all thoughts on the upcoming ceremony.

He reached the bottom and waited on Brianna. She was just a few minutes behind him. He watched her as she came down the steps, his heart full. She wore a dainty robe, one that the wind pushed against her skin, outlining her curves. His mouth watered, and his hands shook. He clasped them together in front of him. Her hair was in a big curly afro, with tiny copper lights twinkling throughout. She wore a veil, one he remembered hearing Cassie insist on. It was held by a diamond comb. She was breathtaking.

Brianna stepped carefully down the wooden steps, sighing in relief when she reached the sand. There was a lit path that led right to the water. The lights cast a yellow glow across the sand. As she got closer, she saw that they were stones. Flower petals littered the path, their color pale and ghostly against the light of the stones.

She was painfully aware that there was nothing underneath her robe as she walked. She'd had her first shot of hard liquor. Afterward, Tahir had come into her room and swept her energy as he'd called it. Whatever he'd done, he'd left her calmer, and less apprehensive of the upcoming ceremony. The fact that there were only three of them on the beach was the only thing that kept her feet moving. That and knowing Fallon was on the bottom of the path. He met her there, and her breath caught.

He was so handsome with his hair blowing in the wind. The copper lights on his skin glimmered in the moonlit night. Sharine had found small pins that lit up the same color and they'd strewn them in her hair. She wanted to match him, even if in that small way. He smiled and reached his hand out to her. She took a deep breath and grabbed it.

They made their way to the shaman who was waist-deep in the sea. She took a deep breath as Fallon paused her at the shore.

He leaned his forehead down against hers. "Relax, *ife.*"

295

His scent rose and surrounded her and her body relaxed, melted, really. He dropped his robe, and she damn near swallowed her tongue.

"Your turn, mate." His voice was a whisper, anticipation in his eyes stealing her shyness.

She dropped the robe and he hissed out a breath. They stepped into the water and magic swelled. She felt it on her skin, in the way the hairs all over her body stood up. The wind picked up until they reached the shaman. She'd underestimated the shaman's height, the water settled just underneath her breasts. Fallon turned her to face him, and she looked into his face, seeing love and acceptance and her heart was full to bursting.

The shaman started chanting in a language she didn't understand. As he spoke, a golden cord appeared and wound its way around their clasped hands, then their body. Next, her forehead warmed and she saw the string wind around Fallon's head. There was a tight gold thread that tethered their hearts together and tears fell from her eyes. She didn't understand the shaman's words, but the sentiment was there, and Fallon's gaze never left hers.

Fallon felt the magic binding him, and the heat built as the threads around them spun faster. His teeth grew, his mate's gaze widened as he leaned over her neck.

"Trust me, *ife*?"

"Yes." She whispered and leaned her head to the side.

The submissive move was exactly right. He leaned down and bit into her neck. She hissed, but he didn't sense any pain from her. The first taste of her blood sent his magic into a tailspin, and his body was on fire. He pulled back and his mate gasped and leaned towards him. Her teeth were sharper, longer than before. He wasn't sure if the magic would work the same with her since she was a Divine. She could only reach his chest, he closed his eyes as her teeth sank into him, right over his pounding heart.

His body temperature skyrocketed and her magic inundated his body. The bond snapped into place, their hearts now pounding together in the same quick rhythm. He needed her...now. She pulled back, her eyes hooded, a drowsy, sated guise on her face. He kissed her, he couldn't stop even if he wanted to. He tasted his blood still on her tongue and the beast in him bucked for control. The shaman continued his chant around them, and the magic built until finally, his mate pulled back. She spoke in the ancient language, declared her love for him, and her soul's acceptance of his, and both he and the shaman were surprised. He gave her back her vow, sensing the magic in the words.

Her eyes cleared and confusion suffused her face for a small moment before she focused on him and smiled. The shaman closed the loop and the bindings on them disappeared. He pulled his mate to him, listening for the shaman to leave the water. Though, whether or not he made it until the shaman left was a toss-up. He needed inside of her or he would go insane.

He lifted her and her legs clasped around his hips. He entered her, never letting go of her mouth. She moaned and arched her back, welcoming him into her body. The magic charged him, let him see into her mind. Their bond was there, strong, and clear. Her lust, her love, was displayed, and it was a heady feeling. It took them no time to reach release, with the magic riding their body.

Brianna was breathing hard, her legs still wrapped around Fallon's waist. Her body was pliant and relaxed.

"Did you even wait for the priest to leave the water?" She said lazily.

Her mate, no her husband, drew lazy circles on her back and nibbled on her shoulder. "He knows what's up. But, for my mate's propriety, I waited."

He was still hard inside her and making no moves to leave the water. "Again, *ife*." He rasped.

She couldn't deny him. Not while her body craved him as it did. He walked them from the water and up onto the beach. He laid her in the sand

and leaned down, sucking a nipple into his mouth. He surged inside her and she arched her back to take him deeper. Their lovemaking was no less frantic than it had been in the water. Even as they both came, he kept a slow pace in and out of her body.

She ran her fingers through his hair, luxuriating in him. The sand should've been bothering her, but nothing could get past the haze she was in. Until she heard a whistle.

She stiffened. "What was that?"

He hummed and licked a path across her chest. "Probably one of my brothers telling me my time is up."

He teased her nipple, his teeth nipping it. She moaned, her body reacting as though she hadn't just had him a second ago.

"Is this the frenzy still?" She held his head in place as he sucked on her nipple.

He didn't answer at first, just plunged deeper into her. "Yes. It will be like this for a few more hours yet."

"We should definitely use that time wisely." She pulled his head up and kissed him.

There was another whistle.

He sighed and stopped moving his hips. "Remind me to apologize to Leo."

She laughed, though she did wiggle her hips to try and coax him into moving again. "For what?"

"One, I plan on punching the shit out of him when he gets down here, and two, I pretty much made a game of keeping him and Liliana at their reception longer than they wanted to be there. I have a feeling he will be exacting revenge."

A robe appeared on her body, a few seconds before she heard shuffling in the sand. She stuck her lip out in a pout.

"That's enough of that, brother. You have a reception to attend. And before you think about hitting me, remember, Karma comes a'calling." Leo stopped a few feet away from them.

Fallon growled and lifted off her. She sighed, missing his body heat. Fallon gave her a hand up and pulled her into his arms. She went there happily, pulling his head down for a kiss.

"Trust me, *ife*?" She whispered, giving him back his own words.

He worried his brothers would be able to keep him at their reception, but she had a plan.

He growled and lifted her. "With my life."

"Then don't worry about your brother. I'll have us in and out in less than an hour." She whispered in his ear.

"Deal." He sealed their lips together.

Leo cleared his throat. "Fallon, I have strict instructions from our mother to bring my sister to her immediately."

She smiled, his sister. She liked the idea of having a new family. Leo grabbed her arm and pulled her out of Fallon's arms. Fallon growled and she laughed.

"The sooner we go, the sooner we can leave, my love." She called over her shoulder as Leo marched her across the beach.

Chapter 35

The next morning Fallon was awakened by his mate's kisses. She'd started at his neck, and was now on the way down his stomach. Her magic was swirling around her, the color deeper. Their connection told him his wife was feeling lustful. It was way earlier than he wanted to be up, but with her tongue tracing the top of his pelvis, in no way was he complaining.

He thought back to their reception last night. She had been so beautiful. The gown she'd chosen made her brown skin glow. True to her word, she'd had them in and out of the reception. She'd smartly enlisted his mother to help her escape. Sharine had given them a distraction and allowed them to leave.

He closed his eyes when she dropped small kisses along the top of his pelvis. Just a few more inches and he'd be in heaven.

She leered up at him and smiled then ran her tongue from the head of his erection down to the base of the underside of his shaft. Planting kissing and blowing across the line of her tongue's path, his hard-on throbbed in response to her attention. She nibbled the base of his head and slid her hands along him, stroking more heat into his member. He watched, mesmerized by her care and pleasure in the moment.

Turning her eyes away from his face, she took him into her mouth. The connection between them broadcasted her enjoyment. His groaning pushed her on and she slid him further into her mouth. Her tongue worked the shaft, sucking on him, immersing him in sensations. Using the pressure of her mouth, she drove him closer to the brink. She reached down with one hand and ran her nails along the inside of his thigh. Squeezing him tightly with her other hand.

He threw his head back, sinking his hand into her hair, languishing in the sensation of her warm mouth. Her magic danced around her, his own reaching up to meld with hers. He shivered as it magnified his pleasure. Her nails raking across his stomach raised his beast, electrifying his body. His powerlines flared, his pheromones spilling from his skin. Brianna moaned, taking more of him into her mouth. He touched the back of her throat and damn near exploded.

He tensed, forcing back his orgasm to savor the feel of his mate's mouth. His muscles tensed, and he fought to keep still under her ministrations. She worked her lips and tongue more, twisting and turning on his shaft, he wouldn't last much longer. She looked up, her face smug, triumphant, she knew what she did to him. His hips jerked as she swallowed, pulling him further down her throat. He let out a deep guttural moan, pulling from her mouth before he exploded. She kissed her way back up to his mouth. He gripped the back of her head once she'd reached his chin, plundering his tongue into her mouth.

"I can feel you inside me," she whispered, pulling away and kissing his neck. "You're feeling some regret."

"Not for this," he turned his body to slide her underneath him. "For being a jackass and taking so long to claim you."

"Well, you finally got it right." She used her hand to guide him inside.

He stroked in and out of his wife in slow movements, taking his time. He would never tire of the feel of her wet heat surrounding him. She came, her pulsing walls dragging him behind her. He pulled out and cuddled into her side.

"How much time did your mother give us?" He kissed her shoulder. He loved the feel of her skin.

"We had last night, she's expecting us back this afternoon. The ceremony will be in the morning. But then, we can have a honeymoon."

301

"Any idea of where you want to go?" He inhaled right into the crook of her neck. Her scent was deeper there.

"How many realms are there again?" Her voice was breathy.

He smiled and turned over. "There are two realms where we won't go to, but the others will be fine. Am I going to spend my bonding period with you traveling and researching?" Not that he'd have a problem with it.

"There will be sex thrown in if that makes you feel better." She straddled him.

He laughed and hissed when she guided him back inside her.

"Gods woman," he whispered, lifting his hips and slamming back into her.

They made love again, the pace slow and lazy. He probed their connection, the closeness filling him with a deep sense of contentment.

He'd pulled her on top of him once they were both sated. He groaned when his communicator rang. He shuffled Brianna under the blanket and answered it. It was both mothers, sitting in what appeared to be Deidre's living room, smiling.

She ducked underneath the covers.

He laughed. "Ladies." He greeted.

"Good, you two are up." Deidre clapped her hands and pulled out a small notebook. "We have a few things to do this afternoon, Brianna, you should head here."

She peeked her head out from under the blanket. "Mom, I don't care what you guys plan, just tell me when to show up."

"Show up now. Luckily the dress Sharine had made will work for the ceremony, but we have last-minute things to do." Deidre didn't look as though saying no was an option.

She sighed and peered over at the dress she'd hastily discarded last night, or rather in the wee hours of the morning. She wanted more time with her new husband.

He nuzzled under her ear. "Bonding period after, *ife*. Just give them this."

She rolled her eyes. "Fine, we're getting dressed."

They took a shower, and headed to the portal station, dragging her wedding dress behind her. On the way there, she thought about the last time they were in the jeep alone. Her body heated, the memory playing through her head in a loop.

He growled. "Gods, I can feel everything, this is going to be dangerous."

She laughed and leaned over to kiss his neck. "Can't you put this thing on autopilot?"

He shook his head. "You are temptation itself, but I know if we start, we'll be at it for another hour."

She smiled and licked his neck. He turned and kissed her deeply. "Behave. We'll have time tonight."

"Fine," she pouted.

He parked the car on the street in front of the portal station and left the keys in the jeep. This time he took her through the main portal terminal and they stepped through the portal along with ten others.

The bright light had her blinking like crazy when they arrived. Soldiers in the area saluted as Fallon passed, some giving her a thumbs up.

She'd only been gone a few days, but coming back through as his mate made her feel different. She looked down at the tattoo that appeared on her wrist last night after their *di êjê* and smiled. She liked being his mate.

He took the dress from her and slung it over his shoulder, reaching down and grabbing her hand.

Their steps didn't slow as they left the portal room and entered the corridors. She held his hand, reveling in their connection. As they reached the main level, Fallon's father was coming through a door. He paused at the sight of them. Fallon stiffened, his wariness transferring down their link.

"Father."

"Fallon, Brianna, you two are back for the Divine ceremony?" "We

are." She answered.

He nodded. "It's good that they still practice the old traditions."

She gave him a polite smile.

"Fallon, if I can speak with you privately a moment."

She nodded her assent and moved away. Ranolph took his son a few feet away and she felt Fallon's anger, his disappointment, and frustration. She wondered what it was about. He came back, his jaw clenched. She grabbed his hand and thought of the advice Tahir had given her when he swept her before their ceremony. He'd told her Fallon would take on his family's problems as his own. He asked her to keep her mate from taking too much of their energy. She wished she could soothe him. As they walked silently down the hall she fumbled with her magic and used their connection to push reassuring energy down their connection.

He stopped her at the garage and turned to her, pulling her into his arms. "Thank you, *ife*."

"You could feel it?" She was surprised, pleased and proud of herself.

He kissed her and she lost the thread of magic she was using.

"Thank you, my love."

She nodded faintly. "What was that with your father about?"

"My father tells me to quit coming to Leo's rescue, but he wants me to intervene between the two of them."

"Why are they fighting? I noticed the looks exchanged between everyone last night." She'd been wrapped up in her mate, but she hadn't missed the tension.

Sharine and he hardly occupied the same space and kept shooting daggers at each other. She'd made an agreement with Sharine so she and Fallon could leave their reception once they'd danced. Sharine had promised a distraction, and boy had she delivered. She'd shuffled Fallon out of the room right as Sharine marched over to her mate.

"My father got hold of a prophecy about a powerful Eshu king bringing the Demi together again to prevent Ofeeree from escaping." He nodded to the guard at the garage

He walked over to a wall and put in a code on the panel. It slid open and revealed a bunch of hanging keys she assumed belonged to the cars in the garage. They walked over to a sleek muscle machine and he opened her door. He walked around the other side. She leaned her elbow on the middle dash, waiting on him to finish the story.

He started talking as he cranked the car. "Well, his best friend is the current king of the Eshu. He and his mate were having issues conceiving. My father thought he and King Leander could bring the prophecy to life. He convinced my mother to sleep with the king and bear the heir."

She gasped and understood all the tension underlying Sharine's words.

"She wasn't aware of a prophecy. She was told that if the queen had a son she wouldn't have to give up Leo. Well, they did, but my father, unable to get over the fact that his mate slept with his best friend, turned Leo from our mother. They fought constantly, and my father made it all

305

seem my mother's fault." He pulled out into the afternoon traffic. "So, Leo is pissed that dad kept him from *Iya*, all in the name of ambition."

"Oh my God, you poor guys. How old were you?"

"Me?" He looked surprised at her question. "Well, you

and Xavier were obviously affected."

He shrugged.

"Hmm, I'm starting to suspect why you ran the world in search of magic. You had to feel pretty powerless in that situation."

He gripped the steering wheel, shocked by her insight.

"So now Leo and your father aren't speaking?"

"He and Baba were very close, he took it very hard." He shook his head.

"You've been mediating the family your whole life, huh?"

He sighed and looked ahead, afraid to let his mate see his face. "I'm so tired of it, *ife*."

"Don't worry, I got your back." She ran a hand down his arm.

Her love surrounded him and he shuddered as his body relaxed. At a red light, he leaned over and kissed her. She cupped his cheek.

"I love you," he whispered and she smiled, a beautiful smile that made him wish they were home. Someone honked the horn behind them. They drove on.

Chapter 36

Brianna waited until they arrived at the front gate before she called her mother. Deirdre directed them to meet her at the temple instead of their house. He got out of the car and stared at the statue of Rugaba that seemed to guard the stone building. He walked over to the passenger side and let Brianna out, glad she'd waited on him. It appeased the beast in him. For some reason, he'd been riled since they arrived at the Esin. He looked around as she got out, unable to quell the uneasy feeling.

Xavier had told him Emilia couldn't be found and that made him nervous. He surveyed the temple, letting his beast off of the leash a bit to heighten his senses. He gripped Brianna's hand, guiding her up the granite stairs leading into the temple. They entered through oversized carved double doors. Inside was unnaturally cool, temperature-wise, like stepping into a cave. Hand-carved stone columns lined the entire temple, from the back to the front.

There were no chairs, only padded kneeling mats shining in the morning light that streamed in through large openings along the wall. There weren't windows or glass, nothing blocking the breeze that perpetually flowed through the gods' temples. The sunlight glinted off the gilded ceilings, the artwork flowing across the ceiling, depicting what he assumed were images of their history.

Their footsteps echoed throughout the temple as they walked to the front where her mother awaited them. Deidre waited for them at the stone altar where ashes from previous offerings stained the marble. Behind the altar was a mahogany shelf shaped into open hands, adorned with rows upon rows of flowers, fruit, and other offerings to Rugaba.

Brianna stopped at the altar and pushed her hands together, bowing her head. "*Opeyemi.*" Her quiet murmur carried in the empty temple.

Deidre smiled and hugged her daughter. "You remember your proper greeting."

Brianna grimaced, lowering her gaze in chagrin. "I don't even remember what it means."

"It roughly translates to 'I give praise'. I'm very happy you remembered and gave respect to Rugaba as you stand at his altar." Deidre rubbed her daughter's back.

Fallon smiled at her abashed face and grabbed a candle from a gold coffer on the right of the altar. He lit it using the candelabra next to it, offering it up to the effigy of Rugaba looming large behind his gifts. He placed it on the altar. The solid ebony version of the god, stood over eight feet tall atop his pedestal. The statue's sharp chiseled features matched Rugaba's likeness, the stern look one he'd seen on the god more than once.

He said a small prayer of thanks for the blessing of his *di êjê* and the safety of his mate while looking into the statue's golden reflective eyes. A shiver of foreboding went down his spine as he finished. He frowned and walked back to Brianna's side, gripping her hand tightly. Worry for her overcame him in a rush and he looked around for hidden danger. He reached into his pocket, his finger caressing the grooves of Azra's coin, in a nervous gesture.

Deidre hugged him as she finished lighting her own candle. "Sharine is somewhere near speaking with the shaman. I want to show you guys the spot we picked outside. It's really beautiful, especially as the sun is rising. Fallon, once we're done with that, Henry will come and get you. You have to be the one to harvest your offering for tomorrow."

Said as they were ushered from the back of the temple, Fallon could only nod as a premonition rocked him. He paused, closing his eyes tight as images of him locked in chains flashed across his mind. He cursed, wishing he could send an offering to Azra for clarity of the vision. He didn't dare do it near Rugaba's temple. Not only would it have been disrespectful, but the Divine were wary of other gods. He didn't imagine Deidre would approve of him praying to a hell god. As a trickster god, Azra didn't have many followers who trusted him.

Brianna turned and lowered her eyebrows. "Everything okay?"

"I'm a little uneasy." Lying to her didn't occur to him. He didn't want to downplay his intuition, not when it could mean the difference between him and his mate being hurt.

"Is it being at the temple, in the Esin, what can I do?" She touched his shoulder.

He shook his head. "I'm not sure. Just stay close to me, please."

He expected an argument, but she simply nodded and tugged his hand to follow her mother. He took his hand out of hers for a moment to send over a message to Haven. He would feel better with a few guards keeping watch over Brianna. He messaged Michel directly and closed his communicator. Hopefully, it wouldn't take the guards long to arrive. Deidre walked them outside and he had to admit it was a beautiful garden.

A rainbow of flowers flanked the stone walkway and went on for at least another two acres. Fragrances from the blossoms competed in the air, reminiscent of the perfumery his mother loved at the Cagyn market. The shift in temperature from the coolness of the temple to the warm breeze of the garden helped Fallon center his swirling thoughts. Following Deidre out into the sun, he held Brianna's hand anticipating the reply from his request sent to Haven.

309

Deidre gave a contented sigh. "This garden didn't look like this until your father got his hands on it. You should see the farm."

Pride shown in Brianna's eyes as she spun to look at it all.

"Bri, you'll pick your offering from this garden. You have to do it yourself, it's tradition."

Brianna rolled her eyes. But she was pleased and excited. It radiated down their connection. He gathered from his interactions with Brianna, she appreciated traditions. Her parents' happiness was also something his mate took seriously. Deidre was brimming with that happiness. Her magic sparkling around her as her hand grazed some of the flowers, their petals seeming to glow in the wake of her touch.

"Is there a restroom near here, mom?" Brianna looked around.

"There's a meeting area for the shaman. You can enter from the side of the temple." Deidre said, pointing around the building.

Nervousness churned in his gut, his magic pulsing. He turned to walk with her and she frowned.

"I can use the restroom myself, love." She tiptoed and kissed him.

"I'm nervous, *ife*, I'd rather go with you."

She studied his face and nodded after a moment. "Fine."

"Thank you."

They walked around to the side of the temple, and tucked into the stone was a small door. They opened it and inside was a meeting area. There was a large stone table with a gold bowl filled with water in the middle. Benches were on either side of the table with a large area rug underneath. There was another door, which he assumed was the bathroom. Brianna gave him a thumbs up after she opened the door and found a light switch. She shut the door and it wasn't until after it closed that he considered going in and making sure the room was clear.

He cursed and knocked on the door. She opened it with a raised brow. "Yes?"

"I should've looked in before you went in." He said sheepish, embarrassed at his mistake.

She sighed and stepped aside. He raised his eyes at the lavish restroom. There were three stalls, all empty as he pushed the doors open. There were no cabinets beneath the vanity, only the three glass vessels under golden faucets on top.

He kissed his mate on the forehead. "All clear."

She snorted and went back in, closing the door. After about ten minutes when she didn't emerge his gut started churning. He looked around the room. There were no additional doors, nowhere else anyone could be hiding, and yet, he was restless. He knocked on the bathroom door expecting Brianna to come out with an aggravated scowl and a few choice words about him rushing her. When that didn't happen, he pushed it open. The bathroom was empty. He checked the stalls, his heart hammering.

She wasn't there.

He rushed from the meeting room, and back around to the garden calling her name. Deidre frowned and met him halfway.

"What's happened?"

"Brianna disappeared from the bathroom."

Deidre dropped a hand to her stomach in shock. "What do you mean disappeared?"

Her eyes frantically scanned the grounds. She turned and rushed towards the meeting area from where he'd just come. She pushed through the door screaming her daughter's name. She turned a panicked circle.

"Not again, Fallon. I can't lose her again." She gripped his arm tight, tears gathering.

"Go alert what passes for security here. I'll keep looking."

311

She nodded and raced out the door. He went back into the bathroom and looked around. This time he was searching for anything that could be a door in disguise. He stopped in front of painting on a canvas that stretched from the ceiling to the floor. He lifted it and saw the seam in the wall.

"Bingo." He whispered, taking the painting down.

It took him another five minutes of searching before he pushed the wall and heard a small snick. Cool air rushed into the room as he opened the door away from him. He turned on light from his communicator and shone it into the dark corridor. He stepped around the door and felt a prick on his arm. He looked down and saw the needle. He growled and reached for it, but his vision swam, his hand missing the needle sticking out from his arm. He reached again and missed, his breath getting choppy. His vision went dim as he took one more swipe at it.

***

Gray walls swam in and out of Brianna's vision as she cracked open her eyelids. She closed them tighter and breathed through the nausea roiling in her stomach. This was much different than the last time she'd awoken in a place she didn't remember. There were no warm eyes from Fallon, and no Kira to take away the pain of her pounding headache. She pried her lids open again, and this time the room steadied. A sliver of panic sped her breathing as a sense of familiarity hit her. Her body temperature dropped as the cold of the concrete seeped through her thin dress. She rolled over, holding her head. It was pounding, a knot forming on the back. She pressed on it gently, wondering how she got it.

In the darkness, she examined the simple stone walls surrounding her. The air was dank and stale in the room. Light crept in through the base of the door, far to the left of her. Beyond the silence pressing in on her, the sound of her pants bounced around the walls. She stilled her breathing as she peered into the corner of the room, seeing a dark bulky shape. She held her breath, and the quiet sound of labored breathing reached her.

She lay on her side, as sitting up was harder than she'd anticipated. She finally worked herself into a sitting position when she realized the shape she'd seen in the corner was Fallon. He lay a few feet from her, his body still. She slid over to him, not even attempting to stand. She was breathing hard by the time she reached him, from both panic and exertion. He hadn't moved in the time it had taken her to scoot over him. His body wasn't stiff, and she was very grateful for that. She touched his arm, reaching for her connection to him. Though new, there was no hesitation in the magic that bonded them together. She breathed a sigh of relief when she felt him there.

"Thank God," She whispered. She rested her head on his chest, happy to hear the rhythm of his heart against her ear. "I need you to wake up, baby, so we can get out of here."

She kept the pitch of her voice low, unsure who was listening.

When he didn't move, she forced herself up and shook out the cobwebs clouding her mind. She was able to stand after much effort, and the room swayed as she stood tall. Her memory of being there slammed into her mind and she gasped.

She had been held here, somewhere in this very room.

She remembered it.

She narrowed her eyes and wobbled over to the wall to brace herself. The stone was cold against her hand and a memory flickered. Her stomach tried to rebel, but she refused to throw up, especially since she didn't know how long she would be stuck in this room with her own vomit. She moved her hands against the wall and found the iron hook where she'd been manacled the last time. Her breath started coming out fast, a panic attack barreling down on her. She hugged against the wall as tears built.

She needed to get a hold of her panic.

"Brianna."

Her name whispered, her mate's voice pulled her back a little. She turned and laid her back against the wall, sliding down to the floor.

He crawled over to her. "Okay, *ife*, I have you."

Tears leaked, her breathing rapid, shallow. He reached her and pressed his hand against her chest. She looked down at his hands and a sob escaped. His hands were shackled together with thick, rusted iron manacles.

"Slow down baby, slow down. Match my breathing." He captured her gaze, and she smelled his scent. It wrapped around her, and her lungs loosened, her breathing slowing. "That's it, *ife*. It's okay. We're here together."

Her eyes never left his. They changed to copper, as his beast pushed to the forefront. His pheromones got stronger until the scent of it filled her. Finally, her breathing slowed, the weight on her chest loosened.

"Better?"

She nodded and let her legs down. He sat next to her and scooped her into his arms, the motion awkward with his hands bound.

"Give me a moment to get the rest of this drug from my body and I will get us out of here," he promised.

She nuzzled into his chin, pulling comfort from the feel of his skin against hers. "There's no way out. This is the same room they kept me in before."

"You remember?"

She nodded. "All of it." She closed her eyes tightly, fighting down the last of the panic attack.

"These restraints are primitive, but they're working and dampening my power. Along with whatever they drugged me with." His voice rumbled against her ear as she curled tighter into his chest. Even with his hands pushing into her stomach between them, she found comfort.

She reared back. "Holmium. How would they know?" She asked, but her mind was quickly filling in the blanks of her memory loss, and collating with everything that had happened in the last few weeks.

"It's not a weakness the Demi advertise, but I imagine the Divine would make it their business to know how to strike at their enemy." He hissed and rotated his wrist within the restraints.

"We need to work on these then." She sat straight, finally having a task with which she could use to distract herself from their situation. She wasn't bound, which was a serious mistake on their part.

Chapter 37

His eyes raked his mate's form. She was okay for the most part. Outside of the panic attack. He ached to pull her back into his arms.

"Are you okay?"

"Yeah, outside of a mega headache." She bit her lip as she studied the manacles wrapped around his wrists.

"Do you think you can get me out of these irons?"

She stared at them for moments, her head cocked to the side, her mind working. She winced a moment, and guilt crossed her face.

"What is it?"

She waved at the manacles on his wrist. "I shared some things about the Demi with the archivists in the Roswell Esin. Maybe they passed the information along."

"There's no way you could've known, my love." He soothed.

She sighed and stared at his wrist. "There are a couple of things I can try."

"Don't touch them with your skin, *ife*." He cautioned. Holmium was a rare earth metal, and toxic to humans in its raw metal form.

She nodded absently. Her magic came to life, the glow of it surrounding her, reaching out to him. His own magic reacted, his skin wavering a little as his beast tried to force his change through the power of the manacles.

Pride expanded his chest. Watching her work was beautiful and reinforced how smart and capable his mate was. "You're using your magic."

"My memory came back," she said absently, her brow furrowed in concentration.

Nerves fluttered as he wondered what she thought of him now that her memory was back. Her head whipped up.

She cupped his cheek. "You're messing with my concentration. Nothing has changed between us."

He kissed her, knowing his insecurities were misplaced and inappropriate at the current moment.

She pulled back from their kiss. "We will be talking though."

He nodded. Brianna was nothing if not blunt and honest. He'd worry about their conversation later.

"Ok. Let me focus." She went back to staring at their irons.

The door to their room opened and she scrambled from his lap and stood. He stood slower, unimpressed with the ragtag couple that entered the room. He moved Brianna behind him, standing between her and the two people.

"Where are we?" He demanded first and foremost.

"It doesn't matter," the woman he recognized as Emilia answered.

Darren stood next to her, his body emaciated, his skin ashen and wet with sweat. He thought of Ade's words about the Divine who had performed the spell that killed his men. Anger filled him. He clenched his hands to stay his temper.

"Why're you doing this?" Brianna growled

"You're a smart girl, Brianna. You know the book can't fall into the Demi's hands. We were going to let it go, but you mated him." Emilia sneered at them both. "We should've never allowed it to go to you in the first place. You don't even believe in the Esin."

"You trashed my aunt's place and still didn't find it." She remembered the fear she'd had the next day as she walked through her aunt's bookstore and saw the damage.

Emilia shrugged. "The book should've come to an archivist who would've taken care of it, and kept it out of the Demi's hands."

"You're responsible for the spell over my mate's memories?" Fury washed through his body.

"We thought the spell would make you forget the book, and give us time to find it before you passed it on to this…thing." Darren spat on the floor in front of them, ignoring him and staring at Brianna. "We'll just have to kill him to keep it out of the Demi's hands."

"You can try," Fallon said in a deadly tone.

The two took a step back.

Brianna's magic was a warm tide at his back as she continued to work on releasing him from the manacles. His wrists were also warm, her magic surrounding them, keeping most of the pain to a minimum. His mate was scared, her fear radiated down their mate bond, and yet, she still made sure he was not in pain. Her head pressed into his back as she concentrated on the task. Love for her filled him, along with anger and frustration at their current situation.

He needed to keep them talking. "How did you get to us without me knowing?"

"It's easier than you think to blind the Demi," Emilia smirked. "I may not be null, like Darren here, but I can mask myself quite well." She pulled a needle from behind her back, her face smug. "I'm also quite proficient with potions."

Brianna stopped working and peeked around him. "Wait, the whole Esin is null?"

"Why do you care, you left us," Darren accused.

"But only the Shaman's descendants should've been nulled." Her hand tightened on his wrist. "That means Elder Cedric is your father?"

"You're smart. I've always hated that about you." Darren crossed his arms over his chest.

Brianna was worried about them being nulled, but his mind was on the fact that they had to still be on the Roswell Esin's land. No way a Divine potion kept him unconscious long enough to move them far. No matter how good Emilia was at potions. His body would metabolize any foreign substance quickly.

"You didn't even realize how close you were to being mated with the next Oliri," Darren announced.

"He's mine now," Emilia taunted.

Fallon snorted. "For however long he has left."

"What does that mean?" The archivist's sharp eyes raked over him in disdain.

"You mean to tell me you spent years siphoning spells out of that library and you didn't bother to learn about the karma that came with using darker magic." Brianna tsked.

Emilia's eyes widened, and guilt stained her cheeks. "You remember?"

Brianna growled. "You spied through my notes. I never would've left them behind. Combine your stolen magic with the notes in my notebooks at the library and you had everything you needed to pull this off."

Emilia shrugged, her eyes darting to Darren. "It doesn't matter where I got the information."

Fallon sucked his teeth. "Shame. Your boy will be dead soon, and it will be everything he deserved for killing my men."

"You don't know I killed them." Darren protested weakly.

"You're the only person around here looking like he's on death's door, so, yeah, I'll take my chances."

"Not a testament to those magical skills you bragged about." Brianna taunted.

Emilia gave Darren a stricken look, her head whipping between them. "That's not true, he's not dying."

Satisfaction flowed down their connection from Brianna and the first tendrils of his magic escaped the dampening spell.

"Look at him," Fallon nodded his head in Darren's direction.

Darren's breathing was labored, and he looked on the verge of collapse.

"What I want to know is, how did the two of you meet?" Brianna asked.

Emilia closed her mouth and crossed her arms over her chest. Darren said nothing either.

"So let me get this straight. You kidnapped me because you didn't want the Demi to have the book. Which tells me, you know nothing about the *Book of Divinity* or how it works." Brianna said casually.

"That means they're being fed a bunch of bullshit by their superiors, don't you think so, *ife*?" Fallon spoke louder to cover the click of the first manacle opening. He didn't dare move his hand for fear it would fall off.

Emilia growled and shared a look with Darren. He sighed as the two of them left the room. There was a loud clang as they locked the door again. They were arguing, the noise of it dampened by the steel door.

"That bought us more time." He turned to face Brianna.

She grabbed his wrist, her magic flaring hotter. "Do you think that? That someone fed them a line about the *Book of Divinity*?"

He snorted. "If they knew anything about that book, they'd know it was spelled to only be read by the guardian. It could be stolen one hundred times, but only the person it was willed to can use it. It's why Xavier never bothered you about it."

"I had wondered about that," she murmured, keeping at her task.

"The only job given to us from Rugaba was your protection. If anything happened to you, the book was useless." He hissed as the second manacle opened and his power flooded his body.

"Something about all this doesn't fit." Brianna rolled her shoulders. "I mean, they didn't even realize I was doing magic while they were in the room."

He rotated his wrists, happy to be out of the irons. "Everything about this stinks. Why would they put us together? Why aren't you chained? I don't like it, and I plan to get answers."

"But not from those two?"

"They're cannon fodder, they just don't know it yet." He swore.

"How will we get out?"

"Through that door." He promised. He changed into his Cagyn form enjoying the burn of his muscles as his body grew. His head nearly touched the ceiling of their prison.

He moved his hands, readying a spell when the door opened. Darren stepped into the room, his eyes wide as he realized Fallon was free. He didn't give the man time to say anything. Fallon blasted him with the magic stored up from the dampening spell. Darren flew from the room and Emilia screamed as he hit the wall.

Emilia rushed into the room, her hands moving as she gathered energy. His mate was faster, her magic sending the woman to the floor. Fallon used his magic to knock Emilia out.

He reached his hand out for his mate. "Let's go, *ife*." He growled.

She rushed into his arms. "That was badass." She kissed his chin, the only part she could reach on her toes.

His eyes softened, and his beast growled in pleasure. "Let's get you out of here and to a healer."

"Happily." She grabbed his hand. "Then we can find out who's really behind this all."

Chapter 38

It took all of ten steps outside of their prison for Brianna to realize something was wrong. The corridor next to where they were kept looked like it was used for underground storage. They passed another steel door, this one with a high window built into it. She frowned and walked over to it, curious. There were grain and various vegetables stored there. She backed away from the door.

"Wait. Wait. This place. We didn't have anything like this at the Douglasville Esin."

Fallon tugged on her arm pulling her further down a corridor. "We can't be far from the Temple where we were taken."

"How can you be sure? We have no way of knowing how long we were out." She hastened her steps to keep up with his long stride.

"She injected our bodies with something. My body metabolizes at a rate that would make it improbable they'd take us far. Not to mention, the sheer mass of my body. Trust me. We're still near the Roswell Esin."

The corridor darkened, and her calves started to burn as they ascended. He kept a firm grip on her hand but didn't slow. She knew his night vision was better than that of a jungle cat, so she didn't worry. She blinked rapidly and processed the fact that she knew he had excellent night vision. With her memory back, it was just a small piece of the things she knew about her new husband. It hit her fully at that moment that her memory was back.

Despite their perilous position, she smiled.

She had her memory back.

He stopped them and she looked around at the pressing darkness. For a moment claustrophobia threatened to take over. Her breathing hitched, but she pushed down the fear as a sliver of light caught her eye. It looked like the bottom of a door. Fallon pushed his shoulder into the door and it popped open. The sound echoed, loudly.

She blinked as her eyes adjusted to the brightness of the sun, well into the afternoon, streaming through the temple walls. Fallon had been right. They hadn't gone far at all. They heard rushing feet and Fallon posted in front of her, his arms up.

"Brianna!" Her mother and father both rushed towards them.

Fallon stepped aside and allowed their embrace. His brothers weren't far behind her parents.

"What happened?"

"Where were you?"

"Are you okay?"

"We've been searching for hours."

Fallon held up his hands for silence. "We've been downstairs. Not of our own volition."

"The Divine kept you," Xavier growled, his eyes changing.

Fallon nodded as they walked towards the front door. They had just passed the altar when a wave of magic moved through the temple, slamming the front doors shut. Divine soldiers, some she recognized from their Douglasville Esin, stepped from behind the columns flanking them on either side. Shaman surrounded them on three sides, soldiers taking up positions next to them for protection.

Xavier moved in front of the group. "What the fuck is going on?"

Deidre clamped a hand over her mouth as two men separated from the group and stepped forward. "Elder Cedric?" She gasped.

The Oliri of their old Esin gave them all a smile that froze her blood. She knew there was no way Darren could've been working alone. Next to him stood another man, his demeanor subservient. As the assistant to Elder Samuel, the Oliri of the Roswell Esin, he was used to being an underling. That he was there, seemingly working with Elder Cedric, was a big surprise.

"Kerric, what is this?" Henry asked the assistant.

"Give us the book." Elder Cedric demanded.

"I'm not giving you shit." Brianna put her hands on her hips, pissed.

Fallon pulled her further behind him. The three brothers shuffled until she and her parents were behind them all. The three of them were a wall of muscle. She had to lean to the side to see anything. Power swelled in the temple. The three brothers in unison started moving their hands, their lips chanting in a language she didn't understand.

They were gathering magic for a spell. She felt the static of it against her skin as they muttered the incantation. With her memory back, she didn't understand the language, but she knew the purpose. There were at least twelve people surrounding them, certainly, more than Fallon and his brothers could take out at once.

Probably.

She actually wasn't sure.

She didn't know the full extent of their powers. Not one to wait around on others though, she was frantically trying to think of a way to get them out of their current situation. It felt great to have her memory back.

Especially since the lessons she'd taken with Tahir were coming back to her, and with them, a way to help. Her mother and father turned and faced each other. Power swelled until her hair was actually blowing around her. Henry's dreadlocks were blowing in a wind. Magic pressed against her skin, her ears ringing until something popped.

Sound around them muffled, the wind only moving in their little group. Magic swelled outside of the circle, and someone hurled magic towards them. It bounced off a shield and Fallon turned to her, surprised. She shook her head, turning an incredulous look to her parents. They were performing the magic. And not simple magic as they had explained to her. They had built a complicated shield around the whole group.

Her mother was sweating as she expended power. She grabbed her mother's shoulder and lent her power to them. She'd planned to lend the power to Fallon and his brothers, but, helping her parents hold the shield would serve them better. She focused her magic on her parents, melding her power with theirs in the way she had practiced with Tahir months ago before she lost her memory. A spurt of pride expanded in her chest when it worked. The barrier seemed to coalesce right in front of them.

"Can we throw anything out of this?" Xavier asked loudly over the swelling power.

Deidre shuddered. "Yes!" She shouted.

"I'll focus fire on the leader when the shield comes down. Leo take the two at your seven," Xavier ordered. "Fallon-"

"I'm taking the Elder," Fallon yelled over the growing noise.

"Fine," Xavier adapted his plan, shifting to put Fallon at the head of the circle, "I'll take the two at my three. Hit the shamans hard, the soldiers won't fight if they fall."

The three of them nodded, their arms moving, amassing power as they fit seamlessly into position. The years of fighting under their brother, Xavier's, orders showed in their cohesive movements and unspoken communication. Pride for her mate bolstered her waning energy.

325

As a single unit, Fallon, Xavier, and Leo started flinging power at the Oliri. It was amazing to see. As Kerric moved closer to him, working his own magic, the determination on his face snapped more of her memories into place. Like a nightmare reel, the memories played through her mind. She remembered him coming down to question her when she was kidnapped the first time. The memory of her guards Mazi and Salim on the ground, their eyes unseeing as she was dragged from her building flashed and her breath hitched. She wouldn't let it happen to her mate and his brothers.

Something solid connected with the shield. They were hurling dark magic, the nasty stain of it coating their shield, trying to taint their magic. She focused her magic on her mother, gathering it from within herself, shoring up her mother's power. She dug deep in her power. Tahir had taught her the Demi way of gathering magic from the atmosphere around her. She chanted the spell, pulling magic from outside the circle, using it to feed their shield.

Her head hurt, her arms were tired, and her body was weakening as the fight between them waged on. Fallon growled and stepped forward, right up against the shield.

"*Ife*," he hollered. He reached into his pocket and pulled out the coin she knew connected him to Azra.

He tugged on their connection, searching for her power. She grit her teeth and closed her eyes to focus. She knew what he needed, she just had to bear down. She fed him some of the outside power, sweat beads gathering on her forehead as she fought to both give her parents and Fallon power. He too had a well of power he reached for. The amount of it was staggering. His hands moved quickly, his brothers stood behind him and both put a hand on his shoulder.

She breathed a little easier as power from both Xavier and Leo flooded their connection. Fallon shouted in the ancient language and the lights in the temple flickered once, twice and then a huge whoosh sounded.

Elder Cedric and Kerric collapsed under the blast, their screams high pitched as the force of Fallon's magic struck them. She and her parents collapsed back and landed in a small heap as their magic was shut off. The quiet lasted only moments before the Divine attacking them stood to renew their assault.

In a blink Leo was a blur of movement, careening into the shaman nearest to him before their hands could rise in defense. Forearms out, he struck both men in the neck, forcibly knocking them over. As they tilted back, falling, he stopped suddenly and punched with both hands downward slamming them into the stone. They were dead the moment their heads cracked against the concrete of Rugaba's temple. The shamans' forms were still on the ground before their guards turned to see them down. The guards protecting the shaman were down behind Leo seconds later as he pulled his sword and swung backward, taking off their heads.

Xavier turned his full attention to the Divine in front of him. Their hands were out, their magic faltering in the face of their fear. With a whisper, he called power to him, his palms open as the magic aggregated around his hands. He turned that power around, shoving it, along with his hands towards the Divine. The men flew up, and backward, their forms twisting under the onslaught of his magic. Their screams added to the bedlam until they struck the temple columns. A clatter of sound filled the room as hands went up and weapons were dropped. The soldiers surrendered immediately after seeing the ease with which their leaders had been dispatched.

She helped her mother to her feet, Xavier helping Henry stand.

"Are you guys okay?" Xavier asked.

She nodded. She looked for her mate and found him stomping over to Elder Cedric's prone figure. He lifted him in the air by his throat.

"Fallon," Xavier called. "He has to be sentenced."

Fallon gripped Elder Cedric's neck and the Oliri gagged. Brianna rushed to his side and placed a restraining hand on his arm. She didn't ask him to stop though. As far as she was concerned, Elder Cedric could choke for what he did and was probably still doing at their old Esin.

"The Demi laws mean nothing to me." The Oliri wheezed as Fallon squeezed tighter.

"I don't give a fuck what you follow. You'll stand before your own tribunal and in the end, we will kill you for the murder of my men." Fallon flexed his hands.

Xavier put canvas gloves on the Oliri and then thick handcuffs around the gloves. There was banging on the doors a moment before they burst open.

Elder Samuel came in. "What is the meaning of this?"

"Your people kidnapped my brother and his mate, and tried to kill us." Xavier got right into the Oliri's face.

Samuel stepped back. "Why should I believe the Demi? We may have a tentative truce, but that doesn't excuse you coming onto our land waging war."

"We were here looking for my daughter. They tried to kill us all." Henry wrapped an arm around Deidre's shoulder.

"I want this man tried for murder." Fallon loosened his fingers and Elder Cedric hit the floor.

Michel and her other guards came in and stood behind Xavier. Sharine came in moments later, her face angry, her powerlines glowing on her skin. She walked up to each of her sons and cupped their cheek, checking them over. She came up to Brianna and did the same. Brianna's legs were shaking, only adrenaline kept her standing. Sharine seemed to sense it and she wrapped her arm around Brianna's waist to steady her. Sharine's scent surrounded her, and she shuddered as her body relaxed further, discharging her residual fear.

Samuel and Xavier were in a stare-off until power imbued the temple. This time, Rugaba stepped from the shadows. Fury had transformed his face into something way scarier than the affable god with whom she'd been meeting. All in the temple went down on their knees. Sharine yanked her down. Fallon moved closer to her before going down on one knee.

Elder Samuel kneeled. "My Lord."

Rugaba waved his hands and the dead Divine disappeared, leaving only Elder Cedric and Kerric, who lay on his side, his breathing choppy.

Rugaba pointed at Kerric and turned his gaze to Elder Samuel. "Do you know this male?"

"He is my assistant." Samuel lowered his body closer to the floor.

"So, there are people under you conspiring to remove the *Book of Divinity* from the guardian's hand and you had no clue?" Rugaba's voice reverberated around the temple.

"My Lord, I was unaware."

Power forced them all lower until they abased themselves before Rugaba. The god stepped closer to the Oliri and bent at the waist to address him.

"This one," he pointed to Elder Cedric, "is from a nulled line, and yet he is in my temple, performing stolen magic. What do you say of that?"

"I have no excuse." Elder Samuel choked out.

"You do not," Rugaba answered. "Gather your tribunal, now. We will get to the bottom of this, or you will forfeit your position, perhaps even your life."

Everyone but the Demi looked surprised by the god's decree. Used to their god's pique, they were unmoved. Rugaba dismissed the Oliri and turned to her and Fallon.

He waved his hand for them to stand. The god's glower transformed into an approachable expression. "Congratulations are in order."

"Thank you, my lord," Fallon answered, his head still lowered down.

Rugaba reached out and touched Brianna's forehead. The throbbing of her headache ceased, and she sighed in relief.

"All is well with you?" Rugaba's dark gaze scrutinized her face.

She nodded, "yes, my lord."

"My lord? You've found some respect?"

She lifted her head and gave him an impish smile. "My mother is watching," she said in a stage whisper.

The god's lips quirked. His gaze raked the rest of them. "You all may leave, this will be handled."

Everyone scrambled from the temple. All except Xavier.

Fallon wanted to lift his mate in his arms and carry her out, but Brianna had fought as well as any soldier and he would do nothing to undermine her strength. He probed their connection as she walked behind him with his mother. Her fatigue was there, along with the adrenaline that went with a battle. He was taking her home and after a Kira inspected her, he was pampering his mate for the rest of the evening.

Despite her fear, Brianna had not bowed under the Divine's assault. He toyed with the coin in his pocket, thankful for his mate. She'd lent him her power, standing alongside him, everything he never thought to ask for in a woman. He'd nearly gave it all up.

Leo stepped up and slapped his shoulder. "Did you know your in-laws had power like that?"

Fallon peered back at Deidre and Henry, answering questions from the Divine in the Esin. "I never would've guessed."

"Your mate kicks ass." Leo fist-bumped him.

He smiled. Yes, his mate kicked ass.

Leo stopped when they reached the group of Haven's SUVs parked in a tight circle in the parking lot. "What about the ceremony? What do you want to do?"

Deidre sighed, coming up behind them. "I personally don't feel comfortable having it here, not knowing whether or not Elder Samuel was involved."

"Do you feel unsafe here?" Fallon asked sharply. His mate would worry about them nevertheless. But if they wanted to leave, he would take care of it.

Henry frowned. "No. The magic doesn't feel tainted as it did in Elder Cedric's Esin."

Brianna yawned, coming up on his other side. She leaned her head on his shoulder. "Dad's right. The magic here still feels light, safe."

Fallon nodded, taking her word for it. "If you have no objection, Deidre, I'd like to take the bonding period with my mate. Once this mess is cleaned up, we'll be more than happy to come back and have the ceremony for you."

Deidre came over to Brianna and kissed her forehead. "I'm just so happy you're okay. Take all the time you need."

Fallon loaded Brianna into the SUV Michel was driving, pulling her into his side in the back seat. "Home, my love?"

She yawned again, and closed her eyes, cuddling into his chest. "Yes, please."

Chapter 39

Brianna was up early again. Fallon had been complaining for the past three days that she didn't sleep like a normal person. She declined to tell him that out of the two of them, she was the normal one. She nibbled on her cereal and played around with the comms tablet Liliana had scored for her. It was better than any tablet she'd ever seen and short of taking it apart, she was determined to find out everything about it. Right now, she was using it to peruse the files the archivist had made available for her.

Penny had been right about the lack of information on the Kokoro souls and it was frustrating. She suggested to Fallon that she try the libraries in each realm. She smiled as she remembered his face. Clearly, he was not sold on the idea and saw through her ruse. She wanted to visit all the realms, this time with her notebooks and explore every corner of them. She closed the files on the Kokoro and opened the ones on the *Book of Divinity*.

She thought about the Divine's attempt to take the book from her. According to Xavier, Elder Cedric had been sentenced to death for his part in both her kidnapping and the attempted theft.

She shuddered.

It seemed harsh, but he was guilty of so many more crimes. She'd not shed a tear over his death. It was strange, their insistence on getting the book from her when they knew so little of it. It niggled at her when she thought about it. Xavier said he cared naught of motive, only that they were gone and no other conspirators were left in the Roswell Esin. She'd make herself happy with that for the time being.

She was the guardian of the book, and she'd be more conscious of that and her security. She never wanted another person to die protecting her. She straightened as she realized something.

She remembered where the *Book of Divinity* was!

Fallon shuffled into the kitchen as she was chugging the milk out of her cereal bowl. He rolled his eyes. She put the bowl in the sink and kissed him on his cheek.

"I gotta go."

He sighed. "Where, my love, where do you have to go so early?"

"I'm going back to the apartment, I need to go get something. I'll take Michel, and it won't take long."

He raised an eyebrow in surprise. "You're volunteering to take a guard?"

"I know you worry." She pecked him on the cheek again.

He turned his head and devoured her mouth until her senses were reeling. His face was smug when they came up for air.

"I nearly lost you. Keep yourself safe."

She smiled. She liked that he left her safety as her responsibility. She gave him a mock salute and left, calling Michel on her way to the ground floor. Funny how easily she navigated the tunnels in Haven now that she had her memory back.

Michel met her in the garage, standing next to the SUV he liked to drive. She was so happy to have her memory back. It pleased her to know all the little things that she'd forgotten about the habits of those guarding her. She wasn't the type of person who treated those that worked for her as strangers.

"How is Isaiah?" she asked, climbing into the front seat.

"Doing a lot better. He was lucky Darren didn't know shit about magic."

She sighed. The thought of another of her guards dying for her constricted her chest. Despite her flippant remark to Fallon, she didn't plan on doing anything to put herself or the men he assigned to guard her in danger.

"Where are we going?" He started the car.

"My apartment." She stared at the dash of the SUV. "Does this self-drive like the cars on Chuita?"

Michel snorted. "And, she's back."

"What? It's just a question." She grumbled.

"You always have a question, or ten."

She rolled her eyes. "Fine, be that way."

It didn't take but twenty minutes to get to her building. She spoke to her bookstore employees as she passed through. The backpack she went with everywhere flopped against her back.

"Wait here." She instructed him in the foyer as they entered the apartment.

She went to her office right away, seeing it with eyes that knew where every secret was held. She closed the door and took off her backpack. She murmured a spell over it, one she'd carefully learned at Haven's library under the watchful eye of Penny so many months ago. She opened the bag when she was done and reached in.

The bag was deeper than normal, and her hands didn't brush any of the notebooks she kept in it. The spelled worked. A smug smile tipped her lips.

She pulled the book bag closer to her chest to reach further. Her hand touched a leather-bound journal and she laughed. She pulled it out and held it in the air, prancing in a circle.

She'd found it.

Happy, she put it back into the void, carefully closing it before zipping her backpack closed. The spell worked seamlessly. Having the book in the void was the only way she was able to keep it on her and travel back and forth to Haven. She put the pack on her back and left the room. She took a final look around the apartment, knowing her place was next to Fallon and the adventures they'd find together. Would she miss the apartment? Absolutely, there were so many memories there. She would more than likely come back and work in the office here, so she wasn't totally abandoning it. Still, it was closure. She would embrace her position as guardian of the *Book of Divine* and a Kokoro soul. She smiled at Michel who stood by the door.

"Let's go home."

Epilogue

Fallon looked around the lavishly appointed room. Sconces along the walls cast writhing shadows on the floor that looked vaguely sexual. A musky aroma filled the room, a menagerie of scents with notes of leather, sweat, fear, and ash. Discarded manacles lay on tables, attached to links of chain at the far side of the room. There were deep maroon, damask covered sofas and divans on either side of him and it looked like a brothel. There was a large circular bed in the middle of the chamber where two female Dzivas worked over one another's body, their purple scales glittering in dim light, completely ignoring him. He frowned in confusion at his surroundings. A tall, lean god appeared, standing inches in front of him. Fallon dropped to one knee. The god in question could not appear on earth, which told him he was dreaming.

Piercing lavender eyes flickered in the light, studying him. Only the sweep of his long lashes lowering in a slow blink broke the god's stare. The god's lips twitched, then moved into an impish grin that transformed his handsome face into the sly being Fallon knew him to be.

"Azra." Fallon greeted, staying on his knee.

With a flourish, the god waved his hand, and the bed disappeared along with its occupants. Azra then folded his hands into his lap and lowered his nearly seven feet tall body towards the floor. The marble of the floor vibrated and rose to meet the god halfway, fashioning into a gilded throne as it conformed around his body.

Azra studied him a moment more before speaking. "You prayed to me. In my brother's temple even. Bold."

He swallowed, trying to ease the restriction clogging his throat as nervousness bloomed. He didn't have an answer for what he'd done, except to say he'd do it again if it meant saving his mate.

Azra chuckled. "Yes, love does make some foolish."

"Did my prayer offend, my lord?" He stood as Azra waved him up.

"Not at all. You and I have an accord. Our exchange allows for some quid pro quo." His face cunning, Azra smiled.

He knew that smile had been on the end of that smile when he'd made a deal with Azra the first time. The god was a trickster, his reputation well deserved. A favor for a favor. He knew the price when he'd called on Azra for the extra power in Rugaba's temple. Yes, his mate and brothers had lent him their power, but it wouldn't have been enough to take out all of the Divine hurling magic at them.

"What can I do to serve you, my lord?" He bowed his head.

"Relax, Fallon. You are my brother's, I'd never ask for anything that would damage that relationship. You're far more valuable to me in the service of Rugaba." Azra snapped his fingers and on the wall beside him, a picture appeared.

It was a woman, her dark skin smooth, a rich creamy brown. Her hair was curly, spilling over her forehead, her features striking…familiar. He squinted.

"This woman needs help. You will provide it."

"Of course." He didn't hesitate. Saying no to Azra the furthest thing on his mind. "Who is she?"

"A modern-day Pandora, in that she could unwittingly unleash an evil even I want no parts of, onto the earth." Azra's voice was thoughtful as he gazed on the woman.

"She's a Kokoro soul?" That the god had found her was a relief. Xavier would certainly feel better knowing who she was and having her protected.

"She is."

"Where do you need me? Am I bringing her to Haven? What would you have me do with her?" All questions to which he needed specific answers. Though, with Azra that meant nothing. The god could easily tell him one thing, but dance along the micro-thin wire of semantics and do something else.

"Careful with your thoughts." Azra's voice had deepened, a hint of temper sparking in his dark eyes.

"Apologies, my lord." He bowed his head again.

"Find her, help her with whatever tasks she needs to clean up her life, and then bring her to Haven." Azra's dark stare penetrated his head. "Under no circumstances is she to open the chest she's going to find."

Fear had his stomach churning. He didn't want to know what could possibly have a god nervous.

"Anything else?"

"Don't tell my brother."

That wouldn't be hard to manage. Luckily for him, Rugaba only came to Haven when there was a problem. Azra stood and sauntered closer to him. Fallon had to look up at the god, his seven feet dwarfed him. Azra touched his forehead with a single finger, and images of the woman, her location, and the danger surrounding her flashed through his mind. The information dump gave him a headache. When he was done, Azra stepped back.

"I thank you for this." The god looked sincere.

Fallon was taken back a bit by the worried look that flickered across Azra's face. He nodded. "It's my pleasure."

"Congratulations on your mating."

Azra stood and his throne vanished from the room. Done with the conversation the god turned and began to walk away. He waved a dismissive hand and Fallon jerked as he slammed back into his sleeping body. He sat up and took huge gulping breaths, the shock of it stealing his breath.

He looked around, happy to note he was back in their hotel suite on Legba. His mate had insisted on seeing the large trading market that drew Demi from all seven realms. They'd spent the day shopping and people watching. They were supposed to spend tomorrow in the library. That would be out of the question now that Azra had given him a task.

Brianna sat up and rubbed his back, her sleepy face frowning in worry. "What's wrong?"

"Remember when I told you I had to occasionally do tasks for the god, Azra." He said after he'd caught his breath.

"Hell god, yes. Where are we going?"

He turned his head to stare at her. "We?"

She snorted, turning back over and settling under the blankets. "You're stuck with me buddy, where you go, I go."

He smiled, warmed by that. Azra had never really sent him any place that was dangerous. He didn't worry he couldn't protect his mate. Besides, since she'd gotten her memory back, he'd seen the way she wielded her magic. It was reassuring on many levels. She'd thanked him the day after their ordeal in the temple. Tahir had told her more things than he'd been comfortable with her knowing. She thanked him for all the things he'd done for her that she hadn't realized. It embarrassed him at first, but her gratitude warmed him.

He laid back down and cuddled up to her back. He kissed her neck, nuzzling her, pushing his erection into her back. "Back to the Earth Realm, Chattanooga, Tennessee to be exact."

She yawned and snuggled in. "That's not too far a drive from Atlanta unless you have one of those handy dandy haven's there."

He inhaled the scent from the back of her neck, rubbing his face against the silk scarf that protected her hair while she slept. "Nope, gotta hoof it like humans."

"That's no fun." She settled back to sleep.

He watched her sleep for long minutes as he waited for the adrenaline to slow. He held her tight, breathing in her scent, calming his body. He loved her more than he thought was possible. Life with her would never be boring, he was certain. He looked forward to traveling with her, learning magic alongside her, and most of all, he looked forward to these moments. He kissed her neck one final time and closed his eyes, hopeful for his future.

About the Author

I am a full-time photographer, and a mom of two. I've been writing my whole life, and after the birth of my first kid, I decided I couldn't very well bring up a fearless human without first trying the things that scared me. So, I wrote my first book, and then subsequently more.

I try to write stories I love to read: love stories that feature brown girls like me. My stories feature gods and goddesses, and creatures I derived from old, African folk tales remixed and thrust into a modern world. Visit my website, www.driaandersen.com for more information on my other novels.

Other titles by Dria Andersen

Destiny Series

A Destiny Awakened

A Destiny Revealed

Haven Series

Haven

www.ingramcontent.com/pod-product-compliance
Lightning Source LLC
Chambersburg PA
CBHW020918110726
47900CB00001B/198